# SEA OF SOULS

R.E. PALMER

FrontRunner Publications

ISBN: 978-1-8383995-3-5
www.FrontRunnerBooks.com

Cover art by Kentaro Kanamoto
www.kentarokanamoto.com

# DEDICATION

For Bern, Tim & Neve

…and Smudge

# ACKNOWLEDGMENTS

Once again, I owe a huge thanks to Erin Kahn (Eryn), Amanda Brand (Amyndra) and Janet Allmey (Janae). The time and effort they put into reading my drafts and giving honest feedback, help to make my stories so much better.

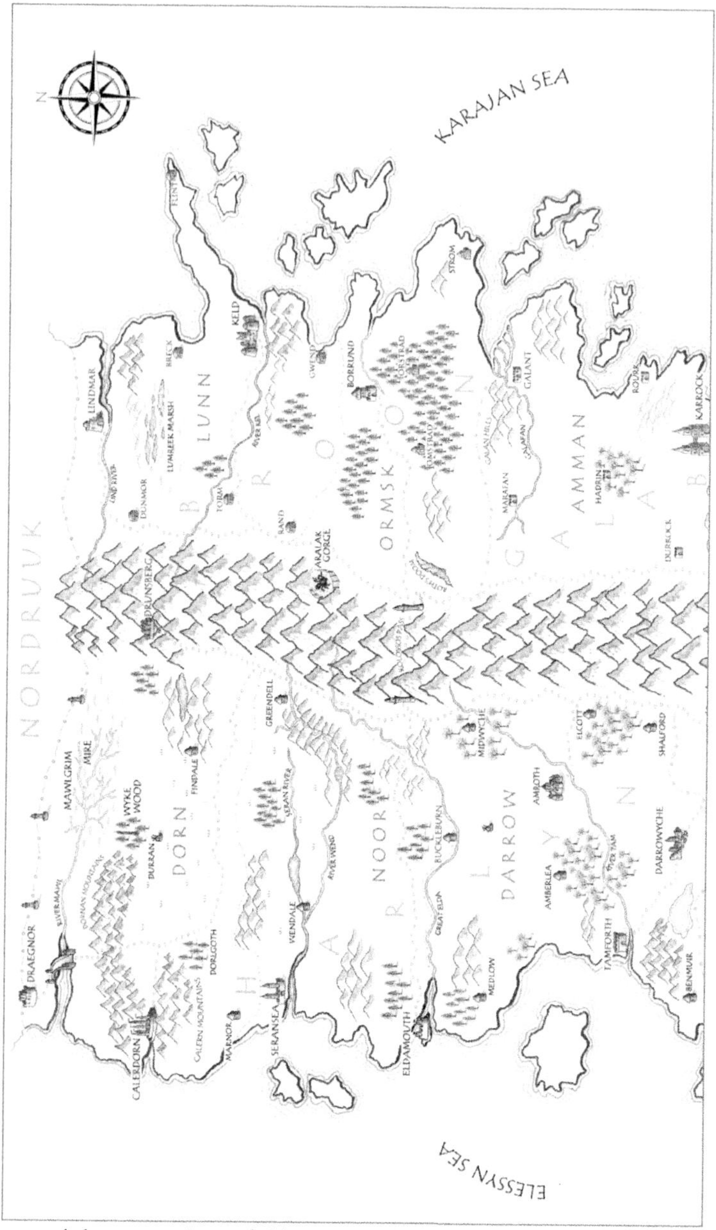


A large version of this map is available to download and print at www.frontrunnerbooks.com/map.html

N
ELESSYN SEA
KARAJAN SEA
KERNLOW
FARRAND
KRANT
PERRAN
PYMOOR
RHYDOR
RANMOOR
PERRAN HILLS
KERNRIM
MERYN
KERN RIVER
KOLOSSOS MOUNTAINS
VORTIMO
VYMARL
TALLABAR
SAPHRIR
VYNMAR
EMRYST
EPHRIM
SALAHA
TELAMIR
KIRIK
STOWE
GWELAYN
CASTER
VINLAYN
HAMM
RIVER MIR
KALIMIR
CAFRA
CASTELDOR
NEVERDOR
SEARITH
FORANFAE
FOREST
PORTLEA
RIVER LOL
TAMARAND
LOROMAR
HURST
MUND
SYRIS
HOLM
CAERMUND
GARAMUND
ABERNOST
WEST HAVEN
ARCHONHOLM
MENON RIVER
TRAITOR'S ISLAND
CAERWAL MOUNTAINS
CAERWAL GATE
MUNDRAKE'S ISLE
THE LOST REALMS

# 1. The Fall of the Seven Realms

A flash stained the dark clouds on the horizon a sickly green. Idraman clenched his staff and set his stance. He waited. During the night he had entered the Song and conversed with Nyomae. She and the last of the Order fled south, pursued by a vast army. They had been caught unprepared, unaware the old enemy could assemble such a force. But it was not the size of the baying hordes that troubled Nyomae — it was the shadows looming behind. Idraman knew of what she spoke. He dearly hoped she was wrong.

The muffled boom rolled in from the plain like thunder, forcing air through the narrow Caerwal Pass. Idraman stood tall against the sudden gale but balked at the foul stench blowing in from Gormadon. His companions had failed to evade the shadow. The army sent north to aid their retreat had no option but to turn and give battle. Fifty leagues north of Idraman, his Order would make what would likely be their last stand.

Another flash. The ground shook. Idraman entered the Song. He searched for Nyomae amid the cries of anguish overwhelming the Verses. He found her. His knees buckled. All was surely lost. It could not be. The true enemy had finally revealed itself. Idraman could no longer cling to the hope that had sustained him these past months. The Seven Realms faced a far deadlier force than they had foreseen. And to his dismay, he saw they were led by one of their own. She had once gone by the name of Sylvena and was the most powerful of their Order. But she had probed too deep into the old Verses and failed to heed the warnings. And the voices of the dark had turned her.

Until now, she was thought lost in her quest for a relic she believed would save them. But Sylvena was deceived and had fallen into the trap set for her. She had been corrupted and become Uluriel, a servant of the Dark Verses. And to Idraman's horror, she had summoned the *Draedalak*. The demons from Ormoroth's dark pits had pushed the mighty Draegelan to the edge of defeat. How could Idraman and his Order counter such evil?

He stared at the dark sky and cried out. The return of the *Draedalak* threatened the very existence of the Seven Realms. Spawned by the Evil One from the Verses of the Maidens' torment, the *Draedalak* once resembled their half-sisters. But their voices wrought despair and destruction, and soon their fair guise fell away to reveal the demons beneath.

Idraman probed the roiling air suffering the presence of the dark beasts. Uluriel alone could not have called them. Few had the authority to summon the *Draedalak* from the darkness. It had to be a warlock, a captain from the armies of old. Ormoroth was believed defeated in the frozen wastes of Talaghir. But, if Idraman had hoped he had been banished and cast into the Great Void, he was mistaken. If a warlock commanded the demons, Ormoroth must still hold sway in the living lands. Idraman pitched forward, clutching his stomach. It could only mean Ormoroth lurked in the Halfway World — a place from which he could return.

Idraman had just moments to strike back. Only months earlier, his only concern was to contain the unrest along the northern borders. He believed it to be nothing more than the mischievous acts of lesser spirits stirring the Ruuk. Nevertheless, they could not risk the darkness and unease spreading to other realms. So, while Idraman had stayed in Elmarand, the remaining six of his Order had gone into Nordruuk to push back the rising shadow.

However, they soon discovered they faced a threat more powerful than anticipated. Idraman had no choice but to rally the full strength of the Seven Realms to rescue them.

No fanfares accompanied Hadrul, the warrior Archon, as he led the greatest army of living memory through the Caerwal Pass. Dwarfed by the sheer rock faces bearing down on their flanks, the vast ranks bearing their proud banners had entered the northern realms in silence. With no thoughts of glory, the soldiers had marched passed their families and loved ones who openly wept without shame.

Yet Idraman, like Sylvena, had been tricked. Lured into a trap, he had sent sixty thousand of their finest soldiers to be trampled into the dusty plain. And not in a forlorn hope of victory, not now the *Draedalak* had risen. Their sacrifice would serve only to delay the enemy and give him time to seal the pass.

Idraman turned and gave the signal. If he were to fail, the reserves would head for the ports in the south and advise those willing to listen to abandon the realms. Many in the north had refused to leave their homes in the face of terror, believing the strength of the Seven Realms would protect them. But the realms had been outwitted, and to Idraman's regret, he could do nothing for them — they were already lost.

He glanced at the cliffs at his side. Idraman did not relish the task ahead. But not to act would condemn many more to death or a life of slavery. The lands to the north would be sacrificed to secure the south. Closing the pass would drain his power, and if unsuccessful, he would be too weak to halt the enemy advance. But he had no choice. Idraman widened his stance, planted his staff, and closed his eyes. Amid the cacophony of screeching demons, he found what he sought. A faint, but clear echo from the Song of Creation, one of the earlier Verses untainted by the horrors that beset the Maidens in later times. He allowed their voices to fill his being and drew upon their power.

The ground trembled. A wide strip of land spanning the pass danced as if boiling from fires raging below. Idraman tipped his staff and thrust it into the air. The dust erupted as the rock beneath burst forth, freed from centuries of constraint. Far across the plain to the north, the battle paused. The heat in his body died as the *Draedalak* searched for the source of the sudden surge of power. Idraman stiffened as their terrible gaze froze him to the bone. The forming rock wall shuddered. He threw back his head, reciting the lines to complete the barrier. The rock stood firm. The foundations held. But in the distance, the enemy mocked him — something was amiss.

Idraman opened his eyes and groaned. A gap at the center of his defense, wide enough for an army to march through fifty abreast, refused to close and seal the wall. This was the work of evil hands groping beneath the earth to deny him access to the bedrock. Again, they had got the better of him, anticipating his every move leaving the pass open to their hordes.

But Idraman was not yet defeated. He drove his staff into the ground and stretched out his arms. Bowing his head, he ventured deeper into the Song. Idraman delved down into the heart of the mountains, seeking the force that had raised them. He found the echo of their birth as the peaks thrust skyward. He embraced its power and clenched his fists. A shimmering blue curtain emerged from the opposing rock faces. The charged air of the pass crackled as Idraman fought to seal his barrier. But the spoiled ground resisted. He strived to bring his hands together against a force pushing them apart. Idraman cried out, imploring the mountains to grant him strength in his hour of need. And they obliged. The barrier closed. But it was yet too weak to withstand a determined assault. Idraman would need another day to consolidate his defense.

The shriek froze the blood in his veins. Uluriel had learned of his strategy. She had promised the spoils of the south to the *Draedalak*. And a price had to be paid. If she could not deliver, Uluriel and the warlock would be that price. The battle had to be won.

One by one, Idraman's Order weakened in the face of the renewed rage of the assault. They began to fall. First Dormarl, the youngest of the Order, fell silent. Idraman staggered as then another, Elsaya was lost. At their side, the soldiers died by the hundred, torn to shreds by the barbed, flaming whips of the *Draedalak*. Yet the dead were the fortunate ones. Idraman knew the fate awaiting the captured. They would be tortured to the point of madness, then drafted into the ranks of the masses emerging from their dark places of hiding. Yet Hadrul fought bravely on. The warrior Archon's skills surpassed even those of Malendra who had fought with Dorlan. Perhaps while he lived, the enemy could be repelled.

The Amayans! Idraman's spirits rose as a host rode to their aid. The first wave crashed into the dark ranks. But they too were forced back by the *Draedalak*. The Amayans wheeled their frightened mounts, forming a circle around the last three of the Order. Nyomae, her courage never wavering, second only to Idraman in the knowledge of the ancient lore of the Song. Then Mordram, both wise and resilient, wielding the Sword of the Realms. And the last, Finromir, the strongest and most skilled fighter of the Order, pushed beyond the limits of endurance as he stood resolute in the face of the maelstrom. They frantically scoured the Verses to open a passage and banish the demons. But their combined strength was almost spent, and their resistance began to crumble. If the enemy broke through now, Idraman had no means to stop them. His work was not complete. The hordes would be upon him all too soon and breach his unfinished defense as if made of straw. There was no other way. Long years of study had brought him to the brink of understanding the earliest Verses. Idraman's jaw clenched as he found what he sought. He hesitated. Before him lay a path only the most courageous and strongest dared to take. Had he the strength? Six centuries of painstaking study would be lost should he fail. To incite the secret word of the Maidens would be to risk his mind... and most likely his life.

Hadrul was lost! Weakened by the baying *Draedalak*, the mighty warrior Archon was trampled by their cloven hooves, then hacked to pieces by the unrelenting onslaught.

The Amayans' light faded. Their circle broke. The demons fell upon the last of Idraman's Order. He cried out at the loss of Mordram as he too was crushed into the plain. He was out of time. Few Amayans remained alongside Nyomae and Finromir as they stood against the might of the enemy. But Finromir faltered. The time had come. Idraman took a breath and uttered the most sacred and powerful lines known to his Order. He screamed as the voices of the Maidens entered his soul. Idraman endured the pain to speak the name of Nyomae. But not her mortal name, her real name, the one bestowed upon her by the Maidens.

Far across the plain, the *Draedalak* paused. Idraman had invoked the pure, unbridled power of the Maidens to grant Nyomae the strength to resist. Her power would be fleeting, but immense. Nyomae responded. Idraman's strength waned as she drained the last of his reserves. No! He read her mind. In the despair of her madness, Nyomae chose a dangerous path. Idraman could not stop her. The eruption seared his eyeballs just as the shimmering edges of his protective shroud melded. He had sealed the Caerwal Pass with a Word of Forbidding, and along with it, the fate of those stranded in the north. The last of his strength seeped from his bones. Idraman fell.

# 2. A Light in the Shadow

Nyomae opened her eyes and blinked in the light streaming into the Archon's quarters. Elodi and Toryn dared to breathe as Nyomae gathered her senses. They had waited two long weeks for her to recover from the encounter with Uluriel. And during that time, Elodi's impatience had grown, frustrated by the lack of urgency from Lord Kernlow and his new Council. She hoped Nyomae's return, and with it, her insight, would force Kernlow to act.

Nyomae shielded her eyes from the light. 'In my deep sleep, I came across Idraman's Verse of the last days of the Seven Realms. That is how events truly unfolded on the Gormadon Plain on that darkest of days. But as you have come to learn, the said plain was not in the south. Instead, it is where the Foranfae now flourishes, seeded by the Nym to cleanse the ruined land following my... intervention.' She collapsed back into her chair, exhausted by her recollection.

Toryn looked down at his clasped hands. 'I saw our forces advance. In the Foranfae. The night we spent trapped in the Nym's circle.' His voice faltered. 'I heard the call of their horns. I saw knights from the old realms, so tall, so strong.' He turned to Elodi. 'The horses screamed. The knights cried out. So terrible to hear. And they died, they all died. Lightning flashed across the sky… and then silence.'

Nyomae met Toryn's gaze. 'I had no choice. The enemy possessed those fine soldiers as they fell. Idraman took a great risk. He called upon the earliest known Verses to give me his strength, also putting my existence in jeopardy. But as he saw it, and I agree, there was no other means to save the day. With the knowledge gained, he invoked my Maidens' Name, the name given to me by the Three.'

Elodi glanced at Toryn. 'I do not know of this Maidens' Name? Do we all possess one?'

'Every living being created by them has one. But it is most sacred. Few will know their true name. I do not know my own. As all appeared lost, Idraman entered my First Verse, the one that brought me into this world. It is our belief that the name of every creature yet to be born was assigned at the beginning of time. When Idraman cried out mine, it opened the way for me to unite momentarily with…' a tear rolled down her cheek, 'the Maidens' voices that proclaimed my right to life as they sang the Song of Creation.'

Toryn's face tingled. 'And would they have spoken mine and Elodi's true names?'

'Indeed, thus enabling your inclusion in the myriad of the Verses to follow.'

Elodi's eyes glistened. 'Yet this name is not made known to us?'

'For good reason. To cite it opens the path back to the earliest of Verses. Draegelan feared it could also be heard by those who wished us harm. If used in conjunction with lines from the Dark Verses, our name could be removed, thus casting us into the Great Void outside of time. Few have the strength to invoke a Maidens' Name. It would have taken Idraman decades to recover. He may yet be weak all these years later.'

Toryn took her hand. 'And it was this that saved the day?'

Nyomae let out a long sigh. 'At great cost. When Idraman spoke my name, it allowed me to reach further back into the Song than any of my Order, save Draegelan.

In a way, Uluriel allowed this to happen. She had ventured deep to bring the *Draedalak* to the battlefield, opening Verses previously beyond our grasp. But as I sought the means to cast back the demons to their own time' — her voice wavered — 'I stumbled upon the Verse of Unmaking. Whether another unknown presence in the Song led me there, I cannot tell. But as all fell about me in the face of unspeakable terror, I saw no other way open to me. With the combined strength of Idraman and Toryn's father, Finromir, flowing through me' — her head dropped into her hands — 'I uttered those dreaded words.'

Toryn put his arm around her trembling shoulders. 'Surely, the enemy would have been victorious had you done nothing.'

Nyomae looked up. 'While my action *unmade* the bulk of Uluriel's army, those not of our time such as the *Draedalak*, shreeks and other unworldly creatures, were expelled but not eradicated. They yet exist, able to fight another day once the Ul-dalak have the strength to recall them. And sadly, I believe that day may come all too soon. From your account of the first attack on Calerdorn, Elodi, we know they already conjure apparitions of these foul beasts, and that alone requires tremendous power. But the Ul-dalak will not be content with mere illusions. Our struggle with Uluriel at the Caerwal Tower proves her confidence grows. And I suspect once she recovers from her expulsion from the Archon, she will have the ability to summon the Draedalak possibly within the year.'

Elodi gasped. 'Kernlow must be made aware of this. He is too hesitant, and his indecision and lack of action will cost us dear.' She glanced to the doorway. 'And what of the Golesh? Do they hold the south?'

Nyomae shook her head. 'A falsehood. When I entered Mordram's mind in the tower, it helped me recover much of my memory. And I found neither he nor I had any recollection of the Golesh.'

Toryn gaped. 'They don't exist?' He looked at Elodi. 'But since childhood we've been taught to fear them.'

Nyomae shrugged. 'The Golesh are purely an invention, created and maintained by Uluriel through the Archon and the whispers of the Ul-dalak. But it is a powerful lie. I suspect the archives have been amended, and the rumors will have spread both quickly, and far and wide among a people fearful of their own shadows. Remember, famine and disease followed on the heels of the devastating losses of the conflict. All who fought at Gormadon either perished, or like me, lost their minds. People in a state of despair are people who can be made to believe in anything.'

Toryn frowned. 'I find it hard to believe the Golesh are not real.'

Nyomae slowly rose from her chair. 'And that is what the Ul-dalak wishes you to believe. A convincing tale told often will soon take on the guise of truth. And of course, Uluriel knew those living in fear and despair are easily led.' She turned to face the door and appeared to take comfort from the mountains turning orange in the setting sun. 'The deceit served its purpose well, perhaps far better than Uluriel could have anticipated. It kept the strength of the old realms secured beyond the mountains while our enemy sought to recover from the last battle and gain control of the north. Like us, they suffered huge losses in the last moments of the battle. But they appear to recover faster than we do.'

Toryn eyed the charts on the wall. 'It's as if the map of the realms has been turned upside down. The threat comes from the north, not the south.'

Nyomae turned. 'I'm afraid it is as you say. We are on the wrong side of the gate.'

Toryn scratched his head. 'So, the blue haze above the gate is the work of Idraman?'

Elodi straightened. 'I too saw a shimmering light on my first visit. But I assumed it was but a trick of the light.'

Nyomae returned to her chair. 'It is a Word of Forbidding. This proves Idraman still lives and somehow retains the strength to sustain it.' She glanced to the sky outside. Uluriel knew the Caerwal Pass was key. The Uldalak ultimately wanted to drive south into the old realms. Idraman was unaware that Uluriel had sealed the bedrock within the Song. Thus, he could not raise the ground in the center to complete his wall. But while Idraman believed she had outthought him, she had also underestimated his strength. The Word of Forbidding across the pass is a powerful Verse. It is a lock, if you wish, on the air between the rock walls, much like the Verse Uluriel used on the ground.'

Elodi looked at the map. 'Then why the need for a gate?'

Nyomae thought for a moment. 'I imagine Uluriel, in the guise of the Archon, built the gate to conceal Idraman's barrier, a translucent barrier at that. If the south side of the pass was visible, we would not see a rabble of the imaginary Golesh, but forces we would recognize as our own. And sadly, I assume the construction workers met with their deaths to prevent word of it leaving the pass. Idraman sought to hold back the spawn of Ormoroth. His barrier has succeeded, but that also includes us.' She held up a hand. 'Ah. And of course, the gate also serves to prevent those in the old realms from looking into the north.'

Elodi sighed. 'Then it is we who are the Lost Realms. And the seas? The Archon promised to open the way to the south for Lord Broon and the Elites.'

'As with the barrier, it was Idraman who bent the seas

to prevent Uluriel's forces sailing *south*. Having lost most of their finest fighters during the last battle, the old realms were also weak. It would take decades to raise an army capable of defeating anything the Ul-dalak could muster at short notice.'

Elodi gripped the edge of her chair. 'But what of Bardon?'

'I fear it is Uluriel who now commands the seas. It's possible she could have calmed the undercurrents only to stir them back to life. All it required was a spy in the Watchtower to inform her when the fleet had entered the trap.'

Elodi slumped. 'Then we are all but defeated. Bardon and thousands of our Elites are at the bottom of the sea, while the remainder lie buried beneath the rocks in the pass.'

Toryn walked to the map. 'Then what of the south?' He ran his hand along the Caerwals down to the plains below. 'Have the old realms recovered?' He looked at Nyomae. 'Could you speak with Idraman?'

'I did not know for sure he lived until now. But I'm certain the voice I heard from over the Caerwals is the same that found you in the Archon's dungeon, Toryn.'

'Then he wants to help us? Could he defeat the Ul-dalak?'

'He must be close to Draegelan's advanced age, but sustaining the Word of Forbidding consumes what little life he has left. He would be a most welcome ally, but I fear he may not be with us for much longer. And the voice I heard was not that of a man in command of his mind. He too sounds confused, desperate even. If he leads a new Order of Echoes in the south, he would not sound as he does. Furthermore, I believe he may be imprisoned, but for what reason I cannot tell. And sadly, he appears bewildered, living under a shadow, as once did I.' She wrung her hands. 'I have tried reaching him through the Song but have failed. It is a skill requiring much practice, and both the speaker and recipient need their minds to be open. I shall attempt to teach you as there will come a time when there will be many leagues between us, and our birds too slow or in danger of interception.'

'Could Elodi also learn? It would be most useful.'

Nyomae looked to Elodi. 'Amayans have their own ways and, as far as I am aware, do not use the Song as those of my Order. I believe it's the stones of the Amanach that provide them with both strength and the means to communicate over distance.'

Elodi frowned. 'How do you use the Song to speak to one another?'

Nyomae sat back. 'It is my belief that every living soul drifts into the Song when sleeping. We have a connection to our own Verse that brought us into this world. Perhaps our dreams come from our nocturnal journeys through the Song, linking with others and their Verses. I and Idraman believed we could exploit this. We arranged to meet in our dreams at a chosen spot. I would recite a line from a poem, and the following day Idraman would attempt to repeat it back. Before long, we were able to engage in a short conversation, but our time together in the dream was always scarce.' She looked about her. 'Ah. This room would be an ideal location for us to meet in our dreams, Toryn. We shall begin our practice at once. We can accomplish this as I teach you the ways of the Song. But we must take care. There will be the Watchers. These are the eyes of our enemy, ever-present, ever vigilant to my, and now most likely, your entry. I will teach you ways to avoid them, but as yet, I am unable to evade the likes of Uluriel if they are present. I shall strive to converse with Idraman but do not hold out much hope.'

Elodi's gaze wandered to the mountains. 'Yet the

question remains, if Idraman created the barrier to protect the south, why is there no apparent defense on their side? Where are the guards watching the gate should Uluriel attack? Why is the pass to the south abandoned?'

Nyomae massaged her brow. 'Alas, that is yet another mystery to solve. It could be a feint. Toryn's eyes may have been misled by a Word of Concealment. It may be the pass is guarded, but the defenders do not wish to be seen.'

Elodi sighed. 'It will be months before the new tower is finished. Can you recall the situation in the south before the gate was built? Could you somehow penetrate Idraman's defense to *see* what lies beyond it?'

'I lived under the shadow for far too long. Much of my former life appears like a dream. At times, I get flashes but I suspect much remains to be revealed. And I do not yet possess the strength to challenge Idraman's Word of Forbidding. But I suggest we wait before investigating the south. The danger lies north.' Nyomae's hands dropped to her lap. 'Uluriel did not possess the Archon solely to cripple the recovery of the Five Realms. Through the Archon, she gained access to the restricted archives secured in the citadel. And I have no doubt she will also have studied the ancient scrolls held at the Seats of Learning of Neverdor and Abernost. The arcane records have challenged our greatest minds, but if Uluriel has read and mastered them, she will soon become a foe too great for our combined strength. I spent many years with her when she was Sylvena, but I cannot pretend to know her mind.' She tipped back her head and rubbed her eyes. 'And another thing troubles me.'

Elodi slapped the arm of her chair. 'Ah! It seems there's not a crumb of comfort to be had. What else should concern us?'

Nyomae exhaled. 'To date, we have faced only three captains of the Ul-dalak. Uluriel, Uleva and Uldrak are corrupt forms of my Order. But there must be others. Ormoroth's warlocks, his commanders of old, would outrank them all. Only a warlock could have captured and transformed one as powerful as Sylvena into the mockery we know as Uluriel. But where are they? They have yet to reveal themselves, but when they do…'

Toryn's scalp tingled. 'Could they be occupied elsewhere?'

Nyomae nodded. 'That is my fear. I suspect they may be far to the north, possibly tormenting your father.'

Toryn's jaw clenched. 'And we're too weak to press beyond our own border at Dorn.'

Nyomae placed her hand on his knee. 'We must be patient. I believe Finromir may yet frustrate their plans. And in a way, he prevents them throwing their full strength at us. Perhaps that is his strategy. But now my strength returns, and I have the two of you at my side, perhaps we may yet strike a blow.' She arched her back. 'But I am exhausted. The lifting of my shadow overwhelms me. There are so many confusing voices in my head, and I struggle to make sense of them.' She glanced at the door. 'Let us take a rest, and some much-needed fresh air.'

Elodi was surprised to discover the sun had already set, and the stars shone brightly in the clear night sky. The first time she had stepped onto the balcony, Bardon had held her arm to support her. But now she stood steady, in awe of the expanse before them. The new moon's dark face looked down from the sky, tinged silver by the thousands of stars, proud to glimmer in the absence of moonlight. Below, sounds from the city barely reached them, and in the silence, Elodi could be forgiven for thinking the land was at peace and all was well. She reached out to take the hands of Toryn and Nyomae, taking comfort from their warmth.

Elodi broke the silence. 'I recall the Archon telling us he came out here every day to remind himself why he fought on. At the time I found his words reassuring. But now we know it was Uluriel eyeing the ultimate prize she wished to take from us.' She turned to Nyomae. 'Was the Archon blind? I recall his eyes sparkling with many colors. But they were white like fog prior to his death in the tower.'

Nyomae nodded. 'He lost his sight as he fought the *Draedalak*. Only Uluriel's presence gave him the semblance of vision, the *farsight*, which I believe Toryn possesses.' She took his hand and ran a finger across the markings on his palm. 'You and I are… Imaari. Ah yes, it comes back to me now. That is the name by which our kind is known. Some hear and enter the Song, but simply observe. While Imaari have the ability to enter *and* use the power within the Verses.'

'You can tell this from my hands?'

"'The lines do not lie. Your father was more adept than I, and I believe you will also attain his full powers with time and study.' She released his hand and looked at Elodi. 'And as an Amayan, you also will have a semblance of the *farsight* and access to the old powers of the land. But we have limited time for me to fully recover my skills, and for you to master yours. That is, if we are to survive the ordeal that lies ahead.'

Elodi's eyes were inevitably drawn to the north. She smiled wryly. 'The Archon dismissed my claim that I could see the peaks of the Kolossos, insisting it was a cloud. It seems Uluriel cannot see everything. She did not sense my Amayan blood. But at the time, I was also ignorant of my heritage.' She gazed upon the jagged spine of the mountains rising from the far side of the Foranfae. They glistened under the bright starlight, appearing as if

Behemora, the great whale, had surfaced momentarily from the gray seas to take a breath before descending to the depths to resume the vain search for his mate. Her eyes shifted to the misty treetops of the Foranfae. 'When one looks at the beauty of this world, one wonders why anyone would want to corrupt and destroy it. What drives such animosity against order and peace?'

Nyomae placed her hand upon Elodi's. 'Sadly, it is difficult to fathom what motivates those who wish to maim this land. It hurts to know how someone as noble and learned as Sylvena could be turned so quickly to their cause. Moreover, I am puzzled as to why she was defeated while Finromir yet resists. She must have endured the most terrible torment.' She grasped the railing. 'I often wonder whether I and Idraman could have done more to dissuade her from seeking the relic. The realms suffered a serious blow that day. And, from what we know from the last words of the Archon, the part of Sylvena that remained true, had the misfortune to witness the result of her actions.'

Toryn shuddered. 'Of that I am certain. When I entered Wyke Wood, the voices whispered such a foul promise.' He turned to Elodi. 'And what a stroke of luck you arrived before Uleva could get inside my head.'

Nyomae smiled. 'Luck, Toryn? Or destiny?'

# 3. Of Sorcerers, Ghosts & Ghouls

'I demand to be informed of what is discussed at Lord Kernlow's Council!' Elodi slammed her hand down hard on the Castellan's desk, dislodging a pile of his papers. 'I am the leader of a realm, one I hasten to add, has suffered the most from the actions of our enemy. And, despite its woes, committed a sizeable force to fight for the Archon. Yet, whenever I try to meet with Kernlow, I come up against a dozen Palace Guards determined to keep me out. At the very least I should receive word of every decision immediately. But tell me, Castellan, why am I denied a seat at Kernlow's table?'

The candlelight made his lined face appear more troubled than ever. '*Lord* Kernlow has a most demanding schedule. He prefers to keep the numbers on his Council limited to hasten the process of decision making. He—'

'What decisions has his so-called emergency committee made in the last two weeks? Do they even acknowledge we face a crisis?'

'I can assure you they are making progress. The working parties to clear the Caerwal Pass were assembled and is proceeding as scheduled. Furthermore, measures are being drafted to ensure crops are harvested and—'

'What of the north? Does the committee know of the movements of the enemy?'

'Reserves have been sent to strengthen the—'

'Reserves? Does Kernlow seriously think the part-time soldiers of Farrand can hold back the might of the evil tide? And who will bring in the harvest if he sends farmers to do the work of the Archonian Guard?'

The Castellan leaned back and folded his arms. 'Lord

Kernlow's priority is to fortify and consolidate here in Farrand. If he sends knights and his guards north, it will weaken our one and only stronghold. But… I can inform you that work has begun at Caermund to replace the ships lost from Bardon's failed mission.'

'That's *Lord* Broon to you. And I trust you're not inferring it was due to his leadership.'

'Err… no, ma'am. But a great many fine ships were lost after all. We have two under construction at Caermund, but more are planned.' He sat forward. 'And plans are afoot to build ships at West Haven to replace the aging *Celestra.* Lord Kernlow has the wisdom to ensure that in the near future, supplies and soldiers can be moved quickly by sea to deal with any potential threat.' The Castellan held her gaze. 'So perhaps it would be wise, ma'am, to not judge him until you are fully aware of the facts.'

Elodi refused to look away. 'Have you not heard a word I have said? That is precisely why I am here.' Her jaw tightened. 'If I was *fully aware*, then I would have the facts to judge where and when I please, Castellan. But, while my knowledge of ships is limited' — a chill ran up her spine as she recalled the dark walls of water crashing against the *Celestra* — 'I do know the hardy trees found only in Ormsk are essential to construct a sturdy hull.' She sat back. 'Has our dear lord made arrangements to secure the only supply we have? Perhaps our enemy already has designs on the forests with the same thought in mind.'

The Castellan glanced down to his papers still scattered across the floor. 'Err… that I… yes, of course he has. The reserves of Ormsk will be supported to secure the forests in question.'

'Reserves? There you go again. Please remind Kernlow, we are up against battle-hardened Ruuk that wouldn't think twice of slitting the throats of their own mothers if they thought it would gain an advantage.' Elodi took a deep breath. 'If we are to make an effort to keep each other *informed*, Castellan, then it's only fair to tell you what I have learned from my own sources.'

'And that would be?'

'Yesterday, I spoke with Nyomae, and I have to tell you, what she said does not fill me with confidence. If she is correct in her reading of the Verses, it will matter little how much strength Kernlow can muster to defend Archonholm. She believes the enemy have yet to reveal their full hand. And she fears they will soon overrun the northern realms while we sit comfortably on our backsides down here.'

The Castellan shifted in his chair. 'Do we take the word of this… this sorcerer? Should we risk all and drive north into the open on the whim of something she has seen in a dream?'

Elodi's pulse rose. 'Using terms such as *sorcerer* and *dreams* only serve to expose your ignorance, Castellan.'

'I will not sit and listen—'

'Then stand and listen if you wish! I will not shirk from saying exactly what I think of you. We both know there is no love lost between us, but I am willing to suspend my contempt as it's imperative we work together for the good of the realms.'

The Castellan's face reddened. 'Agreed, Lady Harlyn. But I ask you to withdraw your accusation of my *ignorance*.'

'That I will do once you have proved otherwise and heeded Nyomae's warning.'

'Yet the fact remains she is—'

'The most powerful of our dwindling list of allies, who, just to ensure you are in possession of all the facts, stood beside our Archon in the last battle. And she commands power beyond anything we currently have at our disposal.' The Castellan sank back into his chair. Elodi placed her hands on his desk. 'Now, if you're willing to listen, I believe Kernlow needs to be made aware there are far greater forces in this world than we have yet faced. Our enemies have driven us to the brink of defeat with just a handful of their captains. What we have witnessed recently is nothing compared to what they are likely to call upon in due course. When that will be, Nyomae cannot tell. And this at a time when we have never been more vulnerable. If we are to stand even a slim chance, we must consider striking north before they can unleash their full strength.'

The Castellan's face paled. 'Yet if we disperse our forces across the realms, they'd simply pick us off one by one. Would it not be prudent of Lord Kernlow to consolidate our position here in the south?'

'Our enemy possesses greater numbers and superior powers. They only need to cut Archonholm off from the rest of the realms, and the farms that supply our food, to ultimately achieve a victory. But we can do much to disrupt the Ul-dalak's preparations with raids on the Ruuk positions and their supply lines. This can be achieved with small bands to cause havoc and perhaps even panic. We must do all we can to delay their efforts to summon the fell beasts from the past.'

The Castellan stroked his chin. 'Yet that will still draw strength from Farrand, and such raids will expose our limited numbers to needless danger. Lord Kernlow is unlikely to undertake a plan involving even the slightest of risks.'

Elodi groaned. 'His current strategy is a risk, Castellan. We live in dangerous times. Is Kernlow aware that his current lack of action concedes territory to the enemy? Our enemy will enslave the good folk of Harlyn and Broon, feeding only those who will be forced to serve them. And don't think the enemy won't commandeer our inexperienced reserves Kernlow sends north into their ranks. If they have the means to control Dorlan and my fallen knights, it would be a simple task to turn them to their aim.'

The Castellan opened his mouth, then paused. Elodi sensed she may have made her argument. He glanced to the door. 'Ma'am, I have no say in the affairs of the committee.'

'That may be so, but I believe you have some influence on who is allowed to petition them. I have made my case before now. Why have you not granted me the opportunity?'

'Due process must be followed. All in good time, ma'am.'

'All in good time? Does Kernlow believe our enemies will wait while he re-arranges the seating at his Council? And, talking of due process, what of my objection to Kernlow's appointment as Steward? I submitted my challenge ten days ago, yet I have had no word, not even an acknowledgment of my letter.'

'As you can see, ma'am.' He nodded at the papers on the floor. 'I have many duties to perform as Castellan. I expect your objection will reach the top of my pile shortly.' He leaned over to retrieve the files, flipped through the first few pages, and pulled out a sheet. 'Ah. Here it is.' He placed it on his desk and flattened the creases. 'I can confirm I have received your objection, ma'am, but I'm sure you appreciate these things take time.'

Elodi snatched the paper from his hand. 'We don't have the luxury of time!' She waved it in his face. 'See to it that my objection is heard. And while you're at it, set up a meeting with Kernlow. As a ruler of a realm, I demand my right to an audience. The Five Realms' Charter states he has five days to comply with my request.'

'But… Lady Harlyn. I cannot recall receiving an official written request for a—'

Elodi slapped her letter on the desk. 'My *official*

objection to Kernlow's appointment *requires* a meeting! And by my reckoning it is already five days overdue.'

The Castellan shrank back in his chair. 'Then I will raise a point of order for the next meeting, ma'am.' He picked up another sheet and rubbed his chin. 'Ah yes. Lady Harlyn. There is another matter I must discuss with you. It's... it's about the young man from Darrow.' He cleared his throat. 'It has come to my attention that he spends many hours in your company.'

'That is none of your business.'

'It is when you grant him access to areas that are otherwise restricted.' He raised his hand as Elodi began to speak. 'In the days following events at the pass, proper procedures were overlooked. But you should know I have since re-instated the measures deemed necessary when we suspected enemy spies were operating in the city.'

Elodi's eyes narrowed. 'Are you suggesting Toryn is working for the enemy?'

'No, not at all. But what do we know of this… this simple farm boy? Can we—?'

'This *simple farm boy*, as you put it, saved many hundreds of lives at the pass, including yours, Castellan. Had he not acted, I doubt if more than a handful would have survived. And may I remind you, Toryn was key to purging the Archon of Uluriel.'

'And this would be the intervention that led to the Archon's death. He would—'

'Still be alive? You cannot think we would be better off if he had survived? Had the Archon defeated Toryn and Nyomae at the tower, we would be none the wiser our leader was controlled by our enemy. She had spent the better part of three hundred years draining the poor man. There was nothing left of him. He was just a shell.'

The Castellan shrugged. 'Perhaps we will never know.'

'What we do know is few would have survived that day

had they not intervened. And for that, I will ask you to grant him, and Nyomae, full access to the same areas I enjoy. They both hold a position on my staff. Therefore, I expect them to be treated with the respect worthy of their position. And while you're at it, I want my captains, Gundrul and Cubric, to be given the same pass. And I would like Gundrul's guards and Harlyn's forces stationed closer to Archonholm. It is not acceptable that all but one of my captains are a three-day ride from the city. And it's not as if we are lacking space in the barracks and stables of Archonholm. Twelve stalls for Aldorman and my knights is not acceptable.'

The Castellan shifted. 'We have laws regarding forces under the command of those outside of Farrand, ma'am. Surely you appreciate that.'

Elodi leaned forward. 'If you're suggesting my soldiers are a threat to Kernlow, I resent that. I have not ruled out taking my force north to take back my realm.'

'Please, Lady Harlyn. I am not suggesting you pose a threat. Simply that we must uphold the laws of Farrand. And—' he shuffled his papers — 'far be it for me to offer advice to one so experienced in the ways of the battlefield, but wouldn't it be folly to take such a small army to face an unknown force?'

Elodi eyed him closely, unsure if he was being sincere. 'I reserve my right to act in my realm's best interest. I am willing to aid Kernlow, but as yet, weeks after the tragic events at the pass, I remain ignorant of his objectives. In the meantime, please arrange for all my soldiers to be brought into the West Barracks.'

The Castellan's eyes shifted to his reflection in the dark window. 'Again, these are matters that will have to be put to the Council, ma'am.'

'Ah yes, the Council. How would the realms function without their wisdom?' Elodi sat back. 'These are unprecedented times, Castellan. Would Nyomae and the Archon have held back the dark forces at Gormadon had a committee deliberated at length every move on the battlefield?' She held his gaze. 'While the Council sit on their oversized… hands, our enemy reaps the rewards of captured territory.' Elodi stiffened. 'Is Kernlow aware of the rumors regarding Nordryn?'

'Rumors? I'm surprised you, of all people, should give credence to idle tittle tattle. We have—'

'Then why was he, leader of easily the strongest force outside of the Archon's, allowed to sit tight in Keld? Uluriel did not request his armies to be present at the pass when she unleashed the landslide. Why do you think she spared his soldiers?'

The Castellan's brow creased. 'If you're suggesting the ruler of Broon, one who has passed their own stringent trials, could possibly be in league—'

'Yet we all failed to notice our very own Archon was compromised. I would question both yours and Kernlow's belief that Nordryn's loyalty is beyond doubt. So, let us assume that something is afoot in Broon of which we remain unaware. But even if all is well and *quiet*, the enemy occupies a third of my realm. And I have next to no chance of stopping them advancing into Noor and Darrow. What then? Will they be satisfied with that when the riches and fertile lands of Kernlow and Farrand are within their reach?'

He scoffed. 'Oh, come now, ma'am. You can't think the Ruuk have the strength to make a move against Farrand and Archonholm this side of next spring?'

'They know we have lost a large part of our forces. Would they sit back and wait for us to recover our strength? Would you if our positions were reversed?'

'Even so, ma'am, Archonholm still represents a formidable fortress to assail. It will take months for them to assemble a force large enough to contemplate an attack. And don't forget, we will have completed much of our outer wall before long. And if they bring these fell beasts you fear they command, I'm certain our defenses will be equal to them.'

'I wish I could share your optimism, Castellan. I have witnessed firsthand how quickly a ruthless and determined enemy can take a city. We thought ourselves safe behind our considerable defenses at Calerdorn. But we had underestimated the strength of the Ul-dalak. And, according to Nyomae, this is only the beginning as their power grows. The outcome of the battles to come will not depend on military might alone. We may face older, darker forces than the Archon fought at Gormadon. And I don't need to remind you that conflict did not end in our favor. So, if you could please see—'

The door burst open. A red-faced guard stumbled in. 'Apologies, Castellan. We have a…' he glanced to Elodi, 'a situation requiring your attendance.'

Elodi followed the Castellan, easily keeping pace as he strode through the gatehouse. He had asked her to stay behind, insisting it was not necessary for her to accompany him. But Elodi had seen the anxious look on the guard's face and had to know what had happened. Three guards stood in a huddle outside on the road. On hearing their footsteps, one came to meet them. 'Castellan. Sorry to bring you out on a chilly night, but we thought you should be made aware of… events. And you had ordered us to report anything unusual, but we weren't sure whether this—'

'Just tell me what happened, Captain. Then let me decide.'

The captain adjusted his cloak. 'We heard someone call, all mournful like, sir. Call may be the wrong word. Almost like a fox, but not a fox.' He glanced at Elodi. His face looked pale and drawn in the torchlight. 'Not pleasant to hear. Made the hairs on the back of our necks stand up.'

The Castellan scoffed. 'And you brought me out here because of the hairs on your neck?'

He stiffened. 'No, sir. Of course not, sir. At first, we thought the cry came from the forest so we didn't bother to investigate. We often hear and see strange things in that place. Well, you know all about—'

'Then I ask again.' The Castellan grew impatient. 'What warrants interrupting my meeting?'

'Ah. Well… it's moved, sir. Now it's coming from our side of the river.' He raised his sword. 'Down there, about a hundred paces along the road.'

Elodi peered to the dark river visible at the edge of the torchlight. 'Did you see anything cross?'

The Castellan held up his hand. 'Lady Harlyn. If you please, allow me to—'

'No, ma'am. Nothing. Nothing at all.'

Elodi ignored the Castellan's obvious displeasure. 'And have you investigated now it's on our side?'

The captain's eyes shifted between the two. 'Yes, ma'am… sir. And that was when we thought it best to send for you. You see when we heard it again, we saw a…' he glanced back to his companions, 'a sort of… ghostly light.'

The Castellan sneered. 'Ghosts? Have you been drinking on duty, Captain?'

'Oh no, don't get me wrong, sir. I'm not saying it was a spirit as such. More like a flickering, pale light. Cast a peculiar reflection on the wall, it did. More so than we thought it should, seeing as it was so faint.'

The Castellan looked to the wall. 'I see nothing.' He turned. 'Lady Harlyn. Do you see a *ghostly light*?'

'Not at this moment. But I have seen many strange

things of late, Castellan.'

The captain shuffled. 'That's because it went out. We've not seen it since two of my guards went to get a closer look. And that's my concern, Castellan. The light went out and my men have yet to return. I've called over, but there's no reply.' He scratched his chin. 'It's a mystery, sir. I didn't want to send more in case it's…' again he looked to his colleagues, 'something unnatural.'

The Castellan shook his head. 'I've heard enough of this nonsense today. First…' he glanced at Elodi, 'I'm urged to heed the warning of a sorcerer's dream. Then tales of creatures of old, and now… I'm called out in the night because my guards are seeing ghosts.' He slid his sword from his scabbard. 'Come with me. I'll soon solve this *mystery*.'

# 4. Face of an Old Friend

'And the guards had no memory of the ghost?' Toryn stood with Elodi upon the North Terrace overlooking the road.

'None at all. We found them wandering along the road as if they'd woken from a deep sleep.' Elodi laughed. 'But when the Castellan approached, they certainly looked as if they'd seen a ghost then.' Her smile faded. 'Yet it seemed odd that they couldn't remember why they were out there.'

'And what of the Castellan? Was he satisfied with their story?'

'I think it's safe to say that he most certainly was not. He's put the whole watch on stable duty for a week. He's convinced they'd been drinking, and it was all in their heads. But it's no surprise. Everyone appears to be on edge. Grim tales are spreading around the city like a sickness. People are frightened. The disaster at the pass has shaken their faith in their leaders and the strength of Archonholm.' Her eyes followed the road east to where it looped around the forest. 'Rightly, they fear what is to come.'

Toryn looked down to the grassy bank where the guards had reported the sighting. 'Still, the *ghost* is worth investigating. It would help put our minds at ease if it turned out it was their eyes playing tricks on a dark night. We know little of the forces our enemy commands, yet our imagination is quick to fill the gaps.' He shuddered. 'Mine keeps me awake at nights, but if there are ghosts and ghouls already on the prowl this far south…'

'My father used to say we fear what we can't see more than what we can.' She sighed. 'But if that's true, I dread to think what yet lurks in the dark. Surely, it can't be worse than what I've seen with my own eyes.'

Toryn recalled the strange creatures on the banks of the Menon River. 'Yet we have to keep our spirits high to have the courage to face them.'

Elodi's hand rested on Toryn's. 'I know how you feel.'

He kept his eyes on the evening mist above the Foranfae, rising like steam from a simmering pot. His face burned. 'You do?'

'I felt the same following the death of my father. To have such responsibility suddenly thrust upon you comes as a shock.'

Toryn's shoulders dropped. 'Ah. I see.'

Elodi clasped his hands. 'But I know competence when I see it. Just as I can recognize someone who is not suitable to hold a position of power.' She turned to face him. 'I would not have appointed you to my staff if I did not think you capable.'

Toryn looked down at his hands in hers. 'It was only a few months ago that I was, as the Castellan described, a simple farm boy.' He chuckled. 'And not a very good one at that. I'd heard the tales of Calerdorn and Archonholm, but I never thought places as tall and as mighty really existed. They were just stories to me. Yet… yet now, here I am, overlooking another wonder of our world I thought was another of Hamar's fairy tales. And… to make it all the more unreal, I find myself holding hands with the fair lady of Harlyn.'

Elodi smiled. 'And I could say the same. I stand beside the son of the most powerful Imaari of Nyomae's Order.' Her gaze went to the forest. 'Neither of us could have anticipated this even a short while ago. But here we find ourselves playing a major part in the very survival of the realms.'

'Then I hope it doesn't rest upon the actions of this

*farm boy.'*

'You do yourself an injustice, Toryn.' She held up his hands and turned them over. 'These markings confirm you have inherited your father's abilities.'

He withdrew his hands and shoved them into his pockets. 'But abilities I have little knowledge of how to use.'

Elodi stepped back. 'That will come with time. Granted time is against us, but already you have accomplished more than the generals of Archonholm. And I'm sure with Nyomae's guidance you will soon be a force our enemies will not take lightly.'

Toryn's stomach knotted. 'From the exchanges I have had to date, I think it's safe to say I currently fear them more than they could possibly fear me.'

She touched his shoulder. 'You have already proven your courage. The journey to Greendell alone was treacherous. Many in your position would have given up long before you reached the town.'

Toryn thought back to stumbling over tree roots the night he had left Midwyche. 'Those days now seem a very long way off. And I wouldn't have gotten very far if it hadn't been for Hamar.'

'Look at how much you've changed. We both have. We've faced significant hardship, but as my father used to say, what doesn't kill you can only make you stronger. And considering our ordeals of late, we must be far stronger.'

'Then I hope you're right. And thank you for your trust.' He turned to her, took his hands from his pockets, and held hers. 'You can count on me. I won't let you down. I'll follow wherever you lead.'

Elodi looked away. 'I'm also aware of how you feel… about me.'

'You… you are?'

Her grip tightened. 'And I feel the same… about you.'

Toryn's face grew hot as his heart raced. 'You do? I didn't think—'

'From the moment you held me as I lay injured beneath the rubble, I sensed… a connection. At first, I wondered if it was due to our lineage, perhaps a bond between the Amayans and Imaari. But lately, I've come to know that while there is undoubtedly an element of that, what I feel for you is… is… perhaps not solely to… to do with that.'

Toryn gaped. 'Well, I… that's…' He dropped his hands as two Palace Guards approached. They nodded to Elodi and continued on their way. He watched them leave. 'I should imagine the ruling powers of this land would frown upon the likes of me standing alone, hand-in-hand with you.'

Elodi grinned. 'I'm sure you'll appreciate by now I do not care what the high and mighty of this land think. Not too long ago, Wendel, my Chief Advisor, suggested I find a suitable partner to produce an heir.'

'But that… wouldn't that mean…?'

She laughed. 'Well, yes. Of course.' Toryn's heart lurched as her troubles fell away to reveal the true Amayan within. An eyebrow raised as she noticed the look on his face. 'I politely, but firmly informed Wendel that it was not the time to be planning so far ahead. And could you imagine leading an army into battle heavy with child?' Her laughter faded. She touched his forearm. 'But I feel I must tell you. I cannot...' she searched for the right word, 'invest more at this moment, not with events unfolding as they are. I lost my father, and I never knew my mother. I can't face losing another I had come to hold dear. And the same must hold true for you. We face a considerable threat, and it's not unthinkable that either one of us, or both, will not see the end of the year. I therefore think it's—'

'Apologies for interrupting, ma'am.' An aide to the Castellan stepped forward.

Elodi glanced at Toryn before addressing the aide. She sighed. 'No apology is needed. I assume this is an important matter.'

'I'm afraid so, ma'am.' He nodded towards the east. 'We received a dispatch from Caermund this last hour.' Elodi's eyes closed. She knew what he was about to say. The aide cleared his throat. 'They report wreckage washing ashore along the entire Mund coast. There's enough to account for at least two dozen ships, and…' his head bowed, 'it's not just the remains of ships. There's also bodies of the Elites and their horses, ma'am. More than three hundred have been recovered as of yesterday.'

Elodi's jaw clenched. 'Thank you. Please inform the Castellan that I would like to read the dispatch in full.' She turned her back. A tear brimmed and ran down her cheek. 'We knew they must have died, but receiving confirmation makes it harder somehow.'

Toryn dabbed her cheek. 'Then Nyomae was right. A traitor on the Watchtower must have alerted Uluriel.'

'So many good people lost.' Elodi's eyes burned. 'We must not let them win. We cannot tolerate more death. We have to find a way to defeat these… fiends.' She turned to leave. 'I believe your tuition with Nyomae commences tomorrow. Let us hope you learn fast.'

Nyomae's pace surprised Toryn. He strode behind, recalling the days they had spent together tramping across the western realms. She spoke over her shoulder. 'You speak fondly of Hamar. He must have been a loyal and dear friend.'

'And even more so than I once thought.' Toryn watched as a rower struggled to steer his boat clear of the sturdy piers of the bridge. 'It wasn't until after his death that I appreciated just how much he had helped me. I was a restless child, never feeling that Midwyche was my home.'

Nyomae stopped at the bridge. 'And now we know why. It was a blessing that he had traveled wide and could satisfy your curiosity with his stories.'

Toryn chuckled. 'I was sure many were exaggerated. But my eyes have since been opened these last few months.'

Nyomae nodded to the boat. 'He's made it. Quite a skilled oarsman. It's a most potent river, not the easiest to negotiate.' She turned to Toryn. 'Did Hamar come this far south to Archonholm?'

'That he did. He trained here and later returned on at least three occasions I believe.'

Nyomae smiled. 'Ah, good. Then he would have crossed here.' She held out her hand and invited Toryn onto the busy roadway. Let us see if we can locate him from times past.'

Toryn gaped. 'I would dearly love to see him as a young man.'

'We'll sit here out of the way of the carts.' Nyomae perched on the parapet and patted the stonework. 'Let us begin your tuition in the ways of the Song.' Toryn sat down beside her. 'Your ventures to date have been somewhat haphazard and fraught with danger. I suspect the Watchers will likely be engaged elsewhere at this time, so we'll make the most of the opportunity.'

'Watchers?'

'My Order called them Watchers. As the name implies, they keep an eye on who enters the Song. They are not Imaari and appear to exist only within the Verses with no presence in our world. Idraman believed they were a creation of Ormoroth, or perhaps another dark force of earlier times.'

'Can they harm us?'

'No, they just *watch*. But the danger comes when they

inform others of our entry. Think of them as a guard dog alerting their master. In time, you'll learn to evade them and enter without detection. But as yet, your entry will come to their notice, and I don't have the ability to disguise you.'

'But you seem to think they'll not be watching this morning, at this place.'

'I imagine their attention will be on the borders of the occupied realms in the north.' She patted his hand. 'But be wary. There will be other, lesser mischief-makers from darker times. They may look intimidating but can be ignored.'

Toryn frowned. 'And who are these *mischief-makers*?'

Nyomae gazed up at the passing clouds. 'The dead who have become trapped or lost within their Verses. For instance, if someone has died in a brawl on this bridge, they may have failed to leave this world and remain trapped.'

'There's more to this Song than I first thought.'

Nyomae laughed. 'The same thought still crosses my mind. Everything you do, and even your emotions, create more lines in your Verse. And the same applies to every living being, even the worms beneath your feet. The Song is therefore complex and ever changing, evolving as the world ages.' She took a deep breath. 'Let's delay no more. Today, we'll start with something simple. I will show you how to navigate through the Verses for this part of the bridge.' She clutched his hand. 'Now, close your eyes and imagine Hamar standing before you. Use a memory of happier times to guide us on our journey.'

Toryn glanced over the parapet at the river. 'What if I fall while in a trance? Or if a cart's wheel runs over my toes?'

'You need not worry. We may spend what seems like hours in the Song, yet only a moment passes here. Our eyes will be closed, but to these traders it will be as if we blink. We will appear as if enjoying the morning sun. Now, what about that memory? Do you have something suitable?'

Toryn grinned. 'There are so many to choose from, but many are at the expense of Hamar's pride thanks to my youthful antics. But I have one still fresh in my mind.' He closed his eyes. Immediately, he saw Hamar sitting alongside Jerrum as they rode in the cart after a long day of setting fence posts. Jerrum chuckled at his jibe at Hamar, while the old guard glowered at the young lad from under his bushy eyebrows. Toryn smiled at the memory of simpler times.

Nyomae's hand warmed. 'Yes, that will do.' She muttered a few lines in a strange tongue, then spoke to Toryn. 'Allow the words to flow through you. The language lies within.' She returned to the incantation, and while he found he knew the words, their meaning evaded him. Other voices joined, harsh and unpleasant, but Nyomae's voice rang out over them. 'Pay no attention, Toryn. These are the mischievous folk I spoke of. They are no match for you. We stand at the gateway. Repeat with me, and we will pass them by.'

Toryn's throat warmed as he spoke the words to aid their passing into the Song. A wind blew in his face as if he rode a horse at speed. Yet, he could still feel the solid stone on which he sat. Suddenly, faces flashed towards him, or perhaps he sped through them, he could not tell. Voices rose. Conversations, arguments, cries for help, threats, and laughter, deafened him. A thousand hopes and fears flooded into his mind. His body on the bridge wavered. Nyomae reassured him. 'Focus on the ground beneath you. You feel both the pain and joy experienced here over the years. We progress through time, but our bodies are motionless. You will soon become accustomed to the sensation.'

His head settled as the movement ceased. Nyomae's voice echoed as if they were standing in a cave. 'Open the eyes of your mind, Toryn.' At first, he saw nothing in the surrounding mist. But as he repeated the refrain with Nyomae, the fog lifted to reveal the bridge. He looked up at the towers of Archonholm, but their tops remained shrouded in a mist Toryn knew to be the limits of his vision. He turned to Nyomae. Her outline wavered as if a reflection in a pond. She smiled. 'What you see is my presence within this Verse. And I perceive you the same way. If you were to release my hand, I would disappear although I would still be at your side back in our time.'

Toryn peered upstream to where the river emerged from a wall of fog. 'I know where we are, but *when* are we? How far have we gone back?'

'Not far. We have come back almost fifty years, barely a blink in terms of the Song.' Toryn glanced across the river but could only see the lower slopes of the Menon Hills. Many leagues to the north, his parents would still be children growing up in Midwyche. And what of his real father, Finromir? Did he still wander under the shadow following the battle at Gormadon? Or had he already met Toryn's birth mother? His eyes wandered across the eerie limits of his world, struggling to come to terms that everything he knew had yet to happen.

He turned to the sound of laughter. A band of young Archonians ambled across the bridge towards them. Toryn beamed as he recognized the young Hamar. He strolled with strong arms swinging from his broad shoulders that could brandish the guard's blade hanging from his belt with ease. Toryn stifled a laugh as he watched Hamar flick the ear of one of his colleagues, then try to blame it on another. But as they approached, Hamar's pace slowed. He glanced towards where Toryn and Nyomae sat. His mouth opened as if about to speak, then he shrugged and walked on. Toryn whispered. 'Did he see us?'

'Some may briefly sense the presence of visitors in the Song. Often people think they're being watched, only to turn around and find themselves alone. So perhaps there is some truth in that.' She stroked his hand. 'I believe that happens when a friendship is deep and the bond is strong.'

Toryn's eyes brimmed. 'That it was. I miss him every day.'

Nyomae smiled. 'That may yet aid us. In dark times, friendship and loyalty are powerful weapons against those who hold no such values. If your strength fails, it may be possible to draw sustenance from loved ones from the past. For now, you can only travel back in time at your current location. However, as your skill grows, you will be able to venture farther and move to other areas within the Song. That is how Uldrak conjured up the apparition of a shreek at Calerdorn as none, to my knowledge, has ever attacked the city. That takes strength, but the strongest can bring back actual dark beings' — she winced — 'such as the *Draedalak* at Gormadon. But we will start with something much simpler. Ah, yes.' She pointed to the ground. 'The apple that has fallen from a cart. Let us see if you can bring it back.'

'To our time?'

'Indeed, and if you do it right it will briefly be edible. Uldrak could only maintain his vision for so long, but Elodi's conviction shattered it, thankfully before it could crush Calerdorn's resolve.'

Toryn looked at the red apple close to his feet. 'Where do I begin?'

'Look at the patterns on your palms. That is how it is done. In the everyday world your hands move when you speak without you being aware of their behavior. Thus, your thoughts acquire a physical form through their movement.' She traced a line across his palm. 'We can reverse this in the Song. We cannot touch that apple here. However, if you move your hands as if to pick it up and place it in your pocket, it will be there on your return to—' Nyomae shivered. A dark figure took shape in the fog clinging to the head of the Menon Valley. She sighed. 'Ah. They come. Time for us to leave. Think back to the bridge as it was this morning and then open your eyes, Toryn.'

He blinked in the daylight unaware that his eyes had been closed. Toryn noticed the trader's cart had barely moved since they entered the Song. He turned to Nyomae. 'Was that a Watcher?'

'Sadly not. I could have dealt swiftly with it if it were. That shadow was most likely a servant of the Ul-dalak. Their power continues to grow if they sensed our presence from so far away, and so soon.' She stretched out her arms. 'That will be all for the day, but it's imperative we continue tomorrow. There is something I must attend to at the gate. If my suspicions are proved to be true, I will send for you.'

# 5. Words on a Stone

'Perhaps you should challenge Kernlow to a duel.' Toryn mimicked a sword thrust.

Elodi parried, side-stepped, and slashed an imaginary blade at Toryn's exposed neck. She laughed for the first time in days. 'Now that would be interesting. But I can't afford to be too confident. When we thought the Caerwal Gate was under attack, Kernlow was confident he alone could defend the Great Hall against the might of the Golesh hordes.'

'Turns out he was right, eh, seeing as they don't exist.' Toryn grinned. 'Although, he probably would have tripped over his own feet and hurt himself, or anyone else unfortunate to be in the way.'

Elodi's smile faded as they approached the chasm. She stopped and looked up at the mountain wall opposite. 'We shouldn't make fun of him. By all accounts he was once an accomplished swordmaster and acquitted himself well serving in the north. But that was many years ago, and I fear his indecision may cost us dear.'

Toryn pointed to the ridge. 'That's where I stood when you led your forces across the bridge. I had the most terrible sense of dread. If only I had known what was about to unfold. Perhaps I could have prevented the carnage.'

Elodi touched his shoulder. 'I remember the feeling. With hindsight, there were a few signs, but only a small part of Uluriel's plan was known to each of us. Perhaps together we could have uncovered what awaited us on that fateful day. But if we had, could we have stopped it sooner? I doubt none would have taken our word over that of the Archon.'

Toryn could not take his eyes off the bridge. 'Just before my punishment, a guard told me another had suffered the same fate the year before for being a *wyke.* A young lass as he described her. I wonder who she was. And how many like me are still out there?'

'I wonder indeed. If there are more, I assume they will be like you, uncorrupted by the Ul-dalak, and therefore potential allies. Perhaps as Nyomae recovers she can locate them.'

They crossed the bridge as the evening sun tinged the mountains red. But as they walked through the Lower Gate and into the pass, the late warmth deserted them. Neither spoke as they approached the site where the Shreek's Rage had obliterated the armies gathered to strike against an imaginary foe. The eerie silence stopped them in their tracks. Raised wooden walkways crisscrossed the ground allowing for easier passage over the rubble, but they both felt uneasy walking over the mass grave of the poor souls beneath.

The work to clear the debris and recover the fallen had finished for the day. Despite the large workforce, little progress appeared to have been made in two weeks, making the enormity of the task seem all the more daunting. Sifting the rocks was time-consuming but vital. Masons selected those suitable for building a perimeter wall around Archonholm to keep the enemy's large weapons far from the city. The rubble was ferried in carts and dumped in the chasm. But the most demanding task was dealing with the dead. By now, the heat of summer had made it a most unpleasant duty. And, as much as it galled Elodi, she accepted their armor and weapons had to be recovered to use another day. Everyone in the city was assigned a role. A field was cleared, graves were dug, but with resources being scarce, burying the thousands with dignity proved difficult. Despite Elodi's frustration with Kernlow and his Council, she could not deny they had organized the grim task of clearing the pass admirably.

'I see Kernlow's tower is taking shape.' Toryn gestured to the wooden framework anchored at the center of the gate. 'I'd say they're about a third of the way up. If they can keep the same pace the higher they climb, they'll reach the top in a month.'

Elodi watched as two men worked the winch to hoist a dozen planks up the precarious structure. 'Then I assume he's asked to install a platform. It would take Kernlow an age to climb a ladder to the top.'

Toryn stopped. 'I hear he's reluctant to open the gate. Doesn't he believe me? I am certain I saw nothing on the other side.'

'I believe you, Toryn, but Nyomae did say it wouldn't be beyond the craft of the enemy to conceal an army, whether by deceiving your sight, or by clever disguise. But of course, while Nyomae believes the Golesh are a falsehood, we don't know if we'll be faced by friend or foe if we throw open the gate.' She glanced to the piles of rubble. 'We're not exactly in the best position to defend ourselves, or even entertain a potential friend. And, if we unlocked it, could we easily lock it again? The engineers predict it would take at least a day to shift a single gate on its rusty runner wide enough for a horse and cart to get through. And if it gets stuck when fully open…'

'I guess it makes more sense to look over rather than go through it. But why did the Archon choose to build a tower of stone in the first place? If he wanted to see into the southern pass, why not use wood and get it done quicker?'

'If we assume it was Uluriel's decision, her ultimate objective was to convince the realms to bring their main forces to the pass. Once the Archon claimed he had looked over and seen the imminent threat, we had no option but to do just that. Perhaps the time it took to construct the tower gave the Ul-dalak more time to prepare their own forces. Had you not intervened, the bulk of our strength would have perished under the landslide and their armies would now be pouring across Farrand's border. Uluriel had already dispatched our elite forces to the bottom of the Karajan Sea. I suspect she thought it wouldn't be long before she could welcome her hosts to Archonholm itself.' Elodi stopped at the end of the walkway. She turned to Toryn. 'But Uluriel hadn't foreseen you and Nyomae showing up at Midsummer. Her expulsion from the Archon has cost her dearly, and thankfully has afforded us a little more time to recover.'

Toryn smiled. 'You underplay your own role. It was your Amayan blade that sent her fleeing back to the north.'

'Then let's agree the three of us just about managed to outwit that foul being.' Her eyes wandered to the head of the pass. 'But how much of her powers were drained by possessing the Archon? What if she's stronger when in her own body? She would prove to be a formidable opponent.'

'There she is.' Toryn spied Nyomae standing by the remains of the old tower. 'I wonder what she's been investigating. She gave no hint following my lesson at the bridge this morning.'

Elodi looked up from a rotting carcass of a horse. 'We cannot know how many spies still operate in Archonholm. For that reason, I urged Kernlow to keep the number of Council members to a minimum. But I did not anticipate that he would exclude me.'

Toryn sighed. 'I blame the Castellan. It's obvious Lord Kernlow is intimidated by the man. One word from him was enough for Kernlow to bar you from his meetings. And from what I've seen of the Castellan, it's obvious to all that he's wary of you.'

Elodi scoffed. 'Wary? I think it would be safe to say he despises me. He knows I can undermine his position given the chance. That's why he's stationed Gundrul, Aldorman and Cubric well outside the city. I've threatened to take them north if he doesn't locate them closer to Archonholm, but I won't hold my breath. And he's only too aware that I hold him accountable for my father's death. I've made it clear I won't rest until I find out what happened that night. And, if I find any proof of his involvement, take my word, the Castellan will suffer. He's vulnerable, at my mercy, and he doesn't like that one bit.'

Toryn grinned. 'I certainly wouldn't want to be in his shoes.'

They reached the foot of the gate. The two had not ventured this far into the pass since their conflict with Uluriel. The hairs on the back of Toryn's neck prickled. He gazed up to the top of the gate, finding it hard to believe he had stood upon its iron beam towering over them. The gate had held firm for over three hundred years, seemingly unperturbed by the recent carnage. The lattice of iron girders and enormous bolts held huge stone slabs in place and stacked impossibly high. Toryn had heard stories of how giant machines with thick ropes and pulleys had hauled each stone into place. Now that he had time to examine it, he could not imagine how it could have been done. But regrettably, it was now obvious all the architects and workers who had observed Idraman's shimmering blue barrier had been put to the sword. It all seemed so cruel and pointless. The years of painstaking work to construct the greatest structure for a thousand years had served purely to hide the truth.

They approached the new cabin used by both builders and Archonians. A short, stooped man strode out. He gasped. 'Well, I'll be. May I shake your hand?'

Toryn glanced to Elodi. She shrugged. 'I think he

means you.'

The man stopped. 'It's Toryn of Darrow is it not? Then I have you to thank.' The builder patted his chest. 'It's me. Don't you recognize me?'

Toryn stared. 'I'm sorry. Have we met?'

The man slapped his forehead. 'What am I saying? Of course not. You won't recognize me. We didn't actually meet in person as such.' He wiggled his finger. 'Does this help? We met through a small hole in the cell wall.'

Toryn laughed. 'Ah yes.' He reached out and shook the man's hand. 'You must be Dravic.' He turned to Elodi. 'We were once neighbors in the Archon's dungeon.'

Dravic beamed. 'And who was to know things would turn out the way they did, eh? One day you're a wyke and enemy of the people, the next I hear you saved thousands.' Dravic held onto Toryn's hand and continued to shake. 'And then you arrange for me and my old crew to be released.' He looked at Elodi. His eyes widened. He bowed low. 'Begging your pardon, ma'am.' He groaned as he straightened his back. 'I hadn't expected to see the gracious Lady Harlyn down here among the death and dust.' Dravic extended his thumb to the gate. 'And what do you make of our new tower? Not as grand as the Archon's, but it will do the job just the same.'

Elodi nodded her approval. 'It's a fine structure. You and your crew have made excellent progress.'

'Couldn't be more proud of my boys. Here. Do you reckon the new lord will let us look over the gate when we're done? Would be a crying shame if we build another and still don't get a peek of the south.'

Elodi smiled. 'If it were up to me, I would have no issue with that. But it is Lord Kernlow's project, so it is his decision to make.' A builder whistled from the tower.

Dravic looked up and waved. He turned and bowed once more to Elodi. 'Better be off now, ma'am. That thing won't build itself. And thanks again, Toryn of Darrow. Another year in that cell and I would have run out of walls to keep track of the days.'

Toryn grasped Dravic's shoulder. 'It was the least I could do. You and your team were treated appallingly after all your effort.' The builder saluted and returned to his work.

Toryn turned as Nyomae called to them. 'Ah. There you are. Thank you for coming.' She nodded at the ruin. 'You may be wondering why I asked for the debris to be cleared here at its base.'

Elodi hooked her arm in Toryn's. 'I imagine you had a good reason, compelling enough to convince Kernlow to assign a work party.'

'Ah. I may have bent the truth a little and told Kernlow what he wanted to hear. I suggested the Sword of the Realms should be recovered without delay.' She smirked. 'He believed me when I said it may hold powers that should be in his hands. I think he likes the idea of having a portrait of him holding it aloft.'

Toryn kicked at the stones. 'Have you found it? Is it a sword of power?'

Nyomae paced across the rubble-strewn ground. 'It's over there by that large stone. But I'm not aware it's anything other than just a well-forged sword. And certainly not alike Elodi's Amayan blade.'

Elodi strolled to the stone and took up the weapon. She spun, drawing the sword from its scabbard in one swift move. She held it up and examined the blade. 'It's not damaged.' Elodi swung it about her head. 'And perfectly balanced.' She lowered the sword to inspect the grip. 'To think Draegelan once wielded this in battle. Do you seriously intend to give this to Kernlow? It may serve the realms far better in another's hands. Toryn? How about you?'

'My skill is with the bow. I've had no formal training with a sword.'

Elodi thrust the tip at Toryn. 'Then I see it as my duty to teach you. While Eryn was especially generous gifting you her bow, it will not serve you well at close quarters.'

He grinned. 'Then I gladly accept your offer. But… I would be more comfortable with a lesser one. Surely, the Sword of the Realms should be in Nyomae's hand.'

Nyomae declined. 'I have no use for such a sword. You keep it safe for now, Elodi. Perhaps a suitable hand will be found in time. But while its recovery may help to raise spirits, it's not the reason I wanted to excavate this site.' She stopped, brought her palms together and closed her eyes.

Elodi exchanged a glance with Toryn. 'So, the reason was…?'

Nyomae clapped her hands and looked down. 'Yes. I was right. It's here.' Her eyes widened. 'When you and I entered the tower, Toryn, I sensed an ill presence beneath us.' She kneeled and scraped the remaining stones aside. 'As our priority was to deal with Archon, I ignored it at the time. Following my recovery, I returned and still sensed something was wrong.'

Toryn joined her to clear the last of the debris. His fingertips brushed against a cold surface. His stomach turned. 'I feel it too. And look.' He scooped up a pile of dust to expose a black marble slab.

Elodi peered over his shoulder. 'And highly polished at that. An extravagant choice of material for the foundation. I know the Archon… or Uluriel were fond of their luxuries, but surely a more suitable stone could have been used.'

Nyomae's gaze remained fixed on the marble. 'This is exactly the right choice for what Uluriel had in mind. The thick stone conceals much of what she intended to keep hidden. And since I was able to detect the wrongness through it, I urge caution. We must remove the slab, but if you become dizzy, or perish the thought, you feel the need to inflict harm upon me, retreat to a safe distance. I fear whatever lies beneath this stone will have the power to corrupt until I can annul its power.' She looked at her companions. 'Let us proceed. Toryn, if you could be so kind to retrieve that rod from the broken platform mechanism, I believe that will help to lever the slab clear.' She grinned. 'It wouldn't be right to use the Sword of the Realms for such a task.'

Toryn eyed the stone. 'Is it possible to make that slab disappear as we did with the droog's collar?'

'Ah yes, that would save us much labor, but I think it wise we limit our time in the Verses. From what we learned this morning we must be on our guard for more than just the Watchers. And besides, we may also need all our strength for what lies beneath.'

Elodi found another rod. 'Then let's press on. It will be dark before long.'

Nyomae picked up her torch. 'Good thing I came prepared.' She whispered a few words and it burst into flames. She placed it next to the slab and found the edges of the stone. Toryn and Elodi worked together, pulling and twisting the rods to lift the marble free.

Elodi spat as they levered it aside. 'Ah! I can taste it. There is the same foulness I detected in the air when Dorlan came to Calerdorn.'

Below, steps led down into darkness. Nyomae retrieved her torch and peered into the gloom. 'I will go first.' Elodi and Toryn followed as Nyomae descended the short stairway. At the bottom, the torch shed light on a small room, revealing what Toryn suspected he would see the moment his stomach churned. A jagged rock jutted up from the floor. Nyomae's flame fell upon letters carved into its sides.

Toryn's nose wrinkled. 'That looks like the same scrawl I saw at Wend Gap. There were three such stones in a cave that destroyed a Singing Stone.'

Nyomae bent and examined the words. 'It is as I thought. The stone emits a powerful invocation to weaken Idraman's Word of Forbidding. It appears this tower was more than just a token gesture from Uluriel.'

Elodi stared in disgust. 'Can we break it?'

'It will be a challenge, but our combined strength will suffice.'

Elodi circled the stone. 'What do you require from us?'

Nyomae thought for a moment. 'Please draw your Amayan blade and place the tip close to the rock, but don't touch it. Be prepared to withdraw should it grow hot.' Elodi followed Nyomae's instructions. She gasped as a faint green glow spread slowly up her sword.

Elodi grimaced. 'My arm tingles.'

Nyomae held her hand over the blade. 'This confirms the stone has been tainted by evil. If you are able, maintain your position a moment longer. But if the light reaches the hilt, withdraw and step back.'

Toryn held his breath as the green light grew brighter. He turned to Elodi. 'Is it getting hotter?' She shook her head, keeping her eyes fixed on the blade but appearing to see something other than her sword.

Nyomae stepped forward and lowered Elodi's hand. 'I have seen enough.'

Elodi staggered back and recovered her balance. Her eyes shone. 'I felt… my mother.' Tears brimmed. 'I know it was her. My mother… and there were others, many more lending me their strength.'

Nyomae smiled. 'The invocation within the stone has stirred the power of your ancestors. It works through you.'

She looked at Elodi's blade, now a dull silver. 'And thankfully it remained cool.'

Toryn kneeled beside the stone. 'And if it hadn't?'

'We would have faced a difficult task. This is a lesser stone, not as potent as the three you saw at Wend Gap. I imagine Uluriel doesn't think Idraman could maintain the power of his barrier for much longer. Therefore, she believed that a single stone would be sufficient to drain its strength over time.'

Elodi sighed. 'And what now?'

'This presents an opportunity to teach you both how to use your powers. It comes from within. The skill is to allow it to flow through you.'

'Ah! *Not to try.*' Toryn recalled his days hanging from the bridge. 'I had no other option when left to rot, and despite my predicament, I somehow managed to relax.'

Nyomae's gaze stayed on the rock. 'When you try, you interfere with the natural course. And Elodi. When your blade first came to life in the gatehouse when you faced Uldrak, you had not the first idea of your mother's kin. You were in a fight for your life. Your desire to survive and defend your people awoke your innate Amayan powers.'

Elodi sheathed her sword. 'And how about a situation such as this? I do not feel threatened as I did when confronting Uldrak. How do I awaken my power now?'

'The Amayans were appointed Guardians of the Amanach, I presume by the race that raised them. But their purpose was to protect. This stone presents a threat.' Nyomae took Elodi's hand. 'Your desire to defend against the dark forces of this world will stir them.' She turned to Toryn. 'You both must learn to calm yourselves, to think clearly, and ultimately, get out of the way and allow your powers to flow. Any thoughts of failure, or conversely, a sense of arrogance, will prevent both the entry into the

Song, and access to your abilities.'

Elodi glared at the stone. 'Then let us act and remove the evil from within this rock.'

Nyomae nodded. 'Good. Toryn and I shall enter the Verse for this place. Elodi, when the wording on the stone begins to fade, please strike with your blade. It will crack in two. But first, let me show you both how to prepare.' She stepped back and held up her hands. 'Please stand tall, poised, not stiff. Feel the ground beneath your feet. Focus on your breathing and the movement of your ribs. Soften your face. Don't fix your eyes. Let the light come to you. You don't need to stare at the stone… or any future threat. This will cause tension and limit the flow of energy through you.'

Toryn slowed his breathing. He watched as Elodi appeared to grow taller and her eyes shone. She turned towards him, and for a moment, he thought he saw Eryn.

Nyomae positioned herself behind the stone. 'You are ready. Maintain your focus on the rock, Elodi. When the time arises, your powers will surge through your sword to destroy it.' She held her hands out to Toryn. 'You and I shall seek to separate the stone from the vile invocation pervading its pure heart. I suspect Uluriel's corruption dates to when construction of the tower began.'

Toryn took her hands. 'So, this is the same process when we *unmade* the droog's collar?'

'Same process, but a little more challenging. And we shall not be alone. Our foray into the Verses at the bridge this morning has alerted the Watchers to our presence. They will be keeping vigil here. Our ancestry will send a strong message to our enemies in more ways than one. I want them to learn they no longer have free rein in the Verses, and they can expect to face worthy opponents from now on. But be wary, they will soon learn of your inexperience and quickly move to corrupt or finish you.

And, Elodi, they may also attempt to work through the stone to reach you. If either of you hear voices promising rewards beyond your dreams, ignore them and stay with me.'

Toryn smirked. 'And trust me, they can be quite convincing.'

Elodi leveled her blade to the stone. 'Then let them try.' She widened her stance. 'I'm ready. And don't worry. I will not let you down.'

Nyomae tightened her hold on Toryn's hand. 'Then I shall begin. Close your eyes, Toryn, and follow my lead. You know the words. Let them come through you. I will draw on your strength to break the spell on this stone.'

Toryn's hands warmed as his vision blurred. He kept his feet firmly planted as his mind hurtled back through time. The movement slowed. His head settled. When he opened his eyes, he found himself inside the tower. He watched bemused as a bright circle above widened, descending towards them as the walls were unmade as they approached the moment Uluriel set the stone. Nyomae spoke. 'The Watchers come. Be ready.' Dark shapes churned the air around Toryn as their voices echoed in his head. At his side, Nyomae shone in the swirling mass. 'Stay strong, Toryn. Draw on your strength within.' The heat in his gut grew. He joined Nyomae, uttering words to resist the efforts of the Watchers to distract them. The dark forms dispersed. The walls of the tower disappeared as if swallowed by the bedrock. The stone took shape at the center of the foundations.

Nyomae's voice strengthened. 'This is the moment following Uluriel's invocation. I do not wish to go back farther as we will encounter her Verse. I do not have the strength to face her at present. In order to weaken her spell, we will draw upon the forces that reside within the mountain roots.' She bowed her head. The rock glimmered as she recited lines from a Verse that Toryn knew to be from early in the Maidens' Song. The words defacing the stone faded, but just as he thought they would vanish, they reappeared. Toryn could not tear his eyes off the words. They burned bright like fire, hurting his eyes.

Nyomae gasped. 'Something's not—' She cried out. 'I've been deceived. Leave! Leave at once.' The air howled, turning dark as if a storm raged about them. Nyomae's hand was ripped from Toryn's. His limbs thrashed out as if a mighty chain dragged his body through a whirlwind. He cried out but made no sound. He crashed to the floor, forcing the air from his lungs.

'Toryn!' Elodi gripped his hand. 'What happened? You were away for so long. I thought you were lost.' She jabbed her sword at the stone. 'It emitted a most terrible screech and threw me back.'

He opened his eyes. Elodi's tear-stained face stared down at him. His voice croaked. 'How long was I out?'

'It's the middle of the night. I've been by your side for hours. You both became icy cold. I thought you were… dead, but then you began muttering in a language unknown to me.'

Toryn turned. Nyomae sat close by, shaking her head. 'It was a trap. I should have known. The stone could have easily been hidden from me by a thicker slab. Uluriel dangled this as if a carrot before a donkey.' Her jaw clenched. 'And I acted without thought. She's always one step ahead.' Nyomae stared at the wording. 'There is something here that I cannot see. This isn't merely a means to weaken Idraman's barrier. There is another spell concealed within, but I cannot fathom its purpose.' She stood. 'I must apologize to you both for putting you in danger. I have become careless. I must return to my studies and learn to be more cautious.'

# 6. Over the Hills & faraway

'I believe we are only seeing half the story, Toryn.' Nyomae looked up from the scroll. 'It appears Elodi's father was correct in his assumption. Based on the gaps in the archive, I would say many records have been removed from this room. And unfortunately, I suspect that includes much of Idraman's early work. My only hope is that Uluriel has not pilfered his scrolls stored in the libraries of Neverdor and Abernost.' She sat back and rubbed her eyes. The Master of Scrolls had retrieved part of the archives studied by Uluriel when acting as the Archon. Nyomae believed she was searching for a discovery made by Draegelan in his later years. But they had barely read a third of the first box, and there were still twelve to open.

Nyomae turned to the small window. 'We have been here since daybreak. I think that will do for today. We could easily miss a vital clue if tired.' She smiled. 'We may have the gift of *farsight*, but it aids us little in such a cramped space.'

Toryn stood and massaged his shoulders. 'I wonder if Elodi has had a chance to speak with Lord Kernlow about that stone.'

Nyomae glanced at the open scroll on the table. 'I wish the Castellan was as vigilant in protecting Archonholm as he appears to be about restricting access to Kernlow.' She frowned. 'Why does Uluriel seek to bring down Idraman's Word of Forbidding? Does she believe she has an ally beyond the Caerwals? Or do they seek to take the lands to the south and drive out the people?' Nyomae groaned. 'So many unknowns. And I fear Kernlow does not have the stomach for the upcoming fight. For too long he has enjoyed the comfort and privileges that come with his title.' She pushed back her chair and stood. 'He must appreciate the luxuries of which he avails himself will soon disappear. His large dinner plate will begin to look sparse if he fails to secure the fertile lands of Kernlow and Galabrant.'

Toryn placed the scrolls back in the box. 'Yet while he surrounds himself with like-minded people, he learns nothing of events in the real world. It seems the Castellan is all too eager to protect Kernlow from those who question his motives.' He held open the door for Nyomae. 'And as Elodi's impatience grows by the day, I worry she may do something that could land her in the dungeon. The Castellan needs no encouragement to remove her from the citadel.'

Nyomae appeared not to hear Toryn as she eyed the boxes stacked by the door. She ran her hand across their dusty tops. 'I am missing something. The years I spent under the shadow of my own making has numbed my mind. It should have been obvious to me that Uluriel would lay a trap beneath the tower. I should never have put you and Elodi in harm's way so early in your journeys.'

'But how could you have known?'

'There is no excuse.' She held up her hand. 'I failed to spot signs I would not have missed even in my youth. Either I have grown weaker, or perhaps worse, arrogant, all too ready to trust in abilities I have yet to fully recover.' Nyomae stopped. 'Prior to the last battle at Gormadon, I could have destroyed that stone at the gate unaided. But I made the grave error of underestimating our enemy and rushed in where more thought was needed.' She turned to Toryn. 'I will retire to the Archon's Tower. I must withdraw and revisit my Verses relating to the period before Gormadon. There are things I must study, things I need to reassess.'

Toryn saw the doubt in her eyes. 'How long will that take?'

Nyomae shrugged. 'I cannot be certain. I am aware that time is against us, but I hope it will not be long. I will also attempt to contact Idraman once more. He will be weakened with his efforts to sustain the barrier. It is quite remarkable that he has been able to maintain it for so long. If I can reach him, we can at least learn about the situation in the south.' She touched Toryn's arm — her hand felt cold. 'I will send for you when I am done. But in the meantime, I suggest you and Elodi double your efforts on making Lord Kernlow listen to our concerns.'

Toryn lifted the lid of the first box. 'Should I continue the search here?'

'No. The best use of your time would be to practice your gift of *farsight*. Look for signs of Eryn and the Amayans to the east of the Kolossos. You will find it easier from a high point. The North Terrace is an ideal location. You need line of sight but remember, you're not seeing with your eyes. Use the same process as if entering the Song, but instead look to the horizon and *invite* the images into your mind. Think of Eryn and your *farsight* will lead you to her. *Farsight* is the act of entering the Song and *seeing* the present verses at the moment they are created. It would be more accurate to call it *firstsight*, but those who initially awoke to its power would have supposed it to be a visual skill. You will not see the past, or the future, but only a few can see what is yet to come. I occasionally get a glimpse of the times ahead, but I cannot be sure if what I see is manipulated by those who wish us ill. Ask Elodi to assist. Amayans appear to have a connection to one another that allows a form of communication. They have a limited capacity for the *farsight*, but her presence will lend you strength.'

Nyomae walked to the door, but then stopped and

took a step back. Her hand rested on the last box. 'Wait.' She opened the cover, reached inside, and pulled out a frayed scroll. Her brow creased as she read the first lines. 'I wonder if Uluriel saw this one.' She slid it inside her robe. 'The Master need not know.'

Toryn waited for the captains of the First Horse to leave the terrace before addressing Elodi. 'The incident at the ruins has dealt Nyomae's confidence a blow.'

'I fear the responsibility lies heavy upon her, Toryn. I hope her retreat will prove beneficial. But it is a warning. We cannot rely on Nyomae alone. You and I must learn to master more of the powers she claims lie within us.'

He watched the roof of the Archon's Tower turn red as the sun slowly slipped to the horizon. 'Then let us try to locate your fellow Amayans. Imagine what another dozen warriors with your skills could do for our cause.'

Elodi held his gaze. 'I wonder what they will make of me. Would they think me an imposter? I know little of their ways, and, by their reckoning, I have lived a sheltered life.'

Toryn laughed. 'If you count fighting shreeks, shrouls, surviving a landslide, and then confronting Uluriel, as sheltered, then maybe… yes.'

She smiled back. 'The shreek was an illusion. But I suppose the rest might impress them.'

'They do set a high standard.' He shuddered. 'Tackling five Nordleng while fending off the attention of a hungry droog takes some skill.'

Elodi's eyes wandered to the road leading east. 'Then let us see if we can locate them. While I was aware the Archon possessed the *farsight*, I assumed it was just good eyesight that allowed me to see things other people could not.'

'And I also. I could see the mighty Caranach from my

village when others struggled.' He checked the sun. 'We have an hour before sunset, but whether we need the light for *farsight*, I am not sure.'

Elodi held his hand. 'I will be convinced if we can see as far as Emryst.'

'Nyomae instructed me not to *try* to see, but to let the images come to me. But what that means in practice, I don't know for sure.' Toryn took a breath. He looked north across the vast canopy of the Foranfae. Dozens of birds made their way back to the treetops ready to settle in for the night. He slowed his breathing, then invited the horizon towards him as if lifting a book to read. The colors changed, becoming brighter, more vibrant. He appeared to move, seeming to fly across the treetops. Toryn stumbled, unsettled by the sensation of speed but continued his journey. Beyond the forest, the pink-tinged, snowy peaks of the southernmost mountains of the Kolossos came into view. For a moment, he was reminded of the day he stood with Jerrum as Caranach had made its appearance. He spoke to Elodi. 'Do you see them?'

'I do, but I don't know their names. They must be seventy leagues from here.'

Toryn arrived at the plains of Emryst. 'Nyomae directed Eryn towards Telamir to locate Amyra. We should start our search there. If successful, Eryn said they would look for their remaining sisters.' He let his eyes wander farther east. He pictured Eryn's face. At first, all he saw was a red haze as the dust from an early harvest caught the last rays of the sun. The field lay to the west of a small town he assumed was Cafra. Toryn recalled the lines on Hamar's map. If accurate, Telamir would be another ten leagues or so north. Eryn's blue eyes came to mind. Once more, the land surged towards him as they sped through the haze and over Cafra.

Elodi clutched at his hand. 'This will take some getting

used to.'

'You see it too?'

'I have yet to visit the lands east of the Kolossos. It looks so strange.' They both gasped. Rising from the evening mists, the forked pinnacle of Telamir Tower jutted impossibly high into the shimmering sky. Elodi stuttered. 'I had not realized how tall it stood. It must be twice the height of the Archon's Tower.'

Toryn gaped at the peculiar structure of the old world. 'Hamar told me of Telamir, but his words didn't do it justice.' He sighed. 'But as much as I'd like to see the sights of the east, we must find the Amayans. They surely took this road if our *farsight* led us here. But where are they?' He tried to picture Eryn's face, but the vision of Telamir dominated. Beyond the tower, a thick fog within the Verse blocked their view. His heart pounded. 'Have they been captured?' The vision shattered. Toryn staggered and grasped the balustrade. He waited for Archonholm to stand still and then opened his eyes. 'Perhaps they have gone farther north, and we cannot reach them. I can't imagine they could have been captured by the Nordleng, or… killed.'

Elodi steadied herself. 'Then let us hope they have found their sisters and are causing havoc with the occupying forces of Dorn.'

Toryn took his hands off the wall. 'The *farsight* drains my strength. We shall require a lot more practice if it is to be of use.' Elodi frowned as she stared at the forest. Toryn asked. 'What's wrong?'

She thought for a moment. 'There is something that has troubled me, but I could not place exactly what it was. But now we stand here overlooking the forest, it comes to me.' Her face paled. 'You said you were assailed by Uleva in Foranfae as you rowed down the river. I believe it was at the time of the full moon?'

Toryn's scalp tingled. 'I remember it well. And yes, the full moon shone that night. But what concerns you?'

'Only seven days earlier, Uleva and her army stormed the gates of Calerdorn.' She turned to face the Menon Hills. 'It would take Sea Mist at least fourteen to make that journey, and that would be at full speed with hardly any rest. How could Uleva cover that distance in half the time that would leave Misty lame? It continues to—' A clash of swords rang out, accompanied by shouts from around the corner. Without a thought, Elodi and Toryn ran towards the skirmish.

They rounded the bend and bumped into those fleeing the fight. A guard hobbled towards them. He held up a hand, gasping for air. 'Have a care, ma'am. He's slaughtered two gentle folk and taken down a guard.' He winced as his hand clutched his blooded leg. 'And injured three.'

Elodi peered past the guard. A large, red-faced man stood astride three bodies on the flagstones. He swung a long blade, raging at the guards circling him. She stared aghast. 'Who is he? Why does he fight?'

'Can't say, ma'am. He's lost his mind. Has the strength of ten.'

'By the Three, what is going on?' Toryn turned to see the Castellan. He yelled at the injured guard. 'How did that scoundrel get his sword past the checks?'

'Not his, sir. Swiped it from a guard.'

'Outrageous! I want that guard's name, he'll—'

'He's dead, sir. The madman slit his throat.' More guards scurried across the terrace.

The Castellan looked on. 'Then finish him. Finish him now. How many does it take to bring down one?'

'He fights like a demon, sir. No skill, just brute force.'

The Castellan shoved the man aside and drew his sword. 'Then get out of my way. Let's see how this animal handles a veteran.'

Elodi joined him. 'I'm with you.'

'No, Lady Harlyn. That will not be necessary. Let me deal with this madman.' The Castellan waved back the guards and bellowed at the aggressor. 'Drop your weapon!' The man staggered back. But Elodi did not see rage in his eyes; she saw fright. He glared wide-eyed at the guards as if he saw shreeks. The Castellan took a step and repeated his demand. 'Drop your weapon.'

The man stiffened. He sneered. 'Come and take it, weasel.'

The Castellan thrust back his shoulders and straightened. 'This is your last chance. You have been warned. Surrender or die.'

The man's mouth twisted. 'Surrender? Never.'

The Castellan shrugged. 'Very well.' He turned to an arriving Palace Guard. 'Your spear! Hurry.' He gripped the weapon and leveled it. 'You have spilled blood in Archonholm. Your life is forfeit.' Elodi regarded the man. His scarlet face and bunching muscles seethed with anger, yet his eyes suggested shock, perhaps even fear.

Elodi stepped forward as the man's jaw softened. 'Castellan! Wait. He may—' With a speed that surprised her, the Castellan lunged and thrust his spear deep into the assailant's gut. He staggered but stayed on his feet. His eyes glared. He cried out a challenge and grasped the shaft, pulling the Castellan towards him. The Castellan reset his stance and twisted the spearhead while he stared into the face of his quarry. Blood gushed from the big man's mouth. His hands fell away as he sank to his knees, gawping at the dead at his feet. He caught Elodi's eye as he slouched and died. She held his gaze, perplexed — they were not the eyes of a madman, but of one who appeared to have woken from a nightmare.

The Castellan propped his spear on the stones, leaving

the man impaled as if a trophy. He turned; his grin sent a shiver through Elodi.

A man pushed past Toryn. 'Muldrin!' But the guards grabbed his cloak and pulled him back. Tears streamed down his face as he gaped at the Castellan's work. He struggled with the guards. 'Please. Let me go to him. He don't deserve to—'

'Throw that man into a cell.' The Castellan rubbed his hands on his cloak. 'He's an accomplice. I shall interrogate him later.'

Elodi stepped between them. 'Castellan. Please, allow me a moment with him.'

He opened his mouth to deny her request but then stumbled. Toryn grabbed his arm to prevent his fall. 'Are you injured?'

The Castellan recovered his balance but looked unsure of why Toryn had a hold on his arm. 'Injured? Of course not.' He shoved Toryn back. 'Unhand me, boy.' He spun around and stepped over the bloody flagstones and strewn bodies as if they were not there.

Elodi watched him go, abhorred by the show of violence. The man held by the guards dropped to his knees, unable to take his eyes from his friend slumped over the spear. But the guards allowed him no time to grieve. They hauled him up to face Elodi. She addressed him. 'You called him Muldrin. Was he your friend?'

He mumbled to himself. 'Why? I just don't get it. We're just builders.' He looked up as if hearing Elodi's question. 'He… he was, ma'am. But he's a gentle giant. I've never seen him hurt as much as a hornrasp.' His shoulder's shook. 'It's not like him at all.'

Toryn joined Elodi. 'You wear a style of cloak worn in Darrow. What brought you to Archonholm?'

He looked down. 'It is, sir. We're from Elcott. Close enough to the mountains so we don't see the sun 'til midday. My name is Seldric. We answered the call for masons to help build the new wall. We only got here yesterday. But if I'd known…' He slumped.

Elodi kneeled beside him. 'I am sorry for the loss of your friend, but please, did you notice anything unusual about him?' She glanced to Toryn as she spoke. 'Surely, a man does not change overnight.'

Seldric straightened. 'I've known him since we were little rascals. But I'd never seen him like that. We came up here to see the view. Then he went mad, grabbed the sword and… killed those poor folk and then the guards.'

One of the restraining guards spoke. 'It may not be my place to say anything, ma'am, but this ain't the first time we've had trouble of late.' His hold on Seldric relaxed. 'Nothing as bad as this, but fights have been breaking out all over the city. Folk are uneasy, ma'am. It seems they're quick to anger and use their fists when words would have done.' He looked down at the dead. 'We'll be in a heap of trouble if they start resorting to weapons.'

# 7. The Fable on the Wall

Elodi looked up at the tapestry. 'The Archon held that same pose just before he brought the weight of the Caerwals down upon our heads.'

Toryn stared in awe at the vivid colors and fine details. 'Now that we know what really happened at the battle, should we ask the weavers to make changes?'

Elodi's eyes were drawn to the gaping mouths of the demons. 'It would mean unpicking much of the drayloks' fire to make room for Nyomae and your father at the Archon's side.' She turned to the doors. 'It seems a different age from when I last stood here with Lord Broon.' Elodi smiled. 'I can't believe I thought this was the Great Hall.'

'I expect most visitors make the same mistake on their first visit.' Toryn took his eyes from the tapestry. 'Will Kernlow listen to your concerns? Or take your challenge to his leadership seriously?'

'I'm hoping a dose of the truth will be enough to make him question his suitability to command. It's obvious to all he enjoys the ceremonial role of being Steward, but I very much doubt he has the courage to meet the enemy in open battle, or even deal with the unrest under his nose.'

'But do we? How can we hope to challenge them when we number just a few thousand? And the majority of those are reserves. And what do we know of our enemy? You said more than ten thousand assailed Calerdorn. But how many more can they muster?'

Elodi held his gaze. 'We must believe we can succeed. It is clear the evil tide will sooner or later surge south. We must stay strong and stand tall in the face of overwhelming odds.' Her hand went to her sword. 'But that requires the kind of leadership Kernlow lacks. We should be making critical decisions now. The city is already in the grip of fear. People distrust their neighbors. And how long before another *gentle giant* turns? We cannot afford to sit here and wait for the enemy to show up at our door. The people must see we're taking steps to counter the evil they know will come.'

Toryn noticed her grip tightening on her sword handle. 'What would you do if you were Steward?'

'Send a dozen raiding parties north immediately.' She turned to face the two Palace Guards standing impossibly straight at the entrance to the Great Hall. 'It would require experienced soldiers, but not in numbers to cause Kernlow concern over weakening Archonholm. Small, well-led groups could inflict damage beyond their size and disrupt the Ul-dalak's preparations. We cannot let them believe we offer no threat.'

Toryn scoffed. 'They have nothing to fear from Kernlow.'

But Elodi's attention was far to the north. 'I would send parties to attack their camps, then move on to find new targets. We currently don't have the numbers to mount an all-out attack. But we can still hurt them. Make them feel uneasy, and perhaps, we can lead them to believe we have more numbers than they suspect. And, of course, we could gather information in the process.'

Toryn waited for her to pause. 'But would you have to remain in Archonholm if you were steward?'

She beamed. 'I would like to see them try.'

The hinges creaked. The large doors opened. The guards stepped aside as the Proctor shuffled between them. Elodi marveled at the ability of the man to stay on his feet with such a bent spine. He beckoned to Elodi. 'Lord Kernlow will see you now, Lady Harlyn.'

She winked to Toryn. 'Wish me luck.'

He whispered. 'It is Kernlow in need of luck if he is to survive your meeting.'

Elodi's smile faded. 'Meet me on the South Terrace at noon. I'm sure we'll have much to discuss.' She turned to follow the Proctor, but the guards blocked her path.

'Ah, yes.' The Proctor pointed to her belt. 'Your sword, ma'am. You cannot enter the Great Hall armed.' She stepped back. The old man smiled and held out his hands. 'It's just a formality, Lady Harlyn. The same rule applies to all who enter, including the Castellan. It will be returned as soon as is… appropriate.'

'And by that you mean…?'

The Proctor gestured to the door. 'Lady Harlyn, Lord Kernlow is a busy man. He will not be kept waiting.'

Elodi regarded the open-handed guard. 'Very well. Then take the utmost care. This sword means a great deal to me. It has served me well. I will not abide mistreatment.' She removed her belt and gave it to him. Her hand dropped to her side, suddenly feeling vulnerable without it.

'Thank you, ma'am.' The Proctor instructed the Palace Guard to step aside. 'You may now enter. And rest assured, your trusty weapon will be handled with the respect it demands.'

Elodi muttered under her breath. 'It had better be.' Then louder. 'Thank you, Proctor.' She entered the Great Hall, and as always, looked up. Bright sunlight streamed through the tall windows only to be trapped by the dust hanging in the thick air. Elodi wondered if she would live to see the day it finally settled.

'Ah! The fair and gracious Lady Harlyn enters.' At the far end of the hall, the ample frame of Lord Kernlow struggled to get up from his chair. But once on his feet, he strode with surprising speed to greet her.

Elodi took a breath. 'Thank you, lord, for granting me this' — she noted the empty seats around the table— 'private meeting.'

'My pleasure. And…' He glanced behind him. 'Ah yes. I gave my council the morning off.' He stretched out his arms and thrust his elbows back and forth. 'I suggested they get some fresh air and exercise on this fine day. Need everyone to be at the top of their game.' He blinked in the sunlight. 'Don't you think, eh, Lady Harlyn?'

'Err… yes. I expect that would be... desirable.' Elodi's anger had grown during the days waiting for this meeting. But now she saw him, she pitied the lord. Did he really believe a breath of fresh air could prepare the people to challenge the formidable forces that would soon come south?

Kernlow pulled out a chair for Elodi. 'Such a shame, all that unfortunate business at the pass. Who would have thought the Archon was in the thrall of that awful woman?' He nodded to the seat. 'Please sit my dear and tell me what concerns you.'

A red-faced Elodi stormed across the terrace towards Toryn. 'They've taken my sword! Can you believe the nerve of these people?'

'I thought you were supposed to get it back following your meeting.'

'As did I, yet still they keep it from me. I gave it to the guards in good faith.' She slapped the wall. 'Ah! I was a fool to trust them. I have been informed the Castellan has it for safekeeping. I ask you. Safekeeping? Who do they think I am?' Elodi looked behind, lowering her voice as two First Horse commanders strolled along the terrace. 'I wonder if the only reason I was granted the meeting in the first place was to let that insufferable man get his grubby hands on my sword.'

'But why? Surely, the Castellan cannot justify confiscating your blade.'

'Clearly, he's wary of a weapon of power over which he has no control. But I'd like to see the look on his face when he discovers it's useless in anyone's hands but mine. The Palace Guard apologized profusely and assured me it would be returned within a few days. But after the scalding I gave him…' Her shoulders relaxed. 'The poor fellow. It wasn't his fault, but by now the Castellan will be in no doubt that if it's not returned by tomorrow, he'll feel the cold steel of the Sword of the Realms where it hurts.'

Toryn laughed. 'I imagine that should do the trick. But what of your meeting with Kernlow?'

Elodi leaned against the balustrade and sighed. 'A waste of a fine morning. He's burying his head in the mire, refusing to face reality. Does he not hear the clashes of swords and cries of anguish in the city? And like the Castellan, Kernlow is suspicious of Nyomae and refuses to heed her warnings. As much as I tried to convince him, he maintained that everything was in order. I told him of our discovery at the gate. However, he appears to think Nyomae is overstating the threat, and therefore it's not an issue that need concern him.'

'And the situation in the north? Could he shed light on events in Dorn?'

'Ah yes! Finally, some rare, good news to report. Ruan and his spearmen made it to Seransea. This gives me some hope. My rider, Lena, deserves much praise. She made it through the Ruuk hordes and reached Ruan. I know little of their journey, but few were lost. Elsewhere, Kernlow states the border at Noor remains quiet. Preparations at Seransea for an evacuation to Eldamouth are in place. But as yet, they see no need to execute the plan, although many have already left on foot and head south.'

'And Nordryn?'

'Ah yes, our *friend in the north*. The new leader who sat in his hall while the rest of us committed our forces here.' Her jaw clenched. 'He wouldn't hear of it. Kernlow accepts that if Nordryn passed the trials, he'll remain loyal to the realms. Apparently, Nordryn has confirmed no Ruuk have crossed into Broon, but I would not trust his word. Ruan expressed his doubts about the man, and I trust his judgement.' Elodi turned to the mountains. 'Kernlow did, at least agree to send a detachment of Archonians to Noor to keep watch and report back on enemy activity. And another to the North Forest of Ormsk. So, perhaps some of my concerns are shared by others.'

Toryn watched the sunlight find its way into the pass behind the Lower Gate. 'Dare I ask, what of your challenge to Kernlow's stewardship?'

'Of that, I am not confident. As the lord was so keen to point out… and pat my leg as he made it, is that proper procedure must be followed. He didn't write the charter, so claims he is only adhering to the law. So, while I can count on the support of the surviving generals and commanders, unfortunately, I require the approval of the Council before I can approach them.'

'And you're certain the generals will back you?'

'I see no reason why they wouldn't. I have more experience of battle than all of them put together. And would they welcome the hardships of the road at their advanced ages? I'm happy to listen to their knowledge of historical conflicts and tactics, but I know the minds of our enemies better than they. But the Council? That is where my problem lies. I doubt they will vote for a measure that would result in their removal from the Great Hall's table.' Elodi grimaced. 'Thanks to my readiness to speak my mind, they know exactly what I think of them.'

'Lady Harlyn? Excuse the interruption, but could I

possibly have a few moments of your time?' Elodi turned to see a man in his late fifties. For a moment, she was reminded of the Archon. The man's hairless head glistened in the sunlight but thankfully his skull was free of the Archon's markings. Elodi recalled seeing him outside the Great Hall the previous day. He glanced at Toryn, then back at Elodi. 'I believe we may be able to assist each other in a somewhat… delicate matter.'

Elodi agreed to his request. 'Very well. But please note, Toryn can be trusted. We are as thick as the thieves of Saphrir when it comes to dealing with *delicate matters*.'

The man relaxed. 'Ah, good. Then I hope it will prove beneficial to us all.'

She held out a hand. 'I'm afraid while I know your face, I do not know your name… or your position.'

He bowed, then shook her hand. 'I am Marrick of Loromar, principal city of Tamarand. But as for my position here…? I am not sure I can answer that with confidence.'

Elodi gestured to a nearby bench. 'Then perhaps we shall sit in the shade while you try to explain.'

'Thank you, ma'am.' They arranged themselves on the bench. Marrick continued. 'I was brought to Archonholm ten years ago. I had previously acted as an advisor to the Council of Tamarand following my service with the Archonian Guard.'

Elodi caught Toryn's eye. 'That is reassuring to hear. I would much rather take advice from a soldier who has served with a sword in his hand, than from those who sit in dusty halls dispensing ill-thought decrees.'

Marrick smiled. 'Every word I've heard about you, ma'am, appears to be true. And I too am pleased to discover that.'

'I believe we are going to get on well, Marrick. Now please, tell me what makes you unsure of your function here in Archonholm?'

'I was appointed Chief Advisor to the Council of Farrand, and then within a year, promoted to the Archon's Inner Council. But I soon came to realize my position appeared to be purely for show as the Archon, and the Vice-Archon for that matter, would not be advised on even the most mundane of matters.'

Toryn looked up at the banner flying from the tower. 'And now we can appreciate why the Archon's ears were not open to advice. And the Vice-Archon would never say or do anything to contradict him.'

Marrick turned at the sound of the workers unloading the rubble into the gorge. 'I admit my spine tingled when I discovered the truth. I'd spent many an hour, worthless hours at that, sitting at his table, but I never thought…'

Elodi sighed. 'Sadly, none of us suspected a thing.' She gestured to the dust blowing across the narrow bridge. 'But we'll live with that regret for many years. But by all accounts, the Archon had always been a difficult man to read.' She scanned the terrace. 'Now, what of this delicate matter?'

Marrick took a step closer and lowered his voice. 'Let me begin by saying my role as *advisor* to Lord Kernlow appears to be no different from before. Permit me to be flippant, but my mouth moves, the words come out, but they don't appear to reach Kernlow's ears.'

Elodi smirked. 'Ah yes. There's something about the air in the Great Hall that allow words to travel solely in one direction.'

Marrick agreed. 'Sadly, I observe that spectacle daily. It explains why so much that needs to be done is neglected. First, the armory is running short of raw materials owing to the loss of Drunsberg, and at a time when so many repairs are required.'

Toryn glanced at the Lower Gate. 'As grim as it

sounds, clearing the pass will recover hundreds of swords and armor plate. But then, many will be damaged.'

Marrick nodded. 'I'll give credit to Lord Kernlow for the work completed to date. But even if we had ample materials to make them battle-ready, practically all of Farrand's blacksmiths served in the reserves, and sadly, the majority were lost at the pass. But that is not all. We have a problem with the upcoming harvest. Hundreds who would have brought in the crop lay buried beneath the rubble. And of course, we have many displaced people fleeing the Ruuk in Dorn. And rumors of more incursions are clogging the roads south. Livestock in the north is falling into the hands of our foes. Therefore, to put it bluntly, much of our food supply is not where the empty stomachs are, ma'am. And last, but certainly not least, taxes will not be collected for the foreseeable future. This means the guards, knights and servants of the realms will have to be paid from Farrand's dwindling gold reserves.'

Elodi looked up. 'Reserves? Farrand has gold in reserve? We never had that luxury in Harlyn. Funds were earmarked for vital projects before it arrived at our treasury.'

'It's perhaps wrong of me to say dwindling, ma'am, seeing as the floor of the vault is gathering dust where the gold once stood. Exhausted would be more accurate. Unfortunately, the Archon, or rather the imposter inside his head, saw fit to all but empty the vaults for what came to be known as the *audacious plan*, plus the odd extravagant project.'

Elodi frowned. 'But surely the money is at least in the hands of the suppliers and workers of the realms.'

Marrick shrugged. 'I'm afraid that is not the case. The largest sums were spent on the wood for the ships from the forests of Ormsk, and that of course, means the gold now sits in Keld's treasury and—'

Elodi slapped the bench. 'In the hands of Nordryn!' The walkers enjoying the afternoon sun turned at the sound of her annoyance. She lowered her voice. 'And who knows what he'll see fit to purchase with his newfound wealth. Is there anything Uluriel did not overlook?'

Marrick leaned forward. 'Ah. Your reaction makes it easier to raise the delicate matter.'

'Am I to assume this regards Nordryn?'

'It does, ma'am. And while I imagine you became suspicious when he failed to show up for the gathering at the gate, I suspect there were things afoot long before that. I have reason to believe the trial to select the new Lord Broon was skewed in his favor.'

Elodi stiffened. 'How so?'

'It was rigged. Through one of my colleagues, I discovered three long-standing members of Broon's Council died suddenly while Bardon attended the opening of the Caerwal Tower. And, I presume the replacements had connections with Nordryn. But the move would have been futile if there was no need for a trial.'

'Of course. The mission south.'

'Precisely, ma'am. Through the Archon, Uluriel sought to weaken the realms from within. I think we can now appreciate how the construction of border fences, and the travel restrictions imposed, slowed our recovery from the dark years. But I believe it went beyond that. Uluriel was not concerned about the lords of Kernlow and Galabrant. They posed her no threat. They are old and obviously reluctant to commit to anything that compromised their position sitting comfortably between Farrand and the northern realms. And, as is the tradition of Galabrant, the title passes to the eldest son of the deceased lord. And as we both—'

'Stay in line.' They turned as a Schoolmaster admonished two girls as one grappled the other to the floor. The man pulled the sparring children apart. 'I brought you up here to appreciate how Archonholm has protected our people for centuries. How can you learn if you are at each other's throats.' Elodi looked on, saddened that not even the young had been spared the dread gripping the city. She wondered if the sound of children's laughter and mischief would be heard again in Archonholm.

Marrick waited for the Master to establish peace in his class. He leaned in. 'And as we both know, many see Galabrant's son as weak, living in luxury in his father's shadow. Whereas Uluriel knew your father and Bardon were a different prospect altogether. Both capable leaders of strong realms with years of experience dealing with the Ruuk. You were also less likely to bend to the will of the Archon without question.'

Elodi's jaw tightened. 'At the time, I assumed the Archon wanted to remove myself and Bardon following an incident in his quarters. But all along it was a plan to send Bardon on a mission he, and thousands of our elite forces, would not survive so Uluriel could install Nordryn in Keld.' Her hand covered her mouth. 'And my father…'

'Killed to remove him and thus bring a young and inexperienced woman to the helm at Harlyn.'

Elodi's eyes burned. 'And it couldn't have worked out better for her. Calerdorn would not have fallen under my father's command.'

Toryn tried to ease her guilt. 'From what I've heard from your soldiers, I don't think anyone could have withstood that assault. Would your father have faced Dorlan?'

'It is good of you to say so, but I harbor my doubts. I had suspected my father was killed because he discovered no enemy stood behind the gate. But now it appears Uluriel's actions have had a greater impact than I at first thought.'

Marrick frowned. 'Your father knew the pass was unguarded?'

'That is my belief. He had read archives that must have roused his curiosity. He climbed the Caerwal Tower that night, but unfortunately never made it back to Archonholm to share his discovery.' She turned to the bridge glistening in the sun. 'He met his untimely end in what should have been the safest place in the Five Realms, and at the hands of cowards who were not fit to look him in the eye.' Elodi clutched Marrick's arm. 'Did the Castellan have a hand in this despicable act?'

'I cannot be certain… as yet. But he must have been responsible for spreading the story it was an accident. Otherwise, he would have to admit he was not in total control of Archonholm. And we all know how important that is to the man.'

Toryn glanced to Elodi before asking Marrick. 'Do you know who could have thrown the lord off the bridge?'

'I have my suspicions. There were nights the Archon would walk unattended on the road to the east. He dismissed the Castellan's concerns, insisting he could defend himself against any perceived threat. He persuaded his staff he needed time alone to contemplate issues beyond their comprehension, and of course, no one dared contradict the Archon.'

Elodi smiled. 'But he didn't convince you?'

'No, he did not. He spent many days alone in his high tower. Sometimes we didn't see him for weeks on end. So, no, I didn't accept his explanation. Therefore, I took it upon myself to follow him one evening. I had to remain some distance as he would more than likely sense my presence. But follow him I did. He walked at least three leagues along the Northeast Road under the boughs of the Foranfae, and at one point I thought he was about to enter. But as night fell, he stopped and waited by the side of the road. By a stroke of luck the clouds cleared, and the full moon rose. I hid in a ditch some fifty paces away when I heard horses. But despite the moonlight, I could not see the riders' faces, but my luck had yet to run out. One of the riders appeared to disagree with the Archon. He went for his sword, which turned out to be his last action. The Archon's hand shot out, a bolt of light brought the miscreant to his knees, then he collapsed. The remaining three were compliant and listened intently before strapping their dead colleague to his horse and riding off. But in that brief flash, I saw the riders clearly. They were tall men dressed in black, all with dark hair and beards.'

'Nordleng!' Toryn lowered his voice. 'They sound like Nordleng from north of the border. I have had the pleasure of their company.'

Marrick agreed. 'After investigation, I came to the same conclusion. They wore nothing to identify their allegiance and spoke with a heavy accent that made it difficult to understand what was said. I knew little about them, but when I described them to my colleagues from Broon, they confirmed they had to be Nordleng. I couldn't understand why the Archon was meeting with these fellows. But following the tragic murder of Lord Harlyn, I came to suspect he was using them for his… shall we say, dirty work?'

Elodi groaned. 'And all the while we sat meekly behind our fences as decreed by the Archon.' She turned to the mountains. 'Do you still hold the post of Chief Advisor, Marrick?'

'I do, ma'am. While I have yet to see any advice I've offered result in any noticeable action, the post does bring certain privileges. But…' he appeared to consider his next words, 'I have been looking deeper into the murder of your father, ma'am. And following the carnage at the pass, more guards have been willing to speak openly to me. I have another I wish to consult, but I believe the Nordleng must have had assistance from someone within the citadel.'

Elodi caught her breath. 'And could that be the Castellan?'

'Please allow me a little more time, ma'am. But if not directly involved, his cooperation was required to cover up the events of that night.'

Elodi's jaw tightened. 'Thank you, Marrick. I have much to digest. We shall meet again, but in the meantime perhaps you could find out what has happened to my sword. I feel there is a good chance I will need it very soon.'

# 8. Return from Evermore

Toryn waited for the last of the rock-laden wagons to clear the bridge. And, as if on cue, the Caerwals put on their red cloak to greet the evening sun. He had spent the day unsuccessfully trying to locate the Amayans and wished to clear his head. He strode onto the bridge and into the cooler air settling in the chasm. Toryn stopped in the middle and turned to face the Archon's Tower, hoping to see signs of Nyomae. But no light came from the single window, and the door remained closed.

Toryn's stomach churned. He spun around, expecting to see the hooded form of Uleva on the bridge, but found he was alone. Yet, the feeling did not leave him. He strode towards the Lower Gate, convinced something was afoot in the pass. He approached the portcullis just as it began to lower. 'Hold on there, mate. The pass is closing for the day.' A large guard ducked under from beneath the gate. 'And you won't want your head caved in by—'

'Odrun!' Toryn strode to meet him and gripped his forearm.

'Why, if it isn't young Toryn.' He turned. 'Oi! Harruld, you'll never guess who's come to visit.'

Harruld squeezed through the narrow doorway of the gatehouse. He beamed. 'Well ain't our young prisoner now the man of the moment. One day you're hanging from the bridge, the next you're saving our skins at the pass.' He took two long strides and patted Toryn's shoulder. 'Me and Oddy never thought you were a bad 'un. You can't fool an old guard… well, maybe once or twice, but never thrice. We've heard all about your heroics. And may I say a personal thanks. Me and Oddy would have been goners for sure had you not brought down that Nordleng swine on the ledge above us.'

Toryn peered through the gate. 'I only wish I could have taken out more.'

Harruld's grin faded. 'Don't be hard on yourself, lad. You did all you could. If it wasn't for you, who knows how many more would have been lost. No one else, besides the good Lady Harlyn, seemed to know what was happening that day.'

Odrun released Toryn's arm. 'Anyways, what brings you out here at this hour. All the workers have left and we're closing up for the night.'

Toryn's hand went to his gut. 'I came out for some air and watch the sunset, but then… this may sound absurd, but I sensed something's not right… in the pass.'

Harruld glanced at his companion. 'If you think something ain't right, then you must have good reason. Lucky you thought something was amiss when we were all packed in the pass making an easy target, eh.' He wrapped his thick arm around Toryn. 'Let's head on over and have a look, shall we? It's not like me and Oddy have much to do on this watch, so we may as well keep ourselves occupied. We'll just secure the entrance and tag along. If that's alright by you?'

Toryn nodded. 'Your company would be most welcome, but perhaps we should wait until there are more of us?'

'No need to fret there, lad. Fidric and a dozen of his lads are on duty at the gate.'

Toryn shivered. 'Then could I trouble you for a cloak… and maybe a weapon of sorts?'

'That certain something's up, eh? Better be wary then. We hear guards on duty at the city gate are seeing ghosts now.' Harrold chuckled. 'And that's even after the Castellan banned their ale. But we don't have to worry about Fidric. He never touches the stuff. A bit odd if I may say so, but as he's overseeing the removal of the unused casks of Shreek's Rage, I reckon that's for the best. It's done at night after the rubble clearers have gone.' Harruld splayed his large fingers. 'Boom! Can't be too careful with that stuff, eh? So, if you think there's something not quite right, we'd better get ourselves down there.'

Toryn sighed. 'There's plenty not right these days. Scuffles are still breaking out even with the inns closed. People are getting hurt.'

Harruld scoffed. 'Now as a man who likes a drop of ale, I'd say that's the problem. After a tankard or three, most I know can't throw a punch without falling over.' He nodded at the gate. 'Right then. Not sure if we can find a sword suitable for a hero such as yourself. But we have a few still sharp enough to do some damage.' Toryn followed Harruld into the gatehouse as Odrun lowered the portcullis. Inside, Harruld soon found a sword and a heavy cloak. Toryn held the blade, hoping it was of better quality than the one that had shattered in his first fight at Drunsberg.

Odrun entered, picked up his cloak and threw it around his broad shoulders. Toryn buckled his belt as the two guards prepared. Harruld secured his breastplate. He held another out to Odrun. The big man shook his head. 'I'll stick with my leather and sheepskin thanks, Harry.' He grinned at Toryn. 'Gets a little chilly at night down the pass.'

'You're sure, Oddy? If young Toryn thinks something's up, then I believe him.'

Odrun patted his sword. 'Got all the protection I need right here.'

Toryn tied his cloak. 'What happened to your captain? The one who shared our breakfast?'

Harruld looked at Odrun. 'Ah… now that's a tragic tale. And one we don't like to tell...' He waited. Odrun nodded. 'But seeing as it's you, we'll break our rule. And maybe you might be able to explain what happened.' Toryn waited while Harruld appeared to think where to start his tale. He took a breath. 'Well here goes then. Our cappy survived the blast that day, all thanks to you I might say. We picked up a few scratches, bruises, and dents in our armor, but we were only dazed and deafened like.' He looked down at his sword. 'But then… as we were helping those less fortunate, suddenly this big, ugly brute appeared out of nowhere. I was sure he was a Golesh fighter, but I didn't stop to think about how he got there. Anyways, he was shaping to cleave Oddy's thick skull in two, so I…' his head shook, 'I… I ran him through. Had no choice. It was him or Odrun.' He rubbed the back of his neck. Then I took a blow to my head and my short battle was done. But when I came round, in the place where the Golesh creature had fallen, our captain lay dead.' He stared open-mouthed at Odrun. 'I'd gone and killed the cappy. Such a fine fellow. Always fair to his men. Well, you saw how he didn't turn us in for arranging that hearty breakfast at the gatehouse. Such a tragedy. He'd survived the landslide only to die by my hand. If only I could…'

Odrun continued. 'But he wasn't the only one. We lost six of our lads that way. Such fine fellows, but why did they suddenly come at us like mad Golesh warriors?'

Toryn strapped on his helmet. 'I'm afraid it was a devious trick of the enemy. One last attempt to divide us and cause terror. It wasn't your fault, Harruld. You only did what you'd been trained to do. And then because Odrun was in danger.'

Odrun hugged Harruld's shoulders. 'I told you, old boy, you weren't to know it was the good captain. We were all tricked. I'm sure cappy didn't want to split my head in two, but if you hadn't acted, he would have done it. And who knows what would have happened after. He could have taken you down as well.'

Harruld fastened his cloak. 'Well, ain't that the most shameful and cowardly thing to do. To make friend fight friend? That's unacceptable in my book.' He grasped Toryn's arm. 'And thank you for clearing that up. It don't bring the cappy back, but now I know I wasn't to… to blame.' He straightened. 'Now then, let's go and see what's causing you to feel a little squiffy.' Harruld tapped his blade. 'And by The Three, if I find the enemy have sneaked under the gate, they'll regret it.'

Toryn's unease grew as they drew nearer to the site of the slaughter. He pulled his cloak tighter as the cool breeze sought to find its way to his bones. The cleared ground still bore scars from the explosion, but thankfully, no signs of the victims' suffering remained. Their footsteps echoed as they walked in silence and Toryn sensed the guards also shared his apprehension. The three stepped onto the walkway that rose above the ground yet to be cleared. The wood creaked as they made their way over the rubble and the dead still trapped beneath. Toryn's eyes were drawn to the partly excavated quarters once used by the knights who kept watch day and night. He tried to imagine how the pass would have looked back in those days, but Uluriel's heinous act had marred the place forever.

Harruld was the first to speak. 'It doesn't matter how many times I come down here, my heart still lurches. These poor beggars never knew what hit them.' He stopped and looked across the bleak site. 'Here, Toryn. Could you help us out with something that's been troubling us of late? It's kept us talking 'til the early hours, and Oddy needs his beauty sleep.'

'If I can. What troubles you?'

'We was wondering if the souls of the Archonians buried here reached the plain. You've taken the Oath, so you know of the promise of a farm on the Plains of Evermore. But we only get one if we die in battle with our weapon in our hands.' He stroked his chin. 'Yet while we thought we were about to do battle, we know now there was no enemy to fight. So... there was no battle to be had, eh.'

Odrun clenched the railing. 'And not forgetting they wouldn't have had their swords drawn. We were listening to the Archon's grand speech when the rocks started flying. And even if there was an enemy, the gate was shut. So it goes without saying, there was no battle.'

Toryn's eyes wandered across the rubble. 'That's a fair point. But…'

Harruld kicked a stone from the walkway. 'Be a terrible business if they didn't get to the plain, don't you think? All those soldiers wandering around whatever place the gentle folk go. I mean, the poor chaps won't know where they are. And maybe don't even know they're dead.'

Toryn thought for a moment. 'Maybe they *have* gone to the plain.'

Odrun scratched his head. 'How could that be?'

'In their minds, they were marching willingly to face what we believed to be a superior force. In their hearts, they were ready to lay down their lives to defend the realms. They weren't to know they'd been deceived. And what soldier wouldn't reach for their weapon as soon as they suspected something was wrong? I bet your hands shot straight to your swords the moment you heard the blast.' Odrun and Harruld nodded. Toryn continued. 'Then that's good enough for me. Every Archonian that died beneath the landslide was ready to fight the battle of their lives… and, if you think about it, we did indeed face our foe.' He pointed to the gate. 'The enemy was in the

Archon's head, standing right in front of us. So, that settles it for me. I'm certain the fallen will be sowing their first crop on their farms as we speak.'

Odrun wiped a tear from his cheek. 'Thank you, lad. He's right eh, Harruld. He is, ain't he?'

Harruld grinned. 'I believe he must be. If you look at it that way, it all makes sense now. We did face the enemy, and they must have had their hands on their weapons.' He looked across the floor of the pass and sighed. 'Kind of reminds me of the lake at Syris.' He ran his hand along the rail. These remind me of the jetties crossing the still waters of the lake. But there's only fat, tasty fish beneath that surface, while here… well, we all know what lies beneath.' His nose wrinkled. 'It's going to take months to recover all these poor souls. But now we know they've got their farms, that's helped to ease the pain. But I'd still wager most never knew what sent them on their way.'

Odrun grunted. 'Well, I ain't going to let that happen to me.' He set off. 'Let's get going and see what's bothering young Toryn and meet whatever's down there with our eyes open.'

Toryn followed. He looked up. The gate stood less than half a league ahead, but all seemed peaceful. He turned to Harruld as they strode on. 'They say the main tower at Syris is as tall as Telamir.'

'I've yet to see Telamir. But this fellow has seen both.' Harruld nudged Odrun. 'What do you reckon about them towers, Oddy? Which is taller?'

Odrun appeared as if he had just heard their conversation. 'Towers?'

'Which of them lake towers would you say is the tallest? Telamir or Syris?'

He scratched his beard. 'Not easy to say. Syris is a larger lake, and the jetties only stretch so far out. And seeing as no one is allowed on the islands, it's difficult to say which is taller. But…' his eyes wandered to the first stars twinkling in the darkening sky. 'The Towers of Syris are the most beautiful things I've ever seen. It's as if they were crafted by the fair hands of the Maidens. All tall and slender they are. Looks like they're stroking the passing clouds, and the clouds seem to like it.' Harruld winked at Toryn, but Odrun continued, unaware of his friend's mirth. 'Now Telamir… that's a very different tower altogether. A strange one, yet fine-looking in its own sort of way. It's like a potter has twisted it out of wet clay on her wheel. But it's a dark one. It almost defies your eyes to see it. At first glance it appears like glass, but look again and it could be stone. And even in the still waters of the lake it don't cast no reflection. Strange, very strange.' Odrun sighed. 'I hope one day to get the chance to see them towers again.'

Harruld chuckled. 'You should talk about such things more often. It would've made all those nights we've spent on watch more bearable. Never had you down as a poet, Oddy.'

Odrun threw a mock punch at Harruld's chin. 'Not just a fearless warrior with a pretty face, eh.'

Harruld ducked. 'Wrong on both counts.' He jumped up and ruffled Odrun's hair. 'But I wouldn't want to spend those cold nights beside a campfire with any other fool.'

Toryn laughed, happy to be distracted as they neared the end of the walkway. In the murky light, the Caerwal Gate appeared taller as it loomed over them, barely tolerating their presence. At its base, a small cabin occupied the spot where the Archon had made his final speech. Harruld squinted in the gloom. 'Here, Oddy. Does that hut look empty? Where's Fidric and his men? Surely, they'd have lit their brazier by now?' He turned to Toryn. 'As Oddy said, it can get pretty cold here at night, even in summer. It's almost like the dead suck the warmth out of the air.'

Odrun called out. 'Hey! Fiddy! If you're sleeping on duty that's two ales you owe us.' His booming voice echoed over their heads and down the pass. But no reply came. He drew his sword. 'Looks like your gut was right, lad.'

Harruld put two fingers to his lips and whistled. But still none answered. He also drew his sword. 'Be ready. Toryn, guard the rear while we check the cabin.' Toryn waited at the end of the pier. He peered over to the remains of the Archon's Tower, convinced the stone in its foundations was the cause of his discomfort. Yet Nyomae had reinforced the ground around it, believing it would reduce its potency. But Toryn's unease was not solely down to the stone — it seemed to come from all around.

Harruld lit a torch, and the two guards entered the cabin. Harruld cried out. 'Fiddy! What the—?' He stuck his head out the door. 'Here. Toryn. Something is up with Fidric. Come and take a look.'

Toryn hurried over. He squeezed between Harruld and Odrun into the small cabin. Harruld held up the torch. Toryn jumped back. Fidric stood ramrod straight at the center. His eyes stared at Toryn, but appeared not to see him. Harruld shook his head. 'Have you seen anything as strange as this on your travels?' He waved the flame in front of Fidric's face and exclaimed. 'He don't even blink.'

Odrun scoffed. 'Never seen him stand like that even when inspected by the Archon.' He leaned closer. 'Is that frost?' He touched the guard's cheek, then snatched his hand back. 'Stone cold.' He rubbed his hands. 'It's like a blade on a winter's morn.'

'Well have you, lad?' Harruld lowered the torch. 'Have you seen anything like this?'

Toryn looked the guard in the eye. 'No, I can't say I've—' He froze. A glint of green flashed behind Fidric's glassy gaze. 'But I've seen that green before... and that wasn't good.' A line spread from the corner of Fidric's lips. The thin layer of ice cracked. His mouth gaped, stretching unnaturally wide. His eyes bulged. His scream chilled Toryn's heart.

The guard lunged at Toryn. He jumped back, but Fidric was too fast. His icy hands grasped his neck and drove his thumbs into Toryn's throat. He staggered, gasping for air as Odrun and Harruld grappled with Fidric. With the little strength he had left, Toryn slammed down hard on Fidric's arms. His body shuddered as if he had struck a stone pillar. Lights flickered at the edges of his vision. Odrun grabbed a spear. He knocked Fidric over the head as Harruld slammed into the guard. The four crashed out of the cabin door. The groping fingers released. Toryn pitched forward and coughed. At his feet, Fidric laid with his arms extended as if still intent on choking his victim.

Harruld kneeled and felt for a pulse. He looked up. 'He's dead.'

Odrun dropped the spear. 'How can he be? I didn't hit him that hard. He's a tough nut. That blow shouldn't have done for him.' He turned. 'You alright, Toryn?'

'I'll survive.' He coughed and rubbed his throat. 'Lucky you came with me, eh.'

Harruld ran his hands down Fidric's body. 'There's no sign of a wound. I've seen him take blows that would have brought down an ox. Could he have been dead before we got here?'

Toryn followed Fidric's glassy gaze to the emerging stars. 'Dead? He moved.'

Odrun shivered. 'But what about them tales… the one's from Nordruuk? Death don't mean nothing to that lot.'

Harruld groaned as he stood. 'Just tales, Oddy. You can't go believing every word spoken around the campfire.

Anyways, best you go and check what's happened to the others. By the Three, I hope they've not suffered the same fate as poor Fiddy.'

Odrun turned to the gate. 'Surely not all of them. They're strong fellows. Well capable of looking after themselves.'

'Then where are they?'

Odrun picked up the spear. 'I'll find them. Then we'll get to the bottom of this.'

Toryn nodded to the fallen guard. 'Did you know him well?'

'Not as well as Oddy, but we're all brothers. I've fought the Ruuk by his side a few times.' Harruld bent and folded Fidric's arms across his chest. 'Just tragic. He survived the carnage at Midsummer, only to die like this. Ah… the poor soul. Trying to throttle a fellow guard won't earn his farm on the plain. Tragic. Just tragic.'

Odrun hurried back. 'Harruld! They're all dead!'

'Dead?' Harruld gaped. 'All of them? You sure?'

'Yes, all of them.' Odrun's eyes widened. 'Worse than dead, I'd say. All shriveled, shrunken even.'

Toryn checked the gate. 'What could have happened? The gate's not breached. Who could have done…?' His heart sank. The stone. Nyomae suspected another spell lay within. It had to be the work of the stone.

Odrun grasped Toryn's arm. 'Something killed them. Their faces. It's like they're still in pain.' Toryn staggered forward as if a dagger had been thrust into his gut. Odrun steadied his fall. 'What is it, lad?'

Toryn's jaw clenched. He spat out his words. 'There's a stone. Beneath the—'

Harruld cried out. 'Over there.' He jabbed his finger at the old tower. 'I don't like the look of that. That ain't natural.' Toryn steadied his stance. He did not have to look — he could taste the wrong. The tower ruins glowed.

Toryn's ears ached as if the air tried to force its way into his skull. A green light rippled across the ground as if a pebble had dropped into a stagnant pond. But Toryn knew this was no pebble. He retched, recalling the foulness that struck down the guards at Drunsberg.

Toryn whispered. 'We need to leave.' But no one moved as the marble slab shifted. The scrape echoed loudly in the silence. A large rock tilted, sending the rubble toppling down the pile. The ghoulish glow spread. The ground trembled.

Harruld gaped. 'What the—? Do they mine beneath the gate? We should raise—'

A sword thrust up from the rubble. 'By The Three!' Odrun gawped. A gray, scrawny hand clasped the handle. The sword-bearer's head appeared. At first, Toryn thought he was looking at a broken helmet. He was wrong. Toryn reeled as the faint glow revealed a shattered skull. The disfigured soldier clambered out of his tomb. Toryn winced at the cracking of bones as the figure straightened. It bent to retrieve its shield and broken helmet. It turned. Gray skin clung to its head. A single, yellowing eye found Toryn. Its lips split as it grinned and raised its sword arm to challenge him.

Harruld spat. 'Them tales… but I never thought. This is wrong. Very wrong. If it ain't enough this poor guard was buried by their evil, they go and fetch him back from the plains to fight us?'

Odrun leveled his spear. 'It's grim, Harry. But it's just the one. We can deal with one. Let's do him a favor and send him back to his farm, eh.'

Harruld drew his sword. 'Agreed, Oddy. As hideous as this poor fellow looks, a swift blow or two will do the trick.'

Toryn stepped to Harruld's side. 'Can he be killed? He's already dead.'

'Can't say I've ever fought a dead man, lad. But he can't cause us harm if he's got no arms or legs. And it ain't killing him. We'll grant him the peace he deserves and let him return to Evermore. This is an outrage.'

The forlorn figure stood still, its lipless grin and solitary eye, sickened Toryn.

A rock moved. Harruld turned. 'Watch out. Looks like he's got a friend.' Toryn clenched his sword as another clawed its way through the debris. His stomach churned as the crushed, disfigured soldier rose from the mass grave. But he was not the last. More followed. Toryn stared in horror as a tall, thin guard, with his arms hanging loose at his sides, dragged his sword clattering across the debris to join the end of a ghastly line. The sorrowful figures limped on bent legs, raising their shattered swords with twisted arms. Then as one, they began their advance. They did not rush; they had no need.

Harruld muttered. 'Get back to the pier. We'll hold our position there. Remember. Not a step back. What will the others say if they find out we turned tail and ran from these skinny fellows? I reckon these fiends can't move fast. We've got a narrow walkway. They can't all come at us at once.'

Odrun spat. 'Ah! That smell. I can taste it.' To their left, another rock shifted closer to the gate.

'Here, Oddy. Can you remember who formed up over there?'

Toryn answered. 'The First Horse. Most survived, but a dozen or so were lost.'

Harruld wavered. 'No… surely not. They can't bring back a—' A mournful squeal escaped from the ground. 'By the Three. They can. That's a horse!'

Odrun stumbled back. 'Horses? No, Harry, no. The horses as well?'

'Ye gods!' Harruld grabbed Toryn. 'They're raising a

ruddy army.' He twisted away. 'Back to the gate. We can't fight a horde of dead out here alone.'

# 9. One More for the Plain

The mountain sides flickered green, growing brighter until the whole pass appeared as if a corrupt sun had risen. Toryn and the guards stumbled across the uneven boards as they fled. Hooves clattered on the wooden slates. Toryn shot a glance over his shoulder. A dozen, once-proud horses, with heads lolling and protruding tongues from fleshless skulls, bore their dead riders. Behind, more guards gathered, numbering close to thirty to form a ghastly militia.

Toryn reached the end of the walkway. Odrun struggled to catch his breath, but the Lower Gate was still some distance away. Harruld hooked his arm under Odrun's. 'Come on, old boy. Can't let the dead outrun you, eh?'

Odrun staggered to a halt. He stooped and gasped. 'This body's made for fighting… not running. Just need to… catch my breath. Just need a moment and I'll be fine.'

Toryn checked behind. 'A moment's all we've got.' On the walkway, the horse leading the charge faltered. Its front legs buckled then snapped. The beast slammed into the boards, throwing its rider over the edge. The knight struck the rocks and shattered like a plate. Toryn grimaced. 'That'll slow their progress.'

Harruld lifted Odrun to his feet. 'Come on, big man. You've had your rest. Now let's get to the gate and hold them ghouls from there.' He laughed. 'We'll have earned our supper today, eh?'

Odrun managed a smile. 'Been looking forward to that ham all day.' He straightened. 'Ready. Come on then, Harry. Nothing gets between me and my supper.'

They set off just as the stricken horse was bundled off the pier, and the chaotic charge of the dead resumed. Fortunately, the First Horse were not what they once were, and their advance was no faster than a stumbling trot. Even so, a trot was still a match for the two large and aging guards, and they barely arrived at the gatehouse in time to close the inner gates.

Odrun slumped against the ancient wood as Harruld rammed the heavy beam into place. 'That should keep 'em out. Can't think those scrawny scoundrels will have the strength to smash their way through solid oak.' He looked up at Toryn. 'This gatehouse was built to keep *our* people out of the pass, not for an attack from the south. That's the job of the big gate. But while it should keep those dead fellows out, we best play it safe, eh? I'll raise the alarm.'

Toryn agreed. 'Wouldn't hurt to have more than the three of us. And what if the rest rise up? There must be at least four thousand yet to be moved.'

Odrun glanced up, still gasping for air. 'Now there's a thought. Thirty or so we could handle from here. But a few thousand? I don't like them odds.'

Harruld made sure the beam was secure. 'Oddy. You take Toryn to the parapet and keep an eye on them. I'll sound the horn and get the boys down here.'

Toryn helped Odrun squeeze his large frame through the narrow doorway and up the spiral staircase. The big guard puffed and blew as he muttered under his breath. 'This is an outrage. It ain't natural. It ain't right.' The horn blared as they emerged from the stairs and into the cool air of the parapet. Toryn rushed to the wall. Below, horses whinnied a pitiful call from their emaciated throats, sounding more like yelping foxes than the fine beasts they had once been. A ragged line of Archonian guards lined up to assail the gate. Above their heads, a faint, green haze hung as if their spirits struggled to free themselves from their broken bodies and return to the plains. A knight of the First Horse nudged his mount. It hobbled towards them just as Harruld crashed through the doorway, carrying three bows and a quiver of arrows. 'Here we go.' He peered over the wall. 'Not sure how much use these will be against the dead, but it might spoil their evening if we can hit 'em in the eye.' A horn replied from Archonholm. He glanced over his shoulder. 'Won't be long. The lads will be here soon.' He chuckled. 'Bet they won't be expecting this.'

The remaining horses limped behind their leader, bumping into each other as they crowded the foot of the gate. The knights raised their blunted swords and hammered the oak with the pommels of their swords. Odrun jeered. 'If that's all they've got, we won't be needing reinforcements. They can do that all night, it'll never crack.'

Harruld nocked an arrow. 'Anyways, can't have 'em scratching the woodwork.' He leaned over and let one fly. Toryn joined him and aimed at a gap in a broken helmet. His stomach clenched at the sickening crack as his arrow struck a rider's skull. But the knight continued his futile attack with the arrow jutting out of his head. 'Keep going, lad.' Harruld leveled his bow. 'Let's see how many we can spike 'em with before they give up.'

They shot a dozen or so arrows but failed to stop them. Odrun laughed. 'Would you look at that? It's an army of huckles.'

Harruld grunted. 'Whatever they look like, arrows are useless against these dead folk.'

'Rocks.' Toryn glanced behind. 'We need rocks. Very useful at Drunsberg.'

Odrun groaned. 'Now ain't that the thing. There are more rocks than we can count out there, and thousands piled up on the other side of the ravine, but not one to be had here.'

To their left, something clattered on the wall. Toryn turned. 'Ladders?' He stuck his head over the wall. 'It's a decoy. The knights aren't trying to break through.' Farther along, the guards had torn the rails from the walkway and propped them against the wall. Toryn ran to the ladder as three soldiers climbed up with surprising speed. He nocked his last arrow and let it fly as the first clambered over. It struck him full in the chest. The soldier stared down at the arrow as if unsure of what had hit him. To Toryn's dismay, the dead man shrugged and drew his broken blade.

Harruld bellowed. 'Swords! Time to get in their faces, lads.' Toryn and Odrun flanked him as they hurtled into the attackers scrambling to their feet. Harruld swung hard, removing the head of the first. He yelled. 'Best way to stop 'em! Don't hold back.' Toryn parried a lunge from the second. Odrun blocked a blow from the third. Yet despite the sorry state of their attackers, they fought with purpose and strength. The experienced guards and Toryn struck back, and soon the headless bodies of the first over the wall lay at their feet. But the weight of numbers forced the defenders back.

Eight formed a line along the parapet. Harruld recovered his breath. 'Careful, ladies. These fellows are getting organized.' Behind the formation, a large hand grasped the wall. A dented helmet appeared, followed by a scarred face with a tufty, gray beard.

'By the Three, Harruld! It's Glamdel.' A giant of a dead Archonian forced his way through the battlements. His wide, yellow eyes stared at Toryn, but whether he grinned, or whether it was the lack of flesh on his face that revealed his broken teeth, he could not tell. In his hand, he brandished a long, broad sword.

Harruld and Odrun edged back and stood with Toryn.

Harruld gasped. 'The brute was a handful when alive. I saw him take down an angry boar with that sword. One blow, that's all it took. Who knows what he can do now he's one of the dead?' The line parted, allowing Glamdel to take his place in the center. Toryn retched. His eyes watered.

Harruld choked. 'Ye gods. That stench! Glammy was never one to wash, but by the Three, he out stinks the rest of the dead put together. That's enough to take us down without a fight.'

Odrun stammered. 'He's… he's got a thick neck, Harry. Hope our blades are sharp enough.' He winced as he set his stance.

'You injured, Oddy?'

'Took a blow to my dodgy leg. Had worse though. Don't you worry about me.' Four more grinning dead joined the green rank.

Harruld looked over his shoulder. 'This ain't the best position, lads. They'll outflank us easy.' The line crept forward, driven on by Glamdel. Toryn's vision blurred. He stared. They moved as if commanded by an unseen force. Within each opponent, he saw the ghostly outline of a figure. Not a guard, but akin to the squat Ruuk soldiers he had fought at Drunsberg. Bile rose in Toryn's throat — it was if the Ruuk were cloaked in the skins of the dead.

The echo of horses' hooves clattered on the bridge spanning the chasm. Harruld sighed. 'They took their time, but help is here. Right then, lads, let's find another line to defend.'

Odrun hobbled on one leg. 'You go. I'll occupy the big man. Give you a head start, eh.'

'Don't be daft, Oddy. There's no need. We can all make it back.'

Odrun winced, grabbing the back of his leg. 'I'm hamstrung, Harry. I won't make it to the stairs. You two go. Glammy's broad sword will take off our heads as soon as we turn tail.' He raised his blade. 'Besides, I've got a score to settle with that lout.'

'It's not him. He's dead. It's just his flesh 'n bones. Who knows what's inside his head now?'

'Don't argue with me, Harry. Just this once, go with what I say. We haven't got all night.'

Harruld clutched Odrun's arm. 'Not here, Oddy. This ain't your time. Not against these stinking ghouls.'

But Odrun stood his ground in the face of the looming menace. 'I can handle this one. Anyhow, I'm ready for the plain should I—' Glamdel tipped back his head and rasped a challenge. He raised his blade. Odrun lunged, forcing the giant to parry his blow. Odrun yelled over his shoulder. 'Go! Both of you.'

'Not a step back, my friend.' Harruld sprang. 'For the Three!' Toryn leaped after them. The heavy sword of Glamdel sliced down, but Odrun was quick for a large man, even when injured. He dipped. Sparks flew as Glamdel's blade struck the flagstones. Odrun jabbed up and caught Glamdel's helmet. The helmet fell, revealing a bald and scarred head. Glamdel staggered. Toryn swung. A jolt shot up his arm as the blade sliced into the giant's brawny neck. Glamdel's eyes bulged. But he refused to drop.

Odrun cried out. 'Keep going! He can't take much more.' He threw his weight at two guards to his right and knocked them back. He slashed, severing the arm of one, and the leg from another. But still the grim line advanced. Glamdel went for Odrun, swinging his long blade as if to cleave him in two. Odrun was distracted by another. Toryn rushed Glamdel, thrusting at the gap between his breastplate and raised arm. His sword jammed into the dead flesh and was wrenched from Toryn's grip as the giant reeled. But his strike only shifted the giant's downward blow by inches. Glamdel's blade slammed onto

Odrun's shoulder. He cried out, dropping his weapon.

'Oddy!' Harruld parried a blow and threw his arm around his friend. But Glamdel would not be denied his victory. With Toryn's blade protruding from his armpit, he launched at Odrun, piercing his leather tunic. Blood spurted from Odrun's mouth as he fell, taking Harruld with him. Toryn grabbed Odrun's sword and drove its tip at Glamdel's groin. The big guard lurched. Toryn pulled back his blade, then swung hard at Glamdel as his neck came into range. The bones cracked. The Archonian's head toppled from his neck but did not fall. And neither did the big warrior. He stumbled forward with his head swaying from gray sinews. He took three steps and collapsed at the feet of the stunned reinforcements pouring onto the parapet.

Toryn and Harruld joined the arriving guards and charged at the stragglers, bundling four over the wall. Now only three remained bearing arms. The green glow emanating from their skin flickered and died, and to Toryn's relief, they crumpled into a heap. He turned back to see Harruld cradling Odrun in his arms. He ran to kneel at his side as Harruld soothed his injured comrade. 'You big, brave fool, Oddy.'

Odrun coughed, spraying blood onto Harruld's breastplate. 'Should've put my best armor on, eh?' He grasped Harruld's arm. 'I'll wait for you, my friend. On the plains, I'll save a farm for you.'

Toryn pushed his hand onto the gaping wound in Odrun's gut. 'You're not done yet. We can get you to the healers.'

Odrun shook his head. 'Thanks for trying, but I know when I'm done, lad.' His eyes stared past Toryn. 'I can see the barley on the plains.' He smiled. 'It's all golden in the sunshine. Here. I can see the cappy. He made it, Harry. He got his farm after all. I'll put in a good word for—' His body braced.

Harruld stroked his old friend's brow. 'You lucky sod. Always thought I'd get there first.' He glanced at the broken bodies of the dead strewn across the flagstones. 'But if we're up against this kind of enemy now, I guess it won't be long before I'll be joining you. Go now my—' Odrun slumped. His last breath was briefly visible on Harruld's breastplate, but soon faded as the big guard departed for the plains. Harruld hugged his fellow warrior close and rocked. His jaw tightened, leaving his last words for Odrun unsaid.

# 10. Of Swords & Tales

'And what if the enemy had raised more than a handful of the dead?' Elodi glared at the Castellan, convinced the man had a hand in her father's death. However, until Marrick could confirm it, she would have to bite her tongue. Elodi took a breath. 'You have no reason to deny access to my sword. If those ghouls had breached the Lower Gate and crossed the bridge, how was I supposed to aid the defense?'

The Castellan edged back and took a position behind his desk as if a shield wall. His faced tightened as he made his excuse. 'Lady Harlyn, I hope you understand that I was duty bound to have your sword examined.'

'Understand! What is there to understand? You disarmed me without explanation, and now you're asking me to *understand*?'

The Castellan sat. He glanced at the door over Elodi's shoulder. 'Your sword wields an ancient power, and one that you wear in the citadel for which I am responsible. I simply wanted Archonholm's scholars to have time to study it, to determine whether it posed a threat.'

Elodi's jaw clenched. 'Then why didn't you simply ask? You did not have to confiscate it as if I were a child.'

He stuttered. 'I… I wasn't sure if you would hand it over.'

'Too right I wouldn't have. But why do you consider my sword a threat? By the Three, if I had not led a charge at the gate, our casualties would have been far worse. I have more combat experience than any living general or leader of a realm. I have looked them in the eye and felt their foul breath on my face. Have you, Castellan? I think not, but still you don't appear to trust me.'

He kept his eyes on the desk. 'I trust you, ma'am, but your sword?' He clasped his hands, straightened, and met Elodi's gaze. 'What do you know of its origins? What do any of us know of the' — his mouth twisted — 'Amayans?'

Elodi exhaled. 'While you obviously cannot hide your disdain for them, let me remind you, they have saved the realms from atrocities in the past. Nyomae tells us they are protectors of the Amanach, the stones that keep the evil in this world at bay... for the time being.'

The Castellan waved his hand. 'Old tales again, ma'am. How can we know if there is a shred of truth in something told long before the Seven Realms were formed? And now we discover we can't be certain whether the archives we took for granted are true.'

Elodi leaned on the Castellan's desk. 'I would rather place my faith in Nyomae's word than anything that came from Uluriel via the Archon's lips. And what about my sword? Your people have studied it for two days. Did your wise and most knowledgeable scholars discover the source of its power? Did they even have a clue where to begin?'

His eyes flicked back to the door. 'Err… no, ma'am. They have made no progress to date.'

'Then I shall have it back… today.' Elodi tapped her finger on the desktop. 'And if I don't, please bear in mind I command the largest force here… be they a two-day march from the city.'

The Castellan's fleeting boldness abandoned him. 'Certainly, Lady Harlyn. I will make sure it is returned to you immediately.' She held his gaze. He glanced down at his papers. 'And I am informed all efforts are being made to accommodate your forces in and around Archonholm within the week.'

Elodi stood. 'Thank you.' She moved to leave, then

turned. 'And I can assure you, Castellan, my sword represents a threat only to my enemies.'

Elodi led the way up the steep spiral stairs. Toryn peered out of the narrow window to his right. 'We must be at least halfway there. I can't understand why the Archon didn't have a rising platform like the one at the Caerwal Tower.'

Elodi spoke over her shoulder. 'I would have thought it was obvious. It provides an excellent deterrent to unwanted visitors.'

Toryn grinned. 'I would have liked to have seen the Castellan's face when you threatened him about returning your sword.'

She laughed. 'Threatened? Negotiated is perhaps a better… no, you're right.' She patted her sword, happy to have it back on her hip. 'I accept my words may have come across as a threat, but that would have been his interpretation. Although, he did look a little taken aback. But I've learned that's the only way to deal with the likes of him. He's keen to dish it out, but he doesn't know how to handle those who give it back.'

Toryn spoke while catching his breath. 'I would still be wary of him. He doesn't know what to make of you, and, like the rest of us, he was unsettled by the attack at the Lower Gate.'

Elodi stopped beside a window looking out onto the mountains. The light streaming through found the furrows on her brow. 'The Castellan has changed of late. He's less predictable than he used to be. One moment he stands up to me, then the next he capitulates. I can't quite put my finger on it. Whenever I turn, he's there… watching me. He used to avoid me when possible. But lately, he always seems to be there in the background… watching me.'

Toryn eyes were drawn to her red hair brought to life

in the sunlight. It pained him to see her troubled, but it pained him more that he could do little to ease her angst. Her joined her at the window. 'It's obvious the man's disturbed by the panic spreading through his precious city. The people can see he's losing control. I fear if he can't restore order, he'll resort to hanging people from the bridge before long.'

Elodi leaned on the window ledge. 'It seems the stronger and bolder our enemy become, the more I have to worry about our *friends*.' She looked up the staircase. 'Is this wise? Nyomae did ask to not be disturbed.'

'She's been shut up here for three days. Nyomae must be made aware of the incident at the gate. It has to be the work of that stone beneath the ruined tower.' Toryn shuddered. 'We'll face far greater numbers if the Ul-dalak can raise our dead to fight against us.'

'You're right. I'm sure she'd rather be informed than left in the dark.' They climbed the last part in silence. Finally, they reached the top. Elodi glanced at Toryn and knocked. The door opened immediately.

Nyomae smiled. 'Good. I have been expecting you.' She stood to one side. 'Please, come in.'

The sun climbed to the top of the sky, shedding its light directly down into the pass. From the Archon's balcony, Toryn could see the iron railing at the top of the gate glinting in the sunlight. Nyomae stood between them. She let out a long sigh. 'Ah, alas for those guards at the pass. Yet another mistake for which I must accept responsibility. I could not determine the stone's purpose, and yet I believed my intervention would constrain its evil. I did not imagine it could be used for such a vile act as raising the dead. I've never witnessed what you describe. Even during the dreadful battles for control of the north, the enemy did not use its victims as such. It defies all that is right in this world to not grant the fallen their well-earned rest.'

Toryn shivered in the heat of the noon sun. 'How could they have done it? Does that power exist in the Song?'

'I would say not. You mentioned you could see others as if they were inside your assailants.'

'Ruuk. And it was if they could see through their eyes, and then move them like a hand-puppet of a jester.'

Nyomae looked down the pass. 'Then I would assume the guards raised from the rubble were simply vessels. I don't believe our enemy could reach into each of their Verses and bring them back to something resembling life. Even if it were possible, it would require tremendous power to raise just one.'

Elodi clenched the railing. 'And you believe Uluriel can work her evil through the stone? Even from the north?'

'Ah. Now there is another reason for concern. I doubt it was Uluriel. I have sensed no sign of her in the Verses at present. I believe she has yet to surface following her expulsion from the Archon. And this act is beyond the means of Uleva and Uldrak. This must be the work of a warlock. It appears they have finally revealed themselves.' Nyomae clasped her hands. 'But either they have become immensely strong, or… one has entered Farrand.'

Elodi gasped. 'How is that possible?'

'They have many ways to disguise their presence, in both the Song and the realms. The Verses are anchored to the place of their creation. To exert influence from the north would be most challenging, even for a warlock. But not so much from the south.'

Elodi's hand hovered over her sword. 'Should we search for this creature? Can you find it in the Song?'

'Regrettably, I do not yet possess the power to locate it, or even if I could, I would not dare confront a warlock at this time. And it would easily overwhelm the both of you and fifty Archonians combined. My hope is that the effort to raise the dead will have consumed much of its power, thus it will return. But we must remain vigilant.' Nyomae spoke through a tight jaw. 'This is their first move of the next stage. And I cannot think of a crueler way to signal their intent.'

Elodi's lip curled. 'Cruel indeed. But should we prepare for a full-scale attack from the thousands that still lie beneath the rubble? And does that mean' — she grimaced — 'we must mutilate the dead to deny the enemy commandeering our dead?'

Nyomae's gaze wandered back to the pass. 'If I am correct about the means deployed, it would require an army of Ruuk to bring the same number against us. And I imagine that would be beyond even a warlock's ability.' She turned to face the door. 'But while that may be so, perhaps it would be a wise precaution to… let us say, remove the means of our dead to wage combat.'

Toryn sighed. 'I agree. The prospect of repeated attacks by even a dozen of our lost guards would be demoralizing at best. And how many of our reduced forces would perish in such actions? But even so, I cannot see that those clearing the pass would be pleased about slicing up their fallen companions.'

Nyomae agreed. 'As unpalatable as that may be, it would prevent the bodies of the fallen suffering the shame of fighting for our foes. Perhaps it could be seen as a kind act to maintain their dignity.' She held out her hand. 'Let us go inside and take refreshment.' Toryn and Elodi followed, welcoming the promise of a cool drink on a hot day. Nyomae filled three glasses. She sat. 'But I believe the attack may have served only as a show, a move perhaps to deal our spirits a blow, and lead us to revise our tactics.'

Elodi tutted. 'Then it has achieved its aim. Kernlow is

now reluctant to send any force of merit north. I had persuaded him to allocate resources to keep an eye on the borders. But now he's convinced we must stay put in Archonholm in case they raise another army from the pass.'

Nyomae held her glass to her lips. 'Regardless, I need to do more to restrict the influence of that cursed stone beneath the tower. My efforts to contact Idraman have come to naught. I sense his presence, but he has weakened to the point I believe he struggles to enter the Song. He still maintains his Word of Forbidding, but that stone will soon drain the last of his strength if I cannot restrain its power.'

Toryn shuddered at the memory. 'Will you require our help?'

'I shall attempt it alone. Now that I understand its nature, I shall not venture far into its past. I shall continue to strengthen the surrounding bedrock and thus hope to consume much of its wrong before it can reach Idraman's barrier. But it's imperative that I come to understand the intent of our foe. I had not imagined anything like the nature of the attack at the Lower Gate. What other cruel and macabre tactics will they unleash against us? There are many ways in which they can attack us that must be brought to Kernlow's attention. He cannot use conventional means to defeat an unconventional enemy.'

Elodi shrugged. 'But to convince him to use any means at present appears to be an uphill struggle.'

Nyomae placed her glass on the table. 'Perhaps we can take one ray of hope from this hideous development. It would have been a significant effort for whoever orchestrated the raising of the dead. It was not a decision made lightly. Therefore, can we assume they would not welcome our forces riding north just yet? It may have been purely an attempt to convince us to concentrate our resources here. Do they yet fear an early strike?'

Elodi glanced at Toryn. 'That may be so, but Kernlow is set on securing Archonholm. But from what you have said, I fear we may miss our chance to hurt them. And we have yet to debate whether we should open the gate and seek help from the south.'

'That is a debate for another day. I would be wary of making ourselves known at present to whoever holds the old realms. If we cannot rely on their support, we could find ourselves fighting a war on two fronts.'

Toryn's eyes wandered to the door and up to the blue skies. 'But I saw an empty pass behind the gate. Surely, if an enemy lies south, they would defend it. And what if a strong ally awaits us?'

Nyomae held his gaze. 'It is not beyond the skill of our enemies to create an illusion. If they wanted us to open the gate, they would show you an unguarded pass. But if it was no trick and the pass is indeed empty, then it is not a sign of a strong realm, be they friend or foe. If we open it and find people in need of help, it places yet another demand on our already depleted resources.'

Elodi took Toryn's side. 'Perhaps a potential powerful ally sees no need to defend it. Or maybe they have fortified the southern end of the pass.'

Nyomae shook her head. 'I am certain that Idraman is being held in a dungeon. I do not believe a strong ally would see the need. It tells me those who live in the south distrust Idraman. But they also appear wary of ending his life, perhaps afraid of retribution from the old Order. No, I would say those in the south are weaker than we in the north. Therefore, I propose we should not concern ourselves as yet with the matter of opening the gate. We have other, more pressing issues.' She looked at her desk. 'You may be wondering what has occupied my time while in isolation.'

Toryn nodded. 'Would this be regarding the scroll you took from the archives?'

'Indeed. It appears insignificant at first glance. It was written by Draegelan's physician, recording the treatment he administered to him in his later years. If Uluriel had scoured the archives for works by the Imaari, she would have neglected the section where it was located. You see, this scroll was stored in the archives relating to curative practice, not a subject I imagine of interest to Uluriel. These are references for apothecaries and healers. But the one I removed contains something that has stoked my curiosity.'

Elodi frowned. 'And this would be because…?'

'The physician made an interesting observation. The old Archon suffered from what he believed to be hallucinations in the last months of his long life. The herbs and tinctures did little to help, seeming to worsen his condition. The physician noted Draegelan's actual words during such episodes, for which I am most grateful. Draegelan spoke in an ancient tongue known only to a few, but thankfully it's a language understood by the healers of the day. But even to those who knew it, the words I could decipher would appear to be the rantings of a confused mind. However,' Nyomae stood and walked to her desk. She picked up the scroll. 'From the little I have been able to translate, I don't believe these words were from a confused mind. I think it's the opposite. Draegelan may have had a fever when he uttered them, but I would say he spoke with clarity. Not only fully aware of what he said, but also why he used the words he did. I believe he knew the physician was documenting his thoughts. I also suspect he spoke as he did to ensure only those with a certain knowledge of the Song would understand.'

Elodi straightened. 'And these words… Do they reveal anything of use?'

Nyomae dropped the scroll. 'That I cannot yet say. But his words have given me much to ponder. But if my hunch is right, they may prove to reveal knowledge that may lend us strength at a time of great need.' She clasped her hands. 'Now tell me of events in the city. I sense a dread sweeping through its streets, and if left unchallenged may defeat us from within.'

The scream awoke Elodi. She leaped out of her bed, bathed in sweat and her head pounding. Her eyes shot around the dark room but while everything looked in place, the cry of anguish still echoed in her mind. A dull glow from the corner of her room caught her attention. She strode to the chair, grasped her sword handle, and drew it from its scabbard. The blade burned with the familiar orange light; but the threat lay elsewhere. Her sisters! She felt their pain — the pain of three Amayans in grave danger.

# 11. Sisters Past & Present

'We cannot afford to lose another.' Nyomae's eyes shone bright in the twilight as she watched the Menon River head for the sea. 'The Amayans are vital to our cause. They may number few, but one is worth a hundred elite soldiers. And not forgetting, the fate of the Amanach stones is in their hands.'

Elodi shivered as the breeze blowing in from the Foranfae found them up on the North Terrace. 'I don't know how, but I'm certain I heard the voices of Eryn, Calestri and Arijan. But the scream that woke me came from another, one I believe to be Amyra.'

Toryn's heart rested heavily against his ribs. 'If Amyra has been caught and taken north…' his head dropped. 'Another was captured many years ago. Tanis, yes that was her name. She was… altered, altered to fight for the enemy.'

'Much like Dorlan.' Elodi sighed. 'The last thing we need is another as powerful as Dorlan taking up arms with the Ul-dalak. It would indeed be a bitter blow to our spirits if an Amayan rides against us.'

Toryn recalled the sad tale. 'According to Eryn, Tanis fought as one possessed. It took three Amayans to defeat her. Apparently, Amyra is a fighter of remarkable skill, superior to most Amayans. How many would it take to defeat her?'

Nyomae turned to face them. 'We cannot sit here and wait for the Amayans to be snatched from us one-by-one. We must aid them. Even four possessed Amayans would prove a formidable prospect. We could lose hundreds from their actions alone.'

Toryn voiced his concern. 'If we sent fifty knights north, what can they do to help them? If the Amayans face a foe that troubles them, surely our knights would be easily overwhelmed.'

Nyomae looked him in the eye. 'I would not send knights. I would send you, Toryn. But not alone.'

'Me? But what could I do?'

Elodi gasped. 'Is it not too soon?'

Nyomae smiled. 'The power within Toryn grows by the day, and it will accelerate to meet the threat of the Ul-dalak as you draw near.' She took his hand and ran a finger across the palm. 'Look at your lines. They have thickened, and the patterns more intricate. Your skills advance at an impressive rate.' She released her hold. 'The enemy will not take you lightly. And remember, you only have to distract their assailants to give the Amayans a chance.'

Toryn looked at his palms. 'And you believe I'm ready?'

Nyomae brought his hands together. 'Ready to face the likes of Uldrak, then possibly Uleva within a month. But this is finely balanced. While they will be wary of you, they will also look to capture you.' She stroked her chin. 'But in a way, this could work to our advantage. If their attention is directed at you, perhaps that leaves them open to attack from your companions who they would dismiss as weak, posing no threat.'

Elodi grimaced. 'When confronting Uldrak at Tunduska, he conjured up a ball of freezing air that reeked of death and weakened our defenses. It was a most effective weapon. Do the Imaari have this ability?'

Nyomae moved her hand as if stroking a dog. 'The hands can shape and bring objects, even living beings, within a Verse back to our own time. But it is only fleeting, and that depends on the endurance of the caller. But there is a price to pay. The more you draw from the Song, the more time is needed to recover, thus only the most powerful can utilize its power readily and often. Uldrak must have released the air from a bitter winter in the gorge. Ormoroth once drove the freezing winds from the north to pack the Draegelan Trench with ice, thus allowing his armies to cross. While that was on a far grander scale, it would be a simple trick for me and Uldrak to achieve for a short time in a limited area.'

Elodi's nose wrinkled. 'It was green. I can still recall the stench.'

'Ah. From what we've learned of Uldrak, I have no doubt he couldn't resist tainting it with some foul concoction of his own.'

Elodi thought for a moment. 'While speed is vital to aid the Amayans, I don't think Aldorman's knights are suited to such a mission. They are better equipped for open battle on horseback, but I would suggest stealth and the ability to fight… how does Gundrul put it in guard's terms?'

'Dirty.' Toryn recalled his time in the wagon with Jedrul.

Elodi smiled. 'Yes, that's the word. I imagine there isn't a bone in Aldorman's body capable of fighting dirty.' She turned from the railing and walked to a sheltered bench. 'I shall speak with Gundrul and ask for volunteers. I trust he will be keen to get back on the road after weeks of being confined to barracks. And his horsemanship has improved, but whether it is enough to manage such an undertaking is another matter.'

Toryn sat beside her, leaving Nyomae to watch over the forest. 'I hear he is a fine fighter. Harruld and Odrun both spoke highly of him. In a way, he reminds me of my old friend, Hamar.'

Elodi tucked her hands inside her cloak. 'It would have been an honor to meet your friend. It is a pity he perished at the mines.'

'He was a' — Toryn grinned — 'as he would say, a

good 'un. I learned much from him, and since his passing I've come to realize it was more than I at first thought. But I believe Hamar wouldn't have had it any other way. He didn't want to fade away and die on his sick bed. He departed this world with his sword in his hand, defending the honor of an old guard.' Toryn looked up to the clouds. 'He'll be happy now sowing his…'

Elodi frowned. 'His what?'

He looked away. 'Hamar was fond of the land. If there's any justice in this world, I'm sure he'll have gone to a better place.'

'I've heard such talk from guards before, only for them to suddenly go silent when I approached.' She patted his leg. 'It's an Archonian secret, isn't it? Something to do with a pledge perhaps?'

Toryn's face grew hot. 'Perhaps.'

Elodi laughed. 'Then it comes as a surprise that it's stayed a secret for so long. You're not the first to come close to revealing it.'

'Yet Hamar, even as his mind started to play tricks on him, never revealed it to me.'

Nyomae joined them on the bench. 'Ah yes, Hamar. Memories from my time spent under my shadow flood back daily.' Her eyes wandered across the sky. 'Yes. I remember sitting in a dark wood, watching you, listening to your conversation with the old guard. Then,' she clicked her fingers, 'another time on a grassy bank as you watched the moon rise over Caranach.'

Toryn gaped. 'It was you? We knew we were being followed, but… Ha! I'd wager you were also the woman Hamar and his guards tracked years earlier believing you to be an Amayan.'

Nyomae sighed. 'I spent too long beneath the shadow. But even in my state, I must have carried out your father's wish and kept an eye on you.'

'And for that, Nyomae, I shall be forever grateful. I hope one day I can fill my father's shoes and serve the realms with honor.'

She nodded. 'I am certain you will. Now, Elodi, we must discuss the matter of locating and aiding the Amayans with the honorable Captain Gundrul. And you and I, Toryn, must continue our lessons in the ways of the Song. I'm afraid we cannot spend as much time as we should. Time is against us, and our enemy moves ever faster.'

# 12. The Traitor in the North

Elodi shivered in the shadow of Archonholm's towers. The sun bid its farewell, sinking behind the Caerwals a few minutes earlier with each passing day as autumn approached. She turned and looked down to the dark edge of the Foranfae. Any other forest would have been cut well back from the road to prevent an enemy advance going unseen until too late. But none dared to raise an axe against the ancient trees. Could the Ul-dalak and warlocks approach the city through the forest? Did the Nym still possess the power to oppose them?

Her gaze rose over the trees. Following practice, she could now see the spire of the Neverdor Tower in clear detail using her *farsight.* But beyond that, her vision would blur as she tried to find the town of Vinlayn in the heart of Gwelayn's vineyards. All seemed peaceful on Kernlow's border, but it was far to the north in her own realm where she longed to look. While the dispatches coming from Seransea and across Noor confirmed no signs of an incursion, Elodi remained on edge. She knew the enemy would eventually come south. And when they did, she knew it would be fast, ruthless, and in numbers they had not yet seen on the field of battle. And from Nyomae's assessment, Elodi grew impatient to strike quickly. But as yet, she was not certain whether her pleas to the Castellan had even reached Kernlow's Council.

Elodi placed her hands on the cool balustrade and waited for her head to settle and normal vision to return. Nyomae assured her that with time, she would be able to move in and out of *farsight* with barely a blink, but that day had not yet come. Elodi had hoped to spend the evening with Toryn, but he was occupied with preparations for the Amayan quest.

A light flickered behind her. Elodi turned to see wardens lighting the first torches lining the walls. Wishing to stay out of sight of the walkers enjoying the evening air, she strolled towards the quieter East Terrace. As she rounded the bend, movement on the road below caught her eye. Elodi watched, captivated by a majestic white horse and skilled rider galloping at speed towards Archonholm. At first, she wondered if it could be an Amayan. Yet, this rider wore a hooded cloak, which to Elodi's knowledge, was not the preferred attire of the warrior maidens. Intrigued, she decided to pay Sea Mist an overdue visit, hoping to encounter the new arrival at the stables. If the rider was here on business with Kernlow, she might not get another chance to meet them.

Sea Mist was stabled close to the stalls offered to travelers. Elodi hoped to meet the rider before the Castellan's men arrived to question the visitor. She entered the stables, nodding to the grooms taking their rest after mucking out. The rider had yet to arrive, giving her time to see her horse. She rubbed his neck. 'Sorry, Misty. I know, I know. It's been a few days. But I promise I'll take you out soon, hopefully tomorrow.'

The clatter of hooves on the cobbles caught her attention. Elodi patted Sea Mist's nose. 'Be good for me, boy.' She turned, feeling guilty for leaving him so soon, but she felt the need to speak to the new arrival. At the entrance, a tall figure led a sweating, but proud beast through the gate. The hood concealed the rider's face, but the belt carried a fine sword that demanded both strength and skill to use. Elodi approached the traveler. 'That is one fine stallion. Please, what do you call him?'

The rider threw back a hood to reveal the weary face of a woman who had spent many days on the open road. She brushed her long, dark hair from her face. 'This beauty is called Warrior.' The woman extended her hand. 'I am Amyndra. And who might you be?'

Elodi clasped the hand, noting the strong grip of a swordmaster. 'Lady Harlyn. And I'm pleased to make the acquaintance of a rider who can handle such a beast as Warrior.'

'Lady Harlyn?' She dropped to one knee and bowed her head. 'Then I must apologize for not recognizing you… ma'am.'

'Please. There is no need. Do not feel you have to follow protocol. I have long since dispensed with such customs.'

'Thank you, ma'am.' Amyndra attempted an ungainly curtsy.

Elodi helped her up. 'Again. Not necessary.'

Amyndra laughed. 'Thank you. As you can probably tell, I'm not familiar with such rituals.'

Elodi smiled. 'I assume you're more accustomed with the ways of the sword, and… judging by the number of scars on your arm, a veteran of numerous conflicts.'

'Now there you would be right, ma'am. From an early age I held a sword. It was a necessity where I grew up. And may I say we were shocked and dismayed to hear of the fall of Calerdorn.'

Elodi's chest tightened. 'It was like a dagger to my heart. But I have sworn a vow, with every fiber of my body, I will take my city back.' The torches behind burst into flames as the grooms completed their last task for the evening.

Amyndra beamed. 'Ah, but of course. Now I see your red hair in the light, I would have known you right away, Lady Harlyn. The returning spearmen of Ruan speak most highly of you. And all in my company are in no doubt that you will be back in Calerdorn before the year is out.'

'That is kind of you to say. And that would be my desire. As for you... am I right to assume you were raised in Lunn, close to the border with Nordruuk perhaps?'

'Yes, ma'am. Although dragged up would be closer to the mark. I was born in Lunn, north of the Lind River, or the Last River as those to the south call it. And unlucky enough to live in the shadow of Fort Lindmar. That is, when the sun can be asked to show her yellow face up there.' Amyndra stroked Warrior's neck. 'Not the most welcoming place for a child, but, as my father used to say, the harsher the upbringing, the stronger the adult. Err… don't get me wrong, ma'am. My father was not cruel. He was kind when he had the chance. But my mother died when I was still but a child, and my father was both a sheep farmer and head of the local militia.'

Elodi ran her hand down Warrior's strong back. 'I'm curious, Amyndra. When you introduced yourself, you did not mention your realm. And now in the torchlight, while I see you're wearing the colors of Broon, I note the absence of Nordryn's crest upon your arm.'

'Ah, yes. I…' she looked about her. 'I am not sure if I…'

Elodi glanced behind. 'Please, be at ease. The fact you shun Nordryn's colors tells me much… much to the good. I am… was a close friend of Bardon, and in my mind, he remains the true Lord Broon until proven otherwise.'

Amyndra exhaled. 'Then perhaps you could advise me. I have a delicate matter to raise with the Council of Archonholm. But I'm a soldier and not one for words, so I'm unsure of how best to present my case.'

'You do yourself down, Amyndra, I would say you're a better speaker than many who claim to be such. I would be happy to help. And I am also keen to hear of—'

An Archonian knight led his horse through the entrance. He nodded. 'Ma'am. A fine, if chilly evening for a canter perhaps?'

Elodi smiled. 'I may well be tempted, Captain.' He took the horse to the trough nearby. She turned back to Amyndra, aware the captain could hear her words. 'I'll arrange for a groom to give Warrior a thorough rub down and ensure he is well attended. Then perhaps you would like to accompany me on a walk on the high terraces. The views make it worth enduring the long road from the north. And' — she glanced up — 'I believe the half-moon will be bright enough to paint the Caerwals silver. That is a sight not to be missed.' The knight headed off to the stalls. Elodi whispered. 'We may talk more freely up there as the evening chill will send many below for a warm cup of mead. And it will allow us some time together before the Castellan's aides come for you.'

'That would be welcome, ma'am.'

'Come, let me see if Warrior can be stabled next to Sea Mist, my horse. I believe they will enjoy each other's company. Perhaps tomorrow we could ride together out west.'

As Elodi had predicted, most of the evening strollers had abandoned the terrace for the comfort of the halls below. She led Amyndra towards the spot where she had stood with Bardon on her first visit. She spoke, keeping one eye over her shoulder. 'Over there, we can evade the ears of the Castellan. I remain suspicious that conversations in my room are not as private as I'd wish. I suspect there may be hidden ducts that carry voices beyond my walls.'

Amyndra's face shone silver in the moonlight. Her mouth dropped open as they rounded the bend and approached the balustrade. 'Now that's a sight not to be missed. I've spent much of my service in the evening shadow of the Kolossos, but these mountains… it looks as if the gods built a fortress.'

Elodi smiled, recalling her first reaction. 'Hence the name. But it's a pity they did not see fit to locate it farther north.'

'A pity indeed. It would have made life much easier.' Amyndra staggered and grabbed the stone railing. 'Oh my. And that must be the famous gorge. I had not thought it would be so deep, and the walls of Archonholm so high.'

'Ah yes. I should have forewarned you. It does take one's breath away.' Amyndra steadied herself. She stood tall, planting her feet as if poised for a fight. Elodi checked the terrace. 'To business. Please, rest assured, your words will not be heard beyond our ears should you wish to keep it so.'

Amyndra let out a long sigh. She stepped forward and grasped Elodi's hand. 'That brings me much relief. I know I can trust the word of Lady Harlyn.' She looked down at her hand and released her grip. 'Again, apologies. I did not mean to encroach on your—'

'Not at all. Now, if you are at ease, please explain the purpose of your visit. I assume it must be an urgent matter to warrant the long journey south.'

'That it is. We have long since lost trust in our messenger birds, but that is another story.' She took a breath. 'Lady Harlyn, I and many of my fellow captains find ourselves in a bit of a quandary. But let me first tell you a few things about myself. I am a captain in one of Broon's elite divisions. I command a force of four hundred, comprising of knights, spears, and foot soldiers who remain loyal to the true Lord Broon. But I should make it clear that I'm not here in an official capacity. In fact, if Nordryn… ah, forgive me, I cannot refer to him as Lord, but if he discovers I am here, my life would be forfeit. I have come, with the knowledge and blessing of my fellow captains and those under my immediate command.' She turned her back on the mountains. 'I wish to petition Lord Kernlow for aid. I had no option but to ride south as Nordryn is in possession of Broon's birds. But now I'm here... I am uncertain how he will perceive such an unconventional approach, and one that could condemn me and my soldiers to be branded as traitors to Broon.'

Elodi let out a long sigh. 'Then I fear to inform you, Lord Kernlow is a stickler for correct procedure. Even I have found it difficult to get an audience with him.'

'You? A leader of a realm? Then what chance do I, a mere captain, have?'

'Then tell me the nature of your petition and perhaps I can help you. Events move fast, while Lord Kernlow moves slowly. The more information I possess, the better my chances of encouraging Kernlow to change course. It has been the lack of reports from the north that concerns me.'

Amyndra's jaw clenched. 'Then I also fear to inform you that Nordryn has invited six Ruuk clans into Lunn. Those in Keld who objected were removed from their posts and banished from the city.'

Elodi sighed. 'Alas, then my distrust of Nordryn is not unfounded. Where have they settled, and in what numbers?'

'It began as soon as he took office. At first, the clans were given land in the region of Lumreek Marsh, and in the towns of Breck and Dunmor. Nordryn convinced the local people that this was to bolster defenses, and the clans could be relied upon for support. As you may be aware, Lumreek is not for those seeking comfort.' She laughed. 'Even by Lunn standards it's a harsh region. Harsher still now we hear rumors of the marsh freezing for the first time in living memory.'

Elodi shivered. 'Then I wonder if the same is true of

Mawlgrim Mire? Long have they provided a crucial line of defense against Nordruuk. And what of the people of Lumreek?'

'Many were originally from Ruuk clans of Nordryn's descent. They have lived there in peace for many generations and been loyal to Broon. Those in Keld were only too happy to have them serve as a shield against what they feared to be the more hostile Ruuk farther north. And not forgetting the fearsome Norgog.'

Elodi's hand went to her brow. 'Ah yes, I have had the pleasure of their company.'

Amyndra's eyes widened. 'Then the stories are all true. Many a battle tale suffers from inflated and improbable claims. So, you did stand in the front line at Tunduska? And looked those Hammerskulls in the eye?'

'To be precise, I was initially in the third line. But I soon found myself at the front following the assault. But that tale is for another day. You said, *at first,* they settled around Lumreek. Have they since moved south?'

Amyndra nodded. 'And not peacefully. In the early days, I was not aware of the extent of the numbers of Ruuk coming south. My force was stationed at Lindmar on the border. The order from Keld was to allow certain clans through. However, I later discovered more were crossing farther inland, and in numbers many of us felt uncomfortable with.' She adjusted her sword belt. 'I'm sure you're aware there has long been a divide between the people of Lunn and Ormsk. Bardon and his recent predecessors had done much to unite the two wards. But sadly, it appears that in the short time Nordryn has been in post, he has undone a century of good work and opened old wounds. This has caused many rifts across much of Broon, and more so, even in the military.'

Elodi leaned against the rail. 'This is bad news indeed. Are we to become the Four Realms? We are already weakened, but to lose Broon would be a hammer blow.'

'Thankfully, not all Broon, ma'am. Many remain loyal to Bardon, but it is folly to openly declare it. While I can be certain those under my command can be trusted, many other captains cannot. And this is the reason for my journey. As soon as I arrived at Torm, I sent riders to the captains I knew were of the same mind. I informed them of my decision to petition Lord Kernlow, and they expressed their support. I left shortly after Midsummer, stopping in Rand to consult my retired commander. Together we drew up our plan. I am to inform Lord Kernlow of the situation in Lunn. He should appreciate that it will not stop there. If Kernlow doesn't help, the unrest will quickly spread south of the River Kel. The loyal captains of Broon are formulating a plan to' — Amyndra took a deep breath — 'to unseat Nordryn, but we'll need support as there are many in our armies who stand with him. If successful, I am certain we can take Keld and remove Nordryn. But our time to act grows ever shorter as the lines of Ruuk flocking to his banner grow longer.' Amyndra looked along the wall. 'I appreciate this is an act of treason according to the laws of Broon, but I and my fellow captains are certain we have grounds to turn the tables and convict Nordryn himself of treason.'

Elodi considered Amyndra's predicament. 'Do you have the means in Broon's Charter to remove him?'

'Our laws state if a sitting lord is acting against the interests of the realm, then yes, they can be brought before a court. But…' she looked back at the glistening slopes of the Caerwals. 'We must be certain he has not appointed new officials from his own people. It may well be that we will have to invoke the law of the Five Realms to depose him.'

Elodi held her gaze. 'That would be exceptional in our times, but as I keep trying to stress to the Castellan and

Kernlow, these are not usual times. And what of Broon's commitment to defend Aralak Gorge? Does Nordryn send support to the Archonians guarding the fences?'

'For the time being, ma'am, as far as I am aware. As you'll know, my road here brought me close to that dark place. While I avoided direct contact as I didn't want word of my journey reaching the wrong ears, I did note the watch on the fence appeared to be at full strength.'

Elodi shuddered as she recalled Ruan's tale of the loss of his brother at the gorge. 'But can we trust Nordryn to fulfill his obligation? I would hope he would not want to see those foul creatures escape, but his actions of late do not fill me with confidence. I therefore think it wise to allocate more Archonians to be absolutely sure.'

Amyndra nodded. 'I agree, ma'am. It's obvious Nordryn does not care for the safety of the wider realms. It was not until I reached Durrock that I learned of the tragedy in the Caerwal Pass. We had no knowledge of the events unfolding here. And I imagine many in Broon are still unaware of the disaster. And, of course, had we known of the Archon's intention to open the gate, many would have ridden to support the cause.'

'Then let us be thankful you did not. In a strange way, the treachery of Nordryn saved many lives, and perhaps many who will choose to ride to the realms' aid in the future.'

'That would be my wish, ma'am. I am hopeful those loyal to the realms will number in the thousands.'

Elodi smiled. 'Then you bring me hope. Now, let us formulate a plan to get your audience with Kernlow.'

# 13. From a Fevered Mind

'I must hasten to Neverdor.' Nyomae burst into Elodi's quarters. 'The physician's scroll has proved most enlightening.'

Elodi lowered her sword and grinned. 'Please, do come in.'

Nyomae sighed. 'Ah, perhaps I should have knocked. I apologize for interrupting your morning drill.'

Elodi propped her weapon against the wall. 'I was about to take a break and some refreshment. You're welcome to join me.'

'I will, thank you.' Nyomae glanced back at the door. 'The guard outside seemed a little too keen to interrogate me on the nature of my visit last time. Therefore, I thought it best to deny him the opportunity. But I may have unsettled him with a trick I learned in my youth.'

Elodi stood and retrieved two glasses from the shelf. She led Nyomae to a table beside the window. 'A wise strategy, but I fear the Castellan will be made aware of our meeting before long. We all know his guards are not posted for our safety.' She filled the glass with cool water and handed it to Nyomae. Elodi lowered her voice. 'I believe this spot is the safest place for us to speak. I can see no grates or ducts that may carry our voices beyond these walls.'

Nyomae gratefully accepted and sat. 'That is good to hear.' She leaned forward. 'Toryn progresses at speed. He is a willing student and I believe he is as ready as he could be given the circumstances. It would have been desirable to allow him longer to prepare, but the risk of losing the Amayans outweighs the risk of exposing Toryn to the likes of Uleva. He is strong and resourceful, and I hope to remain in contact with him using a technique we have explored.' Nyomae snapped her fingers. 'But it is the content of the physician's scroll that has brought me here. I have made what I believe to be an important discovery.'

'Ah! That is good news.' She noted Nyomae's brow crease. 'Is it not?'

'Good in one sense, but not in another.' Nyomae settled. 'Let me start by covering some of the history first. Much of what you have heard about the end of Draegelan's reign as Archon is likely embellished by storytellers keen to fill their pockets.'

Elodi held up her hand. 'Please, assume I know nothing and therefore leave nothing out.'

'Thank you. That will hopefully make it easier.' Nyomae straightened. 'Draegelan was the last Imaari to serve as Archon. At his bidding, before he slipped into illness, he deemed it wise that subsequent Archons should not be of our Order. Perhaps events leading to the ultimate defeat of Dorlan at Talaghir, led him to believe too much power concentrated in one leader had the potential to turn ill.'

Elodi heaved a sigh. 'Ah, a wise man. We've become only too aware of the dangers of that, eh?'

'Precisely. Hadrul was the last Archon before the coming of the disastrous time we call the Age of Shadows. But when he fell at Gormadon, followed rapidly by the rest of my Order, Uluriel took the opportunity to possess Mordram. And then, in the ensuing confusion, appointed herself Archon.'

'And Malendra who succeeded Draegelan, was a knight?'

Nyomae took a deep breath. 'Malendra became the first Archon outside of the Imaari. Having fought alongside Draegelan and Dorlan, she was a warrior of great repute. She lived long beyond the years expected of a mortal. And I can count myself fortunate to have known both Draegelan and Malendra.'

Elodi stared in wonder. 'Of all the people throughout history, Draegelan would be the one I would dearly love to have met above all others. It had once been Dorlan, but… that wish came true, and he was not as I expected. But Draegelan. Was he as the tales tell?'

Nyomae smiled. 'Granted, for most of the time I knew him he was both blind and bedridden. The long years of his rule weighed heavily upon him, and many believed he had begun to lose his powers. Late in life, he left Archonholm to spend his days in Neverdor, followed by Abernost. Then he disappeared for almost a year. Preparations for his successor were underway when he returned to the city. But our initial relief was short lived. Draegelan appeared to have lost much of his memory, leading many to fear he was descending into a state of madness.'

Elodi refilled Nyomae's glass. 'Ah yes, that part is known to me. Such a sad end to a long, illustrious life.'

Nyomae shook her head. 'For five centuries, he had carried the guilt of not being at Dorlan's side when he confronted Ormoroth. They had battled together for decades to drive the darkness from the realms. But he was beset with sadness and regret for not coming to Dorlan's aid at Talaghir. Once he had secured the borders, Draegelan rode north to find his faithful companion, but as we know, he discovered nothing but devastation. None lived to tell what happened at Talaghir, and I can find no Verses of that time. But in witnessing the aftermath, Draegelan understood that while Ormoroth had been banished from this realm, his presence remained in the Song. This left the way open for him to return one day. He knew an opportunity had been missed. From what I have gathered from the physician's notes...' Her eyes widened. 'I believe if Draegelan and Dorlan had ridden together at Talaghir they could have cast Ormoroth into the void and beyond the reach of this realm. Perhaps the same force that transformed Dorlan into his all-powerful state at that darkest of times, also aided Draegelan to discover key Verses that could expel Ormoroth.'

Elodi could barely breathe. 'Do the words from the physician's scroll reveal this knowledge?'

'Not directly. Much of the knowledge of that time has been lost.' Nyomae stiffened. 'Or so I thought.'

Elodi leaned closer. 'And am I right to suspect this *knowledge* is perhaps a double-edged sword?'

Nyomae drained her glass. 'Of the most lethal kind. But as I see it, we have no choice but to grip the blade tight with both hands.'

'And this is why you must go to Neverdor.'

'And most likely Abernost.' Nyomae looked out of the window. 'Would you mind if we continued our conversation elsewhere? I have spent long hunched over dusty scrolls and books. My thirst is quenched, but my eyes need sunlight, and my lungs crave fresh air.'

Elodi and Nyomae strolled along the banks of the Menon away from the city. Elodi turned to look back at Archonholm. The sheer walls cast barely a shadow as noon approached. Behind them, the towers reached impossibly high as if competing to be the first to snare the passing sun. But none could outreach the Archon's Tower. The blue banner still fluttered high above the city as Kernlow believed morale would suffer if lowered. Archonholm was an inspiring sight, but was it impregnable? The footings for the new outer wall were taking shape close to the river. It was to join with the gatehouse of the Menon Bridge, then stretch in both directions to curve back to the chasm.

Kernlow believed the outer wall would help to ease the sense of foreboding pervading the streets of Archonholm. But Elodi was not so confident. The fall of Calerdorn was not due to the lack of iron and stone.

Nyomae stopped. 'This looks like a pleasant spot.' She gazed over the river. 'And the green Menon Hills at least offers some semblance of tranquility. But, alas, the new wall will soon obscure the view.'

Elodi perched beside her. 'While the troubles back in Calerdorn seem so far away, none can deny the influence of our enemy hasn't already infiltrated the very heart of our stronghold.'

Nyomae sat back and sighed. 'And it seems we cannot escape it out here.'

'And for that I apologize. You desired fresh air and rest, and yet I cannot grant you a moment's peace.'

Nyomae sat up. 'You're right to persist. The Ul-dalak will not be satisfied with their gains. And every minute I spend enjoying the view is a minute lost.' She brushed the dust from her robe. 'So… I must return to the business of the aforementioned double-edged sword. But let us not be disheartened, one edge may yet deliver a fatal blow to our enemies.' Nyomae plucked a blade of grass and rubbed it between her fingers. She continued with her tale. 'Draegelan concealed his discovery to prevent its misuse. What his physician thought were the mumbled words of a fevered mind were, I believe, a clue to where his later scrolls could be found. And the nature of his clue suggests a certain amount of knowledge is required to solve his puzzle. An entry in the physician's record is from a childhood rhyme once popular in Elmarand. Draegelan was known for singing it to himself when he began his studies in Neverdor.'

Elodi recalled Wendel's final days. 'But it's well known that an aging mind often relives the days of its youth.'

'That may be so, but he made an error reciting the rhyme.'

Elodi frowned. 'Again, that would not be unusual for one so old.'

'But three times? In the same verse? The rhyme was composed using nonsensical language. While it flowed well, it was gibberish, but was sufficient to amuse the children of that time. Yet, Draegelan inserted a word of his own. *Gwylmadoc.*'

Elodi scoffed. 'That still sounds like gibberish to me.'

'That it would. It's a word known only to the people of West Haven. It's a ceremony. They line the quayside to remember those lost at sea. I had the *pleasure* of being at the port on that day many, many years ago. Although, come late afternoon, most will have forgotten who they're supposed to be remembering. Tradition dictates they raise a toast to those they honor, and there are many.' She laughed. 'Dozens end up in the harbor waters, and it's only thanks to the sober ones that they don't end up joining the ranks of the lost at sea.'

Elodi smiled. 'We have a similar ritual in Calerdorn, and with much the same result come the evening. Oh, what I wouldn't give to return to the days of peace and our quaint traditions. Will that ever be possible?' She turned to Nyomae. 'Could this one, misplaced word hold the key to Draegelan's wisdom? And perhaps peace?'

Nyomae shrugged. 'It's a small hope, I admit. But I'm convinced this word is significant. I have yet to fully appreciate its meaning, but from the short time I spent with Draegelan, I believe he may have set a test, a riddle if you like. While he spent many hours studying the Song, he enjoyed inventing and solving puzzles in his spare time.' Nyomae thought for a moment. 'Something troubled Draegelan in his final years. As I said, I didn't know him in his prime, but Idraman noted he had changed. Of course, this could have been due to his advanced age, but Idraman was convinced Draegelan was wrestling with a dilemma. I would see them strolling along the banks of the Menon deep in conversation, close to this very spot. At times it looked like a heated argument, but Idraman never revealed to me the nature of their debate. But I am beginning to suspect Draegelan had indeed stumbled across the means to defeat Ormoroth once and for all.'

Elodi watched a boat moor at the bridge. 'But I don't understand. Surely, he would have shared this knowledge.'

'Not necessarily. Such knowledge may pose significant risks if used incorrectly. I do not possess half the strength of Draegelan, nor do I believe anyone will ever attain his stature again. So, if he thought it wise to conceal this knowledge it must have been for good reason.'

Elodi shuddered as a cloud shut out the sun. 'What do we know of Ormoroth? Were… are there others like him?'

'He was believed to have been spawned by the first demon god, the one we know as the Evil One. The oldest stories tell of others such as Ormoroth, but the tales assure us they were defeated by the returning gods.' Nyomae's eyes darkened. 'As for Ormoroth, the Imaari believe he is in limbo, what we call the Halfway World. He is neither of here, nor of the other side. Which means he may yet return.'

Elodi stood and strolled to the river's edge. 'In all our history, have we ever been so weak as we are today?' She stared out at the hills. 'Would we not welcome the power to cast our most dangerous adversary to where he could not return?'

Nyomae joined her at the bank. 'It will be a challenge to firstly locate it, then to fully understand Draegelan's mind. Then of course comes the dilemma. If this knowledge contains a dangerous power… do we dare use it?'

Elodi kneeled and dipped her hand in the water. 'Unless Kernlow has some almighty trick up his cavernous sleeves, then we have no other choice but to seek out this power. The commander from Broon, Amyndra is due to speak with our lord and master tomorrow. I shall demand another audience and put the fear of the Evil One in him. Perhaps once he's made aware of Nordryn's schemes, and that the threat moves south on both sides of the Kolossos, he'll relent and contemplate a pre-emptive strike.' Elodi glanced up to see the cloud had retreated to the east. 'Ah. Conditions look perfect. I have arranged to meet with Amyndra this afternoon. Together we'll devise her strategy for tomorrow's audience with Kernlow.' She grinned. 'On horseback.'

'Warrior does not shy away from a duel. He is a horse worthy of his name.' Elodi drew Sea Mist alongside Amyndra at the edge of the plain.

Amyndra patted Warrior's neck. 'If there's a better horse on the east side of the mountains, I've yet to meet them.'

Elodi dismounted. 'That I can well believe. I'd say that was a tie. There are only a handful of horses in the west able to challenge Misty.' She glanced over her shoulder. 'There's a stream close to the road. We'll rest there a while. Then let's see who claims the honors on the return leg.'

Amyndra slid off Warrior's back and led him after Sea Mist. 'It would not surprise me if these two conspired to achieve a tie. They know we won't return to the stables until the contest is decided. But…' she frowned, 'if the tales doing the rounds in the taverns of Archonholm are true, I believe I'm challenging more than just a fine horse. Would I be right in assuming Sea Mist's rider is descended from a line of legendary warriors?'

Elodi smiled. 'The stories are true. I discovered the bloodline of my mother only a short time ago.'

Amyndra beamed. 'Then I am twice honored. To ride with both a Lady of the realm and an Amayan is something the young girl in me could only have dreamed of.'

'You flatter me. I am also honored to ride alongside such an accomplished rider and horse from Broon.'

Amyndra gazed north. 'I would dearly love to fight alongside an Amayan band and drive the Ruuk back over the border.' She turned back to Elodi. 'Do many still live?'

They stopped at the bank. 'Nyomae believes a dozen remain in this land, a dozen very useful allies I should imagine.' Elodi watched the horses drink from the stream. 'But I have yet to meet one, but if you want to know more talk to Toryn, he has encountered three.' She chuckled. 'They certainly seem to have made an impression on him. But that was in the vast forest yonder.' Elodi grinned to herself. 'So, who knows what tricks both the Amayans and the mysterious Nym played on his mind.'

'We too hear tales of the Foranfae, and of folk like the Nym in the forests of Ormsk. But we call them *Faerl*. And now you say the last battle for the Seven Realms took place near here, perhaps these Nym folk have done us a favor by healing the land.'

Elodi eyed the forest on the other side of the stream. 'The Nym may yet prove to be useful—' They both leaped up as hooves clattered on the road coming from the north. Instinctively, they drew their swords. Elodi peered up the road. 'It would be a grave situation if we were not safe here. But we can't be too cautious.'

A horse and rider rounded the bend. Amyndra stepped onto the road. 'They wear the black cloak of a Lunn fighter.' She held up her hand. The rider slowed their steed and drew level.

A man called out. ‘Amyndra!’

‘Moran. What brings you here? Please tell me Lunn hasn’t fallen.’

Moran dismounted and stretched. ‘Not when I’d left. But I’m afraid to say I am not the bringer of glad tidings.’

# 14. The Promise of Glory

'I shall not be denied.' Elodi reached for her sword. 'Stand aside or I will not hesitate to use force.'

The two Palace Guards took a step back. The taller held out his hand. 'Lady Harlyn, please. You must complete the official papers to request an audience with Lord Kernlow. He is currently in a meeting with his inner Council. If you wish to speak with him, you must go through the Castellan to—'

'Enough! The time has long passed for filing official papers.' She set her stance. 'Now. Do you open the door? Or do I have to step over your dead bodies and then open it?'

'Ma'am, no blood has ever been spilled in the citadel, this is not—'

Elodi drew her sword. 'Then you can decide whether yours is to be the first. I do not wish to take such action, but if you do not grant me access, I have no choice.' She raised the tip of her blade to the throat of the first guard.

The guards drew their weapons. 'Please, ma'am. We have our duty to perform, and we will not shirk from carrying out our orders.'

Elodi held the man's gaze. 'And while I admire your dedication to duty, you should know I have faced stronger opponents than the two of you, far stronger I hasten to add. Therefore, I suggest you stand back and grant me entry. One day, the people of the realms will thank you, and you shall live to tell the tale. But trust me, Lord Kernlow will be grateful to hear what I have to tell him. He must be made aware that the time for action is now.' She nodded to the door. 'While he sits on his large…

throne, our enemy is making their move.' Elodi pointed her sword at each in turn. 'You are soldiers, defenders of the realms. You must not stand idle while unarmed people in the north are enslaved and slaughtered. If you insist on preventing my entry into the hall, you will be responsible for many more deaths.' She took a step, leveling her blade. 'This is your last chance.'

The first guard glanced at his colleague. He nodded. They sheathed their weapons and withdrew. 'Very well, ma'am. And please, know we never wanted to cause you harm.'

Elodi scoffed, putting away her sword. 'Then rest assured you would have been disarmed and flat on your backs before you could have laid a finger on me.'

'Thank you, ma'am. I admit we were not confident in taking on an Amayan of your standing.'

She pointed to the door. 'Are you planning to open it now?'

'Ah… yes, but…' he glanced at Elodi's sword. 'I cannot allow you to—'

'No.' Elodi's hand clenched the handle. 'You're not taking it from me again.'

His hand rested on the door. 'But it's not permissible to enter the Great Hall armed, ma'am. Palace protocol dictates—'

'We've had this discussion, Captain. You have my word that I will not even look at Lord Kernlow in a displeasing manner. And if you cannot accept the promise of the leader of a realm, then our enemy has already won.'

The guard relented. 'Then the word of the Lady of Harlyn is accepted.'

Elodi relaxed. 'Thank you, Captain. And I appreciate your understanding. I acknowledge your loyalty to Lord Kernlow, but your ability to place the needs of the realms first is worthy. I will ensure the lord is—'

'Ma'am?' Elodi spun around. Marrick hurried towards her. He recovered his breath. 'Apologies for my interruption, ma'am, but I believe you'd wish to hear of my discovery prior to entering the hall.'

Elodi held her hand up to the guard to delay opening the door. 'Thank you, Marrick. Please, do tell.'

He glanced at the Palace Guards and lowered his voice. 'It is as I thought. While the Castellan was not directly responsible for your father's death, his failure to act allowed it to happen.'

Elodi grabbed her sword. She spat out her words. 'He'll suffer for this! I'll remove his head from—'

Marrick stepped in front. 'Ma'am. You cannot—'

'Out of my way! I will see justice done.'

Marrick stood firm. 'Justice shall be done, but in court. The last thing Archonholm needs is the Lady Harlyn standing accused of beheading the Castellan. He must be brought to trial.'

Her shoulders sagged. 'Now it is I who should apologize. I cannot allow a rash action to hamper the war effort.' She looked at Marrick and took a deep breath. 'How did the Castellan allow my father's murder?'

'He made it possible for the Nordleng to enter Archonholm, arranged for the guard to be changed on the bridge, then stood in the way of a full investigation, ma'am. He will argue he was following the Archon's orders, but he must have known he was complicit in a most cowardly crime.'

Elodi spoke through clenched teeth. 'That he would have. And to think he had the gall to look me in the eye and offer his condolences, and then spin his tale of deceit.' She looked at the door. 'Justice will be done. I will have to be patient, but it will be done. Please, wait here and follow the guards when they enter shortly.'

Elodi turned back to the sentries. 'I see you both wear

the burgundy band of Harlyn beside the palace colors.'

The tall guard nodded. 'Yes, ma'am. We both hail from Darrow and have seen action on the Nordruuk border.'

'Then you would have sworn allegiance to my father before you were enlisted into service here in Archonholm.'

'That is so, ma'am.'

'Then, as Lord Harlyn's successor, I ask one more favor of you. Would one of you inform the Castellan I have *forced* my way into the Great Hall, and then both of you accompany him when he inevitably intervenes.'

The guard could not prevent a grin spreading across his face. 'It will be an honor, ma'am.' He turned and opened the door.

The first time Elodi had entered the Great Hall, she had been in awe of its grandeur, and anxious about meeting the Archon. Today was a different matter altogether. She marched towards Kernlow and his Council, unconcerned by their shocked gasps.

The Proctor clambered to his feet. He opened his mouth, but Elodi's stare trapped his protest in his throat as he fell back onto his stool. Her footsteps echoed through the hall, announcing her purpose before she spoke. Lord Kernlow was the last at the table to look her way.

Elodi spoke as she strode to the table. 'Lord Kernlow. Council Members. I will not apologize for the manner of my entry. If you object' — she patted her sword — 'please take it up with my new advisor.' She stopped opposite Kernlow. 'I appreciate I have not filed the official papers, but I deemed the nature of my interruption overrides that need.' Elodi sheathed her sword and looked at the faces of the Council, still unsure of what to make of the intrusion. She took a deep breath. 'While you have all sat in your long meetings with little to show for it, our enemy have not been idle. I doubt they spend as long debating their next move as do you. But know this. We can no longer call ourselves the Five Realms. Nordryn, I will not belittle the title to refer to him as a lord, has aligned himself with the Ruuk.' Elodi paused, satisfied her message had achieved its intended purpose, judging by the gasps and gaping mouths around the table.

Lord Kernlow stood. 'How… how do you know this? We have received no word from Broon.'

Elodi lowered her voice. 'Would you expect Nordryn to inform you of his treachery, Lord? But if the Castellan had carried out his duties, Captain Amyndra of Broon could have informed you of the situation in Lunn.'

Kernlow scratched his head. 'This news of Lord… of Nordryn changes everything. We must… surely, we have to—'

'There is more, Lord.' Elodi waited for Kernlow to sit. 'A second rider arrived this morning. Much of Lunn north of the River Kel is lost, and thousands flee south. Broon is now in a state of civil war. The enemy are massing on the north banks of the Kel. Forces loyal to the Five Realms have mounted a defense on the south side. But bear in mind this news is at least fifteen days old. It's likely our forces will be heavily outnumbered and may have to fall back to the border at Ormsk before long, if that is not already the case. And I don't need to inform you of the consequences should the Ruuk occupy the forests. Our efforts to extend our fleet will be brought to a shuddering halt should we lose the supply of wood.'

The blood drained from Kernlow's puffy cheeks, and pools of sweat glistened under his eyes. He blustered. 'Ah yes. Wood. We must have wood for the ships. But shouldn't we—'

'I'm afraid that is not all. If they reach… when they reach the plains, more farms will fall into their hands. If that happens, we will experience a food shortage for the increasing numbers fleeing the invaders.' Footsteps echoed outside the door. Elodi's hand rested on her sword. 'I have more I wish to say, but first I have a pressing matter that can wait no longer, Lord.'

The door burst open. The Castellan marched in accompanied by the two Palace Guards and Marrick. He yelled at Elodi. 'You have made a grave error of judgment, Lady Harlyn. This is—'

'Guards!' Elodi drew her sword and jabbed it towards the Castellan. 'Arrest that man.'

Kernlow found his voice. 'Lady Harlyn! What in the name of—?'

'The Castellan is guilty of a gross dereliction of duty, Lord.' Elodi raised her voice over the objections of the Council. 'Under his watch he allowed my father to be murdered by Nordleng cowards acting for the Archon.'

The Castellan gaped at Kernlow. He approached the table, flanked by the Palace Guards. 'But… Lord, I protest. She has no authority—'

'I have every authority, Castellan. Read the laws of the realms. I have evidence you stood by and did nothing. That makes you complicit in the death of Harlyn's ruler, and as the current leader of that realm, I have the authority to place you under arrest until you can prove otherwise.'

Kernlow gasped. 'Is this true, Castellan? Did you know of the plot to… to murder Lord Harlyn?'

The Castellan scowled. 'This is all in *Lady* Harlyn's head, Lord. She has spent too much time in the company of that mad witch, of which we know very little.' He turned on Elodi. 'Retract your accusation now, or I'll see you suffer for this… this atrocity.'

Elodi glared. 'The atrocity was committed last summer by you, *Castellan*. Advisor Marrick has the evidence.' Her face burned. 'I should have you thrown from the bridge, but that would be too good for you. It would be a more suitable punishment to let you rot in your own dungeon.'

The Castellan bellowed. 'This is preposterous, Lord. I will not listen to any more of these fairy tales. I have been loyal to the Archon and to you. I have—' His eyes flashed at Elodi. She stiffened, seeing something in his face she had not noticed before. The Castellan stood taller and grinned. 'I have been observing Lady Harlyn these past weeks, *Lord*.' He kept his eyes on Elodi as he addressed Kernlow. His mouth twisted. 'She plots against you, *Lord*.' He poked his finger at her. 'She is just like her father. Not to be trusted, a traitor even. He had little respect for—'

'How dare you sully his good name!' Elodi leaped onto the table and lunged at the Castellan, thrusting her sword to within an inch of his throat. The Council Members jumped back, sending chairs clattering to the floor.

But the Castellan stood firm and glared back. He folded his arms. 'Ha! The good Lady Harlyn has just proved my point.' He held up a hand. 'See, my lord. She behaves as an unruly Ruuk. She has no respect for the civilized ways of the realms.'

A faint orange glow spread along Elodi's blade. She met his gaze. 'It appears you were right for once, Castellan. My sword is a threat. But as I stated at the time, only a threat to my enemies.'

Kernlow held up his hand. 'Lady Harlyn, we cannot have weapons held at throats in the Great Hall. Please, stand down and let us resolve this in a manner befitting of this place.'

She turned. 'Then allow these guards to escort the Castellan to one of his cells. I demand he is held while he awaits to stand trial. Marrick will present the case. He has evidence the Castellan cannot—'

'Never!' The Castellan lunged at Elodi. Her blade

ignited, blinding her with a blazing, blue light. Heat surged through her arm into her chest. Elodi cried out as a fire burned within. Yet all was silent in the hall. Faces around the table, bathed in her blue light, stared wide-eyed as if into empty space. Time had stopped — except for her and the Castellan. Elodi beheld him. Deep inside, she knew and feared what stood defiant at the end of her sword.

The Castellan's face rippled. Two moist, black eyes formed, bulging from a thin, stone-gray face. The eyes were not those of a man, but those of a warlock. Elodi froze, unable to tear her gaze from the apparition, oddly curious to know more. His hateful mien marred what had once been the face of a noble and powerful ruler. But the centuries consumed by the Dark Verses had long since distorted his features. The warlock's eyes bored into Elodi. The fire within her died. His cruel mouth stretched and grinned, taking pleasure from her curiosity. She saw into his past. He rode astride a monstrous corruption of a horse as it thundered towards a city of breathtaking beauty. But its splendor pained the warlock. Driven by his lust for destruction, his dark hosts stormed the walls, slaughtered its people, and razed its tall towers to the ground.

But Elodi was deceived. Too late did she realize she had not witnessed the warlock's victory from afar — he had dragged her into his Verse. His harsh voice vibrated in her chest, promising her glory and immortality. His will forced its way into her as if icy fingers groped for her soul. She had to resist. Elodi's hand still clenched her sword, but her limbs were numb. She could not move. The dread seeped into her bones, chilling her heart, freezing her blood. Yet… the warlock's words soothed her, and Elodi took pleasure from the cold dulling her angst. He pledged to wipe clean her past, free her from her duties, absolve her failures, and erase her guilt. She need never know pain or sorrow again. Elodi would be free to do whatever she desired without fear of consequence or judgement. And she was tempted. All he asked was she give herself to him — she only need speak his name.

Elodi recoiled as if the fierce sun itself had crashed through the doors. A woman, cloaked in a brilliant white light, strode towards her. But Elodi resisted her offer of help. No. She would side with the warlock and accept the riches pledged to her. The warlock hurled his curses at the intruder but still she advanced. The woman raised her arms, then spoke Elodi's name. A warm hand took hers and led her out of the Dark Verse. Elodi's numb lips formed a word. 'Nyomae.'

The spell was broken. The empty shell of the Castellan fell dead.

## 15. A Change at the Helm

Nyomae placed her cloak around Elodi's shoulders. The Great Hall had emptied of all but Lord Kernlow who sat staring at the floor where the Castellan had fallen. Nyomae spoke softly. 'You did well to resist, Elodi. There are few who can withstand such a confrontation.'

Elodi shivered. 'Fortunately, you came when you did. I was about to… to surrender myself to his will.' The warlock's promise echoed in her mind. 'I must admit I was tempted and came close to joining our enemy.' Her eyes stayed on her clenched hands. 'How is that possible?'

Nyomae rubbed Elodi's back. 'That is the way of their words. But I do not think it was as close as you fear. When the warlock touched your blade it kindled the Amayan Fire. Had I not intervened, I suspect it would have saved you.'

Elodi lifted her head. 'The blue lightning?'

She nodded. 'Amayan Fire. I sensed it the moment it blazed. It also stirred something within me. And thankfully so. How could the will of a warlock pass through our walls without my knowledge? And now the cause for the unrest in the city becomes apparent. Let us hope it will ease with his departure.'

Lord Kernlow found his voice and stuttered. 'A… a warlock you say?'

Nyomae stood. 'It was a *kruul*, the will, or mind of a warlock. Had the foul creature's vessel entered Archonholm it would have been a very different outcome.' She looked to Elodi. 'Have you recovered?'

Elodi threw off the cloak. 'I've had long enough.'

'Good. You are stronger than you think. The encounter has served to strengthen you, and the warlock has learned you are a formidable adversary.'

'Then I hope you're right. The *kruul* alone was terrifying. I would not willingly face one in the flesh.' She turned to Kernlow and took a deep breath. 'Are you ready to talk, Lord? We have much to discuss.'

He muttered. 'We do indeed, Elodi, we do indeed.'

Nyomae took back her cloak. 'Then I shall leave you and attend to the Castellan's body. While I cared not for the man, I shall rid him of the warlock's stain before he's laid to rest.'

Kernlow sagged into his chair as the door closed. His voice croaked, speaking to himself. 'Why did I not suspect Nordryn's treachery?' He stared at the flagstones charred by the warlock's departure. 'And the Castellan. The poor chap. Just like the Archon.'

Elodi moved to his side and sat. 'Then let us be thankful that thing has gone. But we cannot sit back and rest.'

Kernlow turned to her. His mouth gaped. 'I had no idea our predicament was quite so… so precarious. While we've had our setbacks with the actions of the Archon, and then that nasty business with the dead rising in the pass, I still thought we were secure, at least for the summer. But now you tell me of Nordryn's treason, and then… this warlock. This changes everything.'

'Setbacks? Lord, I hardly think…' she bit her tongue. 'If I could make a suggestion?'

He waved his hand. 'Please, go on.'

Elodi straightened. 'The Castellan had too much control over who addressed the Council, even before his possession. I have been trying to arrange a meeting with you for weeks, but he stalled every effort, hence the nature of my entrance, and the Castellan's… exit.'

Kernlow's chuckle surprised Elodi. 'I admit for a moment, when you burst in wielding your sword, I was a little apprehensive.' He leaned on his elbows. 'But now we find ourselves without a Castellan, and at a most inconvenient time.' His brow creased, sending a trickle of sweat down his face.

'May I make another suggestion, Lord?' Kernlow nodded. 'There is a very knowledgeable and clever man already in your employ. He is an Archonian veteran and therefore no stranger to a sword. His name is Marrick, an advisor to the Farrand Council on matters of the realm. He would make an excellent appointment as Castellan and… perhaps also your advisor. I have spoken to him on numerous occasions and found him to be most capable.'

Kernlow looked up. 'I do recall meeting with this Marrick fellow. But must admit I'd not seen him of late until he came in just now. Thought the poor chap had been taken ill.' The lord clicked his fingers. 'Then it's done. As you rate him so highly, I shall appoint him as the new Castellan and my advisor.'

'An excellent choice, my lord. But we have more pressing matters to discuss.'

'Yes, of course. The situation in the north I presume. Ah!' The old lord perked up. 'I may not have been as idle as you think, Elodi.' He pointed behind to a giant tapestry. 'Jolly good idea to commission that beauty of a map, eh. It was for my hall at Kirik, but seeing as I'm now entrenched in Archonholm, I had it brought here.'

Elodi took a breath. 'I had noticed it, Lord. Who could fail to be impressed by such a decorative representation of the Five Realms.'

Kernlow beamed. 'I had thirty-four master weavers in Gwelayn working on it for months.'

Elodi gaped. 'Thirty-four?'

'The very best, Elodi.'

She eyed the lavish map. 'I doubt we have more than twenty in the whole of Harlyn.'

He thrust his fat thumb at the wall. 'And all worth it. Makes strategic planning easier having this here, eh, don't you think?'

'Yes, Lord. It is a fine map, one I'm sure will help our situation immensely.'

'Good. Glad we can agree on something. Now, how about you put it to good use and tell me what you think we should do.'

Elodi stared at the tapestry. All these weeks she had waited impatiently to address Kernlow and his Council, and now she alone had his eyes and ears, she was determined not to waste the opportunity. Elodi strode to the wall. The large map was woven with so much thread, the Kolossos Mountains stood proud from the neighboring realms, even casting a shadow to the west. And now she saw the realms in such detail, the evolving plan in her head took shape. Elodi stood on her toes and stretched up to reach the part of the realms she saw as vital to their cause.

'Elodi. Please.' Kernlow grinned. 'Do make use of that pointer.' She noted an elaborate device on a stand beneath the tapestry. A golden hand with its forefinger extended sat on the end of a long, ash handle. The lord chortled. 'Well, I could hardly have a plain stick for such a fine map.'

'Err… no, I suppose not.' She picked up the pointer and ran it from west to east over the bump of the mountains. 'It's imperative we hold the line here, and not only to secure the forests of Ormsk and the fertile plains of Noor. As I see it, the Kolossos Pass is key. And I believe our enemy are only too aware of its importance. While we hold the territory either side, we can deploy reinforcements rapidly through the gap depending on need.' She traced the pointer south. 'But we'll be hugely disadvantaged if our enemy push us back and take command of the pass. It would allow them to allocate their forces either side of the range to exploit our weaknesses. So, for that reason, I propose we send the stockpile of Shreek's Rage north… immediately.'

'The black powder? Are you sure?' Kernlow shuddered. 'As we've learned to great cost, it is extremely destructive.'

'Precisely, Lord. But it can be handled with care. Then if it becomes apparent the pass will be lost, we can block the exit to the east. It may at least delay their plans for a week or two and give us more time to muster.' She pointed to the port at Keld. 'And what if Nordryn is building ships for our enemy?'

Kernlow blustered. 'But… but the Ruuk are not known for their readiness to sail, are they?'

'That's exactly what we thought before they rowed into Calerdorn's harbor. These are not the Ruuk we have had the misfortune to encounter in the past. They are led by the ruthless Ul-dalak and warlocks. And it is not just the Ruuk clans they command. They grow more powerful every day and summon the creatures of old to their cause. And, if they gain access to the vast supplies of the hardy wood in Ormsk, their ships will circumvent our lines to land raiding parties at' — her eyes slid down the east coast — 'perhaps as far south as the Ravenlode Estuary.' She looked to the Elessyn Sea. 'And what if they land at West Haven? Imagine the disruption they could inflict on the farmlands of Tamarand. We would need to deplete the line in the north to push them out. We'd find ourselves fighting on multiple fronts in the east, west and as far south as Farrand. All on terms dictated by them. The Ruuk could attack both the rear of our defensive line or choose to push onto Archonholm.'

Kernlow's face paled once more as his detailed map now brought the harsh reality clearly into view. 'Oh my… oh dear, and I thought we could sit tight in Archonholm, strengthening our position to eventually let them fail here before we pushed back their weakened forces.'

Elodi turned back to the table. 'No, Lord. I don't think that is a feasible strategy. We can no longer sit out this conflict here. I made that error in Calerdorn. Until now, we have allowed the enemy to hold the upper hand. It is they who make all the moves, leaving us to respond in haste. But they are always one step ahead. They force us to commit to one region, while they have plans to attack another. We saw what happened when Uluriel brought the bulk of our forces to the gate.' Elodi replaced the pointer on its stand and returned to the table. 'It's time we took the initiative. We must turn this about and make them question their strategy. And we can only do this by putting their front under pressure.'

Kernlow looked back to his tapestry. His eyes flitted about the map, looking unsure of where to settle. 'Then where… where should I start? Do I lead a force up the east… or the west? And who do I take? Guards on foot would slow our progress, but then knights alone are not suitable for skirmishes. How would—?'

'Lord Kernlow.' Elodi held up her hand. She formed her question carefully. 'Do you think you are… the right person to lead such a mission?'

He looked taken aback. 'But… but of course. As the Steward it is my responsibility, my duty no less.' The lord pushed his chair back and tried to stand. 'My good lady, I've waited all my life for this very moment. This is the time for strength and an iron will, one that won't bend in the face of adversity.'

Elodi watched as the lord gave up the battle to stand. He landed with a bump and a groan. She lowered her voice. 'I am aware you served with distinction in the skirmishes of the north, Lord. But what experience do you have of leading an army into open battle?'

Kernlow recovered his breath from his exertion. 'Well, I… I have much experience of… let me see.' He stroked his chin as his gaze rose to the ceiling. His finger shot up. 'Ah! Of course. I once captured a clan leader in Nordruuk. Ha! Now that was a mission and a half. Under the cover of darkness, I led a dozen—'

'That sounds a feat worthy of a good story for another time perhaps. But have you led a force of greater than a few dozen?'

His cheeks puffed out. 'Yes. Why of course. I led at least forty men against some ruffians stealing wine from one of our finest vineyards back in the day. Then there was an occasion—'

'And how long ago did these exploits take place, Lord?'

Kernlow's brow creased. 'Now there's a question. Well… let me see, I must have been in my twenties, no, early thirties.' He straightened. 'You should have seen me in my prime, Elodi. There wasn't a rider in the whole of the realm who could beat me in a joust, and when it came to the hand-to-hand business, well—'

Elodi could not prevent the sigh escaping her lips. 'And how many years have passed since you were in your *early thirties*?'

His large frame deflated. 'Gosh. It must be almost forty… no, more than forty years now I come to think of it.' His head dropped. 'Too many… too long ago.'

'And when did you last ride a horse at a pace faster than a trot, Lord?'

Kernlow kept his eyes on the table. 'That may also have been more than a few years back.' He looked up. 'But I'm sure I could still manage a canter, with some practice.'

He stroked his chin. 'Ah, but that wouldn't suffice in battle. I could hardly lead a charge at a canter.' A tear formed in his eye. He stared at the door to the Great Hall. 'I'm old, Elodi, too old for anything more than a ceremonial role. It seems my best days are behind me… well behind me.' His chin dropped. He whispered. 'My inaction could cost the realms dear. What was I thinking? I should never have taken on this role.'

Elodi looked at a man who had finally come to terms with his age. She felt his pain and pitied him. 'You have served the Realms for many years, the people of Kernlow love you and speak very highly of you. But perhaps it's time to… to step aside.'

Kernlow nodded, clenching his jaw, trying in vain to stem the tears. 'You're right, my dear. I should retire to my vineyard and see out my days tending to my grapes.'

Elodi placed her hand on his. 'But that would be a loss, my lord. I'm certain with all your experience you will be an excellent orator for the forces when we need to raise morale.'

His eyebrows raised. 'Do you think?' He clapped his hands. 'Ah, yes! Of course, if there's one thing I can still do well, it's rouse the troops with a good speech.'

She patted his shoulder. 'And there is still the issue of the day-to-day running of Archonholm. You have managed the realm of Kernlow longer than any living ruler. We cannot afford for all that experience to be lost at the moment of our greatest need.'

'That is also true. I may be old and' — he jiggled his belly — 'getting a little too plump for my horse's back, but I can ensure the smooth running of the realms.'

'That you can, Lord. You have achieved wonders with the clearing of the pass and laying the dead to rest with dignity.'

Kernlow took out a handkerchief from his pocket and wiped his face. 'Yes… yes, that I have.' He frowned. 'And that's something we need to accelerate if our foe tries to pull another dastardly stunt and pitch our dead against us.'

'Indeed, my lord.' Elodi judged the time was right to play her last hand. 'But if you're to take on the extra responsibility of delivering your excellent speeches, as well as managing the affairs of the realms… would you consider appointing me as the head of our forces?' She held her breath.

'Hmmm.' His lips pursed. 'That would make sense. But an important position such as that would have to be put to the members of the Council. And I expect some of my generals may have issues with that.'

Elodi leaned forward. 'But you have emergency powers, my lord. You can sign a decree that none can dispute. If you appoint me head of our armies, I will report to you and be under your command. I shall take full responsibility for all matters concerning the deployment of our forces, but you would ultimately have the final say.'

Kernlow thought for a moment. He slapped his leg. 'Very well, Lady Harlyn. I like the sound of your plan.' He beamed, appearing to lose ten years as the weight of command lifted from his shoulders.

'Thank you, my lord. I shall not let you down.' Elodi edged forward. 'And that decree, my lord?'

'Decree?'

'Regarding my position as head of our forces. It's imperative you forgo existing procedures to save time. A Steward's Decree will signal your intent to take control of the predicament we find ourselves in. And it will help give the people of Archonholm confidence, my lord, to see you take such decisive action.'

'Ah yes! Of course. I'll ask my new advisor' — he winked — 'Marrick, to issue it immediately. I shall leave you to determine our strategy and tactics, just as long as you run your plans past me first, eh.' He scratched his head. 'But help me here, Lady Harlyn. Would I still be Steward?'

'Yes, my lord. You remain as the Steward of Archonholm at this most vital time to oversee the affairs of the realms. And may I suggest you allow more trade between the wards, and ensure crops can be harvested and transported to the mills and stores. You have done this for Kernlow for decades. That, in my mind, makes you the ideal person for such an important role. After all, a hungry soldier can't be expected to march the length of the land and then be in a fit state to fight.'

He rubbed his chin. 'Ah. I see. Yet surely, the chief priority for our survival is the forces you now command. Is there any way I could assist there, Elodi?'

She grinned. 'But of course, my lord. Don't forget I shall be needing your expertise to deliver those important morale-boosting speeches.'

Elodi closed the door to her quarters and leaned against it. She slid down to the floor, exhausted by her eventful day. Was Nyomae right? Could she have resisted the warlock had Nyomae not intervened? She took some comfort that she had survived the encounter unscathed. And now she had experienced the Amayan Fire, but would it come at her command?

Her hand went to her face. Elodi felt as she had the night before leading the raid into Durran Wood. That involved a few hundred, but now many thousands of lives were in her hands. What had she taken on? In the Great Hall she was convinced of her objective, but Kernlow's decree had elevated her to a position not even her father could have envisaged.

Elodi looked across the room she had occupied on her first visit to Archonholm. At the time it had seemed such a fine chamber for one so young, and it had made her feel important. Today, its grandeur seemed extravagant, a symbol of past glory that the realms could no longer afford in what could be its last days. Would its contents be ransacked, and the walls daubed with the same cruel words she had seen on the stone at the gate?

The knock at the door startled her. Elodi gathered her composure to open it. Toryn stood outside. He attempted to smile. 'I hear you have met a warlock. It seems events are moving at a pace. Nyomae believes I am ready.' He sighed. 'I leave tomorrow.'

Elodi took his hand. 'You had better come in. We have much to discuss.'

# 16. Fare Thee Well

Toryn looked along the line of the dozen volunteers for the Amayan mission. All had been sworn to secrecy as Elodi was certain spies still operated within Archonholm despite the warlock's departure. He did not know most of their faces but was happy to trust any who met with Gundrul's approval. But even if they were the most skilled fighters, riders, and trackers in the realm, much rested on Toryn's shoulders.

Gundrul stood at his side. 'Not a bad bunch of lads and lassies considering. Few Archonians have experience on horseback, but these folk from Lady Harlyn's forces assure me they're accomplished riders. And all will be better than me in a saddle, or I dearly hope so for their own good.'

Toryn nodded at Elrik, standing first in line. 'And some not so bad at putting a shoe on them either. But you'll be needing a shire horse to carry this big fellow.'

Elrik smirked. 'I don't recall you beating me more than twice on our races to the bridge.'

Toryn grasped his broad shoulder. 'That was down to your ponies.' He turned to Gundrul. 'Elrik took his pick of the fast horses he shod, claiming he was testing his work for their owners.'

Gundrul sighed. 'Your horse talk is wasted on me, lads. So long as my mount doesn't throw me off its back at the first sight of danger, I don't care how fast it is.' Toryn moved on. Gundrul introduced the next in line. 'This fine lady is one of Galabrant's best scouts. If Janae can't track it, it must be on wings.' He laughed. 'But I'd guess you'd still find it's droppings, eh.'

Janae held a straight face. 'I've yet to meet a beast that doesn't leave a trail, Captain.' Toryn held the steely gaze of a woman whose age he would struggle to guess. She may have been in her late thirties, but her eyes hinted many more years of knowledge. Janae shook Toryn's hand. 'Pleased to be of service.'

'And we're very pleased to have you with us. I imagine we'll be relying heavily on your skills, and your knowledge of the east side of the mountains will be invaluable.'

'I have traveled far and wide in my time assisting the Archonians.' She looked along the line. 'But few here will have seen as much of Galabrant as have I.'

Gundrul nodded to her horse. 'Janae also has some of the finest birds for us to keep in contact with Archonholm. I reckon they'll come in handy before long.' The captain took a step. 'This handsome chap is Lorek. Lorek of Tamforth. That's in your neck of the woods I believe.'

Toryn clutched the young guard's forearm. 'Indeed, but at opposite ends of the River Tam. That's close to seventy leagues apart. So, a tad more than a stone's throw.' He peered at the man. 'Wait. Lorek? Did you have two brothers at Drunsberg?'

He bowed his head. 'Dorek and Porek. Sadly they…' he looked up. 'Did you know them?'

'Only briefly. I arrived at the mines on the same day of the attack that tragically claimed both their lives.'

'Did…' Lorek blinked, 'Did they die with honor? And with sword in hand?'

Toryn winced as he recalled the look of shock on Dorek's face as the blood had spurted from his sliced throat — a wound inflicted by a kitchen boy with the captain's own blade. And the cries of Porek and his men as they were struck down by the green poison, still pained him. Toryn straightened. 'That they did. And with bravery that couldn't be surpassed fighting an enemy who vastly outnumbered us.'

Lorek's jaw tightened. 'Thank you. To hear it from someone who witnessed their end helps ease my grief.'

Toryn placed his hand on the young man's shoulder. 'And while I knew them for only a short time, it was an honor to serve with them. And seeing as you're cut from the same cloth, it will be an honor to have you in the company.'

'The honor is mine. I hope to avenge the death of my brothers at your side.'

Toryn looked back to Gundrul. The old captain grunted. 'Winter will be upon us if you insist on hearing the life story of each and every volunteer.' He glanced to the sky. 'Dusk is nigh. All are briefed and know their duty… and the dangers. The official reason they're here is for training for combat on horseback.' He winked. 'But we all know different, eh. And if we're to leave under cover of darkness, I'd say we have time for a decent meal before we head off.'

Toryn nodded to the line of faces. 'I assume you're familiar with the legend of the Amayans, so you'll know why this task is of utmost importance to the Five Realms. We face an enemy—'

'That will hear us coming if our bellies are growling.' Gundrul patted Toryn on his back. 'Maybe continue your speech over a hot supper and a glass of ale, eh.'

Toryn beamed, glad to be back in the company of soldiers. 'That sounds like a good plan, Captain.'

The clouds obliged, obscuring the near full moon to conceal their departure from unwanted eyes. While those in the stables were led to believe they were on night maneuvers, the bulging saddle bags, and back packs may have aroused suspicion. They led their horses to the postern gate on the east of the city where one of Gundrul's trusty guards kept watch. As they approached, Toryn noticed a cloaked figure standing by the wall. His heart lurched as their torchlight fell upon a head of flaming, red hair. He gestured to Gundrul he would catch them up.

Toryn dismounted and went to her. He whispered. 'I thought we'd said our goodbyes last night.'

Elodi sighed. 'That was my intention, but I couldn't let you go without… without saying…' She looked away. 'Am I justified taking command, Toryn?' Her hand went to her sword. 'I know I've been frustrated by Kernlow's lack of action, but I'm—'

'Elodi. There's no one better suited to lead our armies. You have more experience than any, and your skill with a blade is second to none in the realms.'

Her eyes glistened. 'But I lost my city. How can I be sure I won't make the same mistakes?'

He clasped her hand. 'You faced Dorlan, the real Dorlan. How were you to know he would be brought against you? And now we have Nyomae, we know more about the dark arts we're likely to face. And you and I grow stronger by the day.' Toryn looked into her eyes. 'The first time I saw you, I knew I would follow you wherever you chose to lead. And I don't know a guard, knight, or reserve, that doesn't think the same. We believe in you, Nyomae believes in you, perhaps you should start believing in your yourself.'

'That's kind of you to say so.' Her grip tightened. 'But… oh, why do I find this so difficult?' Her hand went to his face. 'Toryn? Please take care. While Nyomae is certain the warlock has left Farrand, we both know this mission is fraught with other dangers. I had hoped we could fight every remaining battle side-by-side. I cannot bear to… the thought that…'

Toryn stepped forward and embraced her. He breathed in her fragrant hair, wishing beyond hope, they could ride off into the night and leave their troubles behind. But Hamar's voice reminded him, *duty*, *lad*, *duty*. He spoke into her hair. 'I will come back. I can't accept this is the last time we'll be together.' He stepped back, holding her warm hands, gazing deep into her eyes. 'I will allow nothing, not even the demons of the Underworld to stand in my way. I promise I will return.'

Elodi patted the horse's nose. 'I know you will. But we both know the dangers you and I will face in the coming months. I will look for you with my *farsight*.' She let his fingers slip from hers and nodded to the gate. 'You… you must go now.' Elodi spun away and strode into the shadows. Toryn watched her leave, his heart yearning to go after her. But duty called.

Toryn turned and led his horse through the narrow opening and out of Archonholm. He mounted, glancing up to see the moon's face appear briefly from behind a thick cloud. He recalled the night he and Hamar had sneaked out of Midwyche, listening to Elrik and his friends singing their hearts out at the inn. He glanced behind to see the towering walls looming over as if standing in judgement of him sneaking out of the city. On the night he had left Midwyche, he was blissfully unaware of what lay ahead. His trepidation had been tempered by the thrill of seeing the world beyond his village. Tonight, nothing could ease the pain and dread of what awaited them on the east side of the Kolossos.

Toryn caught up with Gundrul at the front of the line. The captain grinned. 'Said your goodbyes, eh. She's a fine lady, lad, but don't let that be a distraction.' Toryn stayed silent. Gundrul looked up to the sky. 'Come tomorrow, we'll travel by day. There'll be more enemy eyes on us the farther we go north, but speed is vital.' He nodded to Toryn's belt. 'How's your sword work coming on?'

'Progressing. Elodi taught me much in the limited

time we had for lessons.'

'Good. I know you're skilled with the bow, but you can't always rely on it. I reckon you'll be looking your enemy in the eye before long.'

Toryn thought back to the wild eyes of the Ruuk he had faced at Drunsberg. 'I've no doubt I will.'

Gundrul shifted in his saddle. 'Remember this, our enemy care not for rules and fighting fair. You take them down any way you can, and as fast as you can. It won't be pretty, but if you can walk or hobble away from a fight and the other fellow can't, that's a victory by my reckoning.'

# 17. And Another Departs

Elodi let the light breeze brush the hair from her face. She stood on the North Terrace watching Nyomae and the three accompanying knights ride out from Archonholm. While she would have preferred to have gone with her, Elodi accepted her new role as commander meant she could not leave the city until the strategy to secure the Kolossos Pass was complete. And that depended on news from her scouts bravely tracking enemy movements on the borders.

Her eyes wandered along the road skirting the forest. Should she commit equal forces in the east and west? Did the enemy plan to take the rest of Harlyn? Or would they exploit Nordryn's treachery and strike through Broon and on into Galabrant? Until she knew for certain how far the enemy had advanced, and in what numbers, Elodi was reluctant to make the decision. But she took some satisfaction from their preparations. All the forces at her command were now ready to mobilize. And Amyndra was confident Elodi could rely on many more from Broon's forces loyal to the realms. But her heart ached. The two people she trusted most in the world had departed. Both on missions vital in the struggles to come, and now she had to deliver on her promise.

Elodi followed Nyomae's progress as she crossed the Menon Bridge and disappear behind the trees of Foranfae. Nyomae was a fine rider, as good as the First Horse knights at her side. With good speed, they would reach Neverdor in three days. But how long would it take for Nyomae to find what she sought? Elodi's gaze went as ever to the north. She relaxed and let the *farsight* come.

With each calling it had become easier. Elodi felt as if she flew over the Great Northwest Road as it wove its way between the forest and the Menon Hills. The gentle slopes of Tamarand followed with its fields of barley and wheat that fed many in Farrand. Scattered brown patches appeared where the crops had already been harvested and the fields plowed. But more should have been done by now, and autumn rapidly approached. It pained Elodi to think of the many farmhands and villagers who would have happily gathered in the crops, still lay beneath the rubble in the pass.

Beyond the farms, the road forked. Elodi took the west road that would convey Nyomae to Neverdor. A bridge took shape in the mist. It straddled the River Lor, glistening silver in the late afternoon sun as if a giant snail had wended its patient way home. She followed its path towards its source in the valleys to the north, and Nyomae's destination. Neverdor's spire shone, nestling among the hills that shielded the old Seat of Learning from the woes of the outside world. Behind the tower, the haze confirmed she had reached the northern limit of her powers. What secrets lay beneath its gleaming tower? Would they prove to be a boon or a hindrance? Would the—?

'Ma'am?'

Elodi spun around, steadying herself from the rapid departure from the *farsight*. Amyndra stood a short distance away. Her pale, tight face did not bring Elodi hope.

# 18. Fear Comes South

Toryn stirred. His dreams had been of his time in the Foranfae, but another being had entered — something not of his experience. Nearby, Elrik sat beside the glowing embers of the watchman's fire. Toryn stood and went to warm his bones. His friend nodded. 'All quiet. But I would hope so, eh, seeing as we're only a few days out of Archonholm.'

Toryn held his hands to the fire. 'Did you hear something a moment ago?'

'Can't say I did.' He glanced to the trees. 'A fox was yelping a while back, but she must have realized we're no danger to her cubs.' Elrik placed a stick on the fire. 'Your ears must be better than mine if something woke you.' He leaned over. 'But seeing as you have this *farsight* of yours, does it help with your hearing?'

'Not that I'm aware.'

Elrik chuckled. 'Who would have thought it, eh. My skinny friend from the farm turns out to be a powerful wyke.'

Toryn waved a twig in Elrik's face. 'Ha! Then you better be careful. I might turn you into a fat toad.'

Elrik's smile faded. 'I'd settle for that.' He looked up to the silver-tinged clouds. 'I'd rather be a toad right now. Imagine, living in a wood pile without a care in the world.'

Toryn dropped the twig. 'That does sound tempting. But what would Hamar have to say if he heard us talking of swapping places with a toad.'

Elrik laughed. 'Ah yes.' He hunched his back and made a face. '*Duty, lads, duty.*' He straightened. 'It wasn't until I heard of his passing that I realized how much I admired the old boy. You were lucky to see him fighting the enemy.'

Toryn recalled the speed of Hamar's sword. 'He must have been quite a warrior in his day. It's a shame he's not with us now.' He beamed. 'I saw him in his youth. Nyomae took me back in the Song at the Menon Bridge. He was even bigger then.'

Elrik glanced to the stars between the clouds. 'Do you think he might be… with us in a way? I mean, I know he'll have his farm on the plain, seeing as he fell fighting the enemy, but… what about the deal with All Hallows? Do they really come back?'

Toryn watched the breeze fan the flames. 'Not too long ago, I would have said it was all superstition or wishful thinking. But now…' The grass turned silver as the moon found its way into clear sky. 'I still hear his voice. For every situation I find myself in, there's something from his countless stories to offer advice.'

Elrik grinned. 'There were certainly many. But surely, they couldn't all be true.'

'He must have made some up, but he was right about the little folk.' He thumbed to the forest. 'Although they're not so little.'

Elrik sighed. 'I hope I can be like him one day. We live in more dangerous times than he did. Will we even see next summer? Who would have thought Calerdorn would fall. If the enemy can take that from us, then no other city is safe, except Archonholm... hopefully.'

Toryn nudged him. 'If Hamar was sitting by this fire, he would be telling us that's how the enemy want us to feel.' He put on a gruff voice and jabbed a finger at Elrik. 'Hope is our best defense, lad. Without it, we're beaten before a sword is raised.'

Elrik glanced behind into the dark. "What about this thing you heard then? Was it from the forest?'

Toryn shrugged. 'I reckon it was in my dream. Had to be. It came from above.'

The company rounded the bend and rode out of the shadow of the Foranfae. Ahead, the mighty peaks of the Kolossos rose from the lingering morning mists to greet them. At midday, they crossed the border into Emryst, the prosperous ward of Galabrant. But while the vast farmlands of Emryst produced abundant crops for the realms, the true riches lay beneath the hills to the north. Gifted to them by the gods, the people were ever grateful for the seams of precious gemstones found only in their lands. The cities of Saphrir and Kalimir were said to be the most beautiful ever built by the people of the Seven Realms. With tall, ornate towers with conical roofs decorated with gold, sapphires and emeralds, the cities were not shy displaying their wealth. While intrigued by the stories of Saphrir and Kalimir, Toryn had no desire to visit the bejeweled cities — he yearned to set eyes upon Telamir. Seeing it through the haze of *farsight* had only served to whet his appetite. And even Odrun, a man of little words, had found plenty to say about the strange tower.

Gundrul held up his hand and slowed his horse. Toryn drew level. 'Have you seen something?'

'Your eyesight is better than any here.' The captain pointed. 'What do you make of that?'

Toryn felt a pang of guilt. He had been daydreaming, and thus failed to notice the plume of smoke rising from the plain on their right. Toryn stood in his stirrups. 'It's a farmhouse. But it's the field that smolders.' He grimaced as he tasted the death of Greendell.

Gundrul shook his head. 'Has to be an accident. Can't be the work of the enemy this close to Farrand.'

Toryn's stomach clenched. 'Yet their servants ride through our realms with disdain for our borders. We should investigate.'

'Our priority lies north. We would waste valuable time.'

'Wait. I see a struggle.' Toryn let his eyes wander across the fields. 'Yes. A lone man against three.'

Gundrul stared at the smoke. 'A local dispute perhaps? Or should we intervene?'

Toryn spurred his horse, calling over his shoulder. 'We intervene! I've seen these fiends before.'

The captain waved his arm, wheeling the company after Toryn. They set off at a gallop. The finest horses of Archonholm responded, tearing across the grasslands, pleased to be on softer ground. As they neared the farmhouse, Toryn's heart sank. He could not know how, but a wrong had been committed. It wrenched at his gut, forcing bile into his throat.

Gundrul spat. 'The foul beasts. Who could do such a thing?' Toryn's eyes smarted from the acrid smoke, but they could not shut out the appalling sight. Three charred bodies lay at the center of a burned-out circle in the stubble of the harvested field. Gundrul stared at the smallest. He bowed his head. 'Couldn't be older than ten. The poor child. I hope they were dead before they burned.'

'Captain!' Janae strode across the field. She flinched at the gruesome sight at their feet. She pointed east. 'Three set off at speed but a few minutes ago. They must have seen us coming. And there's a survivor by the farmhouse. An old guard I'd wager. He's in a bad way but he can talk.'

Toryn ran to the house. Two of their company sat comforting a bloodied man slumped against the wall. They had given him water, but Toryn guessed it would only serve to ease his passing. Gundrul caught up. He kneeled and picked up the sword by the injured man. 'An Archonian blade to be sure.' He placed it in the man's hand, closing his fingers around the handle. 'Please. Tell me your name, soldier. Your courage will be remembered.'

The man coughed. 'Adreel. But I failed. I was too late.'

Gundrul clutched the man's free hand. 'Looks to me as if you fought against the odds. That's courage in my book.'

A tear ran down Adreel's soot-caked face. 'Four of them. Big fellows. I came when I saw the smoke. Thought Patrel needed help.' He spat blood. 'That poor family. I knew something was wrong when Shepra failed to greet me.'

'Shepra?' Toryn glanced back to the smoke. 'Was she his… daughter?'

He clutched his stomach. 'His dog. Always scampered to the gate when she saw me coming.' Adreel's hand raised towards the field. 'They did this.' He choked back tears. 'I'd known Patrel since we were lads, and his wife too.' He choked back the tears. 'I held Rayla, his daughter, when she was born…. She…' His jaw clenched. 'I made one of those swine pay. You'll find him in the barn. At least he won't be troubling anyone again.'

Gundrul nodded to Lorek. 'Take Elrik and check out the dead scoundrel.'

Toryn laid his hand on Adreel's arm. 'Had you seen the likes of these men before?'

'No. I'd have noticed four large chaps dressed in nothing but black.'

Toryn cursed. 'Nordleng! I thought as much. I've seen their handiwork before. And to think I felt pity for the one swallowed by a droog.'

The captain glanced to the smoldering circle. 'But why do this? What would they gain from murdering these fine folk?' Adreel tried to speak but slumped back against the wall. Gundrul grasped his hand, ensuring Adreel had a firm grip on his sword. 'Don't fight it, Adreel. It's the plains for you, my friend. You can hold your head up high when the old boys come to greet you. Go in peace, Archonian. May your hops grow, and your beer quench your thirst.' Adreel's eyes closed. He smiled as his last breath left him. Toryn bowed his head as the man died. His Verse flowed through Toryn, recounting the Archonian's long, hard life, serving both the realms and his family with a good heart. He looked up to the sky. Adreel would indeed deserve his place on the Plains of Evermore.

'I've searched the house, Captain.' Janae stopped and placed a hand over her heart.

Gundrul stepped back. 'Had those scum been here long?'

'Several days judging by the mess. There's no food left, and the place has been ransacked. I'd say they used the house for shelter and sustenance.' She shook her head. 'The poor family were just unfortunate to be in the wrong place.'

Gundrul could not take his eyes from the blackened patch where the family lay. 'Please ready a bird. I'll send word to Archonholm. Lady Harlyn will have to consider committing a force to track and capture… or kill these swine.' He turned to Toryn. 'I know you hope to talk with Nyomae with your… your magic tricks, but I think it best if we send a bird, just in case, eh. This cannot go unreported.'

'A good decision. Our trials were not always successful.'

'Captain.' Elrik ran back from the barn pointing north. 'More approach. On the road from Cafra I'd say.' They stood to see a black and white dog bounding across the field with three on horseback following. Toryn and Gundrul strode out to meet them.

The captain grunted. 'That must be their dog. A fine collie if I ever saw one. I reckon she'd have run for help. Poor lass will be gutted to find she's too late.' He held up his hand to the riders. 'Captain Gundrul, Archonian Guard.' The horses slowed, but Shepra scampered past. Toryn followed. She cautiously stepped onto the scorched earth, whimpering as she endured the heat, but the faithful dog would not be separated from her family. Toryn went to her. He removed his cloak and laid it beside the farmer. Shepra crouched upon it and licked her master's clawed hand. Toryn turned and left her alone to mourn.

Gundrul spoke with the riders as Elrik and Lorek returned from the barn. Lorek snarled. 'If only we'd arrived earlier. Our friend Adreel did well to take out one. They are big men, and well-armed, and I would say well-trained.' He looked east. 'But they'll rue the day they did this. If I ever see the likes of them…'

Toryn sighed. 'I think we'll be seeing a lot more of these foul folk before long. They'll be in league with Nordryn and the Ruuk. But be wary. Even the Amayans break sweat to tackle them. They are highly skilled, but ruthless with it. I don't know how they'd fare in open battle. They seem better suited to stealth and raids.'

Elrik grunted. 'And attacking defenseless women and children.'

'As I said. Ruthless. They have not a care for any but themselves and their masters.'

Gundrul approached. 'The riders are from Cafra. They said the dog showed up in the early hours.' He turned to Shepra sitting quietly with her family. His eyes glistened. 'The lass must have run twenty leagues without rest. Now there's a dog I'd have by my side any day.' He looked towards the barn. His lip curled. 'The Cafrans speak of a dozen or so similar acts. But they're difficult to track, and harder to confront. I hope Elodi can aid these people. Can't have them spreading fear, there's enough of that already.'

Toryn turned back to the farmhouse. 'Is that their objective? Do they spread fear? Or is there another reason for being in Emryst?'

Gundrul rubbed his chin. 'The Cafrans are certainly anxious. But they only raid the farms. They've not gone near the mines, or the wealth of the cities.'

Toryn scanned the horizon as the dust kicked up by the fleeing Nordleng's horses cleared. 'No, they're here for something else. They're turning south. But for what?'

Gundrul whistled for his horse. 'We must be going. We have our own mission to complete. The town folk will give these poor souls a decent burial. I'll advise they also send a rider to Archonholm with the news as a precaution.' He glanced up. 'We can't be sure if these Nordleng swine have hawks that will bring down our feathered friends.' Gundrul spoke with the Cafrans as the rest of the company mounted.

Lorek nodded to the farmer and his family. 'What about the dog?'

Toryn turned to see Shepra had not moved. 'I'd say she'll likely stay here.' But as they set off, Shepra barked and ran after their horses.

Lorek cheered. 'Looks like we have another volunteer. I imagine she's keen to avenge her family.'

# 19. The Realms Ride North

'And you can be sure?' Elodi found she gripped Amyndra's arm.

'I'm afraid it is true. My rider arrived in the early hours. The Ruuk have crossed the Kel and taken positions at Torm, and farther east in the foothills of the Kellen Heights. Forces loyal to the Five Realms have retreated. They're forming a new front stretching between Rand and the port of Gwend as best they can. But thankfully, the Ruuk appear to have stopped. Why this should be I do not know. They had us on the run, and had they ridden on, we'd have been routed before our camps were made ready.'

Elodi looked out from her window. 'Fortunate indeed. But I worry when the Ruuk are patient. Nordryn must be waiting for instructions from his new masters.' Her hand went to her mouth. 'The forests! It must be as I feared. Nordryn has his eyes on the timber. He's gathering his forces to take Borrund.' She turned and strode to the doorway. 'Please come with me. Your news has forced the issue. We will have to commit a sizeable force to Ormsk. The reserves will be no match for the Ruuk. We cannot afford to concede a single tree to that traitor. And we must ensure Aralak Gorge remains guarded, and the east side of the Kolossos Pass is not lost.'

Lord Kernlow struggled to stand as Elodi and Amyndra strode into the Great Hall. He glanced down and pushed aside his half-eaten dinner. 'You look as if you've seen a shreek, Lady Harlyn.'

Elodi stopped at the table. 'I've already had that

pleasure, Lord, but it is not the reason the blood has drained from my face, or for my haste.' She gestured to her companion. 'This is Captain Amyndra from the forces of Broon who remain true to the Five. She has received word of Ruuk crossing the Kel.'

'They've crossed the river?' Kernlow shuffled to his map. 'Oh dear, that is bad news. That brings them closer to—'

'The forests of Ormsk. Thankfully, our forces are prepared and ready to ride. I have dispatched a bird to the Knights of Amman stationed at Karrock. They will head north immediately to aid those loyal to Broon. The forces at Borrund have already deployed to bolster the line. I have ordered the First Horse to ride immediately to Ormsk, and my reserves at Amroth to help secure the Kolossos Pass to the west. And at dawn, my knights will ride to aid our forces in the east.'

Kernlow's eyes moved up and down the Kolossos Mountains. 'Excellent.' He groaned. 'I'm afraid my legs aren't what they used to be.' He waddled back to the table and sank into his chair. 'That's better. Now I can think.' His eyebrows raised. 'Ah yes, what of the gorge and the spiders?'

Elodi strode to the map and picked up the pointer. She ran it up the east side of the mountains. 'If Broon's loyal forces still hold the line at Rand, I have instructed a detachment of Archonians to consolidate the watch on the fences at the gorge. I do not believe it's in anyone's interest, even Nordryn's, to neglect them. I'm sure the aralaks don't care into which side they pump their foul poison. But I'll be happier if it were our guards at the fences.' The golden finger slid down the map to Cafra. 'But that is not all. Bands of Nordleng are raiding farms in Emryst.'

Kernlow's mouth gaped. 'So far south?'

'Unfortunately, yes. I have sent a small detachment of First Horse to track them down and… eliminate them.'

The lord's brow furrowed. 'Not that I wish to question your judgement, but do we not need every last one of them elsewhere?'

'That would be my desire, but the Nordleng are a vicious tool of the enemy. While it may be a tactic to draw more of our resources away from the front, I cannot leave the people of Emryst undefended against such a cruel band of hoodlums. My hope is to kill them quickly, then my riders can be sent north.'

'Then it is a wise decision, Lady Harlyn.' He looked to Amyndra who appeared in awe of the Great Hall. 'And you, Captain. What is your mission?'

Amyndra stiffened, suddenly hearing the question. She glanced to Elodi. 'Lord. I am to ride with the First Horse to aid my comrades holding the line.'

'The First Horse? My dear, they are our finest riders and knights.' He looked to Elodi. 'Would it not be preferable for her to accompany the Archonians?'

Elodi replaced the pointer on its stand. She smiled at Amyndra. 'The captain is a fine rider, and Warrior is a swift horse equal to any of ours. She also has more experience of fighting than many here. I can assure you, lord, she will not be the least intimidated by Archonholm's elites. And remember, she knows the lands east of the Kolossos better than any south of Emryst.'

Lord Kernlow pushed back his chair and stood. 'Ah good. I see you have thought this through.' He glanced to Amyndra. 'And I apologize if I have offended you, Captain. You sound a very capable soldier, and one whose service and loyalty will be most welcome.'

Amyndra bowed her head. 'None taken, my lord.'

'Good. Then it sounds as if we have a workable plan.' He glanced down to his unfinished meal. 'Err… do you need me to do anything else, Lady Harlyn?'

A wry smile passed across Elodi's lips. 'If you can arise at the crack of dawn, a short address from you would help to rally the troops, my lord.'

Elodi dearly wished she could ride with Aldorman and her knights. The sight of their banners, shining armor and proud horses trotting across the Menon Bridge had raised her spirits. In two weeks, they would cross the Great Elda and enter Noor. Messages from Ruan at Seransea stated Noor remained free of invaders. But Elodi had come to learn the lulls in enemy activity usually heralded preparations were underway for a decisive strike. Aldorman was to marshal the reserves to form a line along the Seran River, but he was ordered to reform on the south bank of the River Wend if overrun.

A horn blared below. A division of Archonians under the command of Cubric assembled at the bridge. While Gundrul and Toryn had gone east, Cubric would lead his guards on the tails of Aldorman's horses. But even with the fabled brutal Archonian's marching speed, it would be close to three weeks before he could take his position. But Elodi was under no illusion the enemy could be held back for long. So, another tactic had to be deployed. Small bands trained in the art of ambush, were tasked to harass the Ruuk where possible. If they attempted to bridge rivers, cross marshes, or build camps, they were to disrupt their plans and force them to divert resources away from their bigger plan. But even with a concerted effort, Elodi was certain they would have to withdraw before long. The River Wend provided the next line of defense, but inevitably they would surely be pushed back to the Great Elda. But this had to be held — the Elda had to be the line where the Ruuk were stopped. If the Five Realms had any hope of surviving, the Kolossos Pass must be secured. If it fell into enemy hands, their ability to reinforce either side of the mountain range would be lost, and with it, all hope of preventing the darkness reaching Farrand.

Earlier that morning, Amyndra and her two comrades of Broon had ridden with the First Horse, looking every bit the equal of the elites. Despite the loss of many from their ranks on Bardon's doomed sea voyage, they would still pose a serious threat to the enemy. Elodi had used her *farsight* to follow them many leagues as they sped along the Great Northeast Road beneath the shadows of the Foranfae.

Reluctantly, Elodi turned away. The crowds lining the bridge had long since returned to the city, thankfully quieter since the departure of the warlock. Her eyes wandered back across the Menon River. Her forces were tasked to hold a line almost one hundred leagues wide on both sides of the Kolossos. But should the enemy break through, they would be entrapped. Elodi shuddered at the thought captured soldiers could soon be turned against the realms by the dark arts of her foe. Yet, despite the bravery and skill of her army, she believed the plight of the realms ultimately rested on Nyomae's shoulders. But Elodi was aware the secrets Nyomae sought could also work against them.

# 20. The Sky is Falling

Nyomae looked up from the scroll and rubbed her eyes. The melting wax from the candle had seeped into the cracks on the splintered tabletop to form what looked like a map. Nyomae traced the lines of red rivers meandering across the wide, wooden plain. She leaned back and looked up to the low arched ceiling of the vault. Nyomae had smiled to herself as she had stooped to gain access to the scrolls, finding herself in the same gait that had taken her across the realms while living under the shadow. But the shadow reigned no more. That had retreated, likely never to return following the words she had just read. Nyomae stretched. Draegelan was indeed a clever, most resourceful Archon. He must have been aware his physician kept a note of every word he uttered during his fever. Even in his debilitated state, he had devised a way to impart the location of knowledge he dared not take to his funeral pyre.

On arriving at the library of Neverdor, Nyomae had quickly solved the first clue in the test devised by Draegelan. The word he had inserted into the rhyme led Nyomae to a scroll beneath the West Window in Neverdor's library. She simply had to count down the shelves, then along the partitions to find the one Draegelan wished to be found. His plan required trust in the archivists of Neverdor to maintain strict order. And mercifully, it was a role in which they took great pride. It had not taken Nyomae long to unlock the meaning of Draegelan's misplaced word in the rhyme: *Gwylmadoc.* The age-old celebration took place in West Haven on the eighth day of the eighth month. And this turned out to be the shelf and scroll's position situated under the West Window of the library. It was a remarkably simple code, too simple for many minds liable to overthink the conundrum and miss the solution.

Nyomae spent a moment reviewing what she had seen. The scroll did not reveal how Draegelan believed he could defeat Ormoroth, but rather referenced a renowned recluse named Aber. Nyomae was acquainted with the cautionary tale of Aber's troubled life, yet she had always failed to locate the man's Verses, sited far back in the Song before Draegelan's reign. But Nyomae's powers had grown of late. Whether it was her study of Draegelan's scrolls, or the confrontation with the warlock's *kruul* awakening her innate powers, she could not determine. It may have been due to sitting in the library where Aber spent much of his youth, but on entering the Song, she was astounded to locate Aber's Verses with ease.

Nyomae observed the young man as he stood before Imaari seniors seated around a table in Neverdor. The vision was blurred by the passage of time, but Nyomae could sense Aber's desperation as he pleaded with the Order to heed his words. He claimed to have found the last known Maidens' Verse before their capitulation to the Evil One. Later to become known as Aber's Verse, it appeared nothing more than an addition to the Song of Creation. The Imaari held it served solely to bring forth new lifeforms, including birds, and trees that held onto their leaves in the cold, northern climes. But Aber was not convinced. Nyomae watched him pacing the room, waving his arms, arguing it was out of place, situated much later in the Song than others of a similar nature. And despite his lowly status in the Order, he did not relent in the face of the stubborn Imaari. Nyomae listened to his passionate words as he explained the Verse must serve another purpose, and at the very least, required further scrutiny.

Finally, one at the table agreed. And as was the tradition of the day, one was sufficient to act. But if Aber felt his speculation was vindicated, he was wrong. His colleagues took up his challenge, but none came to the same conclusion. And to Aber's protestations, the Verse was dismissed, and while not insignificant, it did not warrant taking any more of their time.

Nyomae moved to Aber's later Verses. In frustration, he had abandoned his studies at Neverdor and headed north. Her heart lurched as she saw him hunched over a candle, shivering in a cave hidden away in the remote coastal mountains of Lunn. The walls were covered with writing, but she could not see clearly to read his scrawled words. Her vision faded as Aber himself weakened and eventually died. He had never returned, living as a hermit, absorbed on the Verse, unaware that it would one day carry his name.

Nyomae sat back. Would their plight be different if others had spent longer listening to him? Many years later, a young Draegelan, intrigued by the tale, had discovered the cave and Aber's life's work. On becoming Archon, Draegelan sanctioned the building of a new library named after the hermit. At that time, it was to recognize Aber's dedication to a life of study and his willingness to question accepted wisdom. Later, Abernost became the Second Seat of Learning, as Draegelan came to appreciate the full implication of the man's work. And from that day on, those inducted into the Order were set the task of exploring Aber's Verse.

Nyomae recalled how the prose had seemed out of place compared to corresponding Verses. But she had struggled to find what secrets Aber believed lay within. When other pressing matters of the day demanded her attention, the Verse had been set aside. But now she understood what had roused the curiosity of both Aber and the Archon.

Draegelan had come to the same conclusion as Aber: the lines of the Verse had two meanings and served two purposes. The Maidens had hidden a message within the Verse. Aber named it the Maidens' Cypher. Yet Draegelan wrote only of the accepted interpretation of the first line: the creation of a songbird. But what caught Nyomae's eye was yet another supposed error. And the name out of place also referred to a childhood rhyme.

Nyomae knew this to be Draegelan's second riddle; a test to ensure the hidden knowledge would not find its way into the wrong hands. She recalled singing the rhyme on her father's lap. It told the tragic story of a bird tricked by her mischievous brother. Jealous of her ability to fly higher than other birds, he had convinced her that the sky was falling, and she alone could keep it at bay. All day, and all night, she hovered in the thin air above the mountains to keep the sky from crashing onto the land. And when she could fly no more, the exhausted bird had plummeted to the ground. When she awoke and all about her was black, she believed the world had ended due to her failure. But unknown to her, she had tumbled down a crevice and lay in a deep cavern. Thus, the bird spent the rest of her days alone in the dark, consumed by guilt, never to fly again. While the young Nyomae had felt sorry for the bird's plight, she had learned the intended lesson. But Draegelan's reference to the rhyme was not to warn of the dangers of believing the word of others without question.

Nyomae entered the Song and found Aber's Verse. Her spine tingled as the Maidens voices sang the Verse familiar to all who had studied it. But she had not ventured so far back to listen to the accepted meaning. Nyomae whispered the bird's name, Avisia. She held her breath as the Maidens' voices changed to sing a different Verse. The new song was solely for the ears of Nyomae and her kind, hidden to evade detection from those determined to corrupt the Maidens' words to serve their own ends.

Nyomae understood the purpose of the new harmony — it was to be recited to the Nym of the forests in a time of need. But for what reason, the line did not reveal.

# 21. Beware the Raven

Toryn watched the campfire imagining tongues of flame bursting from a draylok's gaping mouth. Shepra's warm body lay sleeping at his side. He stroked her back, feeling her pain for the loss of her family. How could a dog begin to understand the cruel acts of the Nordleng? He mulled over the contents of Elodi's message that had arrived at first light. While he was troubled by the news of the Ruuk crossing the Keld, Toryn was relieved to hear the forces of Archonholm had finally mobilized and were heading north. But it was the news Elodi had included of Nyomae's discovery at Neverdor that intrigued him. Toryn had failed to locate Nyomae in the Song, but now he understood why. Nyomae was preoccupied with her studies. The exact details could not be divulged in the message for fear of interception, but Elodi had hinted Nyomae had made progress. And that was most welcome. A gnawing feeling in Toryn's gut had plagued him the farther they had ridden into Emryst. But he wondered whether it was due to the proximity of Telamir. Ever since he had seen the tower with the *farsight*, he knew a power resided within its intricate, twisted structure. Little was known about the towers of Telamir and Syris as none had yet to find a way inside. Their architects and builders had easily surpassed the skills of even the age of Draegelan, and they must have had their reasons to prevent entry. But in his heart, he knew those secrets would be key to the survival of the realms.

Toryn looked to the dark peaks of the Kolossos Mountains just visible against the night sky. If unhindered, by late the following day, he would see the wonder of

Telamir with his own eyes. Could the Amayans have entered the tower? Appointed to guard the Amanach, Nyomae believed they could have descended from the elder race of the stones. And now Eryn and her companions had recovered much of their memories, perhaps they could access such places. It would make the perfect hideaway to escape the attention of the Nordleng. And it would explain their absence from the Song if the towers offered protection.

Gundrul chuckled as he sat beside the fire. 'The lass has taken quite a shine to you.' He tickled the dog's ear. 'Looks like we've got ourselves a new recruit.'

Toryn looked down as Shepra lifted her head. 'Do you have much experience with the Nordleng, Captain?'

His mouth curled. 'I can't say I've come across them often, but I remember every confrontation. Both skilled and devious. Not a pleasant combination. But can't say I've ever looked one in the eye. Always hooded and showed little of their face.'

'If I was capable of doing what they did to that family, I'd not want to show mine either.' Shepra laid down and rested her head on Toryn's lap. He looked to the twinkling lights of Cafra to the north. 'The Amayans reckon the numbers of Nordleng are rising. That, or they're coming south more often these days.'

The captain mumbled. 'Not good news, eh. But when did we last have something to cheer about?'

Toryn lifted the meat from the fire. 'Rabbit's done.' He pulled off a piece, blew on it, and dropped it beside Shepra. 'At least Elodi—'

'That's Lady Harlyn to you and I, lad. I'm not blind. I can see you two have… something else going on. But all the same.'

'Yes… yes of course. Well at least Lady Harlyn has taken over from Kernlow.'

Gundrul nodded. 'Best keep it formal, eh. Can't get too familiar with those in command… well, not in front of the common soldier.'

Toryn sighed. 'I suppose it's—' Shepra sprang from Toryn's lap. She sniffed the air and whimpered. He stroked her back. 'What is it, lass?' He glanced to Gundrul. 'I wonder what's caught her—' He ducked. The campfires spluttered and died. Toryn clutched his stomach. He yelled through a clenched jaw. 'We're under attack!'

Gundrul clambered to his feet and drew his sword. 'Where from?' He scanned the nearby trees. 'Can't see a thing. Elrik! Lorek! Light the torches.' The company formed a circle, standing back-to-back. Gundrul paced the perimeter. 'Toryn? What do you see?'

'Nothing. Whatever it was has gone.'

But the captain remained wary. 'Stay ready, lads. I don't like this one bit.' Then to Toryn. 'Nordleng?'

'No. Worse. Ul-dalak I reckon.' He looked to the trees. 'They must have a fast horse. My stomach is easing. They've gone, long gone.'

Gundrul grunted. 'Stand down. Set those torches twenty paces out and keep your eyes open. We'll have four on watch tonight.' He placed an arm around Toryn's shoulders and walked him away from the company. 'You're sure it was one of them wykes?'

'Certain. I've met two, and each time my gut turns over.' Toryn watched the flames take hold as the torches were lit. 'Are they tracking us?'

'They'd have to be incredibly lucky to stumble upon us in this wide land. Or… they can find you in this Song of yours.'

Toryn groaned. 'That could explain it. Unfortunately, I don't yet know how to locate *them*. If I could, it would give us more warning next time.'

'Then the next question is… why are they tracking us?

Are they preparing a trap? We don't need you falling into their hands. We have enough to worry about with three wykes as it is.'

'Captain.' Janae approached with a bird on her arm. 'She'll be in Archonholm by noon tomorrow at the latest.' She handed the captain the tiny scroll. 'Just need your message and I'll send her on her way.'

Gundrul handed the scroll and pen to Toryn. 'Perhaps it's best if you chose the words to inform the good lady. I may have learned some fancy new ones in her presence, but I still can't claim to be a scribe as such. So, I'll leave it—'

Toryn froze. Shepra barked. The horses reared and screamed. Gundrul's lips moved but Toryn heard no words. The flames flickered green. A pain shot through the back of his head. He spun around. But the threat came not from behind, but from above. Toryn staggered back as a hideous, dark shape passed in front of the moon and shot straight at him. He threw himself to the ground as the beast swooped overhead, freezing and fouling the air with a stench that burned Toryn's throat. He twisted onto his back and saw the grotesque, over-sized outline of a bird resembling a raven. It wheeled, squawking its deadly threat at Toryn. A cloaked figure sat on its back: Uleva. Toryn could see her clearly as the beast circled the company. This time there was no disguise, no tragic, but beautiful face suffering from the injustice of her possession. Uleva's malicious grin stretched the skin across her large skull, and as the raven veered sharply, her hair flailed as if the very whips of the drayloks lashed out at the night sky.

Toryn stood. Nearby, the horses tore at their tethers but could not escape. The large claws of the bird would quickly kill or maim many, and without them their mission would surely fail. He yelled. 'Elrik! Get the horses to the trees.' But he could not be sure his voice carried. Around him, the company laid flat on their faces. He had to act.

Toryn bowed his head and entered the Song. Above, the bird turned, lining up for another dive. Its dark, beady eyes fixed on him. And Toryn knew its name: a corvraak. In the same manner the droog was a corruption of the humble earthworm, the corvraak was a perversion of the noble raven. But the beast despised the open skies. To fly was torture, but the desire to inflict pain on its prey bested its suffering.

The corvraak screeched as it dived. But this time Toryn held his ground. He braced, letting the heat from his stomach spread to his limbs. The company and horses now appeared frozen in time as the monstrous bird loomed large. But it was the creature on its back that demanded his attention. The moon glistened in Uleva's large eyes. The black orbs shot a glance that would have sent him cowering to his knees not long past. But Toryn drew strength from the Imaari who had gone before him. Uleva cackled, taunting her intended victim. *Fool! Do you think you can—?* But Toryn met her glare without fear. He felt the presence of Nyomae at his side. Uleva gawped, leaning back to pull her mount out of its dive. The foul air rushed past Toryn as he turned to watch them go. Uleva glanced once more over her shoulder. He knew she sensed his growing power, and she was taken aback. A wry smile crossed his lips. She would not take him so lightly now.

Toryn kept his eyes on the grotesque silhouette as it shrank to an insignificant dot as if swallowed by the moon. He had stated his aim, sending a message to Uleva and her kind. But how would they respond? Had he forced their hand? He turned to those of his company lifting their faces from the ground, staring wide-eyed to the skies. Toryn sensed their terror. If the Five Realms had any chance of winning this war, he and Nyomae had to convince them they could resist.

# 22. The Battle for the Skies

The cool air rising from the gorge was most welcome. Elodi stood upon the spot where her father was bundled off the bridge. She still could not bring herself to look down to where he met his death hundreds of feet below, and part of her wished the Castellan had lived so he could face trial. She tipped back her head and drank in the fresh air. The stifling heat of the Great Hall had felt like a hot, wet towel draped over her as she held meetings with the generals yet to lead their forces north. Elodi had declined the offer to dine with Lord Kernlow, preferring to escape the cloying air of the citadel. The sun had bid farewell an hour ago, but the warmth looked set to continue its reign through the night and following days. She dearly wished she could remain on the bridge and delay returning to the stuffy halls until autumn. Elodi was a child of the north, accustomed to freezing winters and mild summers. But it was not only the cooler climes of the north that tempted her to leave. Each day since the departure of her forces, she had stood upon the North Terrace and searched for signs of Nyomae and Toryn. Her *farsight* was not as developed as the Imaari, her true powers lay elsewhere, but from the little she could perceive of their progress, she knew she would be leaving Archonholm soon. Sea Mist was also restless in his small stable. The opportunities to ride were limited with her new role, but he would not tolerate another on his back. She visited him when time allowed, ensuring he would be ready to ride out at a moment's notice.

The sky flickered. Elodi looked up as thunder rumbled in the south beyond the mountain wall. Not so long ago she had mistaken Uluriel's sabotage of the Archon's Tower for thunder. But back then, they had been oblivious to the wiles of their enemy, convinced the danger came from an unseen foe in the south. And they had walked right into Uleva's trap and placed their full strength to the Caerwal Gate. Yet all the while, the true threat had lain at their backs.

Elodi's fingers numbed. She glanced down to find she grasped the rail so tight she could almost rip it free of its supports. Another flash. She flinched as lighting skimmed across the sky. Her father had told her it was the gods fighting their battles beyond the dome encasing their land. But all knew that tale was not true. The gods had long abandoned them, leaving them to stand against the darkness alone. But whoever disputed the skies today, lay down their claim with renewed vigor. The night briefly became day as lighting flashed so bright, Elodi believed she could hear it crackle. The breeze picked up and blew the hair from her face. She ducked as more joined the battle above, swinging their great blades with such force, the sky would surely shatter. She turned to face the mountains as another barrage discharged over the Caerwals. The peaks appeared taller, but another flare revealed what she thought were mountains were menacing, dark clouds. Elodi shuddered, reminded of the storm that had almost dragged the *Celesta* to the bottom of the Elessyn Sea.

The clouds gathered, piling ever higher until they had the strength to cross the Caerwals. Elodi edged back. The storm clouds poised as a gigantic wave ready to break over the mountains and topple Archonholm's towers. She watched spellbound, full of admiration for the strategy. This was not to be a reckless attack. The gods took their time, sending their vanguard to weaken the fortress before committing themselves to the battle.

Another crack of thunder tore through the pass, crashing over Elodi's head to hurtle north. It rumbled and echoed, rolling over the land of Holm bringing the fear of the old world to the mortals beneath. Elodi decided that was her cue to seek shelter. She turned her back on the attack and strode towards the citadel. The assault commenced as the clouds unleashed their first deluge. She shuddered as the driven hail struck like arrows at her back. Her soaked dress clung to her body like a sheet of ice. But Elodi laughed as she ran, splashing like a child through the puddles turning silver under the lightning.

Elodi reached the gate where others had taken refuge. The mountain wall suddenly looked small as the storm launched lightning bolts as if trying to break the age-old defense. Then, as fast as it had arrived, the storm passed them by to vent its fury elsewhere. Elodi stood dripping and shivering as the stars returned to glimmer in the calm, clear skies and restore order. She listened to the rumblings fade as the storm swept over the Foranfae, dearly wishing she could command such power to drive north and crush their foes. Elodi smiled to herself. She had survived the attention of the gods of the deep onboard the *Celestra*, and now the gods of the skies had taken their aim and had also failed to defeat her.

Dried and refreshed from her ordeal, Elodi sat at the desk in her room. As was his habit, Lord Kernlow had retired early, leaving her the remainder of the evening alone. She looked at the two messages that had arrived late that afternoon. Nyomae's note was brief. Neverdor had delivered what she needed, and she now headed for the second library. Wary of enemy hawks, Nyomae had not mentioned Abernost by name. And following Toryn's account of a giant bird, Elodi appreciated her caution. Her eyes wandered back to Toryn's message. It did not make for a good read on which to go to one's bed. But at least she now knew how Uleva had been able to find Toryn in Foranfae only days after the assault on Calerdorn. But how many of these foul corvraak beasts did their foe possess? If these creatures held dominion over the skies, Elodi's ability to send messages would be compromised. Could they be brought down by archers? She must act now, taking the risk to send her own birds to inform her forces of the need for skilled archers.

Elodi placed her candle beside the bed and opened the box Wendel had given to her on the *Celestra* before he died. The plan revealing the secret entrance to Calerdorn was always at the back of her mind. She had devised numerous ways to exploit it, but had to remain patient as it would be months before she could be in a position to retake her city… if at all.

She lay down and closed her eyes. Immediately, Kernlow's map appeared. The thick embroidered spine of the Kolossos split the land in two as it did her mind. Would the enemy strike down the west or east side? Or worse, did they have the strength for a simultaneous attack?

The knock at the door startled her. The plan of Calerdorn fell from her hands. She had been asleep, dreaming of the moment she would win back her city. 'Ma'am?' Her guard spoke through the door. 'Marrick requests an audience. Should I allow him entry at this late hour?'

'Just a moment, please.' She slid from the bed, picked up the plan and placed it back in the box. 'Coming.' Elodi threw her gown over her shoulders. 'Yes. Please allow him to enter.' The door opened. Kernlow's new adviser hurried in.

'Apologies, ma'am, but I believe you'd want to see this.' He held out a leather tube used by the birds. 'It arrived minutes ago. I was about to place it with the rest for tomorrow's meeting, when I noticed it came from Garamund.'

'Garamund? We've not received word from them in weeks.'

'Exactly, ma'am. I assumed it would be remiss of me not to bring it to your immediate attention.'

'You assumed correctly, Marrick. Thank you.' She broke the seal and slipped out the message. Elodi reached for the candle. Her hand shook as she read the note. She looked to Marrick. 'A ship! A ship has been sighted off their coast?'

'One of ours? Perhaps a survivor of Bardon's fleet?'

Elodi re-read the message. Her heart hammered in her ears. 'No. It appears not. From what they can tell, it's barely seaworthy, and cannot be one built in Caermund.' She let the paper drop. 'Poor quality or not, it's a ship all the same. It must be from the north.'

Marrick pointed to the dispatch. 'May I, ma'am?' Elodi nodded. He read the message. 'This is what we feared. While Nordyn has yet to take our forests, he must have other sources of timber. Even if not the hardy wood of Ormsk, it's obviously sufficient to build a craft to bring a force south.'

Elodi sat on the bed and invited Marrick to pull up a chair. 'If this single ship is one of Nordryn's… what could be his objective? Would you sail close enough to the shore to be spotted?'

'It could be a scout ship, ma'am.'

'But if I was planning an invasion by sea, I wouldn't make my intention known. I'd stay well clear of the coast and venture in at night, maybe sending a small boat ashore to learn what I wish to know.' Her eyes settled back on the message. 'Besides, Nordryn has maps of the region at hand. Surely, he would already know of the places suitable to land a raiding party. Yet the action of this lone ship alerts the settlements along our shore.'

'Perhaps that's its purpose, ma'am? Those living in coastal regions will now be wary and fearful of an invasion. And… this ship now weighs on your mind, and thus draw our limited resources to the coast.'

'Ah yes, that could explain such a maneuver.' Elodi's heart sank. 'But there is another. One that would account for the drifting nature of its course… and as the fisherman have noted, little sign of life onboard.' Her eyes went to the flickering candle.

'Ma'am?'

Elodi looked up. 'I must leave, Marrick. Muster the last of the First Horse. I shall lead a detachment to Caermund. Send word to all the settlements along the coast of Mund. This craft must not be allowed to put ashore. They must stop it by any means possible.' Elodi reached for her sword belt and strode to the wardrobe.

'Ma'am? Am I missing something?'

She spoke over her shoulder. 'All signs point to the likelihood this may be a plague ship.'

# 23. Tower of Illusions

The encounter with the corvraak had unsettled Toryn's company, especially the horses. He had tried to reassure them the dark creature would not fly under a bright sun, but he noticed it did not prevent them from constantly checking the skies. Toryn had not slept following the incident. He had wandered to a nearby ridge to watch a great thunderstorm coming in from the south, engrossed as it hurled its rage at the Kolossos. The storm sighted its target with great flashes of lightning, then unleashed a ferocious barrage of hail and thunder, determined to shake the mountains to their foundations and topple their lofty peaks. But the ancient mountains stood defiant, dismissive of the storm's endeavors. Toryn had climbed to the highest part of the ridge to follow the path of lightning as it searched for a weakness elsewhere in the range. Then, as the clouds had departed, the snow-clad slopes had glistened under the light of the half-moon as they had done since the days of the gods. Perhaps one day they would crumble and the Evil One would be freed from his deep vault. But Toryn hoped it would take many thousands of storms before the mountains finally fell.

In the silence, Toryn had sat beneath a tree and entered the Song. He was aware of the Watchers, but they appeared to be occupied elsewhere and he had entered undetected. He recalled the vision of the corvraak and traveled back through the ages to when a fort had stood upon the ridge beneath his feet. In the early days of Draegelan, the creatures commanded the skies. Ormoroth had bred them in their hundreds to bring fear and death to the middle realms. But the bowyers accepted the challenge, crafting great bows to send their arrows faster, truer, and ever higher. In time, the corvraak numbers had dwindled until only one survived. But one was too many. Unlike droogs, the surviving corvraak had wisdom, over a thousand years of flight had shaped this cunning creature. Yet the bird recoiled from the bright sun that blinded its keen eyes and scorched its coarse feathers. Regrettably, the inferior archers and bows of the present day caused it little concern, and none could challenge its supremacy of the sky.

'You're sure it won't come back?' Toryn found Elrik rode at his side.

'Not while the sun is up.' He glanced to the dark clouds looming over the woodlands east of Cafra. 'But I can't say for sure if those would be enough to shield it.'

'Then let's hope the wind keeps them at bay. We'll be vulnerable tonight if we can't find shelter ahead.'

Toryn stood in his stirrups. 'We'll be in the shadow of Telamir by the evening. Somehow, I think the tower will protect us.'

Elrik turned back to the clouds. 'I hope for our sakes you're right. Even on a clear night with a full moon, our archers would struggle to bring that beast down.'

The afternoon passed without incident. Toryn believed the Nordleng bands were active farther south, perhaps hiding in the Ravern Hills. But Toryn's attention lay elsewhere. His anticipation grew as their horses sped ever closer to Telamir. Even from a distance, his ears pulsed as if the air carried the tower's voice, urging caution to those who dared approach. Nyomae's knowledge of its architects was scant as little could be found of their Verses. And as great as they must have been, Nyomae feared a catastrophic event had erased them from the Song. If that could happen to a race far stronger than those living today, what chance did they have if those forces responsible had returned.

Toryn looked up. Evening came on suddenly to the east of the Kolossos. The sun had dropped below the peaks to their left, casting much of Emryst into shadow. The horses slowed without instruction as if they too were curious what lay ahead. Then Toryn saw it. Two dark spearheads rose from behind a ridge, looking as if they forced their way up from the world beneath. Ten leagues still lay between them and the tower, yet the twin pinnacles sliced through the evening haze to give Toryn the impression he could reach out and touch them. He gaped. His *farsight* had not come close to revealing its majesty — and he had only seen it's crown.

Gundrul urged on the horses, but Toryn noticed even the grizzled, old captain's jaw had dropped, despite him having seen it many times. They rode on in silence as if in reverence to the ancient structure. As more emerged over the horizon, Toryn found it harder to determine the tower's shape. At times he thought its pinnacles angled towards each other, but then a second glance gave the impression they diverged like the claws of a hawk about to snatch its prey. To Toryn's wonder, its color also evaded his attempts to define. Black one moment, then perhaps silver, then gray as it merged with the sky. It was if the architects challenged the onlooker, defying their eyes to see the whole building in a single moment. And despite the twilight, it still appeared to glisten as if the sun's rays somehow penetrated the Kolossos to caress its surface.

Gundrul waved his arm above his head to bring the company to a halt. 'We'll camp here tonight. Getting too dark to see my hand in front of my face.' Toryn blinked. The lake now sat a hundred paces ahead, yet he had not noticed it before now. The tower had all but disappeared against the night sky. He slid from his horse in a trance, not feeling the ground beneath his feet. A cool, stiff breeze blew, but not even a ripple disturbed the water. The lake would not allow the tower alone to deceive visitors. It too had tricks of its own. Toryn stared. Heavy clouds bore down on the land, yet the lake chose to reflect a clear, starlit sky.

No fires were set, no supper was cooked. The company lay down where they dismounted, and let sleep carry them to far off lands.

Toryn stood at the edge of the mirror-like lake. Hamar was right. He ducked and tried several angles but could see no reflection of the immense tower. Shepra sat at his side. He stroked her head. 'Quite a sight, eh, Sheppy.' The dog's eyes widened. Toryn laughed. 'You see it don't you, girl.' He kneeled and dipped his hand in the cool water but noticed it raised barely a ripple. He turned back to Shepra who appeared keen to know more. He obliged with the little he knew. 'Many have rowed out to the tower, but none have found a way in.' Toryn tipped his head right back and could just see the twin pinnacles amid the clouds struggling to make their way around. 'Have you ever seen anything quite so tall? Apart from the Kolos—' Toryn gawped. The peaks of the Kolossos looked smaller. The mountains stood just two leagues to the west, yet in the presence of the tower they appeared half their height. But when he turned his back on the lake, the peaks assumed their lofty status.

'Don't try to make sense of it, lad. Your head will hurt.' Gundrul strode over to Toryn. He nodded to the tower. 'The whole region don't make any sense. So I say, enjoy its strangeness, marvel at that structure, but just accept it as it is.'

'Good advice, Captain.' Toryn turned back to the tower and gasped as if seeing it for the first time again.

With every viewing something changed, or he would notice a new feature, or perhaps the tower altered itself whenever people had the gall to take their eyes from its beauty. 'Imagine what this land looked like when the race that built that prevailed.' He turned away. 'And now I must see Syris. Odrun…' his head bowed, 'saw them both and believed Syris was yet more beautiful and mysterious.'

Gundrul bent to tickle Shepra. 'I've known only a handful who've seen the two, but you won't find agreement on which holds that title. But you're going to have to put your visit to Syris on hold for now. Not the time to go galivanting around the realms for a bit of sightseeing, eh.'

But Toryn had not heard the captain. He was drawn back to the tower, seeing a new twist at its base. He spoke more to himself. 'How were they built? Archonholm looks crude compared to this, and apparently even Calerdorn can't hold a candle to it.' He sighed. 'Defies belief.'

Gundrul patted his shoulder. 'Like I said. Don't try to understand, just enjoy the view.'

Toryn forced himself to look to the captain. 'But this doesn't help us find the Amayans.' He traced the outline of the lake to the opposite bank. 'I'm certain they came this way. I was hoping they'd taken refuge here. I can't explain it, but I doubt our foes could endure spending time in its shadow… even if it cast one. That tower doesn't tolerate evil.'

The captain nodded. 'I get your meaning. I can't tell for sure if it's on our side, but I'd bet my farm on the plain it would have nothing to do with our enemy.'

'A message has arrived, Captain.' They turned as Janae strolled to the lake with a bird on her arm. 'It's from Archonholm. It bears Lady Harlyn's seal.'

Gundrul thanked her and passed the note to Toryn. Toryn had an idea what it might say. He was right. 'Things are moving, Captain. The Ruuk have crossed the Kel. We can expect to see our forces riding this way in a few days. But Lady Harlyn stresses we continue with our mission. Looks like we'll be needing every available sword sooner than we would have hoped.'

# 24. CHILDREN OF THE MAIDENS

Nyomae stood at the edge of the Foranfae Forest. She glanced along the road and recognized the spot where, as Hope, she had pleaded with Toryn to take the route through the hills to avoid the eyes within the trees. And while she now understood the reason for her terror, the trepidation of entering the forest prevailed.

Nyomae instructed her riders to set up camp and await her return. She did not anticipate she would be longer than a day, but she could not know whether a day in the Foranfae would be the same as a day outside — especially as she desired to consult the Nym.

Nyomae patted her horse's nose and whispered words of encouragement, but his head bobbed as his wide eyes stared at the forest. She took a deep breath, stepped off the road and strode under the shadow of the trees. Her hope was the Nym would come if she recited the Maidens' calling. But they were of a different age, a different world, and would answer at their whim.

Nyomae calmed as she walked. She needed a clear mind to summon the Nym. She looked up to the dark ceiling high above hoping to see the sky. Night would soon be upon her, and the world outside would not wait. Her feet tingled. She stopped. This would be a suitable place. She kneeled and placed the stones selected from the hills around Neverdor in a circle. To draw the attention of the Nym, Nyomae had to create a space outside of time, much like the circle at the heart of the forest. It would take days to trek to the center, so Nyomae had to convince the Nym to come to her. Satisfied the arrangement was complete, she stood, placed her palms together and bowed her head. She slowed her breathing and felt her feet connect with the ground as if taking root, linking to the pulse deep beneath the land.

Nyomae entered the Song, easily evading the attention of the Watchers. The Present Verses streamed past as if she stood in a fast-flowing river. She opened her arms and splayed her fingers, creating a sphere of shimmering air between her hands. The globe expanded to the width of the stone circle, bathing her in a soft blue light as it rose over her head. While her feet stayed grounded in the Foranfae, her spirit in the Song floated up and entered the sphere.

She called the Nym. The Nym came, and Nyomae recited the first line of Aber's Verse.

Of the time she had spent in the company of the Nym, Nyomae struggled to recall exactly what had happened. Convinced she had spent days in the circle, she had hurried back to her escort. Yet on her return they assumed she had been unsuccessful as she had been gone not an hour. Asked if she had learned what she sought, Nyomae could not answer. She knew it would take days to at first absorb, and then more time to comprehend the knowledge the Nym had imparted. True to their nature, the Nym had spoken in riddles, flitting from one age to the next, making it difficult to determine of which age they referred. Nyomae had made it known she wished to discover more about Aber's Verse and the Maidens' Cypher. But the Nym responded with waves of consciousness that overwhelmed her senses. She had come close to collapse as the Nym had led her through thousands of years, a challenge almost beyond the limits of a mortal mind, even of her ability. But as Nyomae and her knights approached Abernost, the revelations bestowed upon her began to emerge.

The Nym had graced the land in the earliest of days. Existing in three forms within the water, forests, and mountains. The Nym of the mountains had long ago withdrawn to the foundations of the great peaks, caring little for the troubles of the surface. The Nym of the waters, chose to reside mainly in mountain streams inaccessible to most, or the lakes of Telamir and Syris, thus had little contact with the peoples of the land. But the Nym of the forests remained ever watchful, ready to intervene to protect the trees from harm.

The Nym of Foranfae had honored their pledge. They led Nyomae through the Verses to the arrival of the firstborn of the Maidens' Song.

They were the Elorym.

As the name became known to Nyomae, it awoke a deep memory. Conceived after the Maidens' struggles, the Elorym were brought into the world to heal its wounds. And at the Maidens' behest, the Nym befriended the newcomers. The Nym taught the Elorym the ways to harness the natural forces to enhance both their race and the land. They became a wise and powerful race, living for many centuries without aging until their last days. From what she could determine, perhaps Nyomae's kind and the Amayans descended from the last of the Elorym, but much weakened by the ensuing centuries of conflict with Ormoroth and his vast armies.

Nyomae recalled her journey through the Nym's Verses. For centuries, the Elorym had grown, learning the ways of the world, channeling the energy from the land to build. Their cities enriched the beauty of the Maidens' creation. With tall, glistening spires, floating gardens, waterfalls of glistening water cascading through the buildings, and trees growing from platforms connecting the structures, they easily surpassed the cities built at the height of even Draegelan's time. Neither Saphrir nor

Kalamir, the most beautiful cities of recent times, could match the work of the Elorym, seeming vulgar compared to those of their predecessors.

And of Ormoroth, the Nym had kept a watchful eye. When the gods defeated and imprisoned his Master, Ormoroth had fled and hid beneath the mountains in the lands that would become known as Nordruuk. And as the Evil One had deceived the Maidens, so Ormoroth sought to win the trust of the Elorym, thus to corrupt the Maidens' children and avenge his Master. But the Elorym had grown in stature during the years Ormoroth had plotted his revenge. Thus, he misjudged their wisdom, and they easily resisted his attempt to win over their hearts. Seeing through his disguise, they challenged Ormoroth, and his deceit was laid bare. The Elorym pursued him to the frozen wastes at the top of the world. But in the uncharted and unforgiving terrain, he evaded capture, and the Elorym gave up their chase, believing Ormoroth had perished.

But Ormoroth had outwitted his pursuers, feigning his death as if consumed by the fearsome beasts that roamed the ice in those times. And so it was, he escaped. In the century that followed, he built an ice fortress atop a great mountain that no mortal has ever set eyes upon. In the caverns beneath the mountain, Ormoroth bred a race of his own from the Dark Verses. From the hardy creatures who could endure the bitter cold of the region, he formed the fierce Norgog. Ormoroth then sent these forth to summon the dark beings driven out by the Elorym. And they came, defying the treacherous terrain to rally to his call.

Yet despite his strength, Ormoroth knew he could not defeat the Elorym with armies alone. Thus, he withdrew to his stronghold to venture deep into the Song in search of the old ways. And so it was, in the silence of his deep vault, Ormoroth unknowingly stumbled upon the means to crush the Elorym. At first, the faint, but steady pulse beating far beneath his fortress, intrigued him. But as the years passed, the constant throbbing taunted, then tortured him, evading his desire to determine its origin. The pulse became a tremor, the tremor became a quake, until it seemed to Ormoroth the very hammers of the gods pounded on the walls of his stronghold.

Driven to the brink of despair, Ormoroth raged, imploring the dark gods to aid his search and ease his torment. The Nym knew not whether the old gods had answered his plea, or whether it was the madness that consumed him, but in that moment, Ormoroth became as powerful as his Master. In the time it took a bird to flap its wing, the Song was silenced, and the harmony disrupted. Time itself faltered, allowing Ormoroth to witness the birth of the world. And so it was, he came to know that which should never be known. Ormoroth had discovered the heartbeat of the land… and the source of the Elorym's power.

Ormoroth tasked the Norgog to dig a shaft. Deeper and deeper, they burrowed until the skies became a distant memory, and the heat of the inferno sapped their strength. But Ormoroth drove them on, and the Norgog dared not to incur his wrath. Finally, they broke through the crust, releasing the hot blood that coursed through the veins of the world.

Ormoroth built a great furnace, channeling the magma to feed its fires. And in this forge, he fashioned a mighty pillar of iron, taller than the highest peaks of the Kolossos. Then he accomplished a task surpassed only by his Master at the height of his power. Twisting the Verses that formed the very foundations of the land, Ormoroth defiled the iron and bent it to his will. It was said the ground trembled as he despoiled the pure iron, cast at the dawn of time. And thus, the Angorlith was made. In the years it took Ormoroth to recover from his labor, the pillar cooled. And in that time, his warlocks drew upon its vile power and spawned a vast army thrice that of the Elorym.

Then Ormoroth struck. He drove the Angorlith down as if a great stake, impaling the deep veins beneath his fortress. The land quaked, astounding the Elorym. But they were yet strong and would not be easily defeated. Before Ormoroth could marshal his armies, the Elorym formed the stones of the Amanach. Seven were made from rock quarried from the Caerwals, yet untainted by evil hands. The seven were set along lines of power, augmenting the pulse of the land to counter the distortion of the Angorlith. Ormoroth was dismayed, but kept his anger at bay, desiring not to repeat his errors of the past. In the darkness, he labored to strengthen his great pillar of iron to drain the power of the Elorym stones. But the Amanach were strong, and Ormoroth would have to bide his time.

Under the protection of their stones, the Elorym flourished, building ever grander and greater cities, and set sail across the wide seas to discover new realms of the Maidens' making. Perhaps it was their faith in the Amanach, or the absence of Ormoroth, but the Elorym became complacent, believing their supremacy could never again be challenged. And so, to celebrate their victory over the darkness, they fashioned the Towers of the Lakes.

Through the Nym's eyes, Nyomae witnessed the height of the Elorym's craft. The immense structures rose from the lakes as if the waters spiraled high into the skies to create their intricate forms. In her state of bewilderment, it took a moment for Nyomae to realize five such towers were made. Two were lost, Cyloris and Qaamir had stood in the lakes now named Benmuir and Ravern. But of the fifth, the Nym did not divulge its location. Nyomae observed the lakes of the four known spires, formed a line across the realms running northwest to southeast straddling the Kolososs — but to what purpose? Were the lakes natural, or formed by the Elorym? Nyomae could not comprehend what could bring about the destruction of such immense towers. And where had the fifth stood? Did it yet stand?

The Nym had then revealed the tragedy leading to the Elorym's demise.

Great indeed had the Elorym become, but Ormoroth had not been idle. His armies had grown until he could no longer conceal them behind the impenetrable walls of ice surrounding his northern kingdom. But still he waited. The Amanach stones yet constrained the Angorlith's corruption, but Ormoroth knew their power diminished. The Elorym's ambition demanded ever more resources until, unbeknown to them, the balance tipped.

In the great battles that raged, both sides were devastated by losses. But Ormoroth cared not for casualties, breeding more creatures faster than the Elorym could fill the gaps in their ranks. Too late did the great ships of the Elorym answer the plea to return. By the time they made landfall, they found their cities besieged by dark forces they had not thought possible, and therefore could not defeat.

Then Nyomae came to understand why the Nym had shown her the demise of the eldest of races. In the final days as both armies were brought to the edge of destruction, the Elorym invoked the power Aber had stumbled upon many centuries later. The Nym hid the Elorym's last desperate action from Nyomae's eyes, wishing to withhold knowledge of this dreaded power. But they made it known, the Elorym had delivered a crushing blow to Ormoroth, but in the act, had consumed the last of their strength. The power sustaining their towers waned, and two collapsed.

Ormoroth retreated north, much weakened and would take centuries to recover, and even then, not to his former glory. But the cost to the Elorym had been great — too great. And once their strength failed, so did their fine structures. The cities crumbled like dying plants, withering to return to the earth from whence they came. Nyomae's heart had broken as she felt their pain and despair as Cyloris, then Qaamir shuddered and fell, sinking into the lakes without trace.

Of the Elorym, little remained. Most had perished in the terrible battles, hewn limb-from-limb by the great beasts of Ormoroth's pits. Of those who endured, many succumbed to the plagues released by their retreating foes. The few survivors mourned the loss of their kin, and devastated by the destruction of their creations, many left these shores never to return. Those who remained tried to rebuild the shattered cities, but their Verses failed, and the Elorym declined. The last of their kin wandered the land, lost, and shattered by their grief. Some strayed too far north and were enslaved by Ormoroth. Chained to the cold walls of his dungeons, he finally shattered their spirits. And so it was, these broken souls became the warlocks who would fight Draegelan in the wars to come.

Nyomae wept for their loss. The Elorym endured years of hardship and suffering, and their eventual demise laid a terrible burden on those who followed. In the ensuing centuries, Ormoroth would return like a dark wave crashing over all before him. But each time, the new realms had the strength and resolve to repel his depleted attacks. But the victories came at a cost, and Ormoroth would recover to return, just as the relentless tides of the seas.

Nyomae looked to the gray walls of Abernost in the distance. Today, the Five Realms commanded but a fraction of their predecessor's strength, struggling to hold back even the lesser forces of Ormoroth's servants. If the warlocks could by some means bring back their master… Nyomae shuddered. If they had any hope of securing their freedom, she had to find the secrets held at Abernost.

As the gates creaked open, Nyomae contemplated the last revelation from the forest. The Nym had mourned the loss of their friends, retreating to the forests, rivers and mountains, never to openly converse with the children of the land… until Draegelan. And they had shown her, what they had once disclosed to him.

Nyomae looked up to the ornate stonework on the arch over the gate. She followed in Draegelan's footsteps. The Nym had disclosed a secret of the Elorym to him, and he had chosen to conceal that knowledge. Should she attempt to uncover what he had found? But she had to know. She had to know what the Elorym and Draegelan had discovered that could possibly defeat the forces of Ormoroth. She had to know how the use of this power had destroyed the Elorym, and what led Draegelan to bury his findings. To achieve this, she must enter the Elorym vault the Nym revealed lay hidden beneath Abernost.

## 25. Upon the Shores of Mund

The towers of Caermund stood dark against the pink of the dawn sky. Elodi slowed Sea Mist to a trot. She patted his steaming neck, pleased he had matched the pace of the First Horse finest beasts. They had completed the long journey in under four days and deserved a well-earned rest. An outrider had met them the previous evening with the latest news on the ship. Mund's knights had tracked the wayward vessel as it continued to meander up and down the coast. But it had anchored off Caermund the night before and had not moved since. The crew had made no attempt to make landfall, convincing Elodi the ship's purpose was to bring the plague south. They could not succeed if the knights put them to the sword the moment they landed. A secluded inlet to put a small boat ashore would suit their purpose — two or three carriers would be sufficient to spread both fear and the plague.

The sound of the waves breaking on the sea cliffs, reminded Elodi of her room in Calerdorn. She stood in her stirrups as the horses approached the land's edge. There were few places to put even a small boat safely ashore outside of the ports of Mund. Thankfully, it appeared the knights' presence had prevented a landing, but why had the ship come so far south when the estuaries of Amman and Emryst offered easier access? She imagined the poor souls clinging to life onboard, infected with some foul disease brought on by the dark arts of the Ul-dalak. But one that progressed slow enough for the voyage, so as not to kill them before they had completed their grim mission. And perhaps the crew could be protected by the same art of the apothecaries. Yet, if they could capture one of the crew alive, the healers could determine the concoction and make an antidote.

Elodi brought the First Horse to a halt. She dismounted and stood at the edge of the cliff. She let her *farsight* take her out to sea beyond Caermund, but all she saw was the white horses racing to the shore atop of the waves driven on by the breeze.

A horse approached. 'Lady Harlyn!' A rider pointed out to sea. 'The ship sailed south in the early hours. We have reports it's dropped anchor off Frescove.'

'That lies at least ten leagues from here.' Elodi nodded to the sweating horses. 'We shall let them rest here for the morning, then head south. Have you anything more to report on the vessel?'

'Nothing I'm afraid. At your request, we sent out boats but dare not get within shouting range and risk infection. But that means we can't get close enough to see who sails her. We could get a craft of archers within range, but we don't want to set fire to the ship and sink the poor blighters if we're wrong.'

'I understand your dilemma.' Elodi looked out to sea. 'Perhaps I can help you. I shall ride south and see if I can solve this riddle from the shore.'

The ship remained anchored half a league off the small fishing port of Frescove. The locals had told Elodi of an inlet to the south favored by smugglers. And now she stood on the low cliffs overlooking the cove, Elodi was certain this was the spot they would come ashore. The captain of the town's reserve pointed to his archers on the opposite side of the inlet. 'I reckon we'd get several rounds off before they could get out of the boat, ma'am.'

'Thank you, that is reassuring.' Elodi took a few paces closer to the edge. 'Now please, Captain. Could you give me a few moments alone?' The captain nodded and withdrew. She turned to the sea. The ship lay close to the shore but was barely visible to the naked eye in the dark waters as the evening closed in. She did not need her *farsight* to determine the state of the passengers on the ship; she could sense the anguish from where she stood. But Elodi had to know for certain if they carried disease. Her vision blurred as she skimmed across the calm sea. Her body swayed as she slowed and her *farsight* arrived at the ship. The vessel was indeed poorly made, and compared to the ancient *Celestra*, looked barely seaworthy even to Elodi's untrained eye. She gasped. The deck was strewn with bodies. Some moved, but Elodi could see they were sick, starved and close to death. These were innocent folk, undeserving of the dire predicament imposed upon them. Could they be treated? A cloaked figure stumbled across the stricken souls on the deck. Their bent frame clambered over the taffrail and took a seat on a small craft lashed to the side. The occupant struggled with the ropes but managed to lower the boat to the sea. Elodi could not see the rower's face, but it was obvious they were very weak and anxious of making even the shortest journey across the water.

Elodi stepped back and let her eyes adjust. The captain stood close by. She pointed. 'One is coming ashore. A man I believe, but very frail.' The boat moved slowly towards them as the rower labored to maintain a straight line in the current.

The captain cleared his throat. 'Shall I instruct my archers to let loose a warning, ma'am?'

'No wait.' She held out her hand. 'May I borrow your lantern?'

He nodded. 'Certainly, ma'am. But you can't be thinking of going to greet him?'

'That I am. If they intended to spread a plague, I would have thought more would come. And surely, they can see our lights. If it were my wish to infect the realm, I would have waited until the dead of night. I shall go and meet him but maintain a safe distance. You wait with your archers, Captain. I'll wave my lantern should I wish you to… intervene.'

Elodi made her way down the rocky path to the pebble beach. She walked out to the shore as the boat grounded. The man climbed out, staggered, then fell into the water. Elodi's heart went out to him, but she stopped herself from going to his aid. He recovered his footing and took hold of the rope. But the task of pulling the craft onto the beach proved too much. He gave up and dropped the rope. Elodi waited with her hand on her sword. Yet she doubted the poor soul could take many more steps as he slipped and stumbled on the wet stones.

Elodi called out. 'Stop right there. Please do not take another step.' The man straightened as best he could, but his wet cloak looked too bulky for his thin body to support. She shuffled a little closer and held out her lamp. 'You have landed in Mund, Ward of Farrand. I am Lady Harlyn, leader of the Armies of the Five Realms.' As she said the words, they sounded hollow, perhaps insignificant for the situation.

The man lifted his head and coughed, bending double as pain wracked his feeble frame. Elodi took a breath. 'State your purpose. Twelve archers have you in their aim. State your purpose or return to your ship and leave these shores never to return.'

He coughed once more. Then stood and lifted his hood. He squinted and croaked. 'Elodi? Is that you?'

She stared and took another step. Damp, gray hair clung to his head. The light from her lantern reached his face. He was painfully thin. His eye sockets were so deep she could barely make out his eyes. But she knew him. 'Bardon?'

The man nodded and sagged to his knees. His arms hung limp at his sides as all his strength deserted him. He sobbed. Elodi rushed to him as he fell into her arms. Tears streamed down her face. 'You survived! You've come back.' But Bardon could not answer. He slumped against her, weighing little more than a child. Elodi gaped at his gaunt face. He appeared to have aged twenty years since the moment she had bade him farewell at the Menon Gate. Back then he had stood strong and tall, looking the right man to command the Elites. Yet now, he lay in her arms looking like a sick child wearing his father's robe.

# 26. Song of the Lark

Nyomae's memory of her time spent in Abernost seemed to be from another life, in another time. Her last visit had been fifty years prior to the battle on the Gormadon Plain. She had come to consult Idraman on routine matters concerning the Order. Draegelan's decree prohibiting Imaari from studying the divided set of scrolls still stood. Therefore, Nyomae was not permitted to read those housed in the libraries, or question Idraman on his own work unless all were present. But back then, they had felt no immediate threat. Their studies seemed more of an academic pursuit as none predicted the return of the dark forces could happen so soon.

Nyomae looked out of the arched window. How had they missed the early signs of the gathering storm? Had they been so entrenched in their arcane research they had neglected to keep an eye on the real world? At first, reports of shrouls and the odd droog had been dismissed as the tall tales of the superstitious folk at the borders. Perhaps the long centuries of peace following Ormoroth's defeat had made life too comfortable, and they had become complacent.

Nyomae's eyes wandered to the low hills outside Abernost. The Ul-dalak had been patient. Not all Ormoroth's commanders had perished at Talaghir. Perhaps anticipating the outcome, he had sent many north to escape Dorlan's wrath. The warlocks had retreated to their strongholds concealed by the great ice sheets of Nordruuk. And in their cold, bleak halls they had planned for the day they would return and avenge Ormoroth. They had outsmarted the Imaari, slowly increasing the number of raids, slowly revealing their hand to tempt Sylvena to seek the relic she believed would aid their salvation. They had yet to show their faces on the battlefields of the recent conflict, but a warlock's *kruul* had entered Archonholm. And Nyomae was convinced more than one was active. Uluriel was powerful, but could she command the *Draedalak* alone at Gormadon? And her hold over one as strong as Mordram could not have been maintained for so long without aid. But this did not explain the warlocks' absence from the battles to date. Surely, they would already be massing on the borders of Farrand had they led the Ruuk.

Nyomae's heart sank. Did they strive in their ice-bound lands to bring back Ormoroth? If successful, the Five Realms would inevitably fall regardless of Nyomae's efforts. Their only hope lay in defeating the Ul-dalak, then by some means thwarting the warlocks' effort to free their Master. If the realms had any chance of resisting, she had to solve the secrets within the Maiden's Cypher. But the risks could not be clearer. The Elorym had misused that power causing their own downfall, and Draegelan had deemed it too dangerous to wield, deciding instead to bury his discovery. But he had left a path to this knowledge, perhaps fearing a time when no other way lay open. And Nyomae believed that time was nigh. She had to unlock Draegelan's second safeguard.

Nyomae massaged her temples. The distinctive scrawl of his hand drew her tired eyes across the page. Draegelan's prose was poetic, and not the dry, scholastic style favored by the Imaari. Nyomae smiled to herself. Before the years she lived under the shadow, she had been very much a serious scholar caring little for the poets of the day. But her time wandering the lands in her confusion had opened her eyes to things that would previously have gone unseen. Had her imposed exile enhanced her mind?

Nyomae sat back and let Draegelan's words flow through her. The words changed into his mellow voice in her head. She watched captivated as the green grasslands took shape beneath a vast, blue sky. The Maidens sang. Tears filled her eyes as she marveled at their voices and the purity of their hearts. In the blue expanse, a shape emerged. Nyomae smiled as the Maiden's created the first skylark. Not blessed with the beauty of other birds gracing the skies, the gray, unassuming bird was gifted with a song to bring joy to the hearts of those who would follow. Nyomae sighed as the skylark first warbled its long, melodious song, hovering above meadows bursting with the wildflowers sown by the Maidens' hands.

But alas, the songbird's life was not to be one of tranquility. It was the skylark who first sensed the disharmony despoiling the Maidens' Song. When they finally heeded her warning of the Evil One's purpose, they bestowed upon her a most vital role. The lark was taught another song, not for the skies, but for those in times of need. Nyomae tilted her head. Another melody emerged as if an echo.

She understood. The second answer was not a word: it was the lark's secret song. Nyomae retreated and sat back. She had the key. Now came the dilemma. Should she enter Aber's Verse and read the second line? Nyomae had no choice. She closed her eyes and recalled the songbird's melody. Her vision blurred as the harmony merged with Aber's words. Before her eyes, the line faded, then reappeared in a different form — a form revealing the location and key to the Elorym's vault.

The clash of swords outside brought her to her feet. But the contest in the corridor was not a close match. Metal tore at flesh and the brief conflict was over. Nyomae faced the door as it burst open. Six Nordleng barged in.

Nyomae held her ground. 'You'll need more than six swords to kill me!'

Their leader threw back his hood. He grinned, baring yellowing teeth through a thick, black beard. The Nordleng struggled with the common tongue, but the threat was obvious. 'We're not here to kill you, *witch*. We're here to take you on a long journey.'

Nyomae slowed her breathing. 'Then you still failed to bring enough men.' She entered the Song while turning to meet the eyes of each of the six. The Nordleng appeared frozen as she found their Verses in turn. All bar the leader was no older than thirty summers, making it easy to find their Maidens' Name. The leader's Verse had protection from the Ul-dalak, requiring a different tactic. For now, she focused on the five. It would take a great deal of her strength to undo their existence by reciting their names, strength she needed for the months ahead. No. There was an easier way. Nyomae grinned to herself as she imagined the outcome. She circled her hands, conjuring up images of her would-be captors as young boys. She watched their motionless faces. They would see a blur as her arms moved, already casting doubt in their minds.

Nyomae removed the last twenty-five years of their Verses — a simple task for one so strong against those so weak. She stayed in the Song, turning back to the leader. His expression had changed. He existed in a different time to his underlings. He appeared to have guessed her action and would be ready when she returned to his time. Nyomae decided on an old Imaari trick she had learned from her early days in the Order. It was simple, but effective, and hopefully one the Nordleng had not previously seen. She quickly found what she needed.

Nyomae stepped out of the Song. The five Nordleng dropped their swords, stared at the strange witch-woman, then ran from the room like the frightened children they had become. The leader scoffed and raised his sword. 'You'll need to try harder—' She unleashed the lightning bolt from the recent storm, followed by a deafening crack of thunder. It worked. The dazed leader staggered back as the light burst through the windows. Nyomae lunged and snatched the sword from his loosened grip. Without a second thought, she grasped the handle and ran him through. She did not kill by choice, but the Nordleng had offered no quarter to any of his victims, so Nyomae reasoned he deserved the same.

She let the sword drop and strolled from the room. Outside, she found the bodies of three library attendants. There would be more victims of these brutal servants of the Ul-dalak, but thankfully their objective had been to kidnap Nyomae and not to slaughter the people of Abernost. The five she had sent back to their childhood cowered in the corner as two guards approached.

'Let them be.' Nyomae raised her hand. 'Have pity. They are but innocent children now in adult bodies. With care, they can be educated and trained to do tasks about the library or sent to work on the farms.' She stood over the huddle of confused Nordleng. 'Perhaps they can do something to atone for their actions. Thankfully, they will have no memory of them. But be wary, many in these parts will.'

# 27. Island of Troubled Souls

'As we approached the East Watchtower, the Karajan was as flat as the marshes of Lumreek.' The flames flickered in Bardon's yellow eyes. 'I had never set eyes on the Archon's sea defenses, but the sailors informed me we would see the giant waves long before we'd be upon it.' Elodi clutched his hand. It remained cold despite spending the evening wrapped in blankets and huddled beside the fire. The innkeeper of the single hostelry in Frescove was reluctant at first to grant them entry. But Elodi had assured him Lord Broon was simply exhausted and malnourished, and not a carrier of the plague. But it had taken three gold coins to finally convince the man.

Bardon kept his eyes on the fire. 'Reassured, I assumed the Archon had calmed the seas to allow us passage.' His head dropped. 'But as we drew level with the tower, a terrible churning of the waters began. From what you tell me of Uluriel's possession, it's now obvious it was our enemy who controlled the seas. They must have waited until our fleet sailed into the trap… and then stir the currents.' His voice broke. 'The sea reared up in places and sank in others. Many ships were sucked into whirlpools.' He shivered, pulling the blanket closer to his chest. 'It's a terrible sight to see a large ship swallowed into a maelstrom so deep you can almost see the ocean floor. The doomed crew tried in vain to stay afloat, briefly sailing on its steep sides, but many fell from the decks into the darkness below.' His jaw clenched. 'We lost so many… so many good souls. Ships drawn close to the edges disappeared without trace with all hands lost. Those of us avoiding those perilous pits, by sheer luck I may add, were lashed by gigantic walls of water. The waves stacked so high they shut out the sky, growing ever taller until they toppled over, crashing onto decks, smashing galleons to matchsticks in seconds.' Bardon shook as he relived the carnage. 'I'm afraid General Kragan's ship was among the first to be lost.'

Elodi chilled at the memory of the storm on the Elyssen Sea. 'How did you survive?'

'We fortunate few who kept our masts and had some sails to speak of, were blown farther east. The more experienced skippers managed with great skill to navigate the waves and steer a course clear of those terrifying whirlpools. But we couldn't escape the clutches of the undercurrents. It was if hands beneath the waters dragged us towards the rocky headlands and cliffs of Mundrake's Isle.' Elodi's grip softened. *Plague Isle.* Had she made a terrible mistake? Bardon continued. 'Of the dozen or so ships that escaped the violent waters, I saw four come to grief on the rocks. The sea is so cruel. They'd survived the worst only to be tossed overboard in sight of shore. They were at the mercy of the waves which mercilessly dashed them against the rocks or dragged them to the bottom.' His shaking hand went to his face. 'Just eleven of the forty-four ships leaving Caermund made landfall on Mundrake's Isle. Although landfall is not the right word, hurled more like. Yes, we were hurled onto the few beaches along the shore. Of these only one ship remained in a state we could possibly repair.' He nodded over his shoulder. 'And as you saw, it's hardly what you'd call seaworthy.'

Elodi rested her hand on his shoulder. 'You must have been on that island for the best part of two months.'

He shuddered. 'And like you, I too was familiar with the tales of Plague Isle… as many refer to it. And I can tell you now, it thoroughly deserves that unwholesome name.

It is indeed a bleak and lifeless place as the stories tell. It's surrounded by the warm seas of the south and should be a land teeming with life. Yet… it's as if the island has drifted in from the north, clinging to the cold, defying the southern climes to melt its icy heart. If it wasn't enough to banish those suffering from the plague from their homes, they had to spend their last, miserable days in that place. Little can live on that wind-battered isle other than insects that drain your blood with a greed belying their size. Storms blow in from the Karajan with monotonous regularity, and when they take their misery elsewhere, the constant chill wind offers little solace. And there's no shelter to be had. Once away from the cliffs, the land is mainly flat, consisting of marshes swarming with midges and those nasty hornrasps. And where the marshes relent, it's rocky land is smothered with thick, flowerless gorse. And their sharp thorns would sooner tear you to shreds than allow you to shelter beneath. It seems the whole isle wishes you dead.'

Elodi rubbed his shivering shoulders. 'But you survived. And you say at least a thousand still live?'

Bardon let out a long sigh. 'More than twice that made it ashore.' His voice wavered. 'If we thought making landfall was the end of our ordeal, we were to be bitterly disappointed.' He cleared his throat and straightened. For a moment, Elodi saw Bardon as she had known him, but the effort soon drained him, and he shrank into the chair. 'It is a gloomy place. Even the sun shuns the isle. We made our way inland in a desperate attempt to shelter from the wind. At first, we thought our luck had changed as we found a small settlement of ramshackle huts. They were on the west side of a ridge, affording us some respite from the gales.'

'Settlement? But I thought—'

'Built, no doubt, by those unfortunate to somehow

survive the plague.'

Elodi's heart sank. 'Survived? And there was no way back. What a terrible way to exist.'

'But exist they did, and for a number of years.' He shook his head. 'If the poor souls hadn't suffered enough, they then had to endure having their flesh torn off in chunks by hornrasps, and then ripped to pieces by the thorns. Those recovering from the curse must have soon envied the dead.'

Elodi stared at the fire. 'I can't begin to imagine the lives of those poor wretches.'

'They were resourceful, I'll give them that. They had to be to scrape a living in that dreaded place. Yet they still went to the trouble of burying their dead with dignity. It must have been a struggle to dig graves with their bare hands, and then in the few places the soil was deep enough.' Bardon groaned as he reached for his cup. 'Over the next few days, more survivors washed up among the many dead. Understandably, none wanted to live in the huts inhabited by plague exiles. We set up our own camps, building huts as best we could with the wreckage from the ships. We had enough food for two weeks or so, but when that ran out, we did our best to fish, or shoot down the few birds foolish enough to approach the coast. But tellingly, few do. And… I'm afraid, we had no choice but to eat the few horses that survived.' Bardon winced. 'Yes, it was not agreeable to us, but we had little fodder for them, and the horses became uncontrollable at night. We lost a few who ran over the clifftops in their panic.' His hands clenched his cup. 'A frightened horse makes a sorrowful sound. The fear soon spreads to all in earshot.'

Bardon straightened. 'But we still had hope in our hearts in those early days. We numbered around two and a half thousand in total, which was more than I could have expected. But alas, that means close to ten thousand perished and yet lie at the bottom of the sea. So many fine people gone for good, betrayed and lost in the most horrifying of ways, unable to fight back. All those souls lost without trace or glory.'

Elodi patted his knee. 'Then we shall ensure their sacrifice does not go untold.' But as soon as she spoke the words, she heard how hollow her promise sounded.

Bardon looked to Elodi for the first time since recounting his tale. 'To think we stood beside the Archon with Uluriel inside his head. And… we stopped him leaping from his tower.'

She grasped his cold hands. 'Not a day passes when I don't think what might have happened had we not intervened. But we weren't to know. Uluriel deceived us all.' She refilled his cup, daring to ask her next question. 'How did you lose so many after you landed? Did they starve?'

His gaze went back to the flames. 'Not all the far-fetched rumors of that isle are… so far-fetched.' He took a deep breath. 'We set about repairing the ship least damaged by the rocks. But few of us had the necessary skills. Thus, the work was painstakingly slow with many mistakes made. And, after what we'd experienced, all were wary of setting sail in a makeshift ship. Mund's shoreline is dominated by cliffs more than ready to lure a wayward vessel to be dashed on its rocks. And yes, sadly, the dying did not end. Many failed to recover on the meagre rations. But it was not just the weather and bleak nature of the land that took them.' Bardon leaned closer to the fire but could not prevent shivering. 'I have never been a superstitious man, Elodi, but I saw things in the darkness that challenged my lifelong beliefs. The tales tell of the spirits of the dead, full of wrath for those that exiled and abandoned them to their miserable fate. At night, many of us believed we… saw them, or at the very least felt their presence.'

Elodi's blood froze. 'Wraiths?'

'Worse. They were more than just apparitions, these had… a presence. They drain your spirits, almost as if they're sucking the very life from your bones, seizing back what was taken from them. Many of us became ill, but from no obvious cause. We were all hungry but fought on. But for others it was like they just gave up hope and departed this realm. But there was another danger. Not all who died, perished in their sleep.'

Bardon stopped as the innkeeper brought food. The lord looked to the plate but chose not to eat. He turned back to Elodi and gripped her hand. 'What I'm about to tell you must not leave this room. It may be a true account, or it may be a trick our troubled minds played upon us. By now we were delirious, half-starved, and frightened by our own shadows. I don't know for certain whether I dreamed what I saw. Or if awake, it was a fever from the marshes that took many of us, filling our heads with nightmarish visions. Maybe in the weeks to come as we recover, we'll come to know the truth of what we saw, but until then I'd appreciate your discretion.'

Elodi nodded. 'You have my word.'

'Thank you. If times are as difficult as you say, the last thing we need is our story adding to the fear if it turns out to be a figment of our fevered minds.'

'Agreed. Please, go on.'

Bardon's eyes widened. 'We woke on the mornings following sightings of… wraiths, to find some of our fellow survivors had gone. It wasn't unheard for those close to madness to throw themselves from the cliffs to end their suffering… but these had not. We came across them near to the old graves… as if torn apart by wolves.'

Elodi gasped. 'But surely there are no wolves on that isle.'

'Indeed. And we soon came to a shocking conclusion. At first, I refused to believe my eyes, but we found graves where the earth was disturbed. It appears…' he cleared his throat, 'it appears not all who died on that isle, rest in peace.'

'What! You mean…?'

He kept his eyes on his cup. 'They are not truly dead.'

Elodi grasped the arms of her chair. 'We had a similar problem at the pass, but they had died recently. Those on the island were exiled three hundred years ago. How could that be?'

Bardon's jaw clenched. 'Perhaps our presence stirred them from their unnatural slumber. As grim as it was, we decided to dig up one of the disturbed graves. We found what can only be described as a ghoul. Blood stained its long nails, and…' he grimaced, 'the few remaining teeth in its skull had flesh stuck in between. By day, we exhumed those with signs of activity and burned the creatures within. As for their nature, I can only assume the poison left by our enemy was more than a plague, more of a curse intended to sow fear and unrest for many years to come. So, while the actions of our ancestors to expel them to the islands appears cruel, it may have been a wise move. I only hope our pyres finally allowed those poor souls to rest.'

Elodi put down her drink. 'I believe you may be right. In Harlyn, those who caught the plague were incarcerated in remote villages until recovered. Those who died were burned, as it was feared even the dead could still spread disease. Perhaps only Mund exiled them and let them be. Regardless, that is a terrible fate these people suffered.' She placed her hand on his arm. 'Do you need to rest? Or are you able to complete your tale?'

He shook his head. 'I'd rather finish, thank you. I find it helps to talk of what I've tried to bury at the back of my mind. And then there is much I'd like to know about the unfolding events here. But from what you've already told me, it seems we are in a tight spot.' Bardon smiled. 'But congratulations on replacing the old fool, Kernlow. I'm sure his heart is in the right place, but had he stayed in command for much longer, the fate of the realms would have already been sealed.' He took her hand. 'You are by far a better prospect for the realms.'

Despite her recent successes, Elodi flushed. 'That is good of you to say. But I feel it is you who should lead now you have returned. As the longest serving leader of a realm, the position rightly belongs to you.'

Bardon sighed. 'I am old and from a different age. I am exhausted and suspect my best days are well behind me. No, Elodi, it is you who is better suited to take on the challenges ahead.' He beamed. 'And now I know about your mother. Ha! Didn't I always say she had the strength and skill to match an Amayan. Well… now I know why. And… if anything, I would say you might even surpass her.'

'Again, that is kind of you to say. But not all has gone my way. The loss of Calerdorn weighs heavy on my mind. We don't yet know where we will meet the enemy, and… Nyomae fears our foe has yet to reveal its full strength.'

He patted her hand. 'Much that happens seems ill at the time. Who can predict how the future will unfold. I will stand beside you, Elodi. I will advise where you think you need it, but I will follow.' Bardon massaged his legs. 'But these old bones creak more than they should, so accept my offer… for what you think that is worth.'

Elodi held his gaze. 'It was not so long ago I made the same vow to you in my room at Archonholm. And to repeat what you said to me at the time' — she winked — 'your support will be worth more than you think.' She sighed. 'But look, I have interrupted your tale. Please, do continue.'

'There is little more to be said. After our gruesome discovery, we decided to set sail before our crude ship was fully seaworthy. But we preferred to take our chances on the open sea, despite our dread, rather than be eaten by a long-dead ghoul. We sailed for days up and down the coast, reluctant to land straightaway. While unaware of Uluriel's hand in our misfortunes, in our hearts, we knew something was afoot, whether through intuition or from our weakness. We feared the Five had fallen in an enemy coup and were thus wary of setting ashore. I apologize if our meandering way caused concern for the people of Mund. But as our health and state of our minds deteriorated, we could wait no longer and found what we thought was a remote bay.' He smiled. 'But how fortunate you were there to greet me, eh.'

Elodi nodded. 'Fortunate indeed. I am informed the rest of your crew have been brought ashore and are housed in and around Frescove. Healers from Caermund will be here by dawn, and dozens of fishing boats have set sail for Mundrake's Isle to bring the remainder back. They, and you, when well enough, will be taken to Caermund where you'll receive the best treatment. I have asked for the healers of Abernost to attend. I trust they will have knowledge of what afflicts you. But from what you say, I will also instruct work to begin on incinerating the buried on the island. Sadly, it is not a task we are unaccustomed to these days.'

Bardon stretched. 'A necessary precaution in the light of what we know our enemy is capable of. With hindsight, we should have sailed into Caermund, but none were thinking straight.' He yawned. 'But perhaps it was fate that we came here and found you.'

'I would like to think it was fate rather than luck. We are in desperate need of something going our way if we are to turn back the evil tide coming south.' Elodi held his hand and was relieved to find it had warmed. 'I know you require rest, but there is much to discuss. We have decisions to make on the defense either side of the Kolossos, and I also have two loyal captains from Broon who should be placed under your command. I'm sure they will be heartened by your return. The unrest in Keld spreads, and—' Elodi turned as a man entered. She stood, annoyed at the interruption. 'I specifically expressed I was not to be disturbed.'

The man fidgeted with a message in his hand. 'Apologies, ma'am. But this seemed urgent. It has the mark of Nyomae.'

'Then please accept my apologies. You did the right thing.' Elodi took the note and dismissed the man. She found her hand trembled as she broke Nyomae's seal. The one line read: *Come to Abernost. Come immediately.*

# 28. Into the Valley of Shadows

Toryn found it difficult to tear himself away from Telamir. While not entirely comfortable within its overbearing and unnerving presence, his awe had overridden his initial caution, coming to believe it stood with them against the dark. But his mission was to locate the Amayans, and Toryn was convinced they had gone north. The company had ridden hard along the Northeast Road, passing between the Kolososs and the green hills of Emryst. The first night, they had camped where the road forked. Toryn had stood at the junction. The road to their right would take them to Tallabar and Saphrir. But they would take the other route in the pursuit of Eryn and her companions.

On the second evening since departing Telamir, they had crossed the old bridge spanning the Vynmar River. Rivalling the Kel for length, and in common with the great rivers of the realms, the Vynmar's source lay deep beneath the Kolossos. From there, it crossed Emryst for twelve leagues, then turned northward to eventually meet with the sea in the shadow of Karrock's twin towers. But that would be a journey for Toryn to take another day.

As they had reached the north bank of the river, he felt a growing sense of unease, and not because it was the last day of summer. Andryn's words had come to mind as he noted the sun abandon them earlier with each passing day. As a child, he had sensed his parent's apprehension of whether their supplies would see them through the cold winter to come. But he had more pressing problems on his mind at present. No. His disquiet was not due to the change of season. Toryn knew its source: Ormoroth's mountain fortress of Vortimo.

'Here looks like a good spot.' Gundrul nodded to the settlement of Vymarl. 'I'll send a rider to catch up with the situation here. Might also see if they can sell us some proper meat. Getting a little tired of trying to fill my belly with skinny rabbits.'

But Toryn barely heard the captain. His eyes were drawn to the valley that suffered the presence of the fortress. He mumbled. 'Thank you. Sounds like a good plan.'

Gundrul followed his gaze. 'You're sure then?'

'Certain.'

The captain groaned. 'Then I'll be needing a whole sheep to myself if we're to go that way. There's a reason why that road is sealed off, overgrown, and why no one's taken the trouble to repair it.'

Toryn shivered. 'And unfortunately, I believe that's the reason why the Amayans are trapped there, and why we have to go.'

'Thought as much. Can't say I know anyone who's been within a league of Vortimo in my lifetime. Even Hamar was smart enough not to let his curiosity get the better of him.'

Toryn smiled to himself. 'Perhaps it's the only part of the known realms he never got to visit. But it didn't stop him having a story or two to tell of it.'

'And stories that for once haven't been embellished by a guard's imagination on a dark night, I should think. It didn't get the name Castle of Wraiths in the old tongue for nothing.'

Toryn kept his eyes on the unkempt road beyond a crumbled wall. 'Well let's not get too carried away with the stories, eh.'

Gundrul grunted. 'Suit yourself, but I'd rather go in expecting the worst. Always found that helps. Then I can never be taken by surprise.' He clasped his hands. 'Now then. Let's get the fires going ready for a decent supper for a change.'

Toryn awoke to a silent dawn. It appeared even the abundant foliage on the nearby trees was not enough to tempt the birds to roost so close to the pass. Before he had slept, Toryn had taken himself away from the camp and entered the Song. Shepra had gone with him and had sat patiently by his side. He felt safer with her on watch, knowing she would alert him while he was distracted elsewhere. Toryn had ventured as far back into the Verses of the region as he dared. He needed to know what they would face the coming day. And to his horror, he appreciated the tales heard by Gundrul and Hamar had not been embellished.

The tragic events of the distant past had rent a deep scar across the Verses. A city had once stood close to the head of the valley. But it had been sacked by Ormoroth's armies, and its inhabitants hauled away in chains to build his immense fortress. Toryn understood the slaves were survivors of a great race weakened by many centuries of war. Thousands had died as they labored to build a stronghold in the south for Ormoroth, said to be fashioned on his castle in the far north. None could withstand the raids on their farms to feed the armies within, choosing to forsake the lands of their ancestors and flee.

Vortimo had stood for over three thousand years until Draegelan had finally wrested it from Ormoroth's grasp. Draegelan had ordered the fortress to be demolished, but even the explosive might of Shreek's Rage failed to break its thick walls, hewn from the mountain sides. And as none could endure long the menace of its shadow, Vortimo was abandoned, the road sealed, and a watch set. But as Toryn withdrew to return to the present, he witnessed the defenses collapse from neglect as the realms believed the threat had gone. Of Vortimo, Toryn would have to wait until he stood beneath its walls to determine its condition, but he supposed the stronghold would likely stand until the mountains themselves collapsed.

'Would you ever have thought we'd live to see something that even Hamar hadn't set eyes upon?' Toryn turned to find Elrik and Lorek at his side.

Toryn turned back to the pass. 'Never. But this is one part of the realms I'd rather leave unexplored.'

Elrik shouldered his pack. 'Shame we can't take the horses. I can feel the weight of that castle bearing down on us from here.'

'We can't risk them bolting. Even Shepra is nervous. The horses will be safe in Vymarl, and it's only a league or two on foot to the fortress.'

Lorek checked his sword belt. 'Mine was getting jumpy before we got anywhere near this place. It would be cruel to take them.'

Elrik eyed the ruined wall. 'Even so, if we need to flee, I'd rather be on the back of a bolting horse than my aching legs.'

Toryn tried to smile. 'You'd be lucky to last one minute on a frightened mare.'

'Perhaps, but at least I'd be a minute farther away from whatever we're running from.' Elrik looked over Toryn's shoulder. 'Janae's back. She's a brave one. Wouldn't accept my offer to accompany her.'

Toryn turned to see Janae walking slowly towards them. 'A scout through and through, eh. A solitary folk. Probably thought your great big boots stomping down the pass would muddy the tracks. I wonder—' Janae stumbled.

Toryn ran and caught her just as she collapsed. She clasped his arm, looked at his face, but appeared not to know him. He pulled off his cloak and wrapped it around her shivering shoulders. 'Janae?'

She glanced back to the pass as if remembering where she was. 'I… I'm sorry. I'm not sure what…' Janae stood and handed the cloak back to Toryn. 'Nothing to report for half a league up that road. Well… nothing that I could see with my own eyes.' She looked to the ground. 'Apologies, but I could go no farther up that pass alone. There's something down there… but I can't be certain what.'

Toryn noted she struggled to take her eyes from the way she had come. 'Have you ever experienced such a feeling before?'

She turned to face him. 'Perhaps. Once in Dorn.'

'Would that be Wyke Wood?' Janae nodded. Toryn looked back to Elrik. 'That was Uleva's domain before Lady Harlyn drove her out.'

Janae found her voice. 'We lost three guards in that wood. It was an eerie place… but down that pass… it's worse.'

Elrik handed her his flask. 'Then just as well there'll be twenty of us, eh.'

Toryn kept his eyes on the mountain sides. 'But it's not going to be easy, even with our numbers. I know their ways. The more minds they have to play with…'

Gundrul approached. 'We're ready as we'll ever be.' He eyed Janae. 'Are you well?'

She straightened, regaining the color in her cheeks. 'Ready for duty, Captain.'

Gundrul turned. 'And you, Toryn. You're absolutely sure we'll find them down there? You've seen them in this song of yours?'

Toryn nodded. 'The Amayans came this way a month back. They did not wish to take their horses so set them free. I can't find them at present, which tells me they must be weak and in danger.' He sighed. 'So yes, that's where we're heading.'

The captain stared down the road. 'But what in the name of the Three possessed them to head to Vortimo?'

Toryn's stomach knotted. 'They were pursued. Perhaps they had no other way open to them. But they entered here. No doubt in my mind.'

Gundrul scratched his beard. 'Do they live? I don't want to sound like I don't care, but we're risking the lives of the company here.'

Toryn shook his head. 'That I cannot tell. They may be held captive, or still fighting. But if they're dead it doesn't bode well for the rest of the realms.'

'Then as always, it's down to the Archonians to put our lives on the line and find out.' Gundrul waved to the company. 'Come on, lads. Can't stand around here all day. You'll soon have more tales to tell your grandchildren around the fire.'

It may have been mid-morning, but the heavy clouds sagging between the mountains kept the sunlight from reaching the pass. They had traveled only a short distance when Toryn felt as if a weight pressed down upon him. It seemed as if eyes on the steep slopes watched them, scornful of their boldness to encroach on their territory. Whether real or imagined, it was an unpleasant sensation that slowed the company's pace. And the farther they went, the harder it became to walk, and even Shepra trotted at a crouch.

Gundrul stopped. Toryn forced his legs to catch up. He whispered, finding his voice hoarse. 'What is it, Captain?'

His mouth gaped. 'I can't go on, lad. I've…' his voice wavered, 'I've never felt anything like this. I'm no coward, but I… I don't think I can take another step.'

Toryn grasped his arm. 'You're no coward, Captain. It's this place.' He turned to see the others had come to a standstill, some were on their knees, and another had turned, attempting to crawl away.'

Gundrul's wide eyes stayed fixed ahead. 'Is there anything you can do?'

'Give me a moment.' Toryn closed his eyes and searched for the moment the Amayans had come their way. He turned back to Gundrul. 'The Nordleng pursued the Amayans, but it's not their presence befouling the pass. Something dreadful happened here many years ago. It's left what appears to be a curse. But… the Nordleng had protection, but by what means…' Hamar's account of the Archon surviving the rockfall in the Caerwal Pass came to mind. He looked to Gundrul. 'Gather the company. We'll head back to that outcrop. This curse is on this part of the road. I can't speak for Vortimo itself, but we'll be through the worst stretch in a hundred paces or so.' The captain turned, seeming happier to have a command to give.

They walked back a short distance until the sense of dread lifted. Toryn explained his plan. 'I'll attempt to shield us from what's draining our strength.' He watched them stand a little taller. 'I can't make any promises, but I'm hoping it will lift the burden to make our progress easier.' He clasped his hands, then slowly opened them to create a sphere over their heads. Toryn explained. 'You can't see it, but you're protected by a shield of sorts. I'll bring the uncontaminated air from this point with us. I'll maintain it for as long as I can, but we must move fast.' He looked to Elrik and Lorek. 'I may need your help, as I will soon tire.'

The company turned and marched back down the pass. Toryn kept his eye on the blue, glimmering dome over their heads as they approached the threshold of the curse. As soon as they entered, the shield shuddered, but the company maintained their pace. Toryn's legs began to weaken. Elrik and Lorek grasped his arms and took some of his weight. But the dome began to splinter. Toryn spoke through his clenched jaw. 'Not far now. Keep going.' The cracks widened as if a great weight crushed down upon them.

Toryn's legs gave way. Elrik caught him. 'I've got you.' A section of the shield fell away. Shepra whimpered. Outside, a battle raged. Ghostly knights fought against gangly creatures taller than shrouls. Their long, scrawny arms wielded jagged swords and maces with barbed edges. Shields and armor shattered, but the knights battled on. Half of Toryn's shield crumbled, bringing the ghostly combatants crashing among the company. Toryn cried out. 'Almost through, keep—'

'We made it.' Toryn opened his eyes. Night had fallen, but the snowy slopes of the Kolososs reflected the faint light of the moon onto Elrik's face. He beamed. 'All thanks to you, Tor.' Elrik whispered, but his words echoed as if carried by the ghost of his breath down the cool valley. He patted Toryn's shoulder. 'That was some magic trick, eh. Don't suppose you could bring some heat from the south. Gundrul thinks it's best not to light fires.'

Shepra leaped onto Toryn's lap and licked his face. He looked back along the route they had come. 'Did you see the battle?'

'Battle?' Elrik grinned. 'The only battle I saw was Gundrul trying to stay on his feet.'

'Perhaps lucky you didn't.' Toryn shivered. 'This place still suffers the pain of what happened here once.' The pass appeared peaceful, but Toryn wondered if the ghosts of the fallen still fought their battles beneath the glimmering light of the mountains. He turned. Ahead, a smooth slab of rock jutted out from behind the slopes.

Elrik grimaced. 'That's just the top of one wall.'

Toryn reluctantly looked back to Vortimo. 'I need to get closer. Then I'll be able to tell for sure if the Amayans yet live.'

'We thought as much.' Elrik held out a hand and helped Toryn to his feet. 'Janae is ready.' He leaned closer. 'I think she's looking for a chance to prove herself. She seems ashamed she couldn't complete her task earlier.'

Toryn winced. 'She has nothing to be ashamed of. To come this way alone was beyond most of us.'

Elrik nodded. 'Janae's coming. Besides, if two of us accompany you, we can carry you back if your legs fail again. Ha! Remember when I used to carry you over the stream because you didn't want to get your feet wet?'

'Perhaps a wise precaution.' Toryn smiled. 'Who would have thought we'd end up in a place like this, eh.' He looked down. 'And who wants to get their feet wet? Especially in the streams that run through this valley.'

Shepra licked Janae's hand as she joined them. She kept her eyes on the dog as she spoke. 'I can find no tracks that could be Amayan, only Nordleng boots and those of other creatures I rarely see. Alas, I suspect at least one droog and a shroul. But shrouls freeze the ground as they tread making it difficult to determine numbers.'

Elrik sighed. 'But no sign of Amayans?'

Janae shrugged. 'They're light on their feet and notoriously difficult to track… if at all.'

Toryn asked. 'How many Nordleng do you think came this way?'

She met his gaze. 'I would say perhaps forty in total, but at different times.'

Toryn held out a hand. 'Then please, lead on. I would be grateful if you could go ahead and check if they watch the approach.'

Janae lifted her hood and wrapped it around her face. 'Follow twenty paces behind. If they've posted a watch, they'll need the eyes of a hawk to see me.'

They did as instructed and watched Janae disappear around the bend. Toryn looked up to the steep slopes, half-expecting to see shrouls or cobtrolls stalking their progress. All around, the mountain snow glimmered pure white, but the slopes opposite Vortimo were gray. Did the fortress defile the moonlight? He spat. 'The air tastes wrong. The last time I felt like this was in the Wend Gap. Hamar and I found a Singing Stone. That didn't end well.'

Elrik whispered. 'Here she comes.'

Janae hurried back. Her wide eyes shone as she reported her find. 'There's no watch, but if I were in that place, I wouldn't see the need either. It's… it's immense.'

Toryn peered ahead. 'I imagine they don't get many visitors.'

The three rounded the bend and stood at the foot of Vortimo. Toryn gawped. The fortress appeared to belittle the great mountain from which it had been hewn. It took a moment for Toryn to comprehend what his eyes beheld. A curved wall connecting two lesser peaks formed an outer defense. Behind, the castle keep looked as if the very gods had rammed a sheer slab of rock into the mountain side. A few cracks broke up an otherwise featureless, monolithic wall. The only windows visible were two rows of arrow slits three-quarters of the way up. Toryn craned his neck. Inside the keep, two dark towers rose to the level of the mountain peak. He groaned inside. How could any hope to assail this monstrosity? But Draegelan had done just that. Toryn stood in awe. Draegelan must have commanded a mighty force to breach its defenses, let alone drive out Ormoroth from his stronghold.

He lowered his gaze to the outer defenses standing between them and the steep road leading up to the fortress. In any other part of the realm, the wall alone would be considered impregnable, yet here it appeared redundant. But perhaps the obstacle was meant to taunt and dishearten those foolish enough to believe they could take Vortimo.

The clouds departed from the strip of sky above the pass. The moonlight revealed a great iron gate at the center of the outer wall, sealed shut following Draegelan's remarkable victory. But centuries of wind funneling through the mountains, aided by ice and driven rain had breached the wall to their right. A pile of rubble lay where a crack had opened into a wide gap to form a convenient, if steep and uneven ramp.

Toryn looked to his companions. 'I dare not enter the Song up here. I need to get to the other side of that wall. From there, I can get a good look at the whole fortress and find the Amayans by other means. I don't ask you to come. You can wait here if you wish.' But they would not have it. Both willingly followed him up the rubble, and Toryn was most grateful for their company. While not as unsettling as the cursed road, standing at the foot of Vortimo overwhelmed them, almost to the point Toryn believed he would be crushed by its giant, towering walls.

They scrambled up the rubble and through the wall. The long, winding road leading up to the main gate was fashioned to leave attackers vulnerable to projectiles from above. Toryn imagined columns of heavily armored soldiers, locking shields over their heads, fighting for every inch as rocks came crashing down from the ledge at the top. And for those surviving the ascent, the main gate resembling a mouth with sharp teeth, awaited them. He wondered once more how Draegelan had managed to win this battle.

Toryn found a position in the shadows and scanned the high walls. He let the *farsight* take him through the odd cracks in the slab of rock. He soon found what he needed to know, but not what he wanted to see. He ushered Elrik and Janae back through the defensive wall and returned to the waiting Gundrul and company.

# 29. In the Maidens' Name

'Uluriel must have known I would come to Abernost.' Nyomae patted Sea Mist's nose. 'The Nordleng have been watching this place. They attacked within a day of my arrival.'

Elodi dismounted. 'Yet I imagine they were not expecting to be disarmed so easily.'

Nyomae smiled. 'Thankfully Uluriel had not fully prepared them for what they would face. But she appears to know my mind before I do. I must wrest the advantage back.'

Elodi rubbed down her horse's steaming neck. 'Will your work here achieve that?'

'Permit me to answer once out of earshot.' Nyomae glanced behind. 'We must assume not everyone is who they appear. But what news of Bardon?'

Elodi lowered her voice. 'Bardon and the surviving Elites are in good hands.' She handed the reins to the stable boy. 'But how long it will take them to recover from their ordeal is another matter.'

Nyomae waited for the boy to lead Sea Mist inside. 'It cannot take too long.' She grasped Elodi's hand. 'The storm is coming. Their power grows. They will not wait long to strike south.'

Elodi slowed. 'Have you heard from Toryn?'

Nyomae ushered Elodi through a door and into a small study. 'He has located the Amayans—'

'That's a relief.' Elodi sighed. 'If we are to have any…' she noticed Nyomae's frown. 'Is it not good news?'

Nyomae ran her hands along the wall beside a bookcase. 'While it is heartening to know the Amayans live, I fear they are much weakened by a determined and well-armed foe.'

Elodi's breath caught in her throat. 'Is Toryn aware of this threat?'

'That I cannot tell. He and his company stand in the shadow of Vortimo, which obscures my—'

'Vortimo!' Elodi groaned. 'Why would they enter that cursed valley? It has been sealed for centuries, and for good reason.'

'He was tasked to find the Amayans. Vortimo is where they are trapped. Toryn is strong and can offer some protection to his companions. But his proximity to that place presents another problem. I can no longer sense his presence, and therefore unable to assist.' Nyomae turned back to Elodi. 'But this is not the reason I called you here.' She placed her palm upon a stone in the wall and muttered beneath her breath. The wall moved.

Cool air rushed through the gap into Elodi's face. 'Am I to assume this is why?'

'Partly.' Nyomae took a torch from the wall to reveal a steep stairwell leading down. 'There were rumors of a hidden vault in Abernost, but Sylvena dismissed them as frivolous chatter.' She ducked through the gap. 'I will go first to light your way.' Her voice echoed. 'But as you can see, Sylvena was wrong, and not for the first time.'

Elodi joined her on the top step as Nyomae whispered another command to seal the doorway behind. 'And was it Draegelan's scroll that led you here?'

'Eventually. The writing was somewhat obscure, but for a reason.' Nyomae continued with her story as they descended the narrow, winding stairs. 'Draegelan was wary of anyone stumbling across his musings so did not make it easy. But he has eventually led me here.' She smiled. 'Not to mention with a little help from the Maidens and Nym'.

'I'm intrigued.'

'As still am I. I believe I'm the first to enter this place since his passing.'

Elodi looked down. 'These stairs were certainly not made for ease of access.'

'Precisely. And not built by stonemasons, but by those wanting to keep this vault a secret. It was here before the Seat of Learning was established. I believe Draegelan sanctioned the building of Abernost on this spot *because* of this vault. And he named it after Aber, an Imaari who made a vital discovery that may be our salvation… or lead to our downfall.' Elodi went to ask, but Nyomae seemed keen to press on. They arrived at the foot of the stairs. Nyomae's torch appeared to dim and cast no light beyond her face. She touched Elodi's arm. 'Stand still for a moment.' She waved her palm and doused the flame.

Elodi blinked in the dark. She gasped. 'The walls! They glow.' The air warmed as a golden light illuminated a long hall with curved walls and a low ceiling just a few feet above their heads. She ran her hands along the smooth wall. 'Is this glass? What causes it to shine? I did not know we had such skill.'

Nyomae smiled. 'We don't. This was not built by our hands. This is the work of the Elorym.'

Elodi gaped as the light spread to reveal a space twice the size of the Great Hall of Archonholm. 'Our long dead ancestors?'

'Long dead, yes, but not the ancestors of most. Although yours, and perhaps partly mine.' Elodi frowned. Nyomae continued. 'I believe the Amayans are descended from the Elorym. And my kind, through our studies, may retain some of their ability to hear and use the power in the Song.'

Nyomae led Elodi towards a small, wooden desk and a single chair at the center of the hall. 'This is where Draegelan spent his days before struck down by sickness.'

She pulled out the chair and offered it to Elodi. 'Apologies. You have ridden hard to answer my call. Please sit.' She picked up a jug from the desk and poured a glass of water for Elodi. Nyomae sighed. 'I have to admit I felt a sense of pride to sit in Draegelan's seat.'

Elodi gladly accepted the offer. 'If only sitting in his chair could impart his knowledge and power upon us.'

'In a way it may do just that. I have learned much from the Elorym. Much that is painful to learn… but learn it I must.' Nyomae perched on the desk. 'Now. Where to start. You recall I told you of Sylvena. Against both mine and Idraman's wishes, she went north in search of a relic which we later learned was a trap.'

Elodi placed down her glass. 'And you know what this relic is?'

'Alas, Sylvena was deceived. She believed it to be a source of power that would aid us. I don't know where she came upon such knowledge as she did not reveal it to the Order. But she made an error in her interpretation of the Verse, one of Ormoroth's Verses at that. The relic was a great iron pillar, known as the Angorlith.' Nyomae's hand ran across the scroll. 'According to the archives it was set by Ormoroth, fashioned to despoil the heartbeat of the land.'

Elodi watched the light reflecting on the water in her glass. 'And where is this pillar?'

'The legends say it is set deep beneath the tallest mountain in the land.'

'Caranach?'

'Caranach may be the highest peak in the *known* land, but there is another. I once heard tales of a gigantic mountain crowned with a fortress of ice, thousands of feet tall.' Nyomae shuddered. 'I remember its name: Vorkirik. It's far to the north where it is said the Evil One sat upon his throne. While I'm uncertain whether that is true, the

Nym revealed Ormoroth cast the Angorlith in a great furnace beneath Vorkirik.'

'And this iron pillar corrupts the Song to this day?'

'Fortunately, the Elorym perceived its forging, thus set the seven stones of the Amanach to counter its corruption. As the Elorym suffered in their wars with Ormoroth, they saw fit to assign a force to protect the stones.'

Elodi's scalp tingled. 'The Amayans.'

'Indeed. Your ancestors were great warriors trained by the masters of Elorym lore. But the seven stones are now six, and their power appears to be in decline. The Amayans draw sustenance from the stones, so your powers also wane. Their location was hidden from the mortal world, yet now our guards stumble upon them by accident. Uluriel, through the Archon, was able to locate the stone at the Wend Pass. Toryn witnessed its end. If we lose more, our enemy will grow yet stronger while we become weaker.'

'And what of your kind? Are you also descended from the Elorym?'

Nyomae nodded. 'I believe that is so. As the Elorym came to accept their fate, they formed the Amayans and the Imaari. The Amayans to protect the stones; the Imaari to resist the corruption within the Song. In their wisdom, the Elorym divided our powers. Thus, it would not be such a blow if either an Amayan or an Imaari fell to the enemy.'

'Wise indeed.' Elodi looked about the hall. 'And what became of the Elorym?'

'Let me show you.' Nyomae stood. 'It will aid us in our battles to come if we know of our collective past.' She led Elodi to a bed beside the wall. 'Here. A small comfort Draegelan allowed himself. It may be best if you lie down. The fate of the Elorym is a little distressing.'

Elodi opened her eyes. She rose slowly from the bed. The tears she shed for the plight of the Elorym had dried on her face. She stared at Nyomae in the golden light. 'Is all lost? What chance do we have if the might of the Elorym could not resist Ormoroth and his warlocks.'

Nyomae sighed. 'We can be thankful Ormoroth remains banished from this realm. But even without him, his forces pose a serious threat.'

'Can we use the power of the Elorym?'

Nyomae sat beside her. 'Ah. Now we come to why I called you here. I have learned how to access the depths of the Song previously beyond my reach. I can now see deeper into the past, and to places farther afield. But I get ahead of myself. Aber, the man this place honors, found a curious Verse within the Song. It became known as Aber's Verse, but at the time it was perhaps more in jest than respect. In his later years, Draegelan devoted much time to its study. And I have found what he learned… and I have come to appreciate why he chose to conceal that knowledge here.'

'Then it is a power you are reluctant to use?'

'To a certain degree. But I believe I can safely deploy some of his knowledge that could aid our fight.' Nyomae looked to the ceiling. She took a breath. 'I have discovered the means to determine the Maidens' Name of the lesser of our adversaries.'

Elodi gasped. 'Does this mean…?'

'I could cast them from this world.'

Elodi released Nyomae's hand. 'But if the Maidens know the names of every living being, could they not have exiled Ormoroth?'

'Alas, they could only create, not destroy. And the dark creatures such as droogs and aralaks fashioned by evil ways, possess no such name. But once the Song was corrupted, the means to unmake is now open to others. But I fear to invoke this power against the likes of Uluriel. To utter the Maidens' Name of one so powerful could open a gateway to the oldest parts of the Song, and possibly even the Great Void. If I falter, my enemy could drag me down with them. That would be a risk I'd be willing to take if I could remove Uluriel from this realm. But… that is not the only danger. Opening the gateway works both ways. I could, with the slightest mistake, make it possible for Ormoroth to return. Invoking a Maidens' Name comes with great danger. It is not an act I would use unless all else has failed.'

Elodi's shoulders sagged. 'That is not a risk worth taking. But what of Uleva and Uldrak, and perhaps Dorlan? I have no doubt Dorlan will lead their armies south.' She looked away. 'And the thought of facing him on the battlefield is not conducive to a good night's sleep. And this time I will have no walls to hide behind… for what that was worth.'

Nyomae placed her hand on Elodi's. 'I may have found a way to confront Dorlan without citing his Maidens' Name. I have ventured as far back to Dorlan's Verse at Talaghir.'

Elodi's eyes widened. 'How is this possible?'

'Draegelan discovered the key to using the power of the Elorym contained in this hall. I have located the final moments of that tragic battle. Draegelan was right. Ormoroth did indeed recite the Verse of Unmaking, as did I at Gormadon. But the fire was great within Dorlan that day. He survived where all others fell. But for reasons I cannot fully understand, Dorlan's years were extended by Ormoroth's action. Perhaps his Verses in the Song were altered, and his fate changed. But I cannot fathom how this occurred.'

Elodi grasped Nyomae's arm. 'You have seen this?

Dorlan's legend is the foundation of Harlyn's strength, or its faith in its strength, no matter how weak we are today. Is it true? Was Dorlan as strong as the legend's tell.'

Nyomae smiled. 'Your legends do not do Dorlan justice. The scribe who accompanied Draegelan wrote of the last time she beheld Dorlan shortly before he went into battle… and what would be his final moments of glory. Something within him connected with the power contained in the Song like no Imaari had ever achieved. I'm sure even Ormoroth must have quailed when he set eyes upon Dorlan at Talaghir.' Nyomae paused. 'It is a tale of triumph, bitter defeat, and ultimately, tragedy.' She stood. 'Perhaps it best I show you. The power in this Elorym hall allows me to take you into his final Verses.' She reached forward. 'May I?'

Elodi nodded. 'Please. I have seen Dorlan in his sorry state possessed by Uleva. I would dearly love to see him as the true hero, Harlyn holds him to be.'

'You are strong, Elodi, but if what you see becomes too painful, raise your hand and I will bring you back.' Nyomae touched Elodi's temple. The room faded as if a fog descended.

Dorlan sat tall on his mighty steed, Draego. The Knight of Calerdorn's eyes shone as he searched the north for signs of Ormoroth. Dorlan was great in stature, greater than the portraits depicted, and taller than the pitiful shell of a man who had confronted Elodi at the gates of her city. Ormoroth's bitter wind battered into the armies pursuing him. Yet Dorlan and Draego rode through the assault, leading a vast force across the ice that packed the Draegelan Trench. As they ventured deeper into Nordruuk, Ormoroth grew ever more despairing as Dorlan gained ground on his depleted legions. Desperate to avoid Dorlan's wrath, Ormoroth whipped up the storms and drove a howling gale, thick with shards of ice at the advancing knights. But Dorlan laughed in the face of the threat. He threw out his arms and yelled lines from an unknown Verse into the vortex. The winds ceased, and the ice fell from the air to land harmlessly at Draego's hooves. When Ormoroth could retreat no farther, Dorlan saw his time had come.

Elodi watched in awe as the great knight led twenty thousand knights onto the ice of Talaghir. The ground trembled at their coming, and not even the great beasts who had served Ormoroth through the centuries, could stand before Dorlan that day. The swirling, dark form of Ormoroth withdrew to the rear and surrounded himself with the last of his warlocks. But as Dorlan moved to end the battle, Ormoroth struck. The battlefield erupted. All perished in a searing, white flash.

The fog lifted. The golden light of the Elorym glass eased Elodi's return. She sat, blinking away tears of pain. 'Such a tragic loss. I cannot imagine a greater force for good could ever have been assembled, before or after the Seven Realms. And all were lost?'

Nyomae sighed. 'Those of my Order riding with Dorlan, died, and their Verses remain hidden. The Imaari who later discovered the devastation, believed Ormoroth was banished the moment he completed his utterance of those vile Verses. But I do not know by what device that was achieved. Perhaps, as Dorlan's strength surpassed all others that day, it was by his hand he cast Ormoroth into the Great Void. Or, another force intervened, but I would not hazard a guess. But if you can bear it, I can show you what my ancestors found on arriving at Talaghir.'

Elodi closed her eyes. 'That I must. If I am to ride against the remnants of Ormoroth's armies, I should know the wiles of our enemy, no matter how painful.' Nyomae obliged.

Elodi stood at the edge of a crater, so wide she could

not see the opposite rim. At her back, ice and snow covered the plain. Before her, fragments of splintered armor and discarded weapons scattered the bare rock. Far to the north, the wind wailed. But this was not a gale of Ormoroth's making. Cries of anguish echoed across the desolate land. Elodi was certain she heard the Maidens lament the fall of Dorlan. Their distress rose, accompanied by the shattering screams of their agony and torment.

'Please. Enough.' Elodi brushed Nyomae's hand away. 'I can't bear to hear their grief.' Her head fell into her hands, and she wept for Dorlan and the plight of the Maidens.

Nyomae placed her arm around Elodi's shaking shoulders. 'Their grief, Elodi? Who did you hear?'

'It had to be the Maidens. It came from the top of the world, far to the north. They wailed for Dorlan. It had to be them.'

Nyomae's eyes widened. 'Then you have heard more than I.' Her hand rested on Elodi's knee. 'I must apologize. Had I known, I would not have subjected you to that ordeal.'

'There's no need. I had to know what happened.' Elodi looked at Nyomae. 'You did not hear the Maidens? Did I imagine it?'

'No, it must be your Amayan blood. This confirms you to be of direct descent from the Elorym. You have a bond with the Maidens. That explains why you, and not I, heard them.'

Elodi collapsed back onto the bed. 'Then the tales do not represent the extent of the Maidens' suffering.' Her hands shook. 'But I don't believe we have the words to portray their woe. If this Evil One can inflict such suffering upon the gods' daughters, he must remain entombed to the end of time. To fight the Ul-dalak presents a challenge almost beyond us, and if Ormoroth returns, it would take a miracle to resist him. But if somehow, the Evil One is freed…' Elodi stood. 'I need some air.' Nyomae rose. Elodi raised her hand. 'If you don't mind, I would prefer to be alone for a while. Perhaps we can continue this afternoon…'

Elodi stood upon the balcony of Abernost's Round Tower, but the warmth of the midday sun failed to ease her anxiety. The peaks of the Caerwal Mountains peered over the horizon far to the south. She made no attempt to use her *farsight*, preferring to remain oblivious of events in the wider world for the time being. Below, the grasslands of Holm shone green in the sunlight. The road wound its way through the gentle hills, yet Elodi took no comfort from the wonder of the Maidens' making. Was this all an illusion? Would the beauty formed by the Song of Creation be but a fleeting moment of order in an otherwise cruel, chaotic world?

Elodi placed her hands on the cool stone rail and let the tears flow.

'Please drink.' Nyomae held out a glass of dark liquid. 'It's an old recipe of my father's. He made it when the children of my village mocked me for talking to animals.' She smiled. 'It always helped, but whether it's due to the blend of herbs, or my faith in him, I cannot tell.'

Elodi clasped her hands around the glass. 'He sounds a wise and thoughtful man. Did you inherit your powers from him or your mother?'

Nyomae's eyes wandered to the glass walls of the Elorym hall. 'While he was a clever and much-read man, my blessing… or curse, came from my mother's side. But she never served the Order. My mother died while I was still young, and therefore never had the chance to explain why I could do things others could not. I was eight when I came to realize I was different to the other children. Until then, I had assumed everyone could hear and see the pictures that came into my head.'

'How did your mother die?'

'From an illness that struck down many in our region. But it was not the Winter Fever, this one appeared in summer. Healers from Elmarand came to our village but failed to find a cure. I was in awe of them. We were only a four-day cart ride from the city, but to a young girl they seemed to be from a distant, magical land. But their potions failed to ease the pain of the fever's victims, let alone prevent their passing.' Nyomae's head bowed. 'If you caught it, you died. But as quickly as it struck, it disappeared, leaving many dead in its wake. Years later, I spent time in Elmarand searching the archives for other such occurrences but found nothing.'

Elodi finished her drink. 'We all know the dreadful stories of the poisoned earth that delayed our recovery following the Archon's *victory*. Did you suspect foul play?'

Nyomae thought for a moment. 'At first. But why my village? Was my mother the intended victim?' She shrugged. 'Or perhaps it was determined by the gods' roll of a dice.' She nodded to Elodi's empty glass. 'Did that help?'

'I believe it has. It must be your father's herbal concoction, or… this time it's my belief in you. We may never know.'

Nyomae took the glass. 'Perhaps there are some things best left as a mystery.'

Elodi sighed. 'So. Back to our present woes. Is there anything you have learned from Dorlan's demise that may aid us in our current predicament?' She grimaced. 'But this time, perhaps it's best you tell and don't show me.'

'A wise precaution. But even my words may cause distress. Dorlan's life after Talaghir is not an easy tale to hear.'

'I imagine not. What transpired after achieving what must be the greatest feat by a mortal, to that sorry state of Dohl in the wood, must be a dreadful state of events.'

Nyomae sat. 'Indeed. After Ormoroth was banished, Dorlan wandered the ice plains of Nordruuk, alone, lost and broken. After many years of a bleak existence, he stumbled upon a Ruuk settlement. But he was sadly mistaken if he thought his life would improve. The Ruuk enslaved him, exploiting the physical strength Dorlan yet retained. Of the duties he was forced to perform for them, I will not tell, for his humiliation was complete. But suffice to say, being a man of the south was enough to seal his fate in Nordruuk. He outlived all who oppressed him, living beyond the limits any ordinary mortal could bear.'

Nyomae poured herself a glass of her father's potion. 'How he continued to survive in such terrible circumstances is testament to the man's resolve. If, like me, his memory began to return, it would only serve to add to his misery. The Ruuk are sly folk, they appeared to know how to mistreat a man to keep them in serfdom, breaking them down so only a shell remains. If events had unfolded otherwise, he may have been granted the release of death, thus bringing an end to his untold years of suffering. But then, either by chance or design, the large man of the south became known to Uluriel. Exhausted by his centuries of a miserable existence, Uluriel found it easy to finally break his damaged spirit. She possessed him, no doubt goaded him and having her fun, then handed him over to Uleva in Durran Wood. There, the poor man continued to suffer and serve as Dohl… until Toryn was brought to one of his cells. Whether it was something about Toryn's presence, or a vestige of Dorlan's lingering memory, Toryn recalled an occasion when Dohl appeared to have a moment of clarity. And, of course, you soon came to witness the power Dohl still held within his body.'

Elodi's heart ached at the suffering of Harlyn's legend. 'Such an appalling tale. I dearly hope his true spirit did not witness his role in the taking of Calerdorn.'

'Alas, I believe the way of the Ul-dalak would be to grant him that torment.' Nyomae's eyes glinted in the golden light. 'But I hope to release him from his plight. If a part of him remains true, I believe I can free Dorlan from the grip of the Ul-dalak.'

Elodi's fists clenched. 'Could he be restored to his former glory?'

'I am afraid not. The power of the Ul-dalak has sustained his life, thus if I can remove the moment of his possession within his Verse, it will bring about a rapid end to his long, and of late, miserable existence.'

'Ah. That is a great shame. What I wouldn't give to have Dorlan riding at our side as he was in his days with Draegelan. Yet, if he continues to fight for the Ul-dalak, our chances of victory remain but a forlorn hope. But how can you release him from the grip of Uleva?'

Nyomae drained her glass. 'I will need to be close, close enough to have access to him and his Verses.'

Elodi patted her sword. 'Then I imagine that would be when we inevitably face our enemies on the battlefield.'

Nyomae rubbed her tired eyes. 'I have more studies to complete, but I believe the Elorym's knowledge will show me how to engage Dorlan's uncorrupt spirit. If this can be done, the part of the man who remains true may side with me. With the right preparation, I can remove Uluriel's curse, and ultimately Uleva's hold over the man. But it will be fraught with danger. If Uluriel senses I have entered the Verse when she broke Dorlan, she will come. I will face her at a time when my physical body will be in peril on the battlefield. My soul would be banished should my mortal self be killed while I am present in the Song.'

'Then we will do all we can to shield you. I shall appoint the best of my knights to the task. If you're successful, defeating Dorlan will save many lives.' Elodi held Nyomae's determined gaze. 'If this can be done for Dorlan, would it be possible to free Uluriel and those who fell at Gormadon?'

'Again, it would be a challenge. But even if both Uldrak and Uleva are present at the coming battle, I doubt I will have the strength following my efforts with Dorlan. It may also prove harder. Neither Elsaya nor Dormarl were as strong as Dorlan. The Ul-dalak's curse has a total hold over them, and while I fear there may still be a part of them that sees through their eyes, they may be unable to assist if I venture into their Verses.'

'But there still remains the hope?'

Nyomae looked to the desk. 'Perhaps. How long do you envisage before we see an all-out attack from the north?'

Elodi was reluctant for her thoughts to leave the Elorym hall. 'There is more activity east of the mountains. I have moved to secure the Kolossos Pass, but knowing our enemy, the activity in Lunn could be a ruse. But if we can hold onto the pass, we can allocate our scant resources quicker and where needed.'

Nyomae picked up the scroll and slipped it into her pocket. 'I expect the main thrust will come down the east side of the Kolossos. Uluriel and her kin desire access to the secrets of Telamir Tower. She knows it yet holds power of the Elorym, and the key to the last line of Aber's Verse. And when she's got what she needs, I believe she will attempt to destroy both Telamir and Syris.'

Elodi stood. 'Then we must ensure we, at the very least, hamper their progress. But to achieve that, we need every hand in the realms that can wield a sword. It may be a while yet before Bardon and the Elites are fit to ride, but they're desperately needed. Bardon will perhaps never fully recover, but it won't stop him offering his service. I shall return to Caermund to speak with him. His council will be invaluable.'

Nyomae took Elodi's hand. 'I will have to be situated close to the front line if I am to end Dorlan's misery. But despite my newfound powers, I'm as vulnerable to an arrow or blade as the next. The more swords you command, the longer you can hold them at bay while I attempt my task.'

Elodi sighed. 'Then I pray to the Three, that can be done before our forces are overrun.'

# 30. The Way of Draegelan

'The Amayans are alive… but only just.' Toryn spoke barely above a whisper to the company. 'They're weak from little food and the constant attention of the Nordleng and other beasts. There are four Amayans inside the fortress. But one is held separately. Three I have met, and trust me, their fighting skills are far superior to ours, even in their current state. The fourth is their leader, Amyra. I believe she surpasses even the others when it comes to combat. They could easily fight their way out if they weren't so drained. All we have to do, is distract the Nordleng long enough to give them an opening.'

Gundrul eyed the gray walls of Vortimo. 'That's easier to say than to achieve. How many Nordleng are we up against?'

'Fortunately, the Amayans have halved that number and killed three shrouls. That leaves about twenty Nordleng, two droogs and the remaining shroul.' Toryn glanced to the younger guards in their company. 'Do not get within ten paces of the droogs. They may look flabby and ungainly, but they can lash out with frightening speed at anything within their range. Go for their handlers. Kill them, and the droog will turn on its master. And avoid taking on a shroul alone. They're stronger than they look, and they'll soon freeze the blood in your veins. Attack in threes or fours. Take out their legs, then decapitate.' Toryn smiled, attempting to make their task seem a little less daunting. 'Trust me, they won't trouble you after that.'

The captain rubbed his chin. 'The Nordleng are a handful. And you reckon there's around twenty?' He looked to the company, then whispered under his breath to Toryn. 'Even if they're exhausted, they're easily a match for most of these young fellows.'

Toryn read the captain's mind. He addressed the company. 'Lucky for us, the Nordleng don't like this place any more than we do. I believe I can exploit that fear to give the Amayans a chance to break out. They're trapped in a hall on the upper floors between the towers. If I could lure the Nordleng out and get them between us and the Amayans, we might take the upper hand.' He looked back to Vortimo. 'The Amayans know we're here. Eryn sensed my presence when I found her. I hope they'll guess our intention and act once we draw the Nordleng from the fortress.'

Gundrul's brow creased as he looked up to the towers. 'And how do you intend to tempt those fiends out? If it were me in there, I'd be happy to sit tight in my stronghold while my enemy wears themselves out climbing the steep road.'

Toryn grinned. 'I shall trick them. They may not fear us, but they'd be wary if I can convince them more Amayans approach. They know they'd stop at nothing to get inside to save their sisters. And they'll also be aware, even from outside, Amayans can lend their strength to those in the hall.' Toryn pointed to the narrow gap in the outer wall. 'I reckon they'd rather confront them at the top of that rubble than on the wide, flat floors of the fortress.'

The captain nodded his approval. 'And that's where we set our trap, eh.'

'Exactly. The stonework either side of that gap is loose and wouldn't need much persuasion to bring down on their heads. But…' he looked to Elrik, 'it needs a few brave folks to scale the wall and attach the ropes.'

Elrik surveyed the ancient stonework. 'I've climbed higher trees. If there's enough handholds in those cracks, I reckon I could do it.'

Lorek stepped forward. 'Then count me in. I have yet to avenge my brothers. The more heads we cave in, the better.'

Gundrul patted Lorek's back. 'I'm sure you'll soon be settling that score.' He eyed the gap in the wall. 'So… how to exploit our trap, eh? If I were in their boots, I'd send half my force here, and hold the rest in reserve. I wouldn't leave the Amayans up there unattended and risk them coming at my back, so I'd leave at least four at the hall.' He scratched his head. 'But once they realize we're not Amayans, I reckon they'd either take up a position at the top of this slope, or close the main gate which means we have no chance to get in. If they choose to attack us as we struggle up that road, there'd be few of us left even if we made it to the top.'

Toryn watched as Gundrul's mind ticked over. 'Archers?'

The captain nodded. 'Exactly. You take four and get as close to the main gate as you dare. Then wait for the first to take the bait and rush out. Once they're clear, you get in and find those Amayans. Take the Nordleng by surprise and avoid hand-to-hand combat, then hopefully our fair ladies will do the rest.'

Toryn looked to the determined faces around him. 'I'm sure they'll be only too happy to oblige.'

Gundrul slapped Toryn's back. 'Good. We'll set a watch inside the wall and make a start. But… how do you convince the Nordleng we're Amayans?' He grinned. 'We don't scrub up too well at the best of times. Surely, they'd never mistaken us for warrior maidens, even in the dark.'

Toryn laughed. 'Certainly not you, Captain. Far too… weather-beaten.' His smile faded. 'I'll have to risk going into the Song. From there, I can plant a vision into the mind of the Nordleng up on that ledge. I'll use the moment when Eryn and her sisters first fled this way. He won't know the difference and assume more Amayans approach.'

Gundrul shrugged. 'I'll settle for whistling my own tunes thanks. But if you can make this song of yours do that, that's good enough for me.' He looked up to the strip of sky above the valley. 'I reckon we've got four hours 'til dawn to get those ropes in place. Then I guess we wait until you've found your gullible Nordleng so we can spring the trap.'

A clash of swords rang down from the walls. Toryn grimaced. 'And we can't spring it quickly enough.'

Elrik and Lorek scaled the wall. It was a challenge climbing by the scant light of the moon, but they could not risk using torches. After much work, they had secured ropes to large stones on both sides of the wall. Elrik believed once dislodged, more would soon follow. Half of the company had used the cover of darkness to hide inside the perimeter. Outside, Gundrul and his men would ambush those surviving the wall's collapse.

Toryn, along with Elrik, Lorek, Janae, and four others had armed themselves with bows and headed up the steep road. Shepra followed, appearing keen to exact her revenge for the loss of her family. The rest of the company had taken positions on the ropes, ready to bring the wall down on the Nordleng heads. But there were risks. How many defenders would remain in the fortress? And once the section of the wall had fallen, could those outside gain entry over the rubble? But time was against them and their options few. The Amayans were close to collapse, and Toryn feared they would struggle to hold out for more than a few days at most.

Now it was up to Toryn. The narrow road had been difficult to negotiate in the dark. Parts had crumbled, leaving gaps with a treacherous drop should they lose their footing. But they had reached the last bend just as dawn did its best to bring light to Vortimo. They squeezed into a crack just below the top ledge, hoping the first Nordleng to rush to the outer wall would be too preoccupied to see them.

Toryn stood and scanned the gray walls. His *farsight* partly revealed what lay within. Of the Nordleng, all but six slept. Four watched over the Amayans, while two stood just outside the main gate, perhaps to breathe the fresher, mountain air. One of the droogs lay secured to a pillar close to those guarding the Amayans. Its skin rippled — it had not long eaten. Toryn's stomach turned as he saw a man chained to the adjacent pillar. The poor soul must have been taken from one of the villages around Vymarl. And knowing the cruel nature of the Nordleng, the prisoner would have witnessed the droog guzzle down his companion and suffered to hear the muffled cries as he was slowly digested.

Toryn's fists clenched. Now he must find the shroul. While not as agile a fighter as the Nordleng, its presence alone was a menace. He shivered as he located the creature. The shroul wandered through the dungeons of the fortress. The walls turned white as the moisture clinging to the stonework froze at its passing. But mercifully, the Nordleng did not have to feed it: Vortimo's pits were full of bones from its prisoners of old, more than enough to keep the shroul satisfied.

Toryn retreated from the darkness and looked back to the Nordleng at the gate. The younger of the two despised the fortress. He sensed he would have fled weeks ago had he not feared capture and being fed to the droog.

Toryn patted Shepra for luck then gave the signal to Gundrul far below. He closed his eyes and sought the vision he would plant in the young Nordleng's mind. By a stroke of luck, the Watchers were occupied elsewhere, perhaps distracted by Nyomae's presence. Luck or not, his path to the recent past was clear. He found the Amayans' desperate rush through the pass, pursued by a large band of Nordleng. They had been surrounded outside Vymarl with only the route to Vortimo left intentionally open to them. Reluctantly, they had set their beloved horses free and fled. But as Toryn had expected, the Nordleng were imbued with some power that had heightened their abilities and shielded them from the dangers his company had encountered.

Toryn turned and directed the vision to the young Nordleng's present Verse. He responded, peering down the pass, then pointing frantically to the gap in the outer wall. The other ran into the fortress. Toryn signaled to Gundrul the bait had been taken. He ran his hand along the Amayan bow. The Archonholm's fletchers had done well to make arrows worthy of the weapon. Now he hoped to put them to good use and thin out the enemy before they could draw their keen blades.

Shouts from inside drew his attention. Footsteps rang out along the tunnel leading to the gate. Toryn pressed his back against the rock. He counted ten Nordleng as they sprinted down the road. Certain no more would come, he led his small company to the gate. They crouched at the side and nocked their arrows, anticipating more would emerge once their trap was sprung.

They did not have to wait long.

A shout went up at the perimeter wall — the signal to haul on the ropes. Toryn held his breath until the satisfying crash of falling masonry eased his nerves. He whispered. 'Watch the gate.' Swords clashed below as Gundrul ambushed the survivors.

More footsteps. Four ran out from the gate. Toryn and his archers let fly and brought them down. By Toryn's calculation, six remained. He waited. Silence. With his heart pounding in his ears, he led the dash to the gate and ducked inside. But just as the first of the party entered, the portcullis dropped, followed by the heavy gate slamming shut.

Outside, Shepra barked, and the rest of his party hammered on the gate. But they may as well have been on the other side of the Caerwal Mountains — the gate would remain shut fast.

'Toryn?' He peered into the dark.

'Is that you, Elrik?'

'Yes.' His breath came in fits and starts. 'We got into some scuffles as lads, but nothing like this, eh.'

'Well let's hope we can get out of it.' He turned. 'Anyone else make it through?' Lorek and Janae answered. Toryn whispered. 'Pleased to have you along. That makes it four of us against six Nordleng. But their foul beasts somewhat tip the balance in their favor.' He took a few paces and bumped into a wall. 'We must locate the Amayans to even those odds.' He reached out. 'Come to me. We'll follow this wall and find a way out of the gatehouse.'

'Toryn?' Janae joined him at the wall. 'Could this be a trap? Someone… or something shut the gate. Did they see us coming?'

'Possibly. But why would most of the Nordleng rush out to greet us? Unless… let me take a look.' His *farsight* revealed only the gatehouse. But it was not due to the dark that he could see no farther. His way was blocked. 'Stand ready. The shroul comes.'

# 31. In the Face of Fear

Toryn's wide eyes sought the creature, but he could see nothing in the gloom. He gasped. 'Don't let it get close. Keep moving. You'll freeze with its touch.' He reached out and found a hand. 'Form a line. Link arms. We'll lose two swords, but we won't strike each other if we know our positions.'

Lorek whispered. 'I'll take the left, it's my sword hand.'

'I've got the other. Elrik, Janae, be ready to take our places if we fall.' Their backs pressed against the cold gate. Toryn pulled them to the right. 'Keep the wall at our backs. We can't allow the shroul to get behind us.'

The air cooled. The sweat on Toryn's brow froze. He tilted his head to look out of the corner of his eye. In the dark, he could just make out the shape of a stooped, spindly figure a few paces from them. Toryn shuddered at the sight. The shroul resembled a great hound, struggling to walk on its hind legs. But this hound had a head too large for its body, and a wide, gaping mouth full of teeth like icicles. With its awkward gait, it took a step, snatching at the air with its long claws, ready to clasp around their throats. Toryn's grip on Janae tightened. Her breath chilled his neck. He whispered. 'I see it… just.'

Janae gulped. 'Me too. It's hideous.'

Toryn gagged on the stench of sour milk. 'Get ready.' He swung at the shadow but missed. Lorek's sword swished thin air. The shroul's icy breath stung his skin like a gale in winter. A claw loomed out of the dark. Toryn ducked, then lunged, thrusting his blade up. His body jolted. A screech tore through the gatehouse.

Janae cried out. 'Here! In front of me.' Her hand crushed Toryn's. Lorek's swing connected, clattering as if he had struck stone. The creature squealed, sending a gust of bitter, rank air into their faces.

Lorek swung again. 'I got his legs!' The rattle of bones echoed from the walls. 'It's down.'

Toryn leaped, plunging his blade to where it had fallen. He struck. Lorek followed and they both slashed wildly in the dark. The dreadful wailing stopped. Toryn sank to his knees and gasped for air. He clutched his chest as the last of the shroul's chill breath tore into his lungs.

High above, the gray light of dawn seeped through a dozen arrow loops to reveal the grim sight of their small victory. Toryn stared at its large, grotesque head laying close to its shattered body. The mouth stayed open as if still emitting its dying screech. Dozens of needle-sharp teeth lined its jaw, poised to crunch on their bones had they failed. But it was the eyes that shocked Toryn. While gray and glassy in death, they could have belonged to a human. He knew the tales of Ormoroth's punishment of those defying his will in the north. Were they true? If so, this poor creature had once been a man or woman. Did those eyes once share a glance with their beloved spouse? Whether true or not, they had ended its miserable existence.

Toryn stood and looked to the faces of his companions, still caked with a thin layer of ice. He let out a long sigh. 'That leaves two droogs and half a dozen Nordleng.' He nudged the leg of the shroul. 'And this was the weakest.'

Elrik turned. 'Could we open the gate? If we can't let the others in… what are our chances?'

Toryn scanned the walls now visible in the growing light. 'I can't see how. There're no chains or ropes. And no stairs leading to an upper floor.'

Lorek banged on the gate. 'And no sign of those outside. I can't hear Shepra.'

Toryn's heart sank. 'Were they ambushed? But where could they have come from? Let's hope Gundrul has been successful at the wall.' More sunlight forced its way through the high windows. He looked up. Two rows of wooden archers' platforms lined the walls of the gatehouse. In the ceiling, dark circles marked what he knew to be murder holes. He dreaded to guess what foul, burning concoctions had rained down on Draegelan's forces as they fought for every yard. The opposite end of the gatehouse was their only way out. But the dark portal appeared only too eager to swallow up unwelcome visitors.

Toryn wiped his blade clean. 'We have no choice. It looks grim, but remember, we follow in Draegelan's footsteps.' He chuckled. 'Although, he did command more than just four.' If his three companions had reservations, they did not let it show on their faces. He looked to each in turn. 'If I had to pick three to go with me, it would be you.'

Elrik laughed. 'I'd rather have an army of Amayans, but you folks will do for now.'

Lorek swished his sword. 'For my brothers.'

Janae whispered. 'And for that poor family at Cafra.'

The portal led them into a network of passages, built to confuse and slow the progress of an invading army. Toryn could only imagine the strength of the Seven Realms at its height. Despite his powers, Ormoroth was obviously wary of Draegelan and Dorlan, seeing the need to build such a formidable fortress to maintain a presence in the south. Yet Vortimo had eventually fallen. But what force did Draegelan bring? And how many fine soldiers were lost taking it?

Janae stopped at a corner and held up her hand. Toryn was impressed by her ability to maintain a sense of direction — he had long since become disorientated in the labyrinth of tunnels. She sniffed the air. 'I believe we're approaching the end. There's a wide, open space beyond. Perhaps a hall. And I can hear water.' She shook her flask. 'I'm empty. We should fill up while we can.'

Toryn peered into the shadows. 'Agreed. Then we need to find a staircase. The Amayans are on the upper levels. But where are the Nordleng?' He waved Elrik and Lorek forward, and together they rounded the bend. Janae was right. They found themselves in a hall with a high, vaulted ceiling. Light streamed through tall, narrow windows to their right but failed to penetrate far into the gloom. Three long, stone tables formed a square as they joined a dais at the head. A giant, ornate chair sat on the platform. A throne? Had Ormoroth once sat in this hall? Toryn stared up to the ceiling. At first, he presumed the dozens of wheels suspended from long chains were candleholders. His scalp prickled as he realized the rusted iron wheels were not for lighting the hall. The pale light revealed the remains of long dead prisoners. Toryn's back arched, remembering the pain he had endured in the days hanging from the bridge at Archonholm. But he had been released. The souls above received no such salvation. His wrists ached as he felt their suffering and humiliation. How long had they dangled from their chains for the pleasure of those feasting below?

Elrik whispered. 'Are those…?'

Toryn turned away. 'Once brave soldiers. If we ever get time, we should free them and give them a proper burial.'

Janae's voice echoed through the hall. 'There's the water I heard.'

Toryn followed her direction. Water trickled from a crack in the far wall to form a pool. Parched, he strode over and scooped up a handful. He drank. 'It's melted ice.

Tastes pure.' They kneeled to drink and refill their flasks, unsure when they might find drinkable water again in such a forbidding place.

Toryn wiped his mouth and looked back to the throne. What foul creatures had sat before their commander? And what purpose did the large space in the middle of the tables serve? He dared not enter the Verses here, but he imagined many unfortunate captives would have met a gruesome death for the pleasure of Vortimo's occupants.

In the dull light, Toryn noticed his friends looked gaunt, perhaps weakened by the fortress. He was reminded of the Amayans in the heart of Foranfae. 'Are you well? You look exhausted.'

Lorek spoke first. 'I've felt better. But it's been a long night, and the day has not brought much relief.'

Janae looked up from the pool. 'Many have suffered here. Many have met a horrible end.' She spat. 'This hall saps our strength. It feeds off us. We should not stay long.'

Toryn nodded. 'Our flasks are full. Now let's find the Amayans and get out of—' A flash caught his eye. A blue light flickered through a doorway at the far end. 'It's them!' A clash of swords echoed through the hall. 'They fight. We must go.' Without a second thought, they drew their weapons and raced to their aid. But as they rushed through the door, the light vanished. Once again, they stood in darkness, deep within Ormoroth's ancient stronghold.

'Where did we come in?' Lorek's voice sounded weak. 'I can't see the doorway. Shouldn't the light from the hall be visible?'

Toryn groaned. 'Another trap.' A wet slap on stone, followed by a deep gurgle turned his stomach. He yelled. 'Droogs!' The tunnel grew a little brighter. A faint, green light reflected off the rippling skins of two droogs as they slithered towards them.

Elrik stuttered. 'How… do we fight two?'

Toryn thought back to his previous encounter. He spoke through a tight jaw. 'Remember what I said about their handlers. Break their—' He gaped. These worms had no restraints, no collars to unmake, no master to set them upon. Who commanded the droogs? Bile rose into his throat. With dread, Toryn understood the threat came not from the droogs alone. He whispered. 'There's something else here.' A tall figure, blacker than the tunnel, loomed behind the worms. Janae gripped Toryn's arm. He struggled to find the air to speak. 'Stay strong. We fight together.' But *what* did they fight?

Toryn pressed into the door at his back. But there was no retreat, no way out. The creature stepped slowly into the light as if savoring the terror of its victims. A tip of a long, thin nose appeared. Behind the nose, a cruel chin, then to Toryn's horror… two glistening, black orbs followed. They glared straight at him. Toryn cried out. An icy hand seemed to grasp his stomach, seeking to wrench it free. All else about him faded. He had forgotten the droogs — it was just him and this creature. Its slit mouth widened into a sickening grin. It knew. It knew Toryn realized what he faced: a warlock. Not a *kruul* that had infiltrated Archonholm. This was the embodiment of Ormoroth's will, a vessel of the Dark Verses. And it stood before Toryn.

The warlock raised an arm. His long, bony fingers splayed, then snapped shut as if seizing the air from the tunnel. Toryn choked. It felt as if the creature grasped his throat. He fought to bring his hands together in a futile attempt to enter the Song, but his way was blocked. A low rumble filled the tunnel. For a moment, Toryn thought the main gate was opening and help was coming. But he was wrong. The warlock cackled. Toryn knew its mind – he relished the chance to enslave and corrupt him. The creature waved an arm and stopped the droogs. Their sweating bodies swelled as they flailed their tails, slapping at the floor, angry to be denied their prey. But the warlock cared not. Toryn was in no doubt the droogs would feed off his friends once the creature had finished with him.

The floor trembled as the warlock spoke. 'Surrender, *Imaari*.' He spat out the word as if it caused pain to utter. But the deep, guttural voice pained Toryn more. The words violated his ears, forcing their way into his head as if to split his skull in two. Toryn's bones shook as the warlock offered him an ultimatum. 'Give yourself to me, and I will release the others. They are weak and of no use.'

At his side, Toryn's companions stood motionless as if in a different time. His mind raced. The warlock had them trapped, commanded two droogs, and wielded an ancient and most terrible power. It could easily slaughter his friends and still capture him. Then Toryn understood. Despite the warlock's strength, his power was stretched to its limits. It curbed the droogs' urge to attack; it barred Toryn's way to the Song, and… yes, he saw it — the warlock sustained the barrier restraining the Amayans. Toryn had to find a way to challenge him, to drain a little more of his strength. If he could distract it, the warlock would have to choose between subduing the droogs, containing the Amayans, or preventing Toryn's access to the Song. He sensed the fear and loathing the worms had for their master, thus the warlock could not risk releasing his hold over them. While Toryn doubted the droogs could kill their master, an attack would give him and his friends a chance to escape.

'Your time runs out, *Imaari*.' The warlock's breath scorched Toryn's face. 'You wish for your friends to be eaten? Surrender, surrender now, or you will witness their fate.'

Toryn met the creature's glare. He took a breath. 'No.' He stepped forward, raising his blade, forcing his body to move as if against a fast-flowing river.

The warlock's thin lips twisted. 'No? You dare to defy me?' A hand extended and twisted. A band tightened around Toryn's chest. The creature stooped. Its eyes met his. 'You know what I am, *Toryn*. Do you think you can defeat me?'

Toryn stammered. 'You… you know my name?'

A deep rattle issued from its throat. 'Granted, it is not the name given to you by your father' – it blinked, coating its dark eyes with a moist layer – 'or the Maidens.'

'My father?'

Its eyes widened. 'I can take you to him, Toryn. But know this. His resistance wanes. He will soon become a servant of the Dark Verses. He will know you.' It raised a finger and touched Toryn's forehead. He saw his father chained to a rockface in a vast cavern. Finromir's head sagged onto his chest. His ribs convulsed, protruding from his starved frame. The warlock hissed the man's name. Finromir raised his head and opened his eyes. Toryn cried out as two empty sockets stared back.

The warlock laughed. 'He has waited all these years. He is longing to *see* his son.'

Toryn yelled his defiance. 'No! I won't let you do this.' The corner of the warlock's eyes twitched. Toryn saw his chance. Revealing the fate of his father had drained his assailant's powers. By only a little, but it was sufficient to exploit. Toryn sought entry to the Song. He did not need a specific Verse, just the attempt would suffice. He drew upon the resources Nyomae knew to be within him. He spoke his father's name. The warlock's hold wavered. Now it had to make a choice.

Toryn's way to the Song opened. The warlock moved to shut him out once more, but the act weakened its claim over the droogs. Toryn pushed back. The barricade surrounding the Amayans shattered. The door behind swung open. A cleansing light flooded the room. But the danger was far from over.

A droog reared and twisted towards its captor. The warlock spat a curse, spun on its heels, and was gone. One droog slithered after him. But the other eyed Toryn and his companions as they staggered forward, released from the warlock's spell. The droog's skin rippled, secreting a glistening fluid down its gray body. Toryn choked on the reek of its desire. He tried to find the worm in the Song but was exhausted. He spat out the foul taste and gasped. 'Quick strikes. In and out. Don't let it look you in the eye.' Toryn lowered his blade and circled the droog. 'Split up. One to distract, the others to attack. Drive deep and jump back.'

The droog slapped down on the floor to face Toryn. It raised its swollen head, fixing its bulging, yellow eyes on its prey. Its drooling mouth gaped. Toryn stared in horror at its pink tongue, writhing like a snake. Move! He leaped aside just as the droog vomited, spraying its poison that splattered, hissing and steaming at his feet. The foul mess filled the air with its sickly, sweet stench. The worm coiled and screeched. Behind it, Elrik stood with his blade dripping with the droog's green blood. It twisted and lunged back at Elrik, but Toryn and Lorek cut short its strike with two thrusts at its exposed belly. Janae cried out as its blood splashed on her arm. But she held her stance. As the droog thrashed and squirmed, searching for a victim, Janae sprang and drove her blade into a deep crease in its neck. Lorek repeated his attack, opening a gash on its slimy skin. But he slipped on the blood and bile gushing from the droog. He lost his footing and sprawled at the belly of the worm. Toryn dashed forward to grab his flailing arm, but the droog flipped and slammed down, trapping Lorek beneath its vile body. Toryn read its mind. It could not afford to eat. To consume one of them would make it vulnerable. It had to kill first. Lorek's muffled cry tore at his heart.

He bellowed. 'Together! It's weak.'

The three rushed the droog, slashing and stabbing at its greasy hide. Blood spurted from its wounds, scalding Toryn's arm as his blade opened more. The droog coiled, then unfurled to lash out, knocking Elrik from his feet. But it knew it was beaten. It gurgled and slithered away to die.

Toryn drew a breath and collapsed besides the lifeless Lorek. They had faced a powerful enemy and had achieved a victory of sorts. But at a high price. He rested his hand on Lorek's shoulder, dismayed to be present at the death of the third brother from Tamforth.

But he spluttered. Toryn gasped. 'Thank the Three. I thought you were dead.'

Lorek rolled on his side and coughed. 'I dearly wish I was. Argh! The taste… the smell.'

Toryn helped him up. 'Can't be many who have lived to tell the tale of being smothered by a droog. But we need to wash that drool off your skin.' He rubbed his burned arm. 'We all do. The melted ice in the hall should help.'

They lay in the pool and let the cool water ease their burning skin. Lorek gulped from the stream trickling through the crack in the wall, swilling and spitting to rid himself of the foul taste. He grimaced. 'Not sure if I'll ever be able to drink ale again and not be reminded of that worm.'

Toryn stared at the unfortunate victims hanging from the ceiling. 'Hamar once told me of a guard who had a close call. He said it took a month to get rid of the stench.'

Lorek groaned. 'Then I guess you're going to shun my company, eh.'

Elrik chuckled. 'Now we have a reason and don't have to be polite.'

Toryn recalled the horror of the Nordleng cut free from the droog in the Foranfae. 'Lucky you didn't end up in its gut. That must be the worst of ways to go. If I had—' Toryn sprang up. 'Swords! That sounds real. The warlock won't have the strength to set another trap.' He ran. 'The Amayans have broken free.'

# 32. The Tangled Web

'Ruan reports little has changed in the west.' Elodi passed on the message to Bardon. They stood upon the high sea wall of Caermund. Below, waves crashed onto the rocks, reminding her of the view from her room in Calerdorn. Bardon took it, but she noticed his hand still shook. The lord had made a steady recovery under the care of the healers, but as yet, appeared unsure on his feet and kept a distance from the edge of the wall.

He squinted at the note. 'I'm afraid my sight is not as good as it was, Elodi.'

'Ah, I apologize. I shall summarize. Ruan and his spearmen are stationed at the Seran River south of the forest. Another of my trusted captains, Cubric, commands an Archonian division stationed to Ruan's east at Greendell. There's still the odd skirmish along their front, but the Ruuk have made no effort to push deeper into Noor in numbers that would cause concern. I have given instruction they are to pull back to the River Wend if outflanked. And if the Ruuk commit to a full invasion, they must ensure the West Watchtower is held.'

Bardon rubbed his clean-shaven chin. 'That's encouraging, but we both know what tends to follow a period of relative calm regarding our visitors from Nordruuk.'

'That is my worry. But at least that has afforded us the chance to secure the Kolossos Pass.' She looked out to the dark skies on the horizon. 'But to what avail? If they come with the strength we know they command, we could find ourselves penned up in the pass, leaving them to rampage south.'

Bardon eyed the approaching clouds. 'But yet, they wait. You say Nyomae believes they may still be wary of us. Otherwise, they would surely have struck south following the crushing of our forces at Caerwal.'

'She may have a point. But Nyomae's recent discoveries reveal a power that could work against us. We could damage ourselves in the act of invoking Draegelan's knowledge. Perhaps that is why they wait.' Elodi let out a long sigh. 'I'm forever trying to guess our foe's intentions while suspicious they are pulling my strings. I feel as if I'm being played, nudged and coerced into taking action that may leave our forces stranded. Am I to view every move of theirs as a feint? How can I tell what the right move is to make?'

Bardon pulled his cloak tighter as the sea breeze picked up. 'They are a devious foe. But then, they will not make it easy for you. Why should they?'

Elodi helped Bardon secure his cloak. 'I do not have anything like their resources to turn the tables on them. I dearly wish there was something I could do to… to use the Archon's phrase, sow seeds of doubt in *their* hearts. But what do I have at my disposal?'

'You have Nyomae, and of course, this young fellow, Toryn.'

'But can I be sure they are also not manipulating every move *they* make? Nyomae is forced to delve deeper into Draegelan's discoveries, those, I hasten to add, he felt necessary to conceal in a secret vault. And Toryn finds himself in Vortimo, helping the Amayans who themselves appear to have been forced to enter that cursed place.' Bardon stumbled. Elodi caught his arm. 'I'm sorry. I burden you much with my woes when you are in need of rest.'

He caught his breath. 'Not at all, Elodi. But you will have to excuse this old man. My legs have yet to make a full recovery… if they ever will.'

Elodi helped him to a bench in an alcove in the wall. 'Please say if you prefer to conduct our discussions inside.' She patted his leg. 'But you're strong. You have many years left in you… and the realms need every one of those remaining years.'

'Thank you for your confidence.' He smiled. 'I try to convince myself I'm still a young man, but my bones are not that easily fooled.' Bardon looked out to the waves crashing into the headland, gaining in height as the wind strengthened. 'I look very much forward to meeting Nyomae. She sounds a very useful ally, a powerful one at that. Is she equal to the Ul-dalak?'

Elodi leaned back against the wall. 'Nyomae's story is a remarkable one. She's had a long and eventful life by any reckoning. She undoubtedly commands great power. But I fear the burden of the demands I place upon her, sit heavily upon her shoulders.'

'And, what of this Toryn fellow?'

Elodi sighed. 'He's come a long way in such a short time. He knew nothing of his heritage until a few months ago, yet he finds himself thrust into the forefront of the fight of our time.' She looked down to her hands in her lap. 'I hope he can handle such a responsibility… and stay safe. Nyomae has done her best to school us both in the ways of our powers. But his presence attracts the dark forces. He grows strong, but he still has much to learn and master.'

Bardon struggled to make his voice heard over the gusts buffeting Caermund. 'But he is obviously a resourceful and resilient young man. It's quite an achievement to trek the length of the realms, and then play his part in foiling Uluriel's plans.' His bushy eyebrows raised. 'Not to mention wrestling with her at the top of the Archon's tower.'

'But having entered Vortimo…' Her gaze wandered back to the sea.

'You fear for him?' Elodi nodded but stayed silent. Bardon pressed. 'And am I right to assume you have… feelings for this man?' Her eyes closed. He squeezed her hand. 'If, as Nyomae believes, he masters more of the innate power within, perhaps he may yet surprise our foes.'

She clutched his cold fingers. 'But… Vortimo, Bardon? Not for nothing has that valley been sealed for all these years.'

'Take solace that he's located the Amayans.' He laughed. 'In my youth I longed to meet one of these warriors, and there was Eleni, the Lady of Harlyn, right before my eyes all those years... and then you. It is a blessing you have Amayan blood. I doubt many could endure the days you have spent in the saddle these last weeks.' Bardon sighed. 'I wish you could have known your mother. You are very much like her.'

Elodi looked away. 'When Wendel first told me of the events leading up to my birth, I felt anger towards her. I know that sounds awful, but I couldn't understand why she would ride north with the others while expecting me. But now I appreciate loyalty and duty override even family.'

'That is a burden we have to bear as leaders, especially in troubled times.'

'And a burden that grows heavier by the day.' Elodi stood. 'Now I must prepare to head north. Ruan's dispatch convinces me it will not be long before our enemy reveals its full hand. They gather both on the west and east of the Kolossos, yet we would be hard pressed to face them on just one front. The pass must be secured, but still we will be stretched thin.' She looked down to Bardon. 'I do not ask you to ride yet, but when you feel ready, your presence would be most welcome in Ormsk… along with any who are fit to ride with you.'

Bardon groaned as he rose from the bench. 'I will give myself a few more days but be assured I will follow. The last survivors from Mundrake's Isle came ashore last night. They are weak, but their training will see them through. I'm sure the healers will work their magic. I would hope to bring close to a thousand swords with me, and perhaps more as they recover. The call went out for horses for the knights. They will not be as well-trained as their own mounts, but we will make do.'

Elodi regarded his face. 'A thousand swords are more than I could have wished for only a few weeks ago. With the Archonians and reserves, I expect to muster a force totaling eighteen thousand, but where they are to be assigned requires careful planning. But I fear the cobtrolls will not tolerate our intrusion through *their* pass.'

Bardon scoffed. 'They would be bold indeed to ambush such a force.'

Elodi turned. 'We once thought that of the Ruuk.'

*The Ruuk are moving*. Elodi's heart sank. She had been roused from her bed by her aide bringing a dispatch from Amyndra. The captain of Broon had ridden deep into Ormsk and witnessed bands of Ruuk raiding settlements south of Torm. While still only in small bands, she believed it was a sign of intent.

Elodi let her eyes wander across the flat grasslands of Mund outside her window. The crescent moon shed just enough light to afford her a view of the Formund Forest. Far to the north, the Ruuk plundered farms of precious livestock, meeting little resistance. She slapped the sill. The east! It became clear. They would strike down the east of the Kolososs. Nyomae believed Uluriel desired to break the waning power of Telamir. Elodi made her decision. She could not wait a moment longer.

Elodi dressed, fastened her sword belt, and called for her aide. The First Horse and Archonian Knights would ride to the pass, freeing the Archonians to head to the forests to support the reserves of Ormsk. Preparations had begun the day before. But now she desired to leave before sunrise. She had to reinforce the guard at the East Watchtower, but time was crucial. Should she arrive a day late, she risked surrendering the pass, and inevitably the middle realms. And if the Ruuk gained a foothold in the dense forests, they would be difficult to extract.

Elodi gave her orders to the aide rubbing sleep from his eyes. In moments, the sound of horses' hooves upon cobbles echoed through the city of Caermund as the stable hands readied them for their riders. She returned to the window to see candles flickering in houses and inns. Her heart quickened, but not from panic — Elodi was ready to ride out.

She nodded to the men who came to collect her trunk. 'On the wagon please. Then head for the East Watchtower at the Kolossos Pass as fast as your horses can manage.' Elodi watched them haul the trunk onto their shoulders and hurry from the room. It would take two weeks of hard riding to reach the pass. The wagons would need twice that time, but most of her belongings were not vital to the cause; Elodi wondered what state they would find her in on their arrival.

She bent to blow out the candle at her bedside, then picked up Amyndra's message. Her hand wrapped around it. The last part had struck a pang of dread. Amyndra had spied a small party of Ruuk hurrying along the Great Northeast Road. The route would take them to Aralak Gorge. Fearing an attack on the fence, Amyndra stated she would take a company of the First Horse to bolster the vital defenses.

Elodi stopped. Could the raids elsewhere be a

distraction? Did the Ruuk intend to free the dreaded spiders? Surely, they would pose as much a danger to them as to Elodi's forces. Or… her blood froze, did the Uldalak believe they could command these vicious, unruly creatures. If that were the case, they could be sent to the Kolossos Pass, or the forests and prove a most terrible threat. The Ruuk could sit back and wait for her ranks to be devastated by the foul beasts. And once pumped full of poison, her forces would be too sick to see off a Ruuk attack.

Elodi strode out into the dark corridor. A faint, orange light cast shadows ahead of her. She glanced down. The sliver of her blade above its sheath, glowed. Her hand warmed, anticipating the battles to come. But her heart froze, fearing how many would die under her command.

# 33. No Way South

Nyomae had spent a restless night on the small bed in Abernost's vault. Her mind had refused to settle, denying her the sleep she so desperately required. Reading the last pages of Draegelan's notes had pushed her to the limit of her endurance, and the edge of sanity. Had she the time, Nyomae would have given herself months to prepare for what came next. But she had just days, and those would be spent on the road.

In the middle of the night, she had tried once more to find Idraman in the Verses. Standing at the top of Abernost's Round Tower, she had faced the white peaks of the Caerwals peering above the horizon. Like the Kolossos, Nyomae believed they were raised by the gods in their battles, long before the Maidens saw fit to bring the Elorym into their world. Despite her recent advances, the Caerwals still hampered her attempts to enter the Verses of the south. Yet, Idraman had found a way to overcome the barrier when he had found Hope on the hills overlooking the Foranfae. But his voice had been as a crude weapon, bludgeoning all those who stood in its path. Nyomae had tried many ways to penetrate the jagged slopes, only to be met by a cacophony of sound echoing back from the wall. Too many voices overwhelmed the Song, leaving an exhausted Nyomae to concede defeat. She had retired back to her bed, but if she had hoped to sleep, the sudden appearance of the warlock in Toryn's Verses, startled her awake. Mercifully, he had survived the encounter, offering her some comfort in the dark hours.

Nyomae had risen before the sun, unsure whether she had slept. But she could not afford even a few hours delay.

She nudged her horse through Abernost's gate and onto the road north. Not for the first time she felt envious of the befuddled woman, a young man had named Hope. Back then, she had wandered the land, oblivious to the troubles of the realms. Her time in the shadow had served to heal the hurt inflicted upon herself from reciting the dreaded Verse at Gormadon. But the Nym had been right — now she must heal others harmed by her action. To achieve that, Nyomae had to negotiate the path through the Song where even Draegelan had hesitated. He believed what he sought lay deep in Elorym Lore, a key to reveal the meaning of the last line of Aber's Verse. Yet, to take that path, Nyomae had to enter the place that had driven their greatest Archon to madness. She had to find a way into Telamir Tower.

# 34. A Curse Upon Your Heads

'You're certain about this?' Elrik patted Toryn's shoulder, but his eyes stayed fixed on the Amayans standing by the wall.

Toryn nodded. 'You should go back.' He looked to Elrik's red skin, noting his own had already healed. 'We've achieved our mission to find the Amayans.' He looked to the three warriors. 'Well, almost. I will go with them to rescue Amyra, but you and the company should head for Vymarl. You'll find Captain Gundrul outside. I sense we lost two in the ambush, and three are injured. You would all benefit from the healers at the town.'

Elrik looked to Toryn. 'And when we're fit? What then? Do you know what's happened since we left Archonholm?'

Toryn recalled his dream. He had done as Nyomae asked and found her while he slept. She had appeared only briefly, but long enough to impart Elodi's strategy. 'Head for the East Watchtower of the Kolossos Pass. Lady Harlyn leads an army there. She intends to keep the way open for our forces in the west.'

Elrik nodded. 'I must admit, I won't be disappointed to get out of this place, but I'm glad we came.' He leaned in and whispered. 'Those Amayans may have spent a month fighting for their lives, but the tales don't do them justice, eh. I have never seen such—'

Calestri called over. 'And the tales also fail to do justice to our exceptionally good hearing.'

Despite the dim light, Toryn was sure Elrik blushed. He blustered. 'No… no they don't. But I didn't mean no offence.'

'None taken.' Calestri smiled and winked at Toryn. 'And not all simple folk are quite so simple as *our* tales depict.' The three walked over. 'And we appreciate your rescue mission.'

Toryn looked to Eryn. Of the three, she appeared to have suffered the most from their ordeal. 'Rescue? I can't think we made that much difference.'

Eryn's eyes flickered blue as she met his gaze. 'But that you did. It was your presence that tipped the balance and allowed us to break out. Defying the warlock gave us that chance. The Nordleng here may be dead, but our work is not done. We came for Amyra and that creature still holds her.' Her mouth twisted. 'That fiend kept her captive in the tunnels under the mountains. His aim was to turn her, then capture the rest of us one-by-one.' Eryn sighed. 'She is strong and yet resists… but even Amyra can be broken.'

Arijan took Toryn's hand. 'That was a brave thing to do. Warlocks pose a most dire threat.' She glanced to her sisters. 'We do not ask you to accompany us into the dark places beneath this place… but you'll be most welcome. We are weak after a month of fending off these foul creatures, and eating vermin does little to sustain strength. But we must not delay. It's vital we wrest Amyra from the warlock's grip.'

Toryn straightened. 'I will come. I was tasked to find you, and while one remains missing, my mission is not done.'

Eryn smiled. 'Then wish your friends farewell.'

Toryn took his companions to one side. He regarded their gaunt faces. 'You have proven yourselves beyond reproach. You have faced challenges many would have fled without a second thought. Yet you stood your ground and fought with skill and bravery. I will make sure your deeds are made known to Lady Harlyn.'

In turn, they clutched Toryn's forearm. Elrik was the last. He placed his hands on Toryn's shoulders and looked him in the eye. 'Do you remember the day the Archon's knights came to Midwyche?'

Toryn nodded. 'It seems so long ago.'

Elrik laughed. 'I couldn't wait to leave and looked forward to living the life of a guard Hamar spoke of. At the celebration, I complained about nothing ever happening in the village.' A wry smile crossed Elrik's face. 'I recall you saying there may come a day when I'd welcome nothing happening. Well… my friend, that day has come. What I wouldn't give to sit and watch the carts come back from the field, and then perhaps enjoy an ale or two, eh.'

Toryn lowered his voice. 'Then I also look forward to spending a long, dull day back home with you soon.' He released his hold. 'Stay safe, Elrik. Let's do Hamar proud. Oh, and please give Shepra a pat from me. I believe she's unhurt.'

Elrik beamed. 'She'll have given as good as she got, but she's too clever to be outdone by the Nordleng. I bet she won't have a scratch on her.' His jaw clenched. 'May the Three be with you, Tor.'

Toryn watched his friends leave. Would he see them again? They faced dangers they could barely comprehend and could easily fall in the challenges ahead. He turned as a hand rested upon his shoulder. Eryn stood at his side. 'We must go. I cannot abide these foul creatures holding Amyra a day longer. She would be seen as a great prize if they can corrupt her. Amyra is strong, but she has endured our enemy's attention for too long. And the loss of one more sister is not something we can tolerate.'

'Ah! Then I have good news.' Toryn turned to the others. 'You told me of Eleni.' He paused. 'I have met her daughter.'

'A daughter?'

'Lady Harlyn. Eleni named her Elodi. She has her mother's sword. And apparently her skills.'

Arijan's eyes widened. 'That explains the awakening we felt. Eleni's sword recognizes her daughter's hand.' She turned to Toryn. 'Her Amayan Fire must have been kindled by a foe she faced.'

'Nyomae called it a *kruul*, a warlock's spirit I believe. It came to Archonholm.'

Eryn spat. 'In Archonholm? They grow bold. But in a strange way it's served a purpose. Our new sister will be stronger for it.'

Toryn heaved a sigh. 'That's encouraging to hear, for her and the people. Elodi has taken command of the armies of the Five Realms. She rides north.'

Calestri beamed. 'If she possesses half of Eleni's ability, she will be a force to strike fear into our enemies.'

Eryn turned to face the doorway. 'Then let us find Amyra and swell our numbers. She must not share the fate of Tanis.'

Toryn's voice echoed as they descended the steep, spiral stairway beneath Vortimo. 'Who, or what is a warlock? I was reluctant to ask in front of my company.'

Eryn glanced over her shoulder. 'You were wise not to. Your friends' spirits must not be shattered if they are to stand any chance of victory. They must fight the Ruuk, while we and Nyomae face the warlocks.'

'Are there many?'

'Their numbers are not known to us. You fought one known as Vordrak. He, as with all Ormoroth's commanders, was once a mighty Elorym warrior.'

Toryn slowed. 'Elorym? I've learned a little of them from Nyomae's thoughts. But if this Vordrak is Elorym, that would make him many thousands of years old.'

Eryn sighed. 'Indeed, it does. And it's that great age that makes him, and his like a formidable foe. At the height of their power the Elorym leaders were a match for Ormoroth, but some were deceived and bent to his dark will. Vordrak has long since forgotten his past, being completely consumed by Ormoroth's hate. But he won't have forgotten standing against Dorlan at Talaghir. He's driven by the desire to avenge his Master.' She drew her sword and looked to the blade. 'I do not know how many warlocks survived the centuries in the wilderness of Nordruuk. But it is now obvious they were not idle. What you've seen on the borders is, I imagine, the result of their deeds. Their powers may be curtailed by Ormoroth's absence, but as you've witnessed, they are not a force to be taken lightly.'

Toryn shuddered. 'He showed me my father's suffering. Nyomae believes he still lives, but she can find no sign of him in the Song.'

'Then I suspect it must be far to the north, perhaps deep beneath the ice of Nordruuk. If it were closer, we would sense his presence.'

They reached the foot of the stairs. Toryn shivered despite the warm air. 'Are you confident we can rescue Amyra?'

Eryn held out her sword and peered into the opening of a dark tunnel. 'Like us, Vordrak is drained by his efforts of the last month. Despite our weakness, we three still present a significant challenge to him. We may stand a chance if we can apprehend him soon.' She touched his arm. 'And your presence will help.'

Toryn wiped the sweat pouring into his eyes. 'How many are we chasing?'

Eryn placed her hand on the walls of the tunnel. 'Judging by their speed and slapping of feet, I would say Vordrak is accompanied by at least two dozen cobtrolls.'

Toryn recalled the clammy touch of the creature in Dohl's cell. 'I've had the pleasure of meeting one.'

Calestri sneered. 'Sly fellows, not skilled but can be a handful down here in their domain. But in our favor, it will require an effort on Vordrak's behalf to keep them under control.'

Arijan and Calestri drew their blades to shed more light in the oppressive gloom. Calestri ran her hand along the stone wall. 'This was hewn back in the days of Ormoroth. He must have come this way when Draegelan took his fortress.' She looked up. 'We're deep beneath the peak of Vylanach. I can feel its weight.' She pointed to the stone surrounding the entrance. 'And see here.' Her mouth curled. 'Runesh.' She turned to Toryn. 'These are ancient symbols of the Ruuk's ancestors. You won't be surprised to learn it's a curse on their enemies if they dare to enter.'

Arijan's nose wrinkled. 'And it doesn't smell too pleasant.'

Eryn took the first step into the maw. 'Then we don't spend too long in this place. The fresh air of the valleys await—'

Toryn froze as a wail echoed through the tunnel. 'A shreek?'

Calestri gasped. 'That was no shreek. I only wish it were. That's Amyra.'

# 35. A Lost Paradise

The four-day journey had been hard, but Nyomae had enjoyed the break from her trials of late and the opportunity to be alone. She arrived at Telamir just as the sun had begun its descent towards the Kolossos Mountains. The tower never failed to fill her with wonder, and now she knew more of its history, her awe for the structure grew.

Nyomae jumped. Night had fallen about her. It seemed the moon had replaced the sun in a mere blink of an eye. She looked back to the tower. Its dark surface reflected a full moon, but it was a crescent that graced the night sky. Yet the lake remained dark, showing no desire to allow the world to gaze upon its likeness. Nyomae watched perplexed as the moon in the sky switched places with its reflection on the tower. The land around her grew lighter. The lake glistened, appearing to approve of the exchange and thus allowed the bright moonbeams to settle on its still waters.

The moon in the lake moved, sending silent ripples towards the shore. The water lapped at Nyomae's feet. She smiled to herself. Even now, a millennium after their fall, the Elorym magic remained. Or… was it the Nym? Regardless, she had to find a way into the tower. According to Draegelan's notes, he had hoped the Nym of the water would grant him permission to cross the forbidden lake. But those were his last lines, and he had written nothing of his experience following his departure from Abernost.

Nyomae followed the path of the bright disk on the lake. As it drew near, it faded, transforming into a dark circle of a new moon. It paused a few feet from the edge. The ripples sat motionless as if suspended in time. The Nym had come. And they waited. Nyomae understood. She closed her eyes and brought her palms together. She sought the skylark. At first, it sang its song known throughout the warmer climes of the realms, but, at Nyomae's request, it tilted its head and sang anew. The disk on the lake glowed and came to the shore. She stepped upon its bright surface. Her body tingled as its power flowed through her. Gently, it glided across the lake but left no wake. Whispers filled the air, but whether they offered encouragement or urged caution, Nyomae could not tell. Ahead, the dark tower had gone. In its place, a slender, silvery spire rose from the lake, spiraling to an even greater height. Her eyes were drawn to its pinnacle, rising above the neighboring peaks of the Kolososs to touch the stars twinkling on the great dome.

Nyomae's feet touched solid ground. Instantly, she knew she was the first mortal to step on the island since Draegelan. But the Nym cared little for the passing centuries and her predecessor's visit would still be fresh in their collective mind. And, as with Draegelan, Nyomae understood her presence would be tolerated for only a short time.

She glanced to her feet. A path led to the tower's base, but then spiraled out of sight as it wound its way behind. With no door or gateway visible, Nyomae followed the path. As she walked, night became day, then the day became night once more. She gazed upon her reflection in the tower's wall. Nyomae watched herself as a curious young girl, then as her time as Hope, before changing to reveal her in the present. But still no doorway appeared. Her reflection changed once more. Now she looked older. Long, gray hair flowed down to her midriff. Her eyes shone from a face lined by centuries of strife, yet she walked tall, unbowed by her struggles. The image changed. A blind woman, bent double, limped with her hands groping the air as she walked alone through a land spoiled by war and disease. The tower showed her two fates. Before long, she would come to a fork in the road. One would lead to victory, the other to a crushing defeat. But the path to take would not be obvious. Both would be dangerous, and the choice difficult.

The vision faded. Nyomae stood before a small door. She pushed and entered the Lake Tower of Telamir.

A chill breeze numbed her face. Despite the dark, Nyomae knew she stood between the twin spiraling pinnacles of Telamir. Of her ascent, she had no recollection, but she understood another had led her to the top. Her guide had gone. She was alone but felt the presence of others who had once stood in her place.

The sky grew lighter. The sun rose to reveal a world far below. But not the world she knew. Nyomae looked upon the land as the Maidens' first Verse still echoed across the sky. The rolling hills of the middle lands, yet to be divided by the mighty Kolossos mountains, teemed with joyful, new life. Deep, blue lakes and flowing rivers glistened under the light of the young sun.

But as the Maidens rested to admire their creation, the land shifted. The ground throbbed as if the beating of a malevolent heart pumped its poisoned blood through the rivers and seas. The sky turned black. Nyomae shrank back as she beheld the coming of the evil from the depths of the world. She watched in despair as the Maidens were deceived, falling under the spell of an evil mind they could not comprehend. The world dulled, losing its splendor as seasons of cold and darkness lengthened to strangle the life nurtured by the sun. The ground shuddered as the peaks burst from the ground as the gods returned to entomb the Evil One.

Fearful their corruption would sully their Song, the Maidens chose to exile themselves far to the north. Centuries passed as they struggled to recover their voices. But recover they did. From the chasms deep beneath the ice, they composed new Verses to heal the world. Nyomae saw the Elorym emerge. Within decades, their fine cities and magnificent towers, flourished like trees to enhance the Maidens' creation. The grim fortress of Vortimo had yet to be built. In its place stood three spires taller than the neighboring peaks, glistening in the dawn sun as if upturned icicles.

Yet the weakened Maidens could not rid the world of the Evil One's servants. And one had grown strong, and unbeknown to them, drained their strength. He became known as Ormoroth in the common tongue and would rise to challenge the might of the Elorym.

Nyomae's gaze wandered to the east. The land extended far beyond where Karrock, Saphrir and Ephrim now perched on the coast. More cities and towers had stood on fertile plains before the land was broken by the terrible wars with Ormoroth, and all now lay at the bottom of the deep Karajan Sea.

Voices sang. They guided Nyomae through the Verses as the Elorym succumbed to Ormoroth, and all but two of their towers crumbled. The voices led her to Aber's Verse and to the hidden meaning of the last line, divulged to Draegelan centuries before. Nyomae gasped as the Maidens' Cypher was solved before her eyes.

Draegelan had not lost his mind. It had been opened. He had been offered the means to defeat Ormoroth — or hand their enemy a victory from which there would be no recovery. He too had seen the bountiful land, untainted by the evil that followed. The Elorym had done a great deal to heal the hurt, reviving much that had been ruined. But the loss of the elder race was a bitter blow. Those coming to the land after their demise, had known only a withered, fading world, condemned to live in the shadow of the great wrong.

Now Nyomae understood Draegelan's mind. In the late stages of his life, he had found it difficult to return to the mortal world after seeing the true glory of the Maidens' creation. He had clung to those visions, and it was only in the last throes of his long life, he had recovered his memory to leave his message in the rhyme. But it was not the vision of the lost paradise that had driven Draegelan to despair. It was the secret revealed to him. It was both a blessing and a curse, presenting him with an impossible choice. And now Nyomae would soon face the same dilemma.

# 36. A Most Cruel Deception

The band of Nordleng could not have been more surprised if the Three Maidens had arrived in the foothills of the Ravern's. Accustomed to raiding defenseless settlements, the sudden appearance of Lady Harlyn and two dozen knights of the First Horse, had turned their vile tactic back upon them. But even outnumbered and outclassed, the Nordleng had refused to surrender, choosing to make a stand no matter how futile.

Elodi wiped her blade on the grass. She had wished the eight Nordleng had chosen to surrender, but it was not their way. The skirmish had been short and brutal, and Elodi gave thanks the casualties were all on the opposing side. She looked at the robed figures strewn across the grass where they had fallen. She had no time to dig graves and return them to the soil. They would rot where they lay as she doubted the locals would grant that honor to those murdering their kin.

Elodi sheathed her blade and turned to the captain. 'We'll burn them. If they consider that's good enough for their victims, we'll grant them the same end.' Elodi turned away as he gave the order. She did not know how many bands remained in Mund, but one less was welcome. She strode away as the flames took, desiring to breathe the fresh night air before the smoke reminded her of the fall of Calerdorn. Elodi turned as the sliver of the moon rose above the dark slopes of the Ravern Hills to the east. Her thoughts turned to Toryn. How did he and his company fare in Vortimo?

'Our work is done, ma'am.'

She turned to her captain. 'Thank you. We should ride on. While fortunate we came upon these scoundrels, we must not delay our journey. Please have your men saddle up and be—' Elodi spun around. A black speck soared high over their heads.

The captain frowned. 'Ma'am? What troubles you?' The horses screamed.

Elodi yelled. 'To the trees!' She pointed. 'A flying beast. A corvraak. The horses will bolt.' She ran to Sea Mist. His wide eyes stared skyward but remained calm while the others pulled at their tethers. Elodi leaped into the saddle, turned him about, and kicked on. She glanced over her shoulder to see the corvraak tuck its wings into its body and plummet towards them. A figure sat upon its back. The foul bird extended its large talons and snatched at the last knight yet to mount. He cried out, then fell silent as sharp claws pierced his armor. Elodi wheeled Sea Mist and drove him towards the beast as it eyed up its next victim. The knights struggled with their frightened horses, but two managed to join Elodi. She drew her sword and shouted her challenge to who she knew to be Uleva. Her blade glowed orange as she closed the gap.

Time appeared to slow as the bird's black eyes fixed on Elodi. Behind, Uleva grinned as she drew a shard of rock from her cloak. Elodi's head throbbed as the stone pulsed green. But she held her course. The horses at her side reared up, throwing their riders. But Elodi was not to be defeated. She rose in her saddle as the corvraak opened his claws. She swung her sword to form a dome of light over her. The raven hurtled into her shield. Its claws snatched at Elodi's head. She thrust her blade up. The bird screeched. A light burst from Uleva's stone. Sea Mist lurched. Elodi was thrown back and landed heavily. She gained her feet as the corvraak hovered overhead, thrashing its ragged wings to send a rush of foul air into

Elodi's face. She gagged as the stench of a rotting corpse caught the back of her throat. Shouts behind. Arrows flew past her, but the raven beat them aside as if twigs slung by a child.

Elodi wiped the burning tears from her eyes. She ducked and rolled to her left as the corvraak's blooded talons sought to crush her skull. Elodi lunged. The tip of her blade dug into its belly. She pushed and twisted, but it felt like she had struck a tree. It squawked a vicious retort, beating its wings to pull her off balance. The heat from Uleva's stone scorched her skin beneath her armor, but Elodi held her ground and drove her blade deeper. Yet still the beast fought back. Just as Elodi thought she would fall, an arrow found its target beneath the corvraak's wing. Uleva cursed. The bird withdrew, leaving its foul stench in its wake.

Elodi recovered her breath and watched the corvraak soar into the night and fly towards the Kolossos. She ran to Sea Mist. Thankfully he appeared unharmed, if a little shaken. Her eyes found the torn body of the knight. Two of his companions stood by with their heads bowed.

The captain strolled over. He glanced to the retreating raven, now a speck as it had first appeared. 'What in the Five Realms was that?'

'It's a corvraak, and mercifully, I believe the last of its kind.' She turned to the trees. 'How are the horses?'

'Spooked, but they'll be fine. Their training will see them through.' He nodded to her sword as the glow faded. 'Our enemy continues to misjudge you, ma'am. If the hag on that creature's back thought she could defeat you, she was very much mistaken.'

'I'm not so sure that was her intention. My blade barely left a scratch, and the arrow caused little injury.' She looked up to the sliver of the moon. 'No, I think that was more to delay us. I believe the intended targets were the horses. Had they bolted, we would have wasted valuable time trying to recover them.'

'All the same, ma'am. You stood your ground, and the horses held their nerve… just. I don't think that creature will readily attack us again.'

'I hope you're right, Captain. I would not wish to face that beast every night.' She looked back to the fallen rider. 'And we cannot afford to lose more knights. We need every last one if we're to defend the Kolossos Pass.'

Elodi appreciated why people struggled to describe Telamir now she stood beneath the tower. She turned to her captain. 'We'll stop here and eat. I cannot explain it, but I feel as if this place offers us sustenance. Perhaps a few hours here would be worth a whole night's rest.'

'Agreed, ma'am. I've heard many tell of its ability to ease the aches and pains of the saddle.'

The fires were soon lit and supper cooked. Elodi's stomach rumbled as the smell of roasted rabbit found her. The horses appeared calm, seeming to care less for the tower than their riders. Her knights had recovered from their encounter with the corvraak, but it was the news from Vortimo that caused her concern. By chance, they had met an injured rider from Toryn's company on the road north of Cafra. At first, his account of freeing the Amayans had been a relief, but dread filled her heart when she heard they had entered the tunnels below the fortress. While she had confidence in Toryn's emerging powers and the Amayans' skill, what awaited them deep beneath the mountains? Would the four be lost in the pursuit of one?

'Ma'am?' Her captain pointed. 'Someone crosses the lake. They head this way.'

Nyomae's dull eyes stared into the light of the campfire but appeared to see another time and place.

Despite her frail state, she refused the food offered by Elodi. The few mumbled words she uttered made no sense and Elodi decided to save her questions until daybreak. She had intended to rest only for a short while, then head off before sunrise. But if Nyomae slept for a week, Elodi believed she would struggle to stay on the back of a galloping horse. She instructed the captain they would camp for the night, hoping the refreshed horses would make up the lost time.

Nyomae closed her eyes and slumped. Elodi laid her down and covered her with a blanket. She checked the watch was set, then tried to ease her troubled mind to sleep.

A warm hand touched her shoulder. Elodi sprang up. Nyomae kneeled beside her. She whispered. 'Please come.' She motioned for Elodi to follow her back to the lake. The moon had made its way across the sky to the north and now sat close to the tower. Elodi was certain it had not yet reached a half-moon, yet its full face glowed bright in stark contrast to the black spears of Telamir piercing the night sky. Elodi tilted her head. The tower's silhouette appeared to no longer rise from the lake. She blinked. It looked to Elodi that Telamir was painted on the great dome that sheltered their world, at once both near and far off in the distance. Her hand moved, certain she could reach through the dark rent that split the sky. She let her hand drop and chided herself. At her side, Nyomae gazed into the dark water as if it had cast a spell upon her. Nyomae's eyes flickered, reminding Elodi of the colors she had once seen in those of the Archon.

Nyomae's quiet voice echoed across the lake. 'I have seen through Draegelan's eyes. I have found the meaning of the last line of Aber's Verse.' Her head dropped. 'But now I fear to use it.'

Elodi dared to breathe. 'A double-edged sword?'

'Indeed. But there's another reason that stays my hand.' Nyomae let out a long sigh. 'Sylvena was an imposter. She was always… Uluriel.'

Elodi gaped. 'But she was a high-ranking Imaari. And was it not Uluriel who brought you into the Order? What makes you think she is an imposter?'

'Despite her powers, why did Sylvena succumb so quickly to the Ul-dalak while Toryn's father yet resists. At first, I believed it was due to the Angorlith as few could withstand its power. But if that were so, they would have taken Finromir to Ormoroth's pillar, thus he would have fallen many years ago.'

Elodi frowned. 'Then for what purpose do they hold Finromir, if not to turn him?'

'Perhaps they seek to discover more of our ways. Finromir is an accomplished Imaari. His knowledge of the Song equaled that of Idraman. That is why I believe Uluriel infiltrated our Order. But not only did she learn much of our knowledge, she influenced the direction of our study. And when she had all she needed, she simply returned to the Ul-dalak. We thought she was captured in her quest of the relic. I led a large force to rescue her, only to walk into a trap. We were deceived.' She wrung her hands. 'That decision cost us dear. We've spent the last three hundred years in decline, blighted by the shadow while our enemy schemed.'

Elodi watched the moon emerge from the west side of the tower. 'How could she have deceived our greatest minds?'

Nyomae closed her eyes and tilted back her head. 'The Dark Verses concealed her past to make her appear young to our eyes. She patiently worked her way into our society, gaining trust with her achievements. When she returned to the Ul-dalak, the warlocks must have manipulated her Verse so we would see the false story of her torture.'

'But why did she bring you into the Order?'

Nyomae sighed. 'That is my concern. Now I must ask, why me? Did she see something in my Verses the Ul-dalak could exploit? Does that explain why the *kruul* inside the Castellan did not attempt to kill me? We suspected nothing. It could have guided the Castellan's hand to slay us both.'

'Ah. Then there has to be a reason. Just as Uleva spared my life on Dorn Plain while I slumbered under her spell.'

Nyomae grasped Elodi's arm. 'Was I… or you, chosen by our enemy? Are we capable of being turned to their cause? Or worse, bring about *our* demise by actions we believe will defeat *them*?' Her voice lowered to a whisper. 'From what I learned in the tower, I believe they need me to open the way for Ormoroth's return. And you may yet play a part in their plans.'

Elodi stuttered. 'By… by what means? How do they expect you to succeed when the warlocks have failed?'

Nyomae turned. 'By some means, Ormoroth removed his name from the Song, knowing it could be used to bring about his end. But despite their centuries of torment, the Maidens remembered the name that granted him life before he became a servant of the Dark Verses. They disguised it, then concealed it from him in a new Verse.'

Elodi's eyes widened. 'The Maidens' Cypher.'

'Precisely. And the last line of Aber's Verse solves it.' Her voice wavered. 'Elodi… I know the name the Maidens gave Ormoroth.'

Elodi's hand went to her mouth. 'But that means you—'

'Could cast his dark soul into the Great Void for good. Or… open the way for his return to this realm. His spirit resides in the Halfway World, where he has been held since his defeat at Talaghir. But to send him into the Great Void, I first need to enter his world. I would have to open the way between the two realms. If I delay invoking his Maiden's Name, he could overpower me and return. Or if his warlocks sense my purpose, they can intervene and aid their Master.' She stared at the lake. 'I… I have the means to either secure or destroy our future.'

Elodi looked up at the glimmering stars, untroubled by the woes below. 'This is what drove Draegelan out of his mind? And you too now bear this burden.'

'And already it drains my strength.' Nyomae kneeled and dipped her hand into the cool water. 'Draegelan deliberated long whether to open the gateway and banish Ormoroth for good. But he dared not share his discovery with the Imaari, not wishing to saddle them with this most dreadful burden. When the force that had sustained him well beyond his years began to wane, I believe Draegelan came to the decision he would invoke the Maidens' Name. He risked spending an eternity in the Void to save the realms, but it was a sacrifice he was prepared to make. But by then, many believed him to be senile, thus his words were taken as those of a confused man and ignored. It was only due to the diligence of his healer that his ramblings were noted, leading me to where I stand now.'

Elodi took Nyomae's hand. 'This is indeed a most terrible burden to bear.'

Nyomae's grip tightened. 'Oh Elodi, I am not certain I can live with this knowledge. I do not possess Draegelan's resolve and wisdom. And now I know of Uluriel's deceit, how can I be sure I am not simply a vessel to bring about our ruin?'

Elodi's heart went out to her. 'Uluriel may have selected you because of something she saw in your Verse. But is it not also obvious the Ul-dalak cannot match your ability? Otherwise, she could have stayed within the Order, studied Draegelan's notes, and then opened this gateway herself.'

Nyomae thought for a moment. 'That may be true. But what she has done is pass this appalling deed onto me. Those who open the way to the Great Void risk being dragged into it. I may banish Ormoroth but also myself. I would be stranded with him until the end of time when the gods are said to return.'

To the east, the sky turned pink. Elodi wiped away Nyomae's tears. 'That is more than any can ask of you.'

Nyomae looked away. 'Yet… there may come the time where I have no choice.'

# 37. River Running Deep

For two arduous days, Toryn and the Amayans pursued the warlock. The tunnel took them deep beneath the mountains, so deep, Toryn feared they would never see the surface again. They stopped only for short rests, yet Amyra still seemed out of reach. They had heard no more cries of her anguish, but whether this was an encouraging sign, none dared to consider. Toryn found the closeness of the tunnel walls oppressive and longed for the open sky. But his mood had lifted once the ground had leveled, and their passage took them through a succession of what must have been vast, underground halls. Eryn believed Ormoroth had hidden his armies beneath the mountains during their conflict with the Elorym. The leagues of tunnels and many caverns allowed him to move his soldiers at speed, emerging to strike and retreat, while avoiding the eyes of the Elorym towers. Toryn's skin had crawled as the Amayans told him tales of the cobtrolls' ancestors. Both larger and more cunning, they presented a challenge even to a skilled fighter. But as Ormoroth's strength waned during the last desperate battles, so had his command over the reluctant subterranean creatures.

Eryn hissed. 'Wait!' Her voice echoed. 'They've stopped. I can't hear the slap of the trolls' feet.' They stood in a hall, large enough for its walls and ceiling to evade the light of the Amayan blades. Eryn turned, stretched out her arms and splayed her fingers. 'There are two, possibly three passageways on the north side, and perhaps on both the east and west walls. We appear to be at some sort of crossroads.' She drew her sword. 'Vordrak may be planning an ambush.'

Toryn wiped away the sweat pouring into his eyes. He bent to catch his breath. He had not wanted to hold up their pursuit, but he did not possess the stamina of the Amayans. Calestri patted his back. 'Well at least you get to rest now.'

Eryn raised her blade and whispered a few words. Calestri and Arijan followed suit. Their light grew and shone like the evening sun, bathing the entire hall with its warm light. Toryn gasped as the vast space came into view. But it was not a place built to please the eye. The hairs on the back of his neck stood up. What foul creatures had once gathered here? He could almost hear their glee as they awaited orders to commit atrocities he dared not to imagine.

Eryn's voice echoed. 'We should all rest. We'll engage them before long, but in a place of their choosing, so be wary. Best we have an escape route planned, but not the way we came. We achieve nothing by retreating.'

Arijan circled. 'Why here? Yes, they could surround us, but Vordrak knows his trolls are no match for the three… four of us. And if I could choose the ideal place to take them, it would be here. I prefer to fight where I have the space to swing my blade.'

Eryn took a step towards the north wall. 'Then we must assume Vordrak has command of more than just his trolls down here. Let us find a suitable route for our escape.' She led them to the northern end of the hall. Eryn pointed. 'Three tunnels. But which one did they take? Ah! I can't find Amyra through this rock. Can you feel anything?' Her companions shook their heads. 'Neither can I, and that's what makes me uneasy.'

Arijan sat. 'If they've stopped, so must we. I need to eat. While I don't fear those little troll fellows, I still need my strength to see off a few dozen. I don't want to give them even a small chance of wrapping their clammy hands around my throat.' She glanced at the nearest tunnel. 'But if you're right, Eryn, we may have more on our hands than cobs.'

Eryn and Calestri agreed. They sat in a circle with their backs to each other, keeping a watch on all directions. Arijan handed out food from her supply and they ate in silence. When done, Calestri spoke first. 'It's too quiet. If an ambush is coming, they're taking their time. We'd hear them long before they reach this hall.'

Eryn stood. 'Something has changed. I can't determine what, but we should be ready.'

Arijan joined her and pulled Toryn to his feet. 'Then whatever he has planned, it doesn't involve the cobs.' They drew their swords.

Toryn stiffened. 'Vordrak enters the Song.' He staggered. 'He's strong. The Verses recoil from him.'

Eryn grasped his shoulder. 'Where does he go?'

'Give me a moment.' He closed his eyes and let himself be drawn into the Song. The dark walls of the cavern flashed passed. The hall changed little as he ventured back through the years. A great murmur arose, rising to a cacophony as Toryn came across the Verses of a distant time. Through the mist of the Song, he spied thousands of beasts crammed into the hall. Large trolls, Ruuk-like creatures, and others resembling Norgog stood ready at arms. They shouted, barked, and growled in their harsh tongues, whipped into a frenzy by a warlock. The air rippled around the tall, cloaked figure as he waved his arms and bellowed an invocation to strengthen the grim host with his powers. Toryn's heart sank as he saw what would come to pass. Warlocks commanded two larger armies, poised to strike from elsewhere beneath the mountains. They would be unleashed upon an Elorym city west of the Kolossos. The city would fall to the onslaught. Hundreds would be massacred, and thousands would be enslaved by Ormoroth's legions.

'Toryn?' Eryn's voice found him in the Verse. 'Can you see him?'

His jaw clenched. 'He's gone far back. Much farther than I am able.' He found the shadow of Vordrak. The warlock stood not more than three hundred paces ahead of them. But he had yet to notice Toryn's presence. Vordrak's attention was fixed on a labyrinth of crudely fashioned passages far beneath their feet. Toryn clutched his stomach. 'He desires to bring something back.'

'What is it? To know what we'll face would allow us to prepare.'

'It... it can't be possible. He's found something. It's solid rock, yet something stirs within.'

Eryn's grip tightened. 'How big?'

Toryn watched in horror as a creature thrashed in the foundations of the mountains. 'It's long, it's like a… droog.'

Arijan cried out. 'A rockworm!'

Toryn looked down. 'It resists. Vordrak wrestles with it.' The warlock's head jerked up. His black eyes fixed on Toryn. Vordrak thrust out his hand. The blow slammed into Toryn's chest, expelling him from the Verse. He stumbled back. Calestri steadied him. He opened his eyes, grateful to see the Amayans. 'What is that beast?'

Eryn clenched her sword. 'It must be a rockworm. An abomination of Ormoroth's making. He formed them to carve out this labyrinth, far quicker than any creature with a pick. But don't despair. Vordrak must be desperate to risk fetching a worm. He knows he hasn't the means to stop us rescuing Amyra. And he'll be exhausted from his efforts to summon such a creature from so far back.' She swished her sword. 'So thankfully he won't be able to sustain its presence for long.'

Calestri grimaced. 'He doesn't need to. If that thing brings down the ceiling…'

The ground trembled. Toryn threw out his hand to the wall. 'It's coming. Does it have a weakness?'

Calestri answered. 'It's thrice the size of a horse. It chews through solid rock like a grub would an apple. Its skin is impervious to jagged edges. Ah yes, and it can vomit up stones faster than a trebuchet. So… no, no weaknesses. Or none that we know of.'

Arijan sighed. 'We could just about outrun it, but that doesn't help Amyra if we take the wrong tunnel. We must keep the way open to all three.'

Eryn glanced to her sisters, then to Toryn. 'Then it looks like it's up to you. The worm has no eyes, so we can't blind it. Our swords are useless against its thick hide. It would be helpful if you can find something in the Verses.'

Arijan cried out. 'It's here!' The floor at the center of the hall burst open. Fragments erupted from the hole and scattered across the floor. A large, droog-like creature coiled out of the pit, spewing stones from its gaping mouth, lined with rows of fangs. They ran, stumbling into the nearest tunnel. The Amayans turned back to face the entrance. Their blades sparked as they struck flying stones out of the air.

Calestri yelled over her shoulder. 'Think of something, Toryn. Make it fast. If Vordrak commands that thing, it'll crush us.'

Toryn stared at the rockworm as it writhed like a fish on dry land. But then it calmed, raised its pointed head and turned towards them. Eryn groaned. 'He commands it.' She threw up her hands. 'Ah! Vordrak's moving. They're in the next tunnel. Quick Toryn. If you have a plan, execute it now. We can't let them escape.'

'I have an idea.' He bowed his head. Vordrak's power was consumed as he fought to control the worm, leaving the way to the Song open. Toryn found his way through the Verses to the cobtrolls running alongside the warlock. They appeared dazed, held by the greater power. He chose three larger trolls and wove a sphere about them. The ground convulsed. Toryn heard the desperate shouts of the Amayans, metal clashing against rock, and the screech of the worm. He directed his attention to the trolls. Vordrak perceived his plan, but chose not to relinquish his hold over the worm.

Toryn snapped the three trolls out of their stupor. Like the droogs, they detested their master. He saw his chance and directed their rage at Vordrak. The trolls fell upon him. They grappled with his cloak, groping with their long fingers to gouge out his eyes. The trolls did not have the strength to defeat a warlock, but they would help Toryn gain the advantage. Vordrak fought back, able to fend off the attack while restraining the rockworm's will. But just as Toryn thought he had failed, his feet tingled. A source of power! Far below, a river flowed. He absorbed its energy. Heat surged through his bones. Toryn flung out his arms and hurled it at Vordrak. The warlock staggered. The rockworm fought back… and prevailed. With the last of his strength, Vordrak threw off the trolls and departed the Song.

Toryn withdrew. Rubble littered the tunnel. A bloodied Eryn cried out. 'To Amyra!' They ran, skidding on the debris as they raced to gain the adjacent passage before their way was blocked. Toryn clutched his ears as the worm shrieked. He lost his footing as the cavern shook. As they entered the tunnel, the worm slammed into the wall and brought down the ceiling. They scrambled clear. Then silence. Toryn looked behind. 'It's gone. It's back in its own time.'

A faint glow lit Eryn's scarred face. 'And not a moment too soon. How did you do it?'

Toryn could not stop the grin spreading across his face. 'I set a few trolls on him. It was just enough to take his attention and loosen his grip on that creature.'

Calestri ruffled his hair. 'You have a habit of making yourself useful.'

He frowned. 'But there was something else. There's a river hundreds of feet below us. It gave me strength. I doubt I could have troubled Vordrak without it.'

Arijan looked to her sisters. 'A river beneath the Kolossos? That is not known to us. Can you be certain?'

'I felt its power. And so did Vordrak. It worked through me.'

Arijan patted his back. 'River or not. You did it.'

Eryn scoffed. 'Congratulate yourselves later. We need to move. If we catch them soon, we have a good chance of freeing Amyra and defeating a weary warlock with one strike. Now that would be something worth celebrating.'

Toryn took a step but stumbled into Eryn. She held him up. 'You look spent. You've done your part, leave Vordrak to us. We'll go on ahead. Follow the glow from our swords when you're ready.' Toryn slumped against the wall and sank to his knees. He watched the Amayans' orange light flicker along the tunnel walls and fade. A deep ache penetrated to his core. He thought about lighting the torch in his pack, but his arms refused to move. He had faced a most powerful force of old for the second time. He closed his eyes, yearning to breathe the fresh air of the surface and see clouds floating across blue skies. He imagined lying in the meadows back in Midwyche after a long day's work. The birds sang. A gentle breeze cooled his brow as he began to drift into—

The scream jerked him awake. Two more tore through the tunnel. But they were not cries of a warlock or cobtrolls… they were Amayan.

## 38. One Chill Autumn Night

The days of hard riding with little respite had taken its toll on both riders and horses, but while Elodi knew Sea Mist suffered, the Kolossos Pass could not wait. The slightest delay could mean an abrupt end to their campaign if the enemy captured the East Watchtower. But even the fittest beasts of the First Horse needed rest and sustenance, therefore Elodi had brought the company to a halt at Vymarl. Four days of the same punishing routine lay ahead, and if they were to reach their destination and still be in shape to fight, she would have to allow a full night's sleep.

The people of Vymarl had cheered Lady Harlyn and her knights as they rode through the gates. Elodi noted her riders would not be the only ones to benefit from their stay. The news of Nordleng raids, and perhaps the flight of the corvraak, had done much to lower the spirits of those in the east. The townsfolk had prepared a commendable supper and entertained them with the folk songs of the region. But as her knights retired to their beds, Elodi was not ready to sleep and wished to speak with Nyomae.

She walked with Nyomae towards the main gate of Vymarl. A guard greeted them. 'Be wary, ma'am. There are more than just the usual night creatures abroad these days.'

She stopped. 'Thank you for your concern, but rest assured I am constantly on my guard of late.' Elodi noted the youthful face beneath the old helmet. 'Please tell me, did Captain Gundrul come back this way?'

The young man stammered. 'Yes… he did, ma'am. And I can say we were surprised, but very pleased to see him return.' He shuddered. 'Not for all the jewels in

Saphrir would I take one step down there, ma'am. But the brave captain and his company went all the same.' The guard straightened. 'But sadly, not all made it out alive. The injured received treatment here, but then they rode out at speed the next day. I believe they're heading for the Kolossos Pass.' He glanced to his colleague. 'Err… ma'am? Is it true what we're hearing from Lunn?'

Elodi took a breath. 'And what would that be? Our enemy is known to spread false stories to sow fear and discord.'

The older guard cleared his throat. 'Please, ma'am, let it be known we're not in the business of spreading rumor and tittle-tattle. But we're hearing from more than one source that Lunn has fallen to the Ruuk… and now they're coming south.'

Elodi sighed. 'Yes, I'm afraid Lunn has been overrun by Ruuk, aided by Nordryn, the usurper. But the true Lord Broon has returned, so please let that be known. Lord Broon commands a thousand elite fighters and will be riding this way before long.' She noted their eyes widen. 'So, take courage and let all know our resistance begins.'

The young guard beamed. 'And how many ride north to defeat our foe, ma'am?'

She smiled at his enthusiasm, but inside knew this was not the moment to tell the truth. 'We have many thousands ready to meet the challenge.'

Both the guards' hands went to their swords. The older asked, 'And should we prepare and ride with you, ma'am?'

'That is very admirable of you both, but your duty is here in Vymarl.' She looked over her shoulder. 'As you say, there are dangers lurking already this far south. While we may be victorious in the north, the threat will remain across our land for weeks to come. Your people will be most grateful for your protection here.'

Their hands stayed on the hilts of their swords. 'Then be comforted we shall perform that duty, ma'am.'

'That I am. That I am…' Elodi turned to the trees. 'Now, we will take a short walk to clear our heads. And… don't be troubled.' She winked at Nyomae. 'We're quite capable of defending ourselves against whatever may lurk in the shadows.' They turned and strolled to the small wood nearby. Elodi looked up to the half-moon. 'I dearly hope those guards do not have to face the full might of our foe. It may be dark, but I could not fail to notice the age of their armor.'

Nyomae groaned. 'The state of their armor will count for little if we fail.'

'Alas, I fear you're right. But their stout hearts may be of some comfort should the enemy strike this far south.' Elodi stopped and turned to the crumbled wall marking the entrance to the Vortimo Valley. 'Have you found any sign of Toryn and the Amayans?'

'None. But if they had fallen, I'm certain I would have sensed their loss from the Verses.' Her gray eyes reflected the moonlight. 'It's my belief they're still in the tunnels beneath the mountains.'

Elodi's gaze wandered up to the high peaks bordering the valley. 'Can our defenses be bypassed? Do these tunnels stretch as far as the southern realms?'

'They once ran the entire length of the Kolossos. Following Ormoroth's defeat at Talaghir, Draegelan ordered they be demolished. He had no purpose for them as few could endure the oppressive air for long. They discovered a labyrinth of tunnels and dozens of underground halls. I don't know how many were destroyed, but it's not beyond the Ul-dalak to have tunneled more, especially if they've enslaved the cobtrolls. And, of course we have no way to determine their activity so far beneath our feet.'

Elodi rubbed her aching shoulders. 'There's yet another task to add to our long list if we survive the coming months. We cannot defend against enemy movements both above and below ground. But I would hope the surviving miners of Drunsberg could make short work of blocking tunnels with a few barrels of Shreek's Rage.' Elodi stopped under the first tree. 'Thank you for coming out at this hour, Nyomae. I appreciate you need to sleep, but I wanted to speak with you away from the others.'

Nyomae laid her hand on the old trunk and bowed her head. 'This is an old and noble tree. It has seen much in its lifetime. I pray to the Three it will live to see the region thrive once again.' She turned to Elodi. 'I have done much thinking on the ride north.'

Elodi sighed. 'And for that I must apologize. I'm sure you would have preferred longer to recover from your ordeal at Telamir, but time is not on our side.'

'There is no need. As challenging as the pace was, it gave me the opportunity to clear my mind and contemplate how to best use the knowledge I have gained.' She took a deep breath. 'While I have the ability to invoke the name the Maidens' gave Ormoroth, I will enact it only in the direst of circumstances, and even then, I would be reluctant.'

Elodi took Nyomae's hand. 'I see doubt in your eyes. You still suspect Uluriel chose you to do her work.'

Nyomae looked up to the stars. 'Draegelan had his reasons to divide the Order's scrolls and forbid Imaari from studying both sets. I accompanied Sylvena to Neverdor, while Mordram and Idraman went to Abernost. And now I have broken that law, I understand why Draegelan acted as he did. However, I am not the first since the edict was passed to visit the libraries of Abernost and Neverdor.'

'You refer to Uluriel.'

'As Sylvena, she was denied entry to Abernost's archives, but when in the mind of the Archon, access was granted. And I can only assume she discovered what I have of late. With that knowledge, she could have visited Telamir. Now whether the Nym would have allowed her to enter the tower, I do not know. Uluriel would have known how to summon them, but did she doubt the Nym would receive her? But regardless, if she desires to bring back Ormoroth, why has she not attempted to do so?'

Elodi leaned back against the tree. 'Then even one as powerful as Uluriel fears to open this gateway.'

Nyomae sighed. 'That is my belief. Those who speak Ormoroth's name risk being cast into the Great Void. Uluriel wishes to drive us to the precipice, to the point where in my despair, I will enact the ritual she dares not to cite. But for that strategy, she must think I will fail and thus Ormoroth will overpower me and return. Or…' Nyomae's hand went to her face, 'does she anticipate I may turn at the last moment and aid Ormoroth?'

Elodi gasped. 'No! Surely not. How could you possibly betray all you hold dear?'

Tears filled Nyomae's eyes. 'She inducted me to the Order. Think about that. An imposter chose me. She invited me to Elmarand to study and become an Imaari.' She grasped Elodi's arm. 'Has she planted something within me? Can she choose to take control and force me to act for her? I spent close to three hundred years oblivious to my past. I wandered these lands as a hermit. My mind was all but lost to me. Could another have taken possession? Perhaps they hide still.' She sobbed. 'Ormoroth's true name is known to me. It consumes me. It takes all my resolve to prevent my lips from uttering that most perilous word.'

Elodi wrapped her arm around Nyomae's shoulders. 'Doesn't that prove you remain true? If Uluriel or one of her kind did indeed have some power over you, would they not have forced you to invoke it already? As you said, why would they wait when they have the means to bring him back? And not forgetting the Nym. Surely, if they had suspected a shadow lay within, they would not have revealed the location of the Elorym's knowledge.'

Nyomae slumped back against the tree. 'Perhaps you're right. I am tired and weak, and my mind is full of doubt.'

'I have faith in you. There is not a bone in your body that could possibly be exploited by the dark forces of this world.' Elodi pulled her cloak around her shoulders. 'It's cold tonight.' Her eyes went to the sky, noting the clouds had all but gone. 'This would be considered cool even in Calerdorn at this time of year.' She shuddered. 'At Tunduska, Uldrak froze the pass enabling those ghastly Norgog creatures to enter the fray. Could they achieve the same trick this far south?'

Nyomae looked up. 'It is not beyond their ability to bring about a temporary change such as a storm or a gale. But to influence the seasons? It would take a concerted effort, and a great power that I hope is yet beyond them.'

But Elodi remained to be convinced. 'The farmers of Harlyn grumble about consecutive cool springs shrinking their yields. What if they can bring the cold of Nordruuk to the middle lands of our realms?'

Nyomae thought for a moment. 'The archives tell of cold spells in Draegelan's early reign as Archon. But also, of decades of warmth. It may be a consequence of the eternal struggle between the Verses of the Maidens' growth, and those of death and decay. Perhaps dominance shifts from one to the other over time.'

Elodi's scalp tingled. 'Do you feel that?'

Nyomae pointed. 'Our feathered friend and inquisitive rider I presume.'

Elodi watched the corvraak head north. 'Perhaps we can take some encouragement Uleva wishes to keep her distance after our last encounter.'

Nyomae turned towards Vymarl. 'We must take all we can.'

# 39. An Act Most Foul

'You must not see her.' Eryn blocked Toryn's way. Her eyes burned red. 'Amyra's humiliation is not for your eyes.' He staggered back, daring not to ask what terrible fate had befallen their sister. The Amayan thrust out her hand. 'You wait over there.' Her voice softened as she glanced back to the cavern. 'We will prepare our sister for her final journey.' She turned and left him. Toryn retreated back through the tunnel to wait as instructed. A little way ahead, the Amayans sang softly through their grief. An orange light flickered across the smooth walls, changing to blue before fading. Toryn sat and let his head rest against the rock wall. He felt the pain of the Amayans deep in his gut. The loss of Amyra went beyond her sisters. Hamar had once said if they had just twenty Amayans, they could defeat the enemy at the gate. Toryn had always thought this was due to Hamar's passion for such tales. Yet having seen the mayhem just three could inflict, perhaps on this occasion, Hamar had not exaggerated.

The singing stopped. Sobs echoed through the tunnel, but Toryn knew he should leave them alone until summoned. Footsteps approached. Eryn stood before him. Her eyes shimmered a soft gray light, but her hurt was obvious. She whispered. 'Calestri and Arijan are attending to her.'

Toryn moved to stand. 'I don't have the words… but I'm sorry for—'

'No, please, stay seated.' She sat beside him. Eryn sighed. 'And thank you. It pains us to lose another, and in such a foul and cowardly way. We shall take her to a place of rest where she'll be returned to the land that gave her life.'

'I wish I had met Amyra. You spoke highly of her.'

Eryn wiped away a tear. 'She was strong, one of the best among us. She will be sorely missed. We number few as it is, so to lose another is a great blow.'

'You once told me you didn't know how old you are. We've not had chance to speak at length since you recovered your memory. Can you now recall your past? Nyomae told us Amayans fought at Gormadon. Did you?'

Eryn ran a hand down her face. 'Gormadon was the reason we lost our way. I rode with many of my sisters into a most terrible scene of slaughter.' She bowed her head and whispered. 'Few would have survived if Nyomae had not recited the Song of Unmaking.' She took a deep breath. 'I also fought in many battles of Draegelan's day, but before then? I have difficulty separating my memories from those who came before us.'

'Would you be older than Nyomae?'

She nodded. 'By many years, I imagine. We once numbered in our hundreds, but now only twelve or so remain… and some of those may have left these shores. But I cannot be certain as the bond we once shared has weakened.'

Calestri approached. 'Amyra is ready.' She looked to Toryn. 'You may come now.' He duly followed them into the cavern. The walls glimmered as if moonlight shone through the mountains to honor Amyra. At the center, she lay with her hands folded across her sword. Toryn kept his distance, but from where he stood, Amyra appeared to be asleep and at peace.

Arijan looked up. 'She will not be left down here in the dark. We will return her to the land she loved.'

Calestri kneeled and stroked Amyra's hair. 'We will lay her to rest beside a stone of the Amanach. It will cleanse and heal the hurt inflicted by this world and prepare her for the next journey.'

Eryn read Toryn's mind. 'A stone lies to the east in the woods of Hadrin. Once we're free of these infernal tunnels, it will be no more than a two-day ride. Our horses await us.' She touched his arm. 'You will ride with me. Once Amyra's horse, Midnight, has borne her to the stone, she will bear you. You have deserved that honor.' She beckoned him to the edge of the cavern. Eryn lowered her voice. 'Vordrak has gone. The effort to call the rockworm drove him to exhaustion. When that worm failed to stop us, he knew we would soon be upon him.' Her mouth twisted. 'Then the only purpose Amyra served was… was to stop our pursuit.' Her eyes brimmed. She looked up and clenched her fists. 'I won't speak of what he did, but he is aware we do not abandon our dead, especially in the appalling state he left her.' Her jaw tightened. 'Vordrak will die by our hands. His spiteful act will be made known to all our sisters. None will rest until Amyra is avenged.'

Toryn took a deep breath as they emerged from beneath the mountains. He shivered in the cool, morning air, thankful to be free of the weight of the great peaks. A craggy path wound its way down to the green Kolossos foothills in the distance. But his delight at seeing the expanse of sky above was short lived. He turned to watch the Amayans carry their fallen sister. To the east, the sun peered over the horizon, tinging the mists clinging to the fields and woodlands of Amman, a soft pink.

By the time they had navigated the rocky path and stepped onto the soft grass of the hills, the sun had risen halfway to the top of the world. No one spoke, but Toryn's spirits lifted upon hearing a skylark. He looked up to see a lone bird hovering over their heads. And true to

Hamar's tale, she sang without pause to spare her the misery of having to endure the Maidens' silence.

'They come.' Eryn called to Moonbeam. Four horses galloped across the slopes towards them. The Amayans laid Amyra upon the grass and stood back. The horses whinnied on seeing them and slowed to a trot. Amyra's horse, Midnight, bowed her head and approached. She kneeled and nuzzled her nose to her rider's face. The other horses circled the fallen Amayan, and they too bowed their heads. Toryn stepped back and watched in awe as the horses and riders appeared to draw comfort from their shared grief. Then Eryn gently lifted their sister onto Midnight's back. She whispered to the horse as she secured Amyra, so her head rested upon Midnight's neck. She motioned to Toryn to join her on Moonbeam as Arijan and Calestri mounted. Eryn called to Midnight. 'Please, lead the way.'

The Amayans spoke little during the ride to Hadrin, and Toryn honored their wish for peace. On the evening of the second day since leaving the tunnels, they arrived at the foot of a small hill. A passerby would not have given a second glance to the dozen trees perched upon the modest knoll, yet Toryn knew this was where Amyra would be laid to rest. He was reminded of the wood in Darrow where Hope had led him to a Singing Stone, but he would not enter on this day. This was to be a ritual for the Amayans only. Eryn asked Toryn to wait with the horses. He watched them carry their sister on their shoulders, then stop at the edge of the trees. The light breeze carried a faint voice lamenting Amyra's passing. It awoke a deep memory in Toryn from a time long before his birth, bringing tears to his eyes and an ache in his heart. The Amayans shimmered in the evening sun, then disappeared.

Toryn stirred with Nyomae's voice still echoing in his head. At first, he believed it to be a dream, but as he woke, he recalled they had met as rehearsed in the Archon's Tower. Their conversation came back to him, but he sensed Nyomae had not told him everything.

He sat to find another mist-laden, breaking dawn. He turned to see the Amayans walking down the slope. Eryn and her sisters looked at ease, relieved to have delivered Amyra to a fitting place for an Amayan to start her next journey. As they neared, he noticed their eyes gleamed as if rejuvenated by the visit to the stone.

Eryn spoke. 'Amyra is laid to rest. I and my sisters will avenge her. Vordrak afforded her no honor, and therefore we shall end his days with the same *honor*.' She held Toryn's gaze. 'I see you have consulted with Nyomae. What news?'

'But how did you…? Yes, and for once it's good. Lord Broon has returned with a sizeable force of Elites. All who can carry a sword, now ride to the Kolossos Pass.'

'Then that is where we shall go.' Eryn whistled to Midnight. She trotted over. Eryn stroked his nose. 'Amyra is at peace, my beauty. You served her well, fast and sure-footed, never letting her down. You are released from your service. But should you so wish, I have another task for you. Would you bear an Imaari? He has proved himself worthy of such a fine horse as you.' Midnight lowered her head, then kneeled before Eryn.

She turned to Toryn. 'She accepts. You ride reasonably well without a saddle. Midnight will tolerate reins, but don't dare tell her where to go. She will not stand for that. An Amayan's horse takes its cue either from our thoughts, or they go where they please.' Eryn managed a smile. 'Believe me, if you try to guide her, you'll soon find yourself on your backside.'

Toryn patted Midnight's neck. 'Then I would not presume to be so bold.'

'A wise precaution.' Eryn glanced up the hill. 'While at the stone, we conversed with one of our sisters. Cymori was due to meet with Amyra. But Amyra was waylaid on the road to Telamir. Cymori tried to ride to her aid but was driven back by a large band of Nordleng. It appears our awakening in Foranfae has stirred us all from the long trance.' She picked up her pack and tied it to Moonbeam. 'We are to unite and avenge Amyra. Cymori will meet us at the pass. Two more come from the north. And another from Saphrir where she has…' she glanced to Calestri, 'perhaps you don't need to know about her antics in that city. We will number seven, more than enough to end Vordrak's miserable existence.'

Toryn beamed. 'Will you then fight for the realms?'

'That we will. Your fight is now our fight. The Uldalak must not be victorious. The Amanach must stand. We will—'

'Eryn!' Calestri called over. 'Do you feel that?'

Arijan looked up. 'Something's wrong. The land is ill at ease.'

Eryn kneeled and placed her hands, then an ear to the ground. 'The land trembles to the north. Hundreds, if not thousands of—' She stood. Her eyes widened. 'It's the gorge. The spiders are free!'

## 40. Of Past Victories

Elodi had barely slept. She had risen long before the sun to take a stroll in the cool, pre-dawn air. The flickering fires of the watches placed around Vymarl, assured her all was well… for now. After clearing her head, she went to find Sea Mist. He had stirred at her approach and nuzzled his head against her. Elodi had never known her mother, suddenly lost her father, and more recently, her trusted advisor, Wendel. Sea Mist had been her companion for eight years through both the good and bad times. But in a way, it felt like he had always been there for her to listen to her woes. Reluctantly, she had to leave him and return to her captains as the sky had turned pink. The day ahead would prove most challenging for all… and those to come would be no better. And what awaited them at the pass? Elodi had watched the sun rise while willing it to return to the world beneath and grant her a day's grace.

Nyomae had greeted her with news of the Amayans and Toryn. Elodi could not suppress the tears of relief on hearing they had emerged from the tunnels. But her joy was tempered by the news of Amyra's death.

After a meagre breakfast, the company prepared to ride. The people of Vymarl rallied and provided supplies they could barely spare, but Elodi had no option but to accept. If her force failed, Vymarl would not need the provisions to see them through the cold season — they would not survive to see Mid-winter.

Elodi secured her pack and turned to see Nyomae approach. 'Will you ride with me at the head?'

'That I will—' Nyomae staggered forward, shooting out a hand to clutch Sea Mist's bridle. She steadied herself, looked to Elodi and grasped her arm. 'Ah! It is as we feared. The fences are breached. The aralaks escape.'

Elodi's heart sank. She groaned. 'Then our enemy must command those foul beasts.'

Nyomae closed her eyes and bowed her head. Her eyes flickered behind their lids. She looked up. 'Alas, that appears to be so. The spiders act as if an army. They have divided their numbers. The larger cluster scurries towards the North Forest of Ormsk. The other—'

'Heads for the East Watchtower?'

'As we speak. The aralaks will attack before the day is done.'

Elodi slumped. 'Not with winged horses could we make it in time.' Her mind raced as she spoke out loud. 'We still hold the west side of the pass. There's been little activity on Noor's border.' She pictured Kernlow's elaborate map hanging in Archonholm's Great Hall. She clicked her fingers. 'It's a risk, but one I can't avoid.' She called to one of her captains. 'Do we have a bird able to reach Eldamouth?'

He nodded. 'Three are trained for all the main ports in the west, ma'am.'

'Then select the fastest… and one that can negotiate the thin air over the Kolossos.' He saluted and hurried off.

Nyomae eyed Elodi. 'You are calling the forces in the west?'

'I have no choice. Eldamouth can send their birds throughout Noor. I shall ask for half of their numbers. I cannot leave the good people of Harlyn and Kernlow undefended. But if our forces remain split, we will be defeated at our enemy's time of choosing. I believe the main thrust will come here in the east. If I can bring sufficient numbers through the pass, perhaps we can defeat the aralaks. Then I might gather a force that will at least cause our enemy to think twice.'

Nyomae gathered the reins of her horse. 'And what about us? Where do we go?'

Elodi's jaw tightened. 'We have a hard ride ahead of us to reach the East Watchtower while it still holds. We will strike the rear of the spiders' ranks. Then if victorious… it will come down to a major confrontation. The release of the aralaks surely heralds the coming of the Ul-dalak's armies. We must be prepared to meet them and fight for our very existence. But I want that to be at a place of my choosing. And for that, we must get there first.'

'And would that place be at Roth's Doom?'

A grim smile crossed Elodi's lips. 'The land narrows at that point. We'd have the chasm to our left, and the hills to our right. That is where I wish to confront them. We may have a chance, a slim chance at that, but it's preferable to engage them at Roth's Doom than elsewhere in the open. I will need to station a force at Borrund. If they skirt the forest to the east, they could yet come up against our rear.'

Nyomae returned the smile. 'How fitting we exploit the supposed damage caused by Ormoroth's great axe. And not forgetting he was injured in the act.' She laughed. 'Not that a word of it can possibly be true.'

Elodi secured her pack to Sea Mist. 'True or not, I hope the irony is not lost on our enemy. And of course, Draegelan won a decisive battle there.' She looked over her shoulder to the column of knights. 'But I imagine he led a far greater and better skilled force than I.'

Nyomae mounted. 'Yet I believe the numbers still favored the enemy on that day. After expelling Ormoroth from Vortimo, Draegelan pursued him. Ormoroth summoned a great army through the pass to waylay him, but a large force of Amayans rode to his aid from the east. Together they routed the enemy, forcing Ormoroth to make his last stand at Talaghir.'

Elodi glanced down to her mother's sword. 'Yet now the Amayans number so few. Even if they all rode to our aid it would make little difference.'

Nyomae drew her horse level with Sea Mist. 'Take heart, Elodi. The legend alone may still cause unease among our enemy.'

The captain returned with a large bird upon his forearm. Elodi took the quill and chose her words carefully. She would summon Aldorman and all his knights, Cubric with half his Archonians, and finally, Ruan and his spearmen. Elodi knew a double line of Broon's trusty spears would be worth twice that of her other forces. If a position had to be secured, Ruan would be the captain to hold the line. Elodi watched with her heart hammering into her chest as the bird gained height and flew towards the Kolossos.

She leaped onto Sea Mist's back, drew her sword, and turned to the assembled company. 'Ride! Our allies are in danger.' She kicked on. Sea Mist obliged, leading close to four hundred horses; Elodi hoped the aralaks to the north could also feel the ground tremble.

# 41. A Grim Prospect

Toryn and the Amayans raced north to Ormsk. Eryn sensed while many spiders headed to the Kolossos Pass, greater numbers scuttled towards the forests of Ormsk. Elodi had stressed the importance of keeping Nordryn away from the vital source of wood for their ships. Toryn had convinced the Amayans that the Archonians defending the forests would need their support. But word of the aralaks escape had traveled fast and far. Hundreds fled along the roads from the Galan Hills with their carts laden with belongings, slowing Toryn's progress. While the people of the Galafan region had been prepared to defend their homes against the Ruuk, the threat of an aralak invasion had convinced them to flee. Toryn had spoken to an old guard on the road. He told of the aralaks occupying much of the North Forest. A desperate defense had failed, and many had died, or worse, had been captured and kept alive for a source of fresh food. Toryn's insides turned. It seemed the long years of confinement in the gorge had served only to whet their appetites for the sweet meat long denied them.

Midnight slowed as Eryn raised her hand. From the northern slopes of the Galan Hills, they could see into Ormsk. Eryn turned to Toryn. What do you see? He slowed his breathing, relaxed his shoulders, and let the *farsight* lead him to the forests. The tall, dark spikes of the trees came to meet him. The borders of the South Forest appeared calm. Toryn ventured farther and arrived at the stockade of Omstrad. The road leading to the woodland town was packed with Archonians, riders, and more carts hauled by frightened horses. Many hurried east along the main road to Borrund — Toryn did not have to look far to see the cause of their panic. Not far into the North Forest, the trees were already strewn with thick webs. Toryn recoiled, despite the distance. Spiders the size of large dogs, scampered over a line of recent victims. Their long, spindly legs wove strands of silk from their bloated abdomens to bind their unfortunate captives. Dozens already hung from the trees causing the branches to sag with their weight. But to his horror, two large aralaks with red markings on their pods, discharged swollen egg sacs close to the macabre food supply.

Toryn readily retreated. 'They have taken the North Forest. They've enclosed a large area with web, and… it looks like they're building a nest.'

Eryn grimaced. 'That is not good news. Not good at all. And Omstrad?'

'It looks as if a defense will be mounted there.' His stomach churned. 'But I can't see how they can possibly survive.'

Eryn looked to the others. 'Then that is where we go.'

Toryn was surprised. 'But what of avenging Amyra?'

'That will come. Our first duty is to defend the Amanach, and one lies within the South Forest. If those beasts occupy it, the Ul-dalak will come in numbers, and the stone will be weakened and destroyed. I shall inform our sisters and bring them to the forest. Another stone cannot fall.' She touched Toryn's arm. 'And we can't let those poor souls in Omstrad fight alone. We have experience of the spinners. They do not. As fearsome as those spiders look, they can be defeated if you know how, and which ones to kill. They may appear a leaderless rabble, but the Ul-dalak only need to command a few and the rest will follow. While unruly, when they fight, they fight in clusters. They will soon turn upon each other if we kill those the Ul-dalak influence. It's not a pretty sight, ghastly to be honest, but they'll tear a fellow spinner to pieces to get to a supply of meat. Even more so if softened and made juicy by their poison.'

Toryn's heart raced. The prospect of taking another step closer to these foul beasts caused his insides to revolt. But he had not backed down from a challenge for many months, and he was not going to start now.

Eryn gasped. 'I remember this place.' They stood upon the last slopes of the hills bordering the edge of the South Forest. She pointed. 'Down there. We fought a great battle on that plain many years ago.' Eryn looked back to Arijan and Calestri. 'Towards Roth's Doom. Do you see it?'

Arijan's eyes widened. 'How many rode that day? It must have been close to a hundred.'

Calestri rose in her saddle. 'I fought alongside Tanis and Eleni. And Cymori battled like a demon. None could stand before her.'

Eryn waved her arm across the grasslands to their west. 'We rode to Draegelan's aid from these very hills. Dorlan led a large company of knights from Calerdorn. I recall their armor glistening in the morning sun. They clashed with the dark masses of Ormoroth's guard.' She clasped her sisters' hands. 'We were a sight to behold in those days. Unstoppable. We plowed through Ormoroth's left flank to join Dorlan.'

Toryn tried to imagine the scene. 'One hundred Amayans? How could even Ormoroth withstand such an assault?'

Eryn grinned. 'He could not. We trounced them, then chased his fleeing forces to the Kolossos Pass. I caught sight of Ormoroth, but before we could engage them, he brought down the slopes and blocked our way.' Her jaw clenched. 'But I would not have willingly faced Ormoroth, not even with Dorlan and my sisters at my side. The very air seemed to shun his presence.' She straightened. 'But that was all in the past. What of the present? What do you see, Toryn?'

He reluctantly shook the vision of the great battle and turned to the north. 'They've extended their web wall. Behind, I can see what looks like a funnel… two funnels.' He shuddered. 'Aralaks are perched on it like guards.'

Eryn grimaced. 'Aargh! You were right. It is a nest. They're claiming a new territory.'

Toryn's stomach clenched. 'There'll be more of them? How long before they hatch?'

Arijan shook her head. 'Not long enough. Four to five days at most. And while the young are only as big as your fist, they're as vicious as a full-grown spinner. It may take a year to reach their full size, but they're hard to kill owing to them being small… and fast.' She spread her fingers and covered her face. 'They'll leap and smother you. Not easy to see or breathe once they latch on.'

Eryn groaned. 'I'd hoped we'd never have to fight those beasts ever again. But we must get to Omstrad without delay. They'll strike soon. Their young will require a substantial source of food if they're to grow.' Her nose wrinkled. 'Defending the town against the spiders will be ugly, but that doesn't compare to what comes next. If we survive the first wave, we'll have no choice but to enter the North Forest. It's the last place in the realms you'd wish to visit, but those sacs will have to be destroyed before they can disgorge their foul eggs.'

The town of Omstrad stood at the edge of the South Forest, giving Toryn the impression the trees shunned its presence. From a distance, he was reminded of the haphazard timber buildings of Drunsberg, but as they drew closer it became apparent the town was designed and constructed by skilled woodworkers. Its stockade stood three times the height of a man, built in the days when the old realms fought each other for the precious timber of Ormsk. Outside the fence, dozens of workers frantically dug ditches while others fashioned large spikes from tree trunks. More townsfolk stacked bundles of hay into the bottom of the trenches and then doused them with lamp oil.

Eryn eyed the activity with pity. 'It appears they do not fully appreciate what will soon come their way.'

Toryn waited for Midnight to draw level with Eryn. 'But they must have hope. Their spirit would plummet if they did nothing and just waited.'

Arijan sighed. 'While it may help raise their hopes, I'm afraid their defenses will do little. Flames will slow them down, but they won't stop fighting until they're burned to a crisp. Not a pleasant sight, or smell. And if you hack off their legs, they still won't give up. They'll spray their putrid spit into your face, and then try to smother you. Opening their flabby abdomens brings about a slow death, but only removing their tiny skulls will slay them dead. But as Eryn said, taking out the heads of their clusters will achieve the best outcome. But they're larger and harder to kill.'

Toryn eyed the stockade. 'Can they mount a defense up there?'

Eryn glanced to Arijan. 'Possibly. But only if they're wise to the spinners' devious nature. We can school them on how best to tackle the beasts, but the lessons in themselves may demoralize the defenders.'

Toryn glanced to the North Forest. 'Do you know much of their history?'

Eryn shrugged. 'Ormoroth spawned them from harmless spiders. But with his corruption, the aralaks grew to a monstrous size and developed a hatred for all living things, even themselves. Aside from the quite spectacular web structures they spin, they've brought nothing but terror and misery to this world. Whether by design or a stroke of luck, confining them to the gorge led them to fight and eat each other. That's the only reason the fences have held for so long.' She pointed to the stockade. 'The villagers have finally seen us. It doesn't bode well that we've gotten so close before they'd noticed.'

Ahead, the workers who had been engrossed in their labor, turned to face the Amayans. They dropped their tools and stared wide-eyed as if seeing mythical creatures from their fireside tales. The Amayans may have numbered just three, but that did nothing to dampen the defenders' glee at their arrival. But calls from the rear soon took them back to their vital work.

A horn blew from the main tower of the stockade. Eryn halted. 'Perhaps it's best we wait to be invited inside.' Three riders emerged from the gate. Now it was Toryn's turn to gape. Two wore the livery of the First Horse, the other was clad in black, adorned with the white spear of Broon.

The leader held up her hand to greet them. 'I am Amyndra, Captain of Lunn, loyal to the true Lord Broon.' Her head bowed. 'Though he is lost.'

Toryn spoke first. 'Then you'll be gladdened to hear he has returned.'

Amyndra rose in her saddle. 'Can this be true?'

'Lady Harlyn met him at the coast of Mund. He leads a thousand spears of the Elites north to halt the enemy advance.'

'Then this is good news indeed.' Amyndra looked towards the ridge dissecting the two great forests. 'And much needed. I fear we'll soon be facing an overwhelming foe.'

Toryn turned. 'I wonder why they wait. Surely, the South Forest has more wood to offer, and a quick strike would have prevented Omstrad readying for such an attack.'

Amyndra glanced to the Amayans. 'And perhaps denied you the open road to come to our aid. I had the pleasure of meeting with Lady Harlyn in Archonholm. For a moment, I thought she rode with you.' She nodded to Calestri. 'You have the same flame-red hair.'

Calestri smiled. 'We have yet to meet our new sister. But we may not have to wait too long. I believe she too rides north.'

Amyndra straightened. 'Then first we need to secure our position and see off those hairy brutes. Come, I shall arrange for an Archonian to show you the defenses.'

Eryn scoffed. 'Then it will not take long. Our time will be better spent training you in the ways of our unwanted guests.'

The Amayans may have been indifferent, but Toryn was impressed by the wooden towers and fences of Omstrad. The builders of Ormsk could have taught those of Darrow how to erect a sturdy border fence that did not shift with the imposition of tree roots. The town bustled with Archonians, First Horse, loyal Broon soldiers and reserves. Food and supplies would soon become a concern, but few realistically believed a siege would happen. Aralaks appeared to have little patience for anything that stood in their way. And all knew, the spiders were not interested in the timber behind them — the people crammed within the town were the prize. Some of the townsfolk had chosen to take their chances and head south through the forest. Yet most decided to put their faith in the defenses, not wishing to present an easier source of food out in the open.

Toryn stood with Amyndra on the parapet. The heavy clouds brought an early end to daylight and the torches struggled to illuminate the ditches in the gloom. He withdrew from the *farsight* and focused on Amyndra's face. 'I sense no movement outside of the North Forest. But they are not idle behind their web wall.' Toryn shuddered. 'They're preparing. And I'm afraid the spiders grow stronger… thanks to the prisoners entangled in their webs.'

Amyndra grasped the stockade. 'Twelve of my company are among them. I and many here were ready to ride to free our brothers. I cannot abide the thought they live, knowing what ghastly fate awaits those pour souls.'

'I'm grateful you did not. It must have taken great restraint. But had you gone, you would most likely be sharing the same fate.'

She glared at the horizon. 'Then let them come. Thanks to the instruction from your Amayan friends, we may stand a better chance here. My blade is sharp, my aim is true. I will make them regret ever escaping from the gorge.'

But Toryn had not finished his report. 'Be wary. The years of confinement weakened them, but now they feast on their preferred food, they grow bigger and stronger.'

'Then let us hope our scouts can still outrun them. I would not wish to be out there on this night, but it is a necessary duty.'

Toryn yawned. 'My use of the *farsight* drains my strength.'

Amyndra surveyed the ditches. 'From what the Amayans tell me, I believe your skills may prove decisive in the coming fight.'

He stretched. 'I will do all I can, but it will be down to every last one of us if we're to hold the town.'

Eryn strode towards them. 'The last have completed the training. They fight well and with some skill. We may yet give those creatures a contest.'

Toryn nodded to the north. 'It's quiet at present. We have scouts posted along the road for a league.'

Eryn shook her head. 'I doubt they will attack at night. It's not their way.'

Amyndra disagreed. 'Why not use the cover of darkness? We would not see them coming until the last moment.'

'That is the point. Whoever commands them *wants* us to see them. The sight of hundreds of those things scuttling towards you, does little for your fighting spirit. Besides, even at night, you would hear them coming a league away. Yes, that also dampens hope, but the sight *and* sound of their advance works better… for them.'

Toryn sighed. 'I trust this is not to be your speech before the battle.'

Eryn smiled. 'Ah yes. Perhaps this is just for your ears. But with a sharp sword, a keen eye, and fast hands, we may hold them. But ensure all defenders have both a long and a short blade. You'll be needing them both.' She raised her sword and pointed to the trench. 'My sisters and I will greet them out there.'

Toryn stared at her. 'In the open? Is that… wise?'

Eryn's eyes glowed. 'We have a few tricks of our own. The first ranks will experience something their ancestors learned to fear. Perhaps we may rekindle a memory of pain buried deep in their puny skulls… and maybe a little doubt. Anything that slows their attack could work in our favor.'

Amyndra threw back her shoulders. 'Then I would welcome the opportunity to accompany you. And I'm certain others would be honored to stand at your side.'

Eryn held up her hand. 'I thank you for your offer, but this is something only my kind can execute. We will not be able to maintain our counterstrike for long, but it will reduce the numbers reaching the wall. And I concede your ditches *will* serve a purpose. A line of burning spinners will slow them a little, giving your archers time to take out a few more. They've been instructed to aim at their underbellies if presented, or eyes if not. It's a waste of a good arrow to aim at anything else. They have a thick shell on the top of their abdomen, and the legs are just as tough.' She grimaced. 'But be prepared for the stench of a flaming aralak. It is most disagreeable, although not quite as bad as a droog's reek.'

Toryn did not relish the thought of the battle. 'What about their saliva? You say they spit.'

'That is to be avoided. While not poisonous, it's unpleasant and will sting. Its purpose is to blur your vision. If that happens, you're in trouble. And note, their spit will easily reach you from the base of this wall, so stay on your toes. But they only get one shot. It takes a good hour for them to produce the amount needed for a second volley.'

Toryn's stomach turned. 'You have an interesting way of describing such foul things, Eryn.'

She grinned. 'I've only just started. Now, on to where it gets physical. When the beast has launched its juice at your face, it's chosen you for its special attention. Regardless of whether it hits you, it's committed to the attack. And it will spring up this wall with a speed and accuracy that is truly something to behold.'

Amyndra groaned. 'That is something I could happily *not* see and still go content to my grave.'

Eryn laughed. 'But if you live to tell the tale, there'll be plenty willing to buy you dinner to hear it.' She glanced to the torches. 'To return to their tactics, we are lucky in one respect.'

Toryn scoffed. 'I cannot imagine what that could possibly be.'

She ran her fingers up his arm like a spider. 'Aralaks are very possessive of their prey. Once marked, they will not allow another to take you. I have seen them stop an attack to fight off a fellow spinner. They will actually defend you against the others, then eat you later. But let us hope it doesn't come to that.' Eryn set her stance with the weight on her back leg, then leveled her blade. 'When you see the spider crouch, you do the same. Squat, rock back and keep the tip of your sword above eye level. But only use a one-handed grip. You'll need to keep your other hand free. If you get lucky, the creature's flabby belly will land right on the tip of your blade. If that happens, hold firm and twist. In defense, its legs will snap around your wrist. And believe me, it grasps with such strength it will feel like it will be severed. The spider will squirm, aiming to pull you off balance. Now's the time to use your short blade and stab at anything within range. Eyes are best as it causes them the most pain. If you can hold your position… and nerve, it will soon drop and scurry away to die.'

Toryn repeated the move. 'And if I'm not lucky?'

'Its forelegs will be at your throat and its pincers will be coming for your eyes. But that's not the worst part. It has a spike at the base of its abdomen. Avoid that, and you'll have half a chance of wrestling it to the ground. If you can flip it onto its back, drive your blade deep into its belly. You've won that fight… but get ready for the next one. But do not turn and run. You're finished if you try to outrun a spinner.'

Toryn looked along the wall. 'What about our shields? Could we push them off the parapet?'

'Shields are only useful for deflecting a volley of spit. Once they're on you, a shield takes one arm out of the fight. They'll land on it, then twist and wrench at it to take you off your feet. Shields should be used by the second line to protect the first from the poisonous volleys, but not in the fight. If you lose your footing, you're as good as done. They'll wrap you up in their web faster than your mother can tuck you into bed.' She winked at Amyndra. 'The flurry of their legs as they spin you a blanket is yet another sight that has to be seen to be believed.'

Toryn lowered his blade. 'And you've given the same talk to all the defenders?'

Eryn nodded. 'It's a grim prospect, I'll grant you that. But as I said, you'll only have to fight one at a time. Duck when they spit, set your stance, then impale the leaping spider. Then look for the next and repeat it all over again.' She sheathed her sword. 'Of course, the unknown is how many will attack. That will determine the outcome.'

Amyndra caught Toryn's eye. 'Have you seen them fight in large numbers before, Eryn?'

'My ancestors will have faced an army at the height of Ormoroth's power, but I have only seen them operate in small bands. Few have the strength to control them.' She frowned. 'And that is a concern. Who commands them?'

Amyndra pressed. 'But you obviously have experience in fighting these creatures.'

Eryn's eyes wandered to the sky. Toryn thought he saw a slight shudder. She recounted her story. 'I came across a nest in a forest in Lunn… long before it was called Lunn. I faced ten or maybe a dozen, I did not count them. It wasn't easy, and I admit I had begun to tire as I finished off the last.'

Toryn looked back to the town. 'We have close to three hundred able to handle a sword or bow. Let's hope we don't have to take a dozen each.' He recalled the gruesome scene within the North Forest. 'And their nests will soon churn out more.'

Eryn gazed out from the stockade. 'They're breeding to establish a new home. Unfortunately, the sturdy trees of this region offer them the perfect place for a productive nest.' Her jaw clenched. 'If left unchallenged, their spawn could overrun Ormsk within a year.'

Toryn clenched his sword. 'Then we must keep them out of the South Forest. But even if we defeat them here, I don't relish the thought of attacking their nest.' He watched the flames flickering in the gloom. 'Is it too simple to burn them out?'

Eryn shook her head. 'Only if you can set the whole forest alight with a thousand torches simultaneously. It's unusual for them to act as one, but they'll throw their bodies on a fire to protect a nest.' Eryn let out a long sigh. 'But it may have to come to that. If they overrun the region, the forest is lost regardless.'

'What of the Nym? Are they in that forest?' Toryn recalled how they had guided the boat when he and Nyomae had escaped Uleva.

Amyndra frowned. 'You speak of the little folk?'

Toryn smiled. 'They're actually quite tall close up.'

She gaped. 'You've met them? This world gets stranger by the day.' Amyndra glanced to the trees behind the town. 'And they're here? In Ormsk?'

Eryn nodded. 'Not in the North Forest, but they're here, deep into the heart where the ancient trees yet stand. This was once a single forest. The folk of that time tell of the troubles when the area was cleared for the Borrund road. Most of the trees over there were planted for their timber supply. But on this side, the trees are ancient, and the ground here still retains the potency of the old days. The locals stay clear of the center, having learned long ago it did not bode well to fell those trees.'

Toryn turned. 'Will the Nym tolerate the aralaks?'

'The Nym will not intervene while they cause no damage to the trees.'

'Yet they offered us assistance in the Foranfae.'

Eryn shrugged. 'What the Nym promise, and what the Nym deliver may differ. They have little love for us, but they may help if we can convince them it's in the interest of the trees.'

Toryn peered over the stockade. 'Yet first, we must convince ourselves we can hold this town.'

# 42. The Coming Storm

The conical roof of the East Watchtower rose over the horizon. Though dwarfed by the highest peaks of the Kolossos Range, it stood proud, and Elodi was relieved to finally set her eyes upon it. Beyond hope, the guards had held back the aralaks' onslaught. But holding the pass had cost the defenders dear. Many fine soldiers had fallen, and many more lay injured, never to bear arms again, and perhaps not all due to physical injuries. Elodi gave a silent thanks to the Three that the spiders had retreated. Had her company fought the aralaks after a grueling ride, the casualties would have been high; casualties Elodi could ill afford.

The mound of the tangled aralak dead, turned her stomach. Even in defeat, they presented a hideous sight. And the defenders' gaunt faces confirmed what an appalling struggle they had endured. Yet it appeared the inexperienced reserves had suffered the most. The glazed look in their eyes had chilled Elodi as she rode through the gate. The ancient wood bore the scars of the ferocious attack. She had flinched at the sight of the claws embedded in the gate, unable to imagine the fear the young reserves had suffered.

Elodi dismounted and greeted the commander. 'Captain Waldryn, I believe.' The Archonian was the same age as Gundrul, yet he too looked shaken by the battle. She clutched his hand. 'I congratulate you on what must have been a hard-earned victory.'

The old guard tried to stand to attention, but failed. 'Hard-earned indeed, ma'am. But I'm not sure I can claim a victory.'

'How so? The pass still holds.'

Waldryn glanced to the injured. 'Just when I thought we were done for, they suddenly stopped. Some fought among themselves, the rest scurried away as if called elsewhere.'

Elodi remembered the morning after her first so-called victory at Calerdorn. 'Then let us give thanks they have gone, regardless of the reason.' She turned to the east. 'But we must remain ready in case they return.'

Nyomae spoke. 'They've retreated. I doubt they'll come back. They occupy the North Forest.' Elodi recognized the look as she used her *farsight.* Nyomae's knuckles paled as she clenched the reins. 'They assemble for an attack on Omstrad.'

Elodi's shoulders sank. 'How many?'

'It's difficult to be exact, but they easily exceed five hundred.'

'Five…? How can the town possibly defend itself against so many?'

Nyomae dismounted. 'Toryn and the Amayans are with them. I also see Archonians and First Horse.'

Elodi let her gaze wander towards Omstrad, but she had yet to master the *farsight* and saw only shadows within the fog. 'Then I dearly hope they can hold out. If only we could ride to their aid, but both horse and rider need time to recover.' She looked to the north. 'And we have to prepare for what I believe will be the main strike.' Elodi turned. 'Captain Waldryn. Do those barrels over by that wall contain Shreek's Rage?'

'Correct, ma'am. We felt it best to keep them out of harm's way.'

'Then I shall place them somewhere they can wreak all the harm we need. Please, Captain, have them loaded onto the wagons. We'll take them to Roth's Doom where they'll serve us better. If Ruan and our forces in the west make it through the pass, you will be hard pressed to set the charges if they're pursued. And I think it best we keep the way open for now. If our forces make it through, accompany them and ride to Roth's Doom. If we fail there, the pass becomes irrelevant. That is where we'll make our stand. Now, are you able to walk me through your defenses? But I'm happy to wait until you're rested if you require time to recuperate.'

'Now is fine with me, ma'am. It will take less than an hour to complete a tour this side of the pass, but perhaps… I would be grateful if you allow time for a light supper.'

Elodi and Nyomae had accompanied the captain as he showed them the gate, the inner wall, and then finally the watchtower. Dozens of aralaks had breached the wall to clamber up the ancient tower. But the scars of their attack reached only a short way from its base, perhaps testament of the fine craft of its builders as the spiders had struggled to find a hold. The archers had done well to hamper their ascent, yet many had been dragged out of their windows and tossed to their deaths.

Elodi had visited the west side of the Kolossos Pass on her first journey to Archonholm, but she did not have the time to ascend the tower. Now, despite the situation, she had found a childish delight in the thought of reaching the top. The watchtowers were built in the early days of Draegelan's reign as Archon, reaching a lofty five hundred feet above the pass. With great effort, the slopes had been hewn to establish a line of sight between the pinnacles of the east and west towers. Thus, in times of trouble, a beacon could immediately warn its twin of danger either side of the Kolossos.

The captain escorted them to the uppermost lookout, then excused himself to oversee the recovery operation below. The two stepped out onto the narrow balcony. Elodi was pleased to see it was fashioned from stone, unlike the precarious wooden structure of the Archon's Tower. She placed her hands on the low wall and looked out along the pass. While the east was in twilight, the sun still shone brightly in the west, daubing the peaks the same orange as an Amayan blade when stirred. On a day in early spring, and another in late autumn, it was said the sun rose in line with the watchtowers. At dawn, those with a keen eye could see the shadow of the east spire upon its twin in the west. And likewise at sunset, those in the west could look back to see their spire return the honor.

But Elodi had not come up to admire the view. She calculated the birds from Eldamouth should have delivered her message two days ago. She peered as far as she could along the road, hoping to see spear tips catching the setting sun, or glistening bridles of the First Horse, but it was a forlorn hope to expect they would arrive so soon. She turned to Nyomae. 'How far to the north can you see?'

Nyomae turned. 'From this vantage point, I should see well into Lunn, possibly as far as the marshes of Lumreek.' She took Elodi's hand. 'Steady yourself. I will take you. We won't linger long. I sense the presence of warlocks, and they may attempt to influence you to do something you would not live long to regret.' She nodded over the side. 'It would be easy for them to convince you to jump.'

Elodi edged back to the wall. 'Then I would appreciate a brief visit.' Her vision blurred as they skimmed the steep mountain slopes, flying north through the twilight. They passed the broken fences of Aralak Gorge, then hurtled on towards the Lunn border.

Nyomae's voice echoed. 'A fog lies ahead. This is not natural.' Elodi saw what looked like a great wall dividing the land. At its base, she saw movement along the roads and across the fields. Small bands of wagons streamed south led by the hardy folk who, up until now, had held onto the belief they could survive an assault. But whatever loomed behind the fog had persuaded them it was a false hope.

Elodi knew the answer before she asked. 'Can you see beyond that wall?'

'Alas, it is as I thought. Warlocks block the way. I cannot penetrate it unless I call upon my full powers. But I need to conserve my strength for the days to come.'

Elodi groaned. 'Either these warlocks want to conceal their assembled forces, or… could it be another ruse? We're all but finished if we assemble at Roth's Doom while they strike in the west.'

'Wait. There may be another way. Take hold of the edge. I will bring us out.' Elodi staggered forward, grateful the wall came up to her chest. Nyomae bowed her head and entered the Song. Her eyes flickered behind her eyelids, but then she also stumbled and grasped the wall's edge. Nyomae straightened. 'You are right. They intend to strike on this side. A huge force gathers in Lunn. I sense the presence of three warlocks. And Uleva, Uldrak and Dorlan lead three great armies of Ruuk. And, behind them… a division of Norgog.'

Elodi's heart sank. 'Then it will be here. By the Three, Nyomae, if this is a trick to make us believe the main strike comes down the east, what forces gather in the west?'

Nyomae kept her eyes on the north. 'I am certain this is no deceit. They will attack here. And, judging by the numbers, I cannot think they will see the need to send a force through Borrund to encircle us. They will be confident they have the strength to defeat whatever defense we can mount at Roth's Doom.'

'And what of Uluriel? It seems all their commanders

are present, except her.'

'I cannot detect her. If she's to play a role, it's not obvious to me.'

Elodi glanced back to the pass. 'I would rather we knew of her location. If she intends to bring some unknown force…' Her mind numbed. 'Can you determine when they will come?'

Nyomae frowned. 'That I cannot tell. Two of the warlocks are engaged in an act that demands their full attention. I cannot fathom its nature, but it consumes their power.'

Elodi found herself pressing back against the wall. 'I knew it would come to this, but in my heart, I'd hoped we could stand against them. But I never thought we would face such a formidable foe. And now we must deal with these ghastly spiders. If Omstrad falls and they enter the South Forest, our right flank is exposed.' She clasped Nyomae's shoulder. 'Will we see out the last days of summer? Is this to be our end?' But Nyomae had no answer.

Elodi turned back to the mountains. The peaks reddened as they caught the last of the sunlight from the west. Movement! She strode around the tower to get a better view of the pass. Less than half a league from the watchtower, a column of knights galloped at speed. At its head she spied a banner. Elodi cried out. 'Aldorman! Help comes. Our line grows stronger.

## 43. THE GRAY WAVE BREAKS

It was as if the sun knew what her arrival would herald for the coming day. She stayed hidden above a thick dome of cloud, not wishing to witness the horror awaiting the defenders of Omstrad. Toryn had risen at dawn to stand upon the parapet and use his *farsight* to venture into the aralak's fortress. Reluctantly, he let himself be taken through the gray wall and beyond. Inside, three bulging sacs dangled from a thick strand of web, strung across two great trunks. Toryn winced as the slimy, gray sacs pulsated as their grim contents anticipated the time of hatching. But the eggs were a concern for another day. A dark, writhing line, formed a little way inside the forest. And behind them, a robed figure sat upon a horse. Toryn groaned. Uleva. She had abandoned the winged corvraak in preference for her faithful stallion. Toryn could not help being impressed by the horse's calm nature in the presence of so many aralaks. The spiders quivered, barely able to contain their glee as they anticipated devouring the fresh meat of Omstrad. But even the sight of the aralaks could not detract from Uleva. She looked taller, more terrible than Toryn remembered. He sensed a warlock, possibly Vordrak, lent her power to command such a large force.

Toryn withdrew as Uleva perceived his scrutiny. He called down to Amyndra. 'They're forming. Recall the scouts.' She gave the signal and three riders raced across the grasslands, soon to disappear over the escarpment that led down to the Borrund Road. A horn blew from the tower. More defenders ran to the ditches to douse the bales with more fuel. Toryn watched the knights of the First Horse lead their mounts to the rear of the town.

Their horses had no experience of Ormoroth's spiders and would be tethered well out of harm's way. Today, the knights would fight on foot alongside the Archonians and reserves. Today, it would be a fierce scrap. Skill with a blade would count for little. It would be brute force and stamina that determined who survived. The Amayans stood outside the gate, ready to take their position in front of the ditch. Following the first strike, they would return to fight on the stockade and boost the morale of the defenders. And, as Toryn hoped, they could identify the beasts Uleva commanded to keep the masses under control. Unlike the other horses, the Amayans' mounts would be kept ready at the gate. Should the battle be going their way and an opening appear, they would ride out to assail Uleva. It would be a great blow indeed if the Amayans could defeat her, but much depended on the initial clashes. Eryn had emphasized the first encounter with an aralak was the most important. To survive one, gave you courage to take on the next… and the next. But how long before exhaustion blunted their blows, skewed their aim, and slowed their strikes?

The first Archonians and archers arrived at the parapet. They greeted Toryn with a resolute nod, but they could not conceal the fear in their eyes. And who could blame them? While crucial, Eryn's instruction had done little to ease their battle nerves. Most of the defenders had fought only training bouts against two-legged opponents. Tackling an eight-legged beast that could spit poison in your face, then leap at your throat, was an entirely different challenge.

The crackle and smell of burning braziers reminded Toryn of his first taste of battle at Drunsberg. That fateful day, he had stood alongside the veteran fighters of Hamar and Elwold. Today, aside from the Amayans, he was likely the most experienced fighter on the parapet. But at this moment that counted for nothing. He had spoken long into the night with the Amayans, trying to find a way he could thwart the aralaks using the Song. But whenever he attempted to enter, he found his way obstructed. And now he knew it was Vordrak, the same warlock commanding Uleva. To commit such forces, revealed their enemy regarded this as a vital battle in the wider strategy of the war. This was more than just a fight for resources. The Amayans knew the enemy's ultimate objective was the Singing Stone in the South Forest.

Toryn turned to focus on the coming conflict. His eyes were drawn to the ridge as three riders raced down the gentle slope, eager to get behind the stockade. Another appeared but stayed on the crest. The three weaved their way through the ditches and approached the gate. One called up to report the aralaks had yet to emerge. But Toryn sensed it was imminent. Four leagues lay between the two forests of Ormsk, but the spiders could cover that distance in little time.

A dog barked. Toryn looked up. A company of riders galloped along the road from the west. At their side raced a black and white dog. Toryn's spirits rose: Shepra! He bound down the steps and through the gate as she raced to meet him. He bent and ruffled her fur as she licked his face. 'Good to see you, girl.' The horses caught up. Toryn stood and beamed. 'Captain Gundrul. Of all the people I didn't expect to see today.'

The captain slid from his saddle like a seasoned rider. 'Ha! This is a most welcome reunion.' He grasped Toryn's forearm. 'Glad to see you made it out of the tunnels. I feared you'd never return.'

'It was a struggle, but that is a tale for another day.'

Gundrul released his grip. 'And one I look forward to hearing.'

Elrik joined them and slapped Toryn on the back. 'It

seems like we can't get away from you.'

Toryn frowned. 'What brings you here? I thought you were heading for the pass.'

Gundrul's smile faded. 'The spiders got there first. From a distance, I would say we still hold the pass, but I wasn't keen to take on those creatures out in the open. Those fleeing told us of more heading for the North Forest, so we came here to lend a hand.' He nodded to the wall. 'And I'd rather face them on the other side of that.'

Toryn grasped Gundrul's shoulder. 'Then you're just in time. They'll be here all too soon, and the more swords, the better.' A horn blew on the ridge. The last rider hurtled down the slope. Toryn's heart raced. 'Get your horses to the rear. You'll find the First Horse have theirs stabled at the south gate. They'll be set free if we're… overrun. And ask the guards on the parapet to give you a quick lesson on how to fight these brutes.' Elrik's face paled. Toryn tried to reassure him. 'According to the Amayans there are ways to kill them. Not easy, but they can be beaten.'

The scout from the ridge rode in as Amyndra directed the new arrivals to their positions. The Amayans stood inside the gate. Their eyes shone with a faint blue light, and Toryn was convinced they were taller. Eryn touched his arm. 'Will you stay at the gate and see us in?' She glanced to the sentries. 'I fear they may panic and leave us stranded when they see the horror coming their way.'

He nodded. 'You can rely on me. We can't risk losing you out there. You're needed—'

She clasped his arm. 'If we get overrun, close the gate. I don't foresee it, but don't sacrifice the town for our sakes. If those beasts get inside, you're finished. You cannot fight them front *and* back. You'll get ripped apart in no time if caught between two spiders competing for your flesh.'

Toryn looked to each Amayan in turn. 'Then please,

don't let it come to that. Don't sacrifice yourselves for *our* sakes.'

The three warriors turned and strode to the ditch. Toryn wished he could stand with them but knew he would serve no purpose. They took a position in front of the ditch, bowed their heads, and lowered the tips of their swords to the ground. The murmur on the walls above him stopped. An eerie silence descended on the stockade — only the whisper of leaves could be heard as they danced in the breeze. Toryn turned away from the Amayans and looked up. Defenders lined the parapets two deep, with a third line held in reserve on the ground. The tactic was for the front line to kill three aralaks, then the second would take over while the first recovered. It was a sound plan, one that would help focus their minds on the grisly task, but whether it would work in the heat of battle, remained to be seen.

Toryn took his place alongside the sentries, poised to swing the gates shut and heave the thick beams into place. He checked his sword and dagger in his belt. His skill with a blade had improved with Elodi's tuition, but today's fight was all about the cut and thrust to keep your place in the line. The defenders looked resolute, but none had encountered what was about to stampede over the ridge. And none knew how they would fare, or whether they would see the end of the day. But it would not be a quick death by sword, or even a drawn-out end following a mortal wound. Those who fell faced the appalling threat of being dragged away and consumed by a ravenous spider. Or possibly worse, becoming fodder for an egg sac. Toryn wondered how many Guard's deaths would be readily meted out today to save many from that fate.

The hairs on the back of Toryn's neck tingled. The ground trembled as if remembering the horror of old. A sound akin to rain hammering on a tin roof, echoed over the ridge. With dread, he looked up as the horizon turned gray and a dark smudge poured down the slope at frightening speed. Toryn stared aghast at the hundreds still emerging over the crown — it was if the world had been flipped upside down and a storm cloud rolled in across the earth. Their clawed legs tore up the grassland, churning up a billowing cloud of dirt as if the ground caught fire. As they drew ever closer, individual spiders within the mass took shape. Through the *farsight*, Toryn had only seen shadows and outlines, whereas now he saw them in the flesh. Black, spindly legs pulverized the ground as they scuttled at the speed of a galloping horse. A swollen, gray abdomen bobbed behind their bony heads. From a distance, it looked as if a small rider sat upon a fat pony, but a pony with eight legs. Toryn shuddered as a large aralak in the front rank, fixed its cruel eyes on the Amayans. A cluster of three moist, black eyeballs glowered on either side of an almost human face. Beneath, its slit mouth quivered and drooled at the prospect of its prey.

Ahead of the horror, the Amayans stood defiant. Toryn wanted to cry out a warning. They appeared undaunted by the squall of dust, legs, and unblinking eyes hurtling towards them. A handful of guards attempted to sing their battle song, but throats were dry, hearts raced, and it soon petered out.

Beyond the ditch, Eryn's voice could be heard above the cacophony. Her clear voice recited words from a distant time. The earth hummed beneath Toryn's feet. But this was the Amayans' doing. He knew their mind. They reached out to draw upon the power of the nearby Singing Stone. The ground beneath the three sisters burned blue. But it did not seem to trouble the spiders. The aralaks' front ranks raised their forelegs and twitched their claws, anticipating the treasured prize of sweet, Amayan flesh. Eryn yelled. They raised their weapons. A blinding, blue fire burst forth and formed a single blade. The air crackled as their blazing sword of light scythed through the first line. Legs, heads, and bloated bodies were flung in all directions as the aralaks were sliced to pieces. The defenders cheered. The Amayans reset and aimed at the next rank. Many disintegrated, but more readily took their place, not to be denied the quarry on hand. For a third time, they swept the lightning blade, but Toryn noted it had dimmed and caused less havoc.

He yelled to the sentries. 'Stand ready!' The Amayans turned and sprang over the ditch. Drained by their efforts, Toryn feared they would be caught by the spiders scrambling over the smoldering ridge of charred bodies.

Above, Amyndra bellowed. 'Archers! Release!' They let loose their first volley of flaming arrows. The ditched ignited. A wall of flame flared, scorching the first ranks swarming over the spikes. Toryn clenched his jaw as the burning spiders screeched. The fire failed to stop them, but it slowed the advance, allowing the Amayans time to reach the gate. Eryn nodded and grasped Toryn's hand. 'We'll need a moment. Get to the wall. It must hold.'

The gates swung shut and sent a shudder along the stockade. The sentries threw the bolts and wedged thick trunks into place to bolster the old gate. But the battle would be won or lost on the parapet. Toryn gagged on the stench of burning spiders as he raced up the steps to take his position. The archers released volley after volley, desperate to thin their numbers before they could gain a footing at the wall. The heat from the bales drove the smoke at the defenders. Toryn's vision blurred as the noxious fumes stung his eyes. He wiped away the tears and blinked. If he had hoped the efforts of the Amayans and archers would win the day, he was to be disappointed. The fire in the ditch had died, and the smoke had cleared. The opening skirmish was done. The battle for real was about to begin. A seething mass of spiders, enraged by the fire, surged towards the barricade.

Amyndra called out. 'Cover!' The first line ducked as the bearers behind thrust their shields over their heads. Gouts of foul, green liquid spewed over the top of the parapet. Most splattered onto the raised shields, but some found the eyes of an unfortunate few. They staggered back, desperate to avoid the attention of their predator. The shields held as the front line crouched and thrust their blades through the gaps. Toryn's sword hand tightened, while the other clenched his dagger. Six eyes of an aralak locked onto him. Toryn froze as he read its mind, bent on feeding off his flesh. It sprang. Its legs splayed, its claws twitched, as it fought for space in the air crammed with leaping spiders. Toryn braced. His blade held true. The spider shrieked as it impaled itself on his sword. Its eyes bulged just inches from Toryn's as he drove deep into its soft belly. Eight clawed legs snatched at his sword arm. Blood streamed from his wounds, but he felt no pain. He plunged his dagger in and out, in and out, stabbing at anything within reach. The clustered eyes burned deep into Toryn as the reflection of his own pale face grimaced back. He kicked out at the spike as the spider tried to pierce his gut. The guard to his left fell. Another rushed to take his place. But he also fell as a volley of saliva splattered into his face. But Toryn had no time to help. This was a battle to be fought alone; one-on-one, repeated a hundred times along the parapet. The aralak's grip loosened. It dropped with a sickening thud, curled into a tight knot and perished.

Toryn had no time to celebrate his victory. He ducked as the next spider spat out its claim. Wearily, he set his stance. The creature sprang, but this time Toryn's blade failed to find its belly. Two pincers clenched his throat. He dropped his sword and grabbed the legs. The sharp hairs cut into his hand as Toryn wrestled to free its grip. He thrust blindly with the dagger as six beady, black eyes filled his vision, and its fetid breath clogged his throat. The guard behind slammed the edge of his shield down but struck the hard shell of its back. The aralak's eyes bulged, sensing victory. But Toryn was not finished. He twisted, pulling his left arm over his head, then plunged his dagger at the spider's eyes. It shrieked. A dark fluid splashed onto him, scorching his forearm, but the pressure on Toryn's throat eased. He crouched, grabbed his sword, and slashed down at its thin neck, severing its head with one blow. The aralak's body flopped; its leg sagged like old rope. Toryn shoveled both his victims off the parapet with his feet. Then, gasping for air, he squatted as the next aralak launched its attack. One more. Just one more. Then he would take his place in the second line.

The defenders fought bravely on, but their lines thinned as exhaustion took its toll. Toryn killed his third and made way for his replacement. He turned to see many aralaks now fought each other over their dwindling supply of food. His spirits rose as he dared to think they might yet repel the attack.

Hoarse voices cried out as the Amayans returned. Toryn marveled at how they ran along the railing of the parapet, dispatching swiftly any spiders who dared to snatch at their legs. He glanced over the wall to see only dozens remained. But they were driven by lust and appeared undaunted by their losses. Toryn flinched and ducked as another singled him out. He cried out a curse as it coiled and sprang. He felt his sword pierce its gut, but Toryn lost his grip on the blood-soaked handle. The dagger was knocked from his other hand, and he tumbled back under the weight of the largest spider he had yet faced. Toryn's head hit the boards hard. The spider's dark eyes widened as it fell upon him. He twisted away as its drooling mouth and pincers snapped at his throat. Toryn's hands bled as he tussled with its legs, but his strength was failing, and his attacker was too strong. Its mouth gaped, baring shiny, black fangs. Toryn stared into its wet throat. Was this the end?

An eye burst, spurting warm, sticky liquid into his face. Sharp, white teeth gnashed at the creature's eyes. Shepra! She yanked back hard, tearing at the aralak's skull. It gurgled and slumped onto Toryn. He struggled to breathe under its weight. His eyes and skin stung with the fluids oozing from the dead spider. Shepra dragged it off and flung it from the parapet. He clambered to his feet to find a space had opened. Shepra gagged and spat but looked unharmed. Toryn hugged her and panted his gratitude.

To his left, Eryn yelled. 'Archers! There!' Toryn grabbed the stockade and pulled himself up to peer over. Eryn pointed to a large, squat aralak by the ditch. Its head shook, its body twitched, and its legs flailed at the ground. Toryn guessed it was one of the creatures Uleva restrained to command the others. And now the ranks had thinned, Toryn spied three more aralaks on the smoldering bales. They convulsed, fighting to free themselves from Uleva's hold to join the attack. But her will was strong, and Toryn was certain the spiders would rip themselves apart before Uleva released them.

Flaming arrows streaked from the parapet towards the largest aralak. Four bounced off its back, but the fifth struck the eyes. It recoiled, exposing its belly. The archers were quick to exploit its weakness — they did not miss. The beast twisted, grasping at the air with its long legs as if trying to find a tree. Then it collapsed, twitched, and died. The aralaks' left flank paused. The line of command had gone. Some fought on, clutching their precious prey in their claws. But others scattered, perhaps searching for easier plunder that did not fight back.

More arrows flew. Another large creature was taken. Uleva cried out and gave up the battle. The last two aralaks under her command, collapsed, exhausted from their efforts. Then, like chastised dogs, they skulked up the ridge to lick their wounds. With her control broken, those without a kill in their sights, duly followed. The defenders with air left in their lungs, cheered. The Amayans rushed to their horses. 'Open the gate!' Toryn wiped the slime from his face to see the Amayans jump the ditch and race after Uleva. He wanted to cry out and recall them, but he knew they would not pass up the opportunity to take out an enemy commander.

Toryn's skin burned. His vision blurred as he struggled to breathe. He slumped against the wall as Shepra nuzzled his neck. He fought against the fatigue seeping through his body, but this was a fight he would not win.

# 44. The Setting of the Board

Elodi stood as close to the edge of Roth's Doom as she dared. In years past, a fence had prevented visitors from meeting their own doom as their curiosity got the better of them. But while the fence had long since fallen into a state of disrepair, few took the trouble to visit the chasm following the fall of the Seven Realms — the danger had become all too real once more. The myth was known to all, and although none truly believed it possible, it did make for a good story. At the height of his power, Ormoroth sought to free his Master from the dungeon beneath Caranach. Perhaps inspired by the feat of Tunduska to separate his kingdom from the south, Ormoroth forged a great axe of iron, mined from the seams beneath his ice fortress. It was said even the peaks of the Caerwals shuddered when Ormoroth split the bedrock. But his might proved too much for the craft of his blacksmiths. On reaching the foundations of the mountains, he swung with such force, the axe head shattered. His once fair face was disfigured by the splintering iron, and as the tales claim, the scars still pained him when Dorlan expelled him from the realms.

Elodi peered down into the depths, perhaps as deep as Caranach was tall. The chasm was deserving of such a spectacular tale, but the mountains lay five leagues to the west. If Ormoroth had intended to free the Evil One, he would surely have attempted the feat on the east side of the Kolossos where Mount Caranach reared its head. Elodi smiled to herself. While none had set eyes upon Ormoroth for a thousand years, she was certain he could not be tall enough to wield a weapon capable of causing such a deep rent.

Elodi turned. Across the plain, the banners of the First Horse, Archonian Guards, Knights of the Archon, and forces from all regions of the Five Realms, fluttered in the stiff breeze. She tried to take encouragement from the size of her assembled army, now close to fourteen thousand following Bardon's arrival. And more came. Earlier that day she had received news of Ruan and Cubric leading two thousand swords and spears into the pass. But would they appear in time? The reports from her scouts fleeing south had filled Elodi with dread. Rank upon rank of well-armed and disciplined Ruuk, marched south at a frightening speed. Yet it was not the size of the army alone that caused concern. The scouts had spied Dorlan riding at the head of the Knights of Calerdorn corrupted at Durran Wood. Accompanying these poor souls were those of fighting age from Dorlgoth, and many more from Dorn Plain, captured and turned to the Ul-dalak's cause. And if that was not enough to chill her to the core, the enemy's right flank was bolstered by clusters of aralaks. That morning, her rider had returned from Omstrad, but while relieved to hear Toryn and the Amayans had defended the town, word of the nest in the North Forest disturbed her.

Elodi's eyes wandered back to the colors proudly flown in the camps. She pondered how many would survive the coming winter should they fail. Did the land remember Draegelan's victory? She tried to envisage his formidable force at the height of the Seven Realms' power; a force that even Ormoroth could not take lightly. How she wished she could cause even the slightest doubt in the hearts of her foes. But first, she had to rid the uncertainty from her own.

Elodi shivered. The air had chilled noticeably since their arrival at her chosen place to do battle. And as if to announce the coming of the dark forces, grim clouds billowed high as if waiting for the command to unleash a storm onto her army.

'I cannot find them.' Elodi turned to see Nyomae stood beside her. 'My *farsight* is compromised, and my attempts to enter the Song have all been thwarted.'

Elodi spoke to herself. 'Then we are blind to what happens elsewhere.'

'And they expend much effort to ensure we remain so.' Nyomae touched Elodi's shoulder. 'But this at least will consume the warlocks, and I'm certain they will not be able to maintain it for long. At some point, they will have to stand aside if they are to participate in the battle.'

Elodi scanned the plain. 'Then I assume their efforts are to prevent me positioning my force to best meet their attack.' She turned to face Nyomae. 'You believe the warlocks will fight?'

'I do. They have a large force to command. Not all their combatants are committed to their cause. They require coercion to fight. And nothing drives a warlock like the prospect of a kill, especially when they hold the upper hand.'

Elodi looked to the horizon in the north. But it could not be seen; the land and sky had merged in the untimely darkness. 'Is there the slightest chance we can achieve a victory?'

Nyomae smiled. 'A slight chance, but a chance all the same. The warlocks will have to cede their influence over the Song at some point. And when they do, I will seek to gain some advantage. But first, we'll have to endure an onslaught not seen for many a century.'

Elodi glanced back to the encampment. 'Then we shall rise to the occasion.'

Nyomae sighed. 'And now I must go and prepare if I'm to deliver on my promise.'

Elodi clasped her hand. 'I have faith in you, Nyomae,

but if we fail…'

'We will have done our duty and not backed down where many would have capitulated.'

Elodi watched Nyomae leave. While she expected a conventional battle had to be fought, she was under no illusion the outcome relied on Nyomae. And for that reason, Nyomae required protection. A detachment of the First Horse and Bardon's Elites would form a ring around the Imaari while she attempted to free Dorlan. And if successful, she would then focus her attention on Uleva and Uldrak. But if the enemy smashed through the ring and Nyomae fell…

Elodi strode back to the command tent. Her captains had gathered and awaited her arrival. She took a deep breath, threw back her shoulders, and entered. Her gaze fell on the hastily drawn chart of the region showing the positions of her forces. The thin defensive lines moved under the flickering candlelight, and to Elodi's eyes they appeared to retreat. And who could blame them? The large, dark squares depicting the likely enemy formations, dominated the sketch. But the map looked too simple, too neat, to represent what would be the biggest battle any had fought in their lives. And a battle against an enemy concealing unknown horrors in the shadows behind its vanguard.

## 45. Alliance Gained, Alliance Lost

'That was a fine animal. I can't recall seeing a faster horse.' Eryn looked over the red skin on Toryn's arm. 'Moonbeam is swift, but not in a month of full moons could he catch Uleva's beast.' She dabbed his arm with a balm smelling of a wildflower that flourished in the meadows of Midwyche. Eryn winced as she turned his arm to see another patch of damaged skin. 'Is this helping?'

'The swelling has reduced.' He nodded to her leg. 'I see yours has healed already.'

She smiled. 'It appears there's some advantage to being a thousand years old.' Eryn drew her sword and grimaced at the dried stains from her kills. 'A pity it's only spiders' gore. Uleva was vulnerable after leading the attack. But I'm certain a warlock assisted her. And she was lucky to have a horse of such ability.' She wiped her blade clean. 'The three of us would have been more than a match. But it would have been a fool's mission to pursue her into the forest.'

Toryn felt the pain ease a little. 'I doubt we can hold them off if they return any day soon. With forty dead and close to a hundred injured, we'll struggle if they can replace their losses quicker.'

Eryn sighed. 'Then you won't be pleased to learn the aralaks who assailed the East Watchtower have withdrawn and joined those in the North Forest. Arijan and Calestri keep watch from the ridge, but as yet they have seen no movement.'

Toryn groaned. 'Then we can't sit here and wait. We must take the fight to them. And that means—'

'We need the Nym.' Eryn picked up the cloth and

daubed the red skin on his shoulder. 'And that is down to you, Toryn. You alone have stepped into a Nym circle and returned. If the Nym of the forest here are willing, I hope they will sense that connection. Then maybe they'll honor the vow made by their kin in the Foranfae. If they do, then they'll come at your bidding. But then you'll have to convince them it's also in their interest to aid us.'

'And if they don't?' Toryn knew the answer.

'We have a difficult choice. We either abandon Omstrad, and with it, the South Forest, the Amanach, followed by the rest of Ormsk, or' — her nose wrinkled — 'we have to destroy the aralak nest alone.'

Toryn stiffened. 'Then I must choose my words with care.'

The old trees at the heart of the South Forest grew tall and strong. But Toryn had little time to appreciate its ancient beauty. He could ill afford to fail. At best, they had two days to strike before the egg sacs hatched. Toryn and the Amayans had ridden as fast as they had dared through the close-knit trunks in the gloom. The forest would be dark at the best of times, but the heavy, overcast sky kept out what little light the sun could muster. They had come across a few secluded settlements akin to the Amayans' home in the Foranfae. And Toryn was surprised to find people still lived in them. He wondered if they had dealings with the Nym, but the few they encountered quickly retreated, preferring to take shelter in their moss-covered huts.

Eryn judged the best place to reach the Nym would be the oldest part of the forest. But whether Toryn could persuade them to join their fight was another matter. Yet, they had no other choice. Without the Nym, an attack on the aralaks' nest would likely result in a costly failure. And even if they had the numbers, few would welcome venturing into the giant web engulfing the North Forest.

Toryn's scalp tingled. Eryn pointed at a clearing ahead. 'There lies the forest's heart.' They dismounted, tethered the horses, and stepped out of the shade of the trees into bright sunlight. Toryn squinted in the sudden light. The clouds that had sat heavily upon the towering trees throughout their journey, appeared not to trouble the center. The soft ground felt pleasant beneath his feet, and he was reminded of a meadow where he and Elrik had played as children. But this was not Midwyche. In the middle of the clearing, an ancient tree lifted its bare branches up to the sky. Although leafless, Toryn knew it to be alive, seeming to grow without gaining height — or did it move?

Eryn whispered. 'We will do what we can to assist you.' The Amayans formed a circle around him and linked hands. Toryn's feet, then legs tingled. He had spent the journey forming the words he thought suitable to call the Nym, but now his mind was empty. 'When you are ready, Toryn.' Eryn's voice echoed as if far away. 'We wish you well.'

He took a deep breath and spoke, but could not be certain if it was out loud or in his head. 'The Nym of the Foranfae made a vow to my kind. I call upon you in our time of need to honor that vow.' He waited. Nothing. He tried again. 'A great evil invades the forest to the north. Your trees are under threat.' Still no response. 'If they are not stopped, they will come here.'

A mist formed about the circle and the air chilled. Within the swirling, thickening fog, Toryn saw the Nym. The Amayans faded until just shadows. Toryn entered the world of the spirits.

His head burst as a myriad of voices challenged. *Who calls upon the Nym?* He tried to answer, but had no voice, and the question was not intended for him. A faint, hooded figure formed before him. It stooped. Two gray eyes appeared from the mist, followed by an oval face upon a slender body, similar to those he had seen in the Foranfae. The eyes looked into Toryn's soul. *It speaks truth. It is named in a vow.* Another emerged. It stood twice the height of the others. The Nym spoke out loud. Toryn's chest vibrated. 'You have need of the Nym?'

He found his voice. 'The North Forest is in danger. The aralaks of old lay eggs. The trees are choked with their thick webs.'

The Nym loomed over Toryn. 'It was your kind who divided the forest, and thus put it in peril.'

Toryn struggled to form his words as his face chilled. 'And for that act, we will atone one day. But they did not know what hurt they caused.' The cold eyes stayed fixed on his. Toryn pleaded. 'The spiders will inflict more harm if left unchallenged, harm that would be difficult to heal.'

The Nym's head bowed. 'The old trees in the north died many centuries ago. It is a young forest.'

'But the aralaks will come here if you do nothing. They, along with the Ul-dalak, crave the trees of the old forest. The people of Ormsk have left its heart untouched, but our enemy care not. Many more will follow. If the Ul-dalak get here first, they'll fell all these trees for their own ends.' He pointed to the single tree in the clearing. 'Servants of Ormoroth will destroy your power. But if the aralaks get their way, they'll choke the entire forest with their nests, then devour every living creature under its boughs.'

The Nym faded and dispersed like smoke in a breeze. Toryn found himself back among the Amayans. They released their hands. Eryn groaned. 'Ah! We have failed. They do not come.'

Toryn gaped. 'You didn't see them?'

Arijan shook her head. 'They came?' She looked to

Eryn. 'We live in strange times. One of the simple folk could see them, while we could not?'

Eryn sighed. 'They came. That's all I care about. Did they listen?'

Toryn shrugged. 'I made our plea, but they left. I don't know if—' His head spun as the air stirred, swirling around them as if a storm threatened. This time the Amayans came with him. Six Nym formed a circle. Once more, the tallest spoke to Toryn. 'A vow was made by the Nym of the south. You speak of an old menace. The Nym heed your warning and will aid you.' Its outline wavered. 'But the Nym's strength wanes. The Nym no longer possess the powers of old.'

Toryn staggered, grabbing hold of the parapet to prevent a fall. 'A dark veil hangs over the road. I can't see a thing beyond the ridge.'

Eryn took his arm. 'This hasn't happened before. It appears the warlocks reveal their hand. Only they have the means to obscure your *farsight*.' She helped him to sit beside the brazier, warming the watchmen on the stockade. 'Then I'm thankful Calestri and Arijan keep vigil on the ridge. A surprise attack would be disastrous in our present state.'

Toryn groaned. 'Yet even if warned of an imminent assault, we could no longer defend this town.' He held his hands to the flames. 'Thank the Three the Nym are with us.'

Eryn watched the fire dancing on her blade. 'Indeed. I hope they can protect us with the same mantle that evades prying mortal eyes. But not just to conceal us. They reside in a timeless state. Their cloak would grant us more time to destroy the sacs before the spiders come. And when they do, we would appear as a blur to them, thus hopefully causing confusion, perhaps even panic.'

Toryn recalled his first sighting of the Nym as they abducted Hope in the Foranfae. 'Ah. Much as they appear to us.' His skin crawled. 'But for how long? Do they have the power to hide us all for the duration of the task?'

Eryn lowered her sword. 'That depends on who is present in that forest. A warlock could possibly force entry, or perhaps drain the Nym's strength by other means.' She held Toryn's gaze. 'I suggest you and your companions torch the spiders' sacs, while I and my sisters stand ready should the defense fail.'

Toryn shuddered. 'I don't rate our chances of getting out if that happens.' He prodded the fire with the poker. 'But even if we destroy the nest, the aralaks still need to be driven out. If they stay, they will simply lay more eggs following our retreat.'

Eryn stood. 'My hope is once the Nym see the damage those beasts have done, they may take it upon themselves to banish them. But as they have warned, they are not the power they once were. And while the warlocks are also weaker without Ormoroth, they appear to grow in stature.' She spun around. 'Cymori!' Her eyes glimmered as she searched the ridge. 'Quick. Our sister draws near.'

They ran to the gate. The torches burned bright, throwing their warm light on the scarred ground outside the stockade. But beyond, the land was dark. Toryn drew his cloak around his shoulders as he struggled to keep up with Eryn. He called out. 'When did you last see her?'

'When we rode north on that fateful mission with Eleni. That resulted in a most tragic outcome, but now I hope we—' She froze.

Toryn caught up. 'Eryn? What is it?'

'It's Arijan. I hear… she's in… Now Calestri. They're in trouble!' She drew her sword. The sound of galloping horses approached. Eryn called out. 'Arijan! Here.'

The horses slowed. Arijan yelled. 'Cymori has fallen.

She is possessed.'

Eryn cried out. 'This cannot be!'

Calestri pulled up. 'She fights with the strength of three.' She dipped and held out her hand. 'Come. If we don't confront her now, she'll get stronger.' Eryn leaped onto Calestri's horse.

Toryn yelled. 'I'll get help.'

Eryn called out as the horse sped off. 'Not your battle, Toryn. Go back and rouse the town in case of attack.'

His stomach convulsed. A horse appeared on the crest. Its rider held her sword aloft and circled it about her head, defiling the air with the same sickening green he had seen at Drunsberg. Cymori turned and disappeared behind the ridge. The Amayans charged; Toryn hoped it was not into a trap.

Toryn spent an anxious night upon the barricade. Blue and green lightning flashes lit up the sky, then fade, only to resume elsewhere. At times he thought he could hear cries, but he could not be certain if they came from Amayan throats, or whether it was the wind whistling through the cracks in the stockade. The watch stood ready, but to Toryn's relief no attack came. At last, in the dead of night, he spied three horses limping into the glow of Omstrad's torches.

Toryn rushed to meet them. The old gates creaked as they swung on their rusty hinges. The Amayans entered. Eryn slid from Calestri's horse and stumbled into Toryn. She looked up as he held her. Blood streamed from a gash across her temple. She sobbed. 'We have lost another.' She glanced to the third horse — an Amayan laid across its back. 'We had no choice.' Eryn collapsed. Toryn lifted and carried her to their hut. He laid her on a bed as Calestri and Arijan staggered in.

Eryn muttered. 'How did we not know? How could

she keep her corruption hidden from us?'

Calestri kneeled by Eryn's side and placed a hand on her brow. 'Our enemy indeed grows strong. But we defeated her. There is still hope.'

Arijan turned to Toryn. 'You must leave now. We will attend to Eryn.' She led him to the door.

He glanced over his shoulder. 'Will she recover?'

'When ready, we shall take her to the stone. Eryn fought like no other I've seen, but she bore the brunt of Cymori's wrath.' She sighed. 'The Nym must have known. That is why they showed themselves only to you at first. Our enemy seeks to divide us, and they appear to be succeeding.'

Toryn looked to the sky. 'Dawn will be here soon enough. How far to the stone?'

'But an hour from here. The stones untainted by the Ul-dalak remain out of mortal reach. Many have passed by but will have seen nothing.' Arijan read Toryn's mind. 'Don't worry. The hours it takes for the stone to heal Eryn, will be just minutes here. We may yet be able to assist you come daybreak.'

Toryn looked back to Eryn. 'Regardless, we must destroy the nest without delay. We will make the attempt with, or without you.'

Arijan opened the door. Her hand rested on his shoulder. 'We shall do our utmost, but I cannot tell how long Eryn will need to regain her strength.'

Toryn stood upon the ridge shivering in the chill, morning air. For the first time in weeks, the sky had been clear, but the initial relief on seeing the sunrise was quickly crushed when the northern horizon had turned black. Though many leagues away, the clouds seemed to form an impenetrable wall, billowing ever higher, thrusting against the dome shielding them from the Great Void beyond.

Toryn observed them with a growing sense of dread. It was as if the clouds had been summoned and now assembled, preparing to unleash their fury upon them.

But Toryn could not afford the distraction of what may come. His gaze dropped to the North Forest. If he took any courage from the Nym's vow, it suffered a blow when the day had dawned. Ahead, the trees cocooned in the aralak webs, glistened with morning dew. The barely visible trunks, appeared as tall soldiers awaiting their doom in the thick fog of a battlefield.

Toryn glanced to Gundrul. If the ageing captain shared his doubt, it did not show. But the rest of the company could not hide their unease. Elrik, Lorek and Amyndra had endured and survived much hardship these last weeks, but even they struggled to contain their fear. Janae had also volunteered. Although a tracker, she refused to abandon them as they faced their most grueling challenge yet.

Gundrul nodded to the clouds. 'I'd wager there's rain coming.' At another time, Toryn would have chuckled at the captain's trite observation, but he wondered whether they would live to feel the rain on their heads.

Gundrul threw back his shoulders and addressed the twelve members of the company. 'Yes, a grim task awaits. But you have a choice. You can either enter that place as a soldier consumed by fear, and be beaten before you've swung your sword. Or… you can storm it as a defender of the realms and everything you hold dear.' He grinned. 'And I know which one I'd rather be.' As always, the old captain's words struck home. Gundrul looked to the trees behind. 'Will the Amayans be joining us today, Toryn?'

He looked to his friends' pale faces. 'The Amayans fought a battle of their own last night to strike a blow to our enemy. Today, we must do the same. We may, or may not have the Amayans with us, but we'll have the protection of the oldest force in the land.'

Elrik stammered. 'Can the Nym be trusted?' He looked at the other guards. 'We've heard tales about these little folk. It's said people can lose their minds when those fellows show up.'

Gundrul grunted. 'We're about to attack a nest surrounded by a web the size of a fortress. It's defended by hundreds of giant spiders, and who knows what's going to ooze out of those sacs.' His eyebrows raised. 'So, who here can say with hand on heart, they've not already lost their mind?'

This time Toryn laughed. 'Thank you, Captain. But you needn't worry. I've met the Nym, and as you can see, I'm still of sane mind.'

Now Elrik chuckled. 'Well, that's up for debate.'

Gundrul held up his hands. 'If Toryn says these Nym fellows can be trusted, that's good enough for me.' He searched the grassland. 'Now. Where do we find them?'

Toryn pointed along the ridge. 'They will meet us at a place sacred to them. They'll protect us with their magic so we can go about our task of destroying the nest.' But Toryn could not yet see the tree stump where they were due to meet, and they were exposed until the Nym brought them under their mantle. And not for the first time, Toryn pondered whether they understood the urgency of their mission.

# 46. The Chaos of Order

'Amayan Fire!' Nyomae guided Elodi's gaze to the night skies to the north and east. They sat upon their horses on the foothills bordering the Borrund Road. Elodi wished to see for herself what lay to her right flank, keen to determine whether the enemy could make it unseen through the valleys.

Elodi's pulse raced. 'My blade blazed blue at the warlock's touch in the Great Hall. But what of the green?'

'Alas, it means they fight one another.' The sky lit up. 'Yes, there. That flash of green tells me another has fallen to the Ul-dalak.'

Elodi nudged Sea Mist a little higher up the slope. 'Ah, that is most regrettable.' Her hands clenched. 'Our allies shrink each passing day.' She stood in her stirrups. 'They're close to Omstrad. It must be Eryn and her sisters. Can they free the possessed warrior? We cannot afford to lose just one Amayan.'

Nyomae turned her horse. 'Sadly, she's already lost. Only a warlock can turn an Amayan, perhaps even two committed the act. And once a servant of the Dark Verses, only death will release her.'

'Then I pray another doesn't fall in this tragic conflict.' They rode to the last ridge and looked down to the South Forest. Elodi dismounted. 'Our riders report Omstrad still stands. If our foe intends to outflank and attack our rear, we can hope their progress will be at least slowed through the dense woodlands. And thankfully, there has been no sign of them attempting to circle the forest.'

Nyomae slid from her saddle. 'I don't think that's part

of their plan. As I've said before, I believe they'll focus all their strength against our main force. They'll want to finish us with one blow. Warlocks see themselves as invincible, but that is also their weakness. They cannot envisage a defeat by conventional means, and I believe they've yet to learn of my discovery at Telamir. My hope is they will come to rue their overconfidence too late in the day. If I can free Dorlan, and perhaps Uleva, or at the very least, Uldrak, we may yet win the day.'

Elodi kneeled and dipped her hand into a stream that glistened under the starlight. 'Yet many will die while you make that attempt.'

Nyomae sat by her side. 'I've seen too many good people perish in this seemingly eternal conflict.' She looked up to the stars and let out a long sigh. 'Is this what the gods had in mind when they brought order to the chaos? And if this is order, what horrors did the chaos inflict upon the land?'

Elodi searched for the lights of Omstrad, but the forest was too thick. 'I am informed Toryn's company will attempt to destroy the aralaks' nest come dawn.' Her hand rested on Nyomae's. 'We will undoubtedly lose more good people tomorrow. But if left untouched, more will die in the weeks to come.'

Nyomae plucked a blade of grass from the hillside. 'Perhaps this is the order the gods intended.'

Elodi scooped up water from the stream and let it trickle through her fingers. 'Surely, this cannot be considered *order*?'

Nyomae rolled the grass between her palms. 'In a strange way, perhaps it is. If the aralaks outgrow their food source, they'll fight each other, and their numbers dwindle. But if we defeat our enemies, will we grow to the extent we don't have sufficient land to feed every mouth? Would we then fight over scarce resources?' She sat and scattered the grass. 'It may be painful, but over the centuries, the balance asserts itself and order is maintained.'

Elodi's gaze wandered back to the plain. 'If we fail tomorrow, will we ever recover? Or does the darkness become the new order?'

Nyomae lay back and brought her hands to her face. 'None can claim to know the mind of the gods.' Her voice faltered. 'And… I can't be sure if I know my own at this time.'

Elodi placed a hand on Nyomae's shoulder. 'Then you're not alone. I too have my doubts. But this is the enemy's doing. They wish to wear us down, break our spirit to make us believe we can do nothing to counteract their evil. But we mustn't lose heart. If we do, they have won before they raise a single weapon against us. Perhaps…' she looked to the brightest star, 'perhaps the Maidens may yet aid us. The light must prevail.' Elodi stood. 'Ah. The green fades, the blue triumphs.' She took Nyomae's hand and pulled her to her feet. 'A good omen perhaps.'

Nyomae took a deep breath. 'Thank you, Elodi. You speak the truth.' She grasped her horse's rein. 'Tomorrow's outcome…' she glanced to the horizon, 'today's outcome will determine what unfolds for centuries to come. A victory will save many thousands of both the living and those yet to grace these lands. We must not condemn them to a life of slavery, spending their days longing for the release of death.'

Elodi leaped onto Sea Mist. 'Then we shall fight like the demons that seek to destroy us.'

# 47. Beneath the Mantle

The company walked in silence. Shepra trotted beside Toryn with her tail tucked in between her legs. The soldiers had volunteered aware of the dangers they faced, but Shepra would not be tethered, and had whimpered until Toryn relented and set her free. He patted her head, thankful for her company but hoped she would not suffer in the coming raid. He had done his best to treat her wounds, but her fur had been scorched, and Toryn noticed she constantly licked her teeth as if trying to rid herself of the taste of aralak blood.

Toryn stumbled over a stone. He looked down. His trousers up to his knees were soaked by the long grass still damp with the morning dew. But in parts, the grass was burned away by the Amayans' conflict with Cymori. He glanced over his shoulder, desperate to see them ride out of the forest. But Toryn knew it was unlikely. They would need time to recover from their ordeal — today they fought alone. He searched the grassland for the old tree stump where the Nym were due to emerge. Toryn guessed it would have stood at the old forest's center before his ancestors had built the road. But as yet, he could not locate it and grew anxious as they neared the web-laden trees ahead. Their pace began to slow as others shared Toryn's trepidation.

Gundrul held up his hand. 'Halt.' He turned to Toryn. 'We're getting a little too close for my liking. If those brutes see us out here and attack… well, you don't need this old guard to explain.'

Toryn checked their path of flattened grass back to the point they had left the South Forest. 'We've followed their directions. It has to be here somewhere. If I could enter the Song, I could find it, but my way remains blocked.'

'Then I assume you can't cover us as you did at Vortimo with your... magic.'

'Toryn.' Janae tapped his shoulder. 'Could that be the stump over there?' A patch of brown grass stood proud of the ground to their right. Toryn and Janae hurried over. She kneeled. 'It's here beneath the turf.' Toryn turned and waved the company over.

Gundrul prodded the remains of the tree with his foot. 'Not exactly a landmark of repute, eh.' He looked about them. 'Now what? Do we call them?'

Toryn could not take his eyes from the cobweb-strewn trees ahead. What if the spiders came for them now? The captain coughed. 'Toryn? The Nym?'

He looked to Gundrul and the expectant faces of the company. 'I had hoped our presence would summon them. I will—' His face chilled. A shimmering curtain rose from the dewy grass encircling the stump. It grew, forming a barrier many times their height. The veil glistened with the colors of the rainbow as the Nym rose from the ground. Toryn saw dozens of tall, wispy figures within the haze. Shepra cocked her head, then looked back to Toryn.

Gundrul gasped. 'I guess these must be the fellows we're waiting for.'

Toryn whispered. 'You may all feel a little strange. We're about to leave the world we know.' The veil curved to form a dome over their heads. Toryn glanced to the web still visible outside the Nym's curtain. He did not voice his fear they were about to enter a nightmare. But for the moment, the glimmering mantle made them forget what lay ahead.

Toryn looked at his companions' faces. They appeared as children, enthralled by the old magic as they entered a different time, and briefly, one of wonder, and one without danger. But they could not stay under the protection of the Nym at the stump for long — they had a nest to destroy.

A lone Nym beckoned Toryn towards the veil. It spoke. Then Toryn turned to instruct the company. 'No fire is to be used. It will make our task harder, but the Nym will not tolerate our flames amid the trees. They will strike down any who bears a torch. We must act fast. The aralaks alone may not be able to break the Nym's shield, but if the spiders have help…' Gundrul nodded — none needed reminding of the dangers.

The company reluctantly set off and the dome moved with them. Toryn peered through the Nym's mantle. Now only a short distance ahead, the dew-laden web resembled a glistening wall of stone. But the sentries on this wall had six eyes to watch their approach, and eight legs ending in sharp claws to defend their territory. Toryn found a spot between two large aralaks. It looked wide enough for them to enter without the Nym's veil engulfing the watchers. They stopped short of the web. Toryn checked no spiders sat inside the wall where they would enter, then waved the company forward.

The Nym's shield passed through the close-knit gray strands. Toryn had hoped its touch would dissolve the web. But the veil served only to slow the passing of time within, and not undo what had been made in the mortal world. Two Archonians slashed at the thick strands, but their heavy blades proved useless as the damp web wrapped around them. Janae stepped up. She drew her light sword and with a few swift strokes, sliced a gap wide enough for them to enter in single file. Ahead, Elrik took a deep breath as he ducked through the sticky strands. Toryn recalled the times they would dare each other to dive into the River Tam's icy waters in the middle of winter. Elrik had always gone first back then, shaming Toryn to follow his lead. Toryn found he too took a breath. A wry smile crossed his lips as he squeezed through the tattered curtain. The disturbance would attract the attention of the spiders poised on the gigantic web. He imagined their frustration when they could find no trace of intruders. But he knew their entry close to the nest would soon bring many more enraged aralaks their way.

Inside, Toryn choked as he took a breath of humid, stale air. This would likely be the most difficult day of his life, and the eerie sunlight filtering through the gray wall did little to raise his spirits. He whispered, but his voice seemed to carry deep into the trees. 'Remember, any spiders we encounter at the nest, and whatever hatches out of the sacs, will be within *our* time and need to be dealt with quickly.' He glanced to the mantle. 'And don't forget the lessons of how to kill an aralak… if this is penetrated.' He could say little else. All knew the nest would eventually be encircled once the aralaks found the damaged web. And none believed they would make it out of the nest if their shield was breached. Toryn hoped the Nym would act and attack the spiders, but that could not be guaranteed. The thought crossed his mind the Nym could just as easily abandon them to protect the trees.

The forest darkened. Toryn glanced up and groaned. They had found the nest. Three large, bulging sacs hung from strands as thick as mooring ropes. The trunks sagged under the weight and looked ready to snap. A large aralak perched beside the nest. Toryn pointed. He whispered. 'Be ready. It will see us the moment our shield passes over it.'

Hands tightened on spears and swords as they edged closer. The spider's features sharpened as it was brought into the mantel. Its legs flexed. Its small head twisted towards them, startled by the company's sudden appearance. It sprang. Elrik set his stance and planted his spear. The spider was committed and could not change course. Its great weight landed on the spear tip, piercing its abdomen. Its squeal was cut short as Lorek removed the head with a swift blow. Its long legs splayed and twitched as the spider died. Elrik grunted as he tugged his spear free. He laughed nervously. 'Well, if they're all as easy as that…'

Gundrul gave the command. 'Let's not be standing about admiring Elrik's kill. Time to get this done… and done fast.' He split the company into three with each surrounding a sac. Two kept watch on the Nym's shield, now looking too fragile to defend against what would inevitably come their way. Toryn drew his sword and approached the base of the sac hanging above his head. Gundrul whispered. 'Not like the nests we get in our barns, eh.'

Toryn grimaced. Inside the translucent skin, dark shapes the size of his head wriggled. Gundrul called out. 'Right. On three, lads.'

They raised their blades. The captain completed the count, and the gruesome undertaking began. Toryn instinctively jumped back as the contents spilled onto his feet. The company slashed with their blades and stamped with their feet, crushing the soft skin, splattering themselves in a gray liquid that stung at the touch. But they could not afford to stop and rest. It was a grim task. The unborn aralaks had yet to develop the hard shell on their abdomens. But they were soft and slimy. Both Elrik and Lorek slipped and fell into the gray mess, now thick with short legs like twigs on a forest floor. Toryn looked up as more cuts opened the sacs to release more eggs. He groaned. This would take hours. Gundrul bellowed. 'Don't stop! Don't stop until every last one is squashed.'

Toryn gagged on the stench. He clamped his jaw shut to hold down his revulsion. Outside, the light dimmed.

The first spiders approached. They moved slowly compared to the time within the mantle, but ominously, the shimmering air of the shield darkened as more gathered.

Whether it was the proximity of the aralaks, or just bad luck, the eggs began to hatch.

The man next to Toryn fell back as a newborn sprang and latched onto the guard's face. Toryn grasped the soft body and squeezed. With a sickening squelch, it burst, leaving its orphaned legs wrapped around the man's head. His hands went to his face as he frantically wiped the slime from his eyes. But Toryn had no time to help. A spider scampered up Toryn's arm. He grabbed two of its legs, but the rest jabbed at his forearm, all the time its tiny black eyes glowered at him. Despite its size, it was strong. Toryn yanked hard and hurled it against a tree. It ruptured, leaving its legs clutching at the bark before they twitched and dropped to the ground. He twisted as another snatched at his ankle. Shepra dashed forward, bit into a leg and tore it off.

The company were covered with dozens of squealing spiders. Swords were useless as they risked injuring their fellow guards. They punched, kicked, and grappled. Pulling spiders off the backs of the soldier next to them, while struggling to keep them off their own faces. Toryn saw Lorek fall. As soon as he went down, he was buried under a seething swarm of gray bodies and legs. 'Elrik!' Toryn and his friend rushed to Lorek's aid. They had no choice but to draw their swords and slash across the dozens of tiny aralaks scrambling to claim their first kill. Lorek's hand reached out. Elrik grasped and pulled him to his feet. They slapped, punched, and stabbed until Lorek was free. He bent forward and spat. 'Aargh. Damn thing got into my mouth. Don't think I'll ever be able to eat anything again.' Toryn swiped the last one from his back. The ground and tree trunks had stopped moving. The screeching had stopped; only the gasping and retching of the company could be heard.

Shepra sat panting by Toryn's side. He crouched and used the only dry part of his tattered shirt to wipe Shepra's face clean. 'There you go, girl.' He stroked her damp head. 'Quite the bravest dog I've ever met.'

Behind, Gundrul sagged against a tree trunk. 'Well… I've never seen anything quite so… so vile.' All about them, the ground was covered with twitching legs, split gray skin, and a glistening fluid that clung to their boots. The captain clapped his hands. 'Now let's get out of here and wash this—' He gawped at the mantle. Toryn's shoulders sagged. He had been so engrossed with the horror's inside, he had failed to notice their shield was almost black. Aralaks surrounded them. Some had risen onto their hind legs, appearing as if frozen in their frustration and rage. But they must have had help. How could so many have gathered already in the short time that had expired outside their shield.

Toryn saw their next challenge. As soon as the company attempted to retreat, their shield would bring the spiders at their rear into their time. But his companions were exhausted and in no state to fight angry, full-sized aralaks bent on revenge. They would surely be torn to pieces.

Gundrul staggered to Toryn's side. He struggled to breathe. 'We're finished.' He nodded to the way out. 'We can't move without one heck of a fight. If we had a day to recover, we'd still be done for. Can you do anything with this magic of yours?'

It took all Toryn's resolve not to sob. 'I cannot gain access. My way is still barred.'

The captain pointed to the shield. 'Will the Nym help? Or will they stand aside and watch us die?'

'I cannot vouch for them. Their first duty is to the forest. But if I can convince them the aralaks could still lay more eggs, then perhaps they will act.' Toryn searched for the Nym. Only one was visible, and barely visible, even for a Nym. It appeared weak. The shield still held, but for how much longer? Toryn pleaded with the Nym. 'Will you fight the aralaks? Can you get us out?'

Toryn strained to hear its weak voice. 'Our power lies south. The mantle requires all our remaining strength. We can move, but progress will be slow.'

Toryn thought fast. 'That may help.' He turned to Gundrul. 'I have an idea. We'd struggle to fight a fully-grown spider, but we can fight them one bit at a time.'

Gundrul picked a spider's leg out of his beard. 'I don't get what you mean.'

Toryn held up his hand and interlocked his fingers in the shape of the shield. 'If we retreat slowly, the mantle will overlap their forelegs first, then their eyes and heads. Their back legs will still be outside. They won't be able to leap. If we act quickly, we can cut them to pieces. We won't have to fight a whole spider.'

Gundrul's eyes lit up. 'I get it. Slice and dice, eh. It won't be pretty, but by the Three it could work.' He turned and called the company to him. He formed them into three lines and faced the rear of their shield. 'Now listen up, ladies. Another ugly task I'm afraid, but this may be easier.' He ran his sword across the rear of the mantle. 'When we move, whatever pokes through that wall will be met by our keen blades. Keep swinging, keep stabbing, and keep slicing. Then on my command, rotate like we would in a shield wall.' The captain glanced to Toryn. 'Best we also keep an eye on the other side. I'll put Lorek onto it, he's still a bit wobbly following his early lunch.'

Toryn checked none could overhear. He lowered his voice. 'I don't want to dampen their spirits, Captain, but I sense there's another force out there. And we both know what that might be.'

Gundrul nodded. 'I do know, lad. But let's keep that to ourselves for now, eh.' He threw back his shoulders and turned to the company. 'Ready, folks. Let's get out of this hole and back in time for supper.' Toryn signaled to the Nym. The first line readied their weapons and edged forward. Toryn followed in the second row with Shepra still by his side. The shadows of the aralaks loomed on the mantle; their wrath evident in their raised forelegs hung in the air ready to strike.

Another step. Dark tips of their pincers poked through the barrier. Gundrul whispered. 'Hold it. Not yet. Save your strength for when there's more to lop off. It'll be like pruning a hedge.' The captain crouched. 'Ha. These brutes won't know what's hit them until their heads are rolling on the floor.' Another step. Toryn wondered whether the spiders would see their own claws disappear as they pierced the Nym's mantle. Another step. Pincers twitched, more of the legs emerged as if reaching through a curtain to steal food. Gundrul gave the command. 'Now, ladies! Now!'

Swords sliced through the forelegs. Their pincers snapped, then dropped to the ground, falling like dead birds from the sky. They took another step, hacking at anything entering their domain. The first head appeared, and Toryn was certain the spider looked stunned. Gundrul bellowed. 'Change!' The first row retreated through the supporting lines, gasping from their efforts. Toryn leaped forward and slashed at the head peering through. But it became harder. As they advanced, they had to walk over the still twitching body parts oozing dark blood and making it slippery underfoot. Toryn skidded on a piece of shell but regained his stance as more claws and forelegs penetrated the shield. He swung and chopped through a large claw, desperately grasping for a throat to choke. Six eyes emerged. Toryn lunged, driving his blade deep into the aralaks skull.

'Change!' Gundrul roared. 'It's working. Keep this up and we'll soon be—'

'Toryn!' Lorek yelled from behind. 'Something's here.' Toryn turned to see a tall, dark shape loomed at their rear.

Gasping for air, he ran to Lorek. Shepra barked at the shadow. Toryn gaped. 'As I feared. A warlock!'

The captain called over. 'Need help?'

'Not yet. Keep going. Don't stop.'

The warlock circled its arms and brought its hands together. Toryn noted with dread, it moved at the same speed as those within the mantle. Eyes locked onto Toryn from beneath its hood. He froze as its glare pierced the veil. The warlock grinned as a sword formed in its hand. Toryn balked at the long, glistening blade that resembled the shard Uldrak had used to end the resistance at Drunsberg. It oozed wrongness. Toryn could taste its corruption. Lorek grasped his arm as he realized he had been shouting. 'What do we do? Toryn! What can we do?'

Toryn's mouth moved, but no words came — too many thoughts raced through is mind. *What could he do?* The warlock held out its arms. At its side, two monstrous aralaks took shape, and to Toryn's horror, grew to the size of a horse. Their bulbous bodies quivered, their legs twitched, and a steaming yellow drool oozed from their jaws. Toryn staggered back as their eyes met his. And Toryn knew their mind. Consumed by rage, they eagerly anticipated tearing to pieces the mortals who had destroyed their nest. 'Toryn!' Lorek tugged at his arm. 'What can we do?'

He snapped out of his stupor. The Song! The warlock directed all its power into commanding the beasts and the weapon that would split the mantle. He turned to Lorek.

'Get Gundrul and four guards with spears. I'll take the warlock. You and the guards hold back those spiders.' Toryn shuddered. 'Any way you can.'

He straightened and slowed his breathing. Outside, the warlock raised its blade in both hands, ready to plunge it into the shield. His thin lips muttered a curse that struck Toryn like a hammer blow. But he held firm. He knew the warlock was now bent on splitting the shield. Toryn entered the Song as the blade struck. His vision blurred. The Nym cried out. Their mantle trembled.

Toryn surged back through time, seeking the old forest before its division. He strived to find a source of power to strengthen the Nym. The warlock's blade screeched, paining Toryn's ears as it tore through the Nym's veil. Lorek and the guards cried out. Shepra barked. But Toryn could not allow himself to be distracted. He saw the world change. Trees shrank back to the saplings that had replaced the great, dying giants of the old world. A thick fog surrounded him. Toryn reached the limit of his powers and could go no farther. Through the haze of the Song, he saw the crack in the mantel widen as the warlock plunged the blade deeper. He had to act. Toryn withdrew, retreating towards the present day. A droog! During the drive south, leading to the battle at Gormadon, a captain of the Ul-dalak had entered the forest with a droog. Toryn's stomach turned, but he had no choice. He would have to bring the droog back and hope it would turn on the warlock. He weaved his hands around the shape of the worm's bloated body and hauled it to the present day. The droog writhed and flopped onto the ground at Toryn's feet. He recoiled as the droog sensed who dared to command it. But just as it was about to turn on him, the warlock stepped into the shield… and into the wide, slavering mouth of the worm. The splinter in the mantle snapped shut. The droog guzzled down the warlock and slithered away from the spears to digest its catch. Toryn fell back, drained by his efforts but content the worm would soon return to its own time. He leaned against a tree, ready to collapse. But Gundrul, Elrik and three Archonians spun around to face a threat Toryn could not see. He turned. Shepra faced the wall. Her fur stood up on her back. Toryn groaned.

One of the monstrous aralaks had entered before the mantel had sealed. It reared up and sprayed the face of the nearest spearman. The Archonian cried out as the creature sprang. Four drove their spears at its back but could not pierce its thick shell. Large pincers clamped into the Archonian's throat, but his suffering was not over. The spider yanked him into the air and shook him. The guard's limbs flailed as the aralak flung him at Gundrul.

Toryn barely had the strength to watch the unfolding terror. To his left, Elrik had slipped on the wet ground and lay on his back. But it gave him an advantage. As the aralak leaped to crush him, Elrik thrust his spear deep into its belly. It writhed, wrapping its hind legs around the shaft. It snapped. But the others saw their chance and struck. Gundrul lunged as Shepra jumped onto its head and clamped her teeth into the spider's eyes. Its claws snatched at the air, desperate to find its assailants' throats. But the more it struggled, the deeper the spear tips pierced, and the deeper Shepra's teeth sank. It fell dead with a sickening squelch as its body split.

Toryn could barely stand. His vision blurred as he tried to steady himself against a tree trunk, slick with gore. With all his effort he raised an arm. 'The droog. It will fade soon. But be wary.' The worm's yellow eyes found Toryn. Why had it not gone? Did the warlock inside prevent its return?

The droog's skin bulged. Toryn cried out. 'Get back!' He threw an arm across his face as the worm burst. Flesh and putrid bile splattered the guards. The droog was dead, but the warlock had not accepted defeat. It stumbled from the carcass. But even a warlock was not immune to a droog's innards. The warlock lurched, but before he could recover, Gundrul struck. He thrust his spear into the chest of the most daunting foe the old captain had faced. The screech knocked them from their feet. The shaft burned bright, then disintegrated. Gundrul flung the ash from his scorched hands. But before the guards could regain their feet and finish the wounded warlock, it reopened the split and staggered beyond their reach.

Gundrul gasped for breath and brushed his smoldering hands on his tunic. He turned to the lines of guards still slicing their way through the aralaks at their rear. 'By the Three, let's get out of this place.'

Toryn was carried along with the injured and fallen. Although no longer under the command of the warlock, revenge for the destroyed nest had united the spiders. The Nym's mantle had held, and they left a gruesome trail of legs, heads, and bodies of their foe. After what seemed like hours, they finally emerged from the gloom of the forest. But the aralaks had also gathered beyond the trees. But just as Toryn thought the exhausted survivors could fight no longer, they arrived at the stump where the Nym had emerged earlier that day. The mantle strengthened. It swirled about them, expanding, ripping to shreds any creature daring to approach the Nym's source of their old power.

Toryn let his head rest on the cool grass. He stared at the reddening evening skies. The clouds spun as his head had yet to settle. He was vaguely aware of raised voices. With all his remaining strength, he pushed himself up onto an elbow, dreading another attack. Toryn blinked, unsure of what he saw. His vision cleared. Three figures strode across the grass. The Amayans came. But something had changed. At first, Toryn thought it was a trick of the late evening sun, but as they drew near, he saw the air about them shimmered with a blue light, and their eyes shone brighter than ever.

Eryn kneeled at Toryn's side and laid her hand on his brow. He felt her warmth spread through his body. She looked down and smiled. 'You and your company have struck a major blow today.' Toryn tried to speak, but his throat was dry and sore. Eryn read his mind. 'We took Cymori to the stone. She is free now. Her true Amayan soul will prevail. And our time in the presence of the Amanach has prepared us for the next challenge.' She tussled Shepra's fur. 'This lass has done you proud. I've only known horses, but perhaps I should get a dog.' Toryn smiled. He tried to keep his eyes open. Eryn stroked his face. 'Sleep now, Toryn. We will heal and keep watch over your company. Sleep, for tomorrow we shall ride together into battle.'

# 48. The Power of the Stones

Toryn woke to find he was back in Omstrad. He looked down to his arms and found no sign of the wounds sustained at the nest. The dark window confirmed dawn had yet to break, but he felt as if he had slept for a week.

Gundrul strode into the hut. 'I can see by your face you feel the same as me.' He drew his sword and swung as if taking the head off a shreek. He beamed. 'I can't say I've felt this good since… actually, I can't claim I've ever felt as strong as I do now.'

Toryn stood and rolled his shoulder. 'Look at that. No pain. After yesterday I thought I'd barely be able to move.' He reached for his sword belt. 'What news of the wide world?'

Gundrul glanced to the door. 'I would have lost my wager about the rain. It's the oddest thing. Those storm clouds haven't moved. Above, the stars shine bright in a clear sky. But those clouds sit piled high in the north as if waiting to make their move.'

'That's exactly what they're doing.' Eryn entered. 'They gather over our enemy. The clouds carry a heavy load of snow and ice. A barrage of that in our faces will slow anyone's hand.' She looked to the captain. 'But as you know, that is not the only reason to bring the freezing air this far south.'

Gundrul's sword arm dropped to his side. 'Norgog. They came close to caving in my skull at Tunduska. Can't say I'm looking forward to another encounter with those thick-skinned brutes.'

Eryn clasped his broad shoulder. 'Take heart. You and your company have received sustenance from the

Amanach. You will each fight with the strength of three.' She smiled. 'That may help to even up the numbers. And as for you, Toryn. You can now go deeper into the Song. For the coming days, you will have the ability approaching that of your father's. Use it, use it well. We need all the powers at our disposal if we are to survive the coming onslaught.'

Toryn looked at the door. 'And what of your sisters? Do more ride to our aid?'

Her head bowed. 'I know only of three. Of the others I can now sense nothing, they are either no longer on these shores... or have shared the same fate as Cymori. But the three will be here soon.'

'And you can be certain they have not been corrupted?'

Eryn's eyes shone. 'Of that, I am sure. We drew deep from the well of power at the stone. We are stronger than we have been for many a year. The three who ride from the north are skilled fighters. Six Amayans will ride together for the first time since our failed mission to save Tanis.' Her outline shimmered in the dull room and she appeared to grow taller as her voice rose. 'We shall avenge both Amyra and Cymori today. Vordrak comes. He will not see the end of this day.' The light dimmed. She turned to Gundrul. 'Your company are ready?'

'As they'll ever be.' The captain grinned at Toryn. 'Eryn thought it best we let you have a lie in. You looked so peaceful it seemed cruel to wake you.'

Eryn laughed. 'What he means is you required longer to recover and be ready for this day.' She strode to the door. 'But now we must ride. Lady Harlyn and the remaining strength of the realms, hold the line across the plain to Roth's Doom. We will best assist by attacking the enemy's left flank. Those clouds will be upon us by noon, and that is when they will strike. With speed, we'll make the battlefield shortly after it's begun.' Her eyes flashed. 'We'll give those swine the surprise of their miserable lives.' Eryn whistled. 'Our horses come. They are also well rested and will ride faster than any in the realm.' She threw an arm around Toryn. 'And don't look concerned. Your newfound strength will ensure you can stay on Midnight's back.' The horses whinnied and trotted to meet them.' Eryn mounted. 'We shall meet the last of my sisters on the way.'

Gundrul patted Toryn's back. 'You and the Amayans will ride on ahead. Our ponies won't have a hope of matching your speed. We have two hundred riders, and Amyndra will lead fifty more who arrived in the night, still loyal to Bardon. If we can fight with the strength of three, that makes us a force those creatures can't take lightly.' The captain grasped Toryn's forearm. 'Good luck, my friend. May we meet on the battlefield as victors.'

Toryn returned the grip. 'I dearly hope so, Captain.' He jumped onto Midnight's back. The lines of Hamar's old map formed in his head. He called to Eryn. 'Do we ride the same path as the Amayans when answering Draegelan's call?'

Eryn tossed back her hair. 'You have the strength, Toryn.'

His mind raced. 'That would be a spectacular sight, eh.'

Gundrul looked from one to the other. 'Can you explain to this old, befuddled guard of what you speak?'

Toryn grinned. 'Let's just say, those on the enemy's left flank will see something that'll make them regret ever crossing the border.'

# 49. To Deny the Reapers

Sea Mist's head bobbed as he edged sideways. Elodi leaned forward and patted his neck, but her words failed to calm him. He knew her too well and sensed the anxiety of his rider. They stood at the center of the forces gathered to hold back the dark tide. Elodi glanced to both flanks. Spear tips and armor glistened under the sun as it climbed in the clear sky above them, but the thousands rallying to her call looked too few on the wide plain. The birds sang, unflustered by the army trampling across their grasslands. For a moment, Elodi could be deceived into expecting a pleasant autumn day. But as the breeze picked up, the cool air from the north soon chased away the warmth of the middle realms.

To Elodi's relief, Aldorman had arrived in the early hours and now formed a line behind her. Despite having little time to recover, Aldorman assured her they were fit for duty following their arduous journey through the Kolossos Pass. Her captain had reported only sporadic raids by small bands of Ruuk, and mercifully his losses were few.

Elodi scanned the plain. Her forces stretched half a league along a ridge running from Roth's Doom to the hills in the east. On her left, the chasm presented a solid defense; on her right, the hills offered little. But the enemy's formation suggested the hills would play no strategic part. Nyomae had been right, and the sky told Elodi all she needed to know. And that is exactly what the invaders wanted her to know. They would clash head on. The slope she chose to defend was shallow, but taking the high ground offered a slight advantage. Elodi may have had close to fifteen thousand at arms, yet they looked stretched thin along the long front. But she had little choice. Had she chosen a narrower and deeper formation, they would soon be surrounded with no route open for a retreat, if that was ever an option. Elodi had wished for a more detailed account of the threat, but a vast army of at least thirty thousand would cause even the stoutest heart of her scouts to falter. Understandably, they had not risked capture, but some had waited long enough to spy unworldly, dark creatures moving in the shadows behind the front ranks.

Elodi gawped at the gathering darkness on both land and in the sky. Her stomach churned as she recalled the sea and sky merging just before the maelstrom had slammed into the *Celestra.* On that day, Horace and Blowers had guided the old lady through that battle — could she safely negotiate the one to come? She stood in her stirrups to check the defensive ditch running across her entire front. Hundreds of Archonians had spent the night digging the shallow trench, achieving the remarkable feat in quick time. Dozens of wagons rolled across the line depositing the barrels of the Shreek's Rage retrieved from the pass. While it would not stop an attack, Elodi hoped to thin out the advancing hordes before they fell upon her lines. But her plan for archers to ignite the powder had changed thanks to the looming storm clouds. Elodi had been brought close to tears when so many had volunteered to light the short fuses from the trench. It would be fraught with danger, and not only from the risk of being slaughtered by the advancing enemy. The powder had to be left in their casks to keep it dry, therefore the resulting explosions would be huge and could easily obliterate those retreating.

Elodi looked back across the formation once more. She dearly wished Gundrul and Ruan could be at her side.

Neither had experience of such a large, set piece battle in the open, but their company would have helped settle her nerves. Her captains knew their part, but whether their battle plan could work, would soon become apparent. A series of trumpet calls would command her forces, but one glance at the ominous clouds, cast doubt on whether they would be heard over a storm. She had arranged her main strength at the center. On her flanks, the reserves and archers were supported by mounted knights. Behind, the First Horse shielded Nyomae. If they failed, the realms would most likely fall. While Elodi had done all she could with her limited resources, much depended on the actions of the enemy. She believed Dorlan could not resist assailing her position on spying Harlyn's banner. Nyomae needed to be close to the great warrior if she was to succeed. But one thought nagged Elodi above all others. Should she sit back and wait for the attack? Or if the explosives disrupted the enemy's advance, would a strike by her mounted knights help to drive home an early advantage? But riding out would leave a gap and could risk losing the battle before it had fully begun. As Elodi saw it, she had no choice but to wait and see what the enemy brought against her.

Bardon pulled up alongside. He had yet to fully recover from his ordeal on Mundrake's Isle, but he sat with confidence upon his horse. He nodded. 'The First Horse are in position. Nyomae is well defended.'

Elodi glanced over her shoulder towards the rear. 'She is as close to the front as we dare. It's a risk, but she could determine the outcome of the battle if she can free Dorlan from the Ul-dalak. If successful, the First Horse will be free to join the fray.'

Bardon's brow creased as his gaze shifted to the storm clouds. 'I fear *fray* will not do the coming battle justice.'

Elodi tried unsuccessfully to smile. 'Apologies. That

was a poor attempt to calm my nerves.'

'Nerves can be good, Elodi. They can drive us on when otherwise we may falter.' He pulled his cloak around his shoulders. 'And perhaps, they may also make us oblivious to the cold. These old bones appear to have long forgotten my upbringing in the north.'

Elodi glanced to the ditch. 'I also worry the sleet will dampen the fuses. I had hoped to devastate their front ranks at the very least.' Elodi's face chilled. Harlyn's banner lifted and tugged at its pole as if eager to retreat. She turned to Bardon. 'The wind picks up.' Ahead, the clouds billowed ever higher. She now had to tip back her head to find their tops. And as if they detected her attention, they began to tumble towards them. Elodi whispered. 'It begins, Bardon. This is it.' Her gaze reluctantly dropped to the plain. At first, she thought she saw the shadow from the clouds, but this was no shadow. She stiffened as she saw the clouds' front served to guide the mass ranks of the enemy. The plain north of the Borrund Road appeared to rise against them, writhing as if a giant worm slithered beneath the surface.

Elodi stared, dismayed as the green plain turned gray. How could they raise such an army? Nyomae had to succeed if the realms were to survive. Above, the clear skies reminded her of what she fought for, but the blue expanse would soon be smothered by the dark storm. Once more, she looked to her lines. Did the glistening ranks of her army standing defiant upon the high ground, cause even a moment of doubt among the approaching hordes? But the frightening speed the enemy closed the gap, suggested not. Elodi groaned. Her scouts had underestimated their size, perhaps by as much as ten to fifteen thousand — they were outnumbered four to one. She took a deep breath as she tried to calmly assess the threat. The front line consisted of three large formations of heavily armed Ruuk. She guessed it was close to a league wide; twice that of Elodi's front. And, as she predicted, Dorlan's banner flew at the center, with Uleva not far behind.

At the head of both flanks, two cloaked figures rode large horses, easily three hands taller than Sea Mist. Elodi's heart pounded into her ribs: warlocks. Again, Nyomae had been proven right. The warlocks intended to lead from the front to savor the slaughter. But where was Uluriel? Elodi strained to determine the threat of the second and third ranks. Her jaw clenched. The jittery movement in the formation opposing her left flank suggested aralaks. And the rider at their side had to be Uldrak.

But the full horror had yet to be revealed. A solid mass strode behind the main force at the center. Her head throbbed as she recognized the cruel hammers of the Norgog that had almost ended her days at Tunduska. She did not have to read the enemy's mind to know the ghastly role the Hammerskulls would play. They would be held back until the storm unleashed its hail and froze the air over her forces.

But what awaited her right flank? She rose in her saddle to see a solid line of Ruuk marched on their left. But it was the swirling air behind the Ruuk that plunged the dagger into Elodi's heart. Tall, rangy forms of shrouls and shreeks teetered on their long legs as if stepping over the dead of past battles. But how many, Elodi could not begin to assess. Behind the mass ranks, the ground had turned white. The enemy had brought the freezing skies of Nordruuk with them. Even if the realms could repel the first wave of Ruuk, they faced the grim prospect of the Norgog battering their exhausted and depleted lines.

Elodi adjusted the strap on her helmet, doubting it could withstand a hammer blow. She muttered. 'Bardon? How… how do we even begin to…?'

In the silence, she heard the leather of Bardon's gloves tighten on his reins. 'For the sake of us all, you must stay strong. Remember your ancestors. You are an Amayan, Elodi.'

She straightened. 'Yes, yes I must.' She kicked Sea Mist forward, then turned to face her army. Elodi took another deep breath and let the warmth flood her limbs. She cried out. 'We are the defenders of the Five Realms! This is our land. The enemy before you have no right to trample our fields, burn our villages, and enslave our loved ones.' She drew her sword and held it high. 'This is where we hold the line. This is where we drive them back!' She looked to the Archonians. 'Not a step back!' She let loose her power. Her blade glowed orange, reflecting across the armor of her front lines. The army cheered and thrust their weapons up to the sky. She watched the display but dared to think what lay at her back. What show of force would the warlocks unveil to belittle hers?

Elodi rode back to her position and turned Sea Mist. The front ranks of the enemy had halted just one hundred paces from the ditch. A dark line stretched east to west across the land and sky, dividing the realm as if they stood in two worlds. But alas, they would soon clash. Dorlan positioned his stallion, Draego, to face her. Elodi had avoided a confrontation at Calerdorn — today, she would not. The great knight looked up as the clouds rolled over the open ground between the two armies. Elodi could not help following his gaze, determined not to allow the weight of the sky crush her spirit. But she failed. Yet she was thankful Dorlan had not brought Meloni with him. The sight of the young girl laughing as Sea Mist's blood had splattered her white nightgown, still haunted Elodi. She often wondered what had become of the sole survivor they had found in the smoldering grass of Dorn Plain. Did she still reside in Calerdorn?

Bardon leaned over. 'May I say, Elodi, there is no other I would rather follow on this day. The enemy may look a daunting prospect, but believe me, they will also be wary of you.'

'Thank you, Bardon. I only wish I shared your confidence. But I am most grateful to have you by my side.' Her voice wavered. 'Bardon. If I don't get the opportunity to—' Three lightning bolts tore the words from her mouth.

Midnight slowed and came to a halt beside Eryn. She pointed. 'They come.' In the early light, Toryn saw three riders to the north.

Calestri drew level. 'I sense no ill as we did with Cymori.'

Arijan agreed. 'I see Igrayne, Madraal, and if I'm not mistaken, the third is Neeve.' She turned to Toryn. 'You'll never seen anyone throw a spear as far or as true as Neeve. I saw her pierce the throat of a warlock before he saw her coming.' She grinned. 'The look of surprise was still on his face as he perished.'

Eryn held up her hand. 'Wait here please, Toryn. We have matters to discuss with our sisters.'

He dismounted, happy for the chance to stretch his legs after the strenuous journey. He patted Midnight's nose. 'Good girl. We'll rest here while—' but she trotted off along with the Amayans to greet the three riders. Toryn looked up. It was if the sky was sliced in two. To his left, the calm starlit skies of mid-autumn; to his right, the angry clouds of a bitter winter. They had risen even higher, but still held back. But as the day all dreaded approached, the stars began to fade, happy to withdraw from the world and avoid the carnage to come. Toryn watched the stars depart as he would dear friends. He wondered if Hamar looked down from the Plains of Evermore and dearly wished the old Archonian was at his side. Would he soon be with Hamar? He had made the Archonian vow, and it was highly likely he would die today with his sword in his hand. But whatever the outcome, he hoped Hamar would be proud of him. Toryn had come close to walking away from his duty while resting on the Menon Hills. The urge to explore the shoreline of the restless Elessyn Sea had beckoned — and he was sorely tempted. He could have easily turned his back on Hope, happy to stroll through the sunlit barley fields of Tamarand and onto the coast. But Hamar's words had stopped him. Toryn had achieved much since that moment, but that would count for nothing if the realms fell today. He looked to the horizon now visible in the dawn light. Would he live to see the oceans?

Horses approached. Although they rode out from beneath the cloud creeping over the plain, the six Amayans glowed. And despite the dread growing in his gut, Toryn felt heartened by the sight of the warriors. They pulled up in front. Eryn slid from her saddle. She held out her hand to the three in turn. 'Toryn. Meet Igrayne, Madraal, and Neeve. He stood entranced, not hearing Eryn's words as she explained Toryn's heritage to her sisters. Neeve sat the tallest on a fine chestnut horse and could easily be mistaken for Eryn from a distance. But despite their appearance, Toryn sensed their recent awakening from the shadow had troubled them.

He jumped as Eryn touched his arm. She winked at him and addressed the Amayans. 'And don't be fooled by the strange expression on his youthful face. You will see it often when he's in our company. But beneath it lies a brave man, and perhaps one day' — she smiled — 'a wise man.'

Toryn cleared his throat. 'I don't need to be *wise* to say how pleased the realms will be to see you.'

Igrayne dismounted and laid her hand on his shoulder; Toryn's face tingled at her touch. 'Eryn tells me you may yet turn the battle in our favor.'

His cold skin welcomed her warm hand. 'It's well beyond anything I've attempted before.' Toryn glanced east. 'But I guess the same applies to most of us this day.'

Igrayne held his gaze. 'That it does. We've had a difficult passage south. Lunn, and now many parts of Ormsk, lie under a thick blanket of snow and ice. The storm leads an army the likes we've not seen in centuries. It's stopped at the Borrund Road, poised and ready to strike where your forces assemble.'

Eryn wheeled Moonbeam. 'Then we ride. More follow, but we cannot wait. Ride on.'

The horses reared and screamed. Three lightning bolts shot from the clouds, scorching the earth close to Elodi's trench. But this was not natural. The bolts struck in a line at equal distances apart. Elodi checked the dugouts of the volunteers ready to light the fuses. None moved. They had not run. Did they live?

The sky darkened as the clouds rolled overhead to suffocate the sun, and with it, the hope of the realms. The ground trembled. Elodi's hair stood on end beneath her helm. Where the bolts had punctured the surface, the earth boiled as if scorched by the fires below. The three patches widened, then spun like whirlpools to open dark pits down to the Underworld. In the sudden silence, Elodi swore she heard the earth sigh as coils of thick smoke billowed forth. What vulgar beasts did the enemy summon from the depths? Elodi's breath caught in her throat as three figures took shape. Had Uluriel called upon the drayloks? She quailed. The tapestry in Archonholm depicted the hags spewing fire and ripping mortals to shreds with their long, barbed hair. The *Draedalak* had all but defeated the Archon and Nyomae's Order. Did they return?

The creatures grew to a monstrous height. Their knotted spines cracked as they unfurled to stand taller than Uleva's hideous tower at Wyke Wood. The smoke vanished. These were not the drayloks from the weavers' imagination. Elodi's mind raced. These beasts were not from any tale she knew. She gawped in horror as they stretched out their limbs as if released from an age of confinement. They raised their elongated, hairless skulls from their scrawny necks with great effort. Deep within, Elodi knew no mortal had beheld their fearsome faces for many a century. Despite her revulsion, Elodi could not tear her eyes from them. When still a child, she had been terrified by the outlandish face of a sea monster stranded on Calerdorn's shore. But that was long dead, now three such monsters loomed over her. Yet who had the power to awaken these eldritch beasts? Had Ormoroth returned?

The ground shook as their long arms dropped to their sides as if too heavy for their gangly bodies to support. Yet no hand or claw touched the plain — their arms ended in long, curved blades that tore at the earth as if giant plows. But the horror had just begun. Their slit eyes opened. The plain convulsed as the demons' gaze fell upon the mortal lands. Elodi shrank back as the dull, red eyes of a beast found her. And in that moment, she understood it had come for her soul.

Its cavernous mouth gaped. Elodi's eyes were drawn into its throat, slick with a gray slime that glistened in a dull light glowing from within. The demons announced their return. Three voices boomed, rising and falling as if the Evil One himself blew his foul breath through a great horn. Elodi's heart vibrated against her breastplate as the stench of death turned her guts to water.

The creatures moved, taking long, lumbering strides towards Elodi's line. Once more, she searched for the guards posted at the trench. Should she give the signal to light the fuses? Or were these creatures an apparition, sent for the purpose of wasting her powder. Something stayed her hand.

The burning eyes of the beast opposite Elodi, fell upon her. She cowered as if the very air desired to crush her bones into the dirt. Sea Mist took a step back. Elodi clenched her jaw, vowing to herself, 'No! I will not be afraid.' She swallowed her fear and found her voice. 'By the Three, Bardon. Surely, they cannot be real. But the ground trembles. Do the old tales speak of these craven beasts?'

Bardon stuttered. 'I… recall just the one. A story of Gildorul of Keld. Before a great battle in Nordruuk.'

'Then what are they? How are we supposed to fight them?'

His mouth gaped. 'Reapers. They were named Reapers. They come from the Underworld to lay claim to the souls of those about to die.'

She grasped his forearm. 'But are they real, Bardon? Should we retreat?'

His wide eyes stayed fixed on the creatures. 'I… I'm afraid I don't know, Elodi. I never thought they existed. I assumed they were a creation of our storytellers.' The ground shuddered as the Reapers stepped over the trench and swung their giant scythes. Elodi ducked as a gust of foul air blew over their heads. The Reaper at the center stopped, then leveled the tip of its long blade at Elodi's heart. It stooped, thrusting its large head forward to lock eyes with Elodi. Slowly, it lifted the blade above its head. She froze. The Reaper made its intention known — it would slice her open, rip out her heart, and banish her soul to its vault deep beneath the mountains in the north. There she would be confined for eternity, and at the mercy of the beast's dark desires. Through her tight throat she managed only one word. 'Bardon?' But he too was held in the grasp of the Reaper.

Elodi clutched her chest and screamed. The Amayan within resisted. The hold released. She gasped for air as the Reapers' blades swished again across their ranks. Elodi cried out against the reek of decaying flesh. 'They want to take us all!' Some fell on their faces, crying out, some braved the assault, but others turned and fled. Elodi forced herself upright. She found her voice. It rang clear across the plain. 'Hold the line! Do not fear them!' Her body burned. *Amayan Fire!*

Elodi threw off her helm, tossed her breastplate and armor into the dirt, then urged Sea Mist forward. 'Be brave, Misty. Be brave for me once more.' Her loyal horse answered her call. His back rose as he surged towards the danger. Elodi yelled at the Reapers. 'I am an Amayan! Begone, craven beasts. You do not belong here.' She thrust her sword to the sky. A bolt of blue burst forth, flooding the plain, and blasting the eyes of all who dared to challenge her.

The Reapers halted. She drew up Sea Mist twenty paces short. All three fixed their gaze on Elodi. But horse and rider refused to cower. She praised her mount. 'Brave boy, Misty.' She met the glare of the creature at the center and bellowed. 'I deny you. The souls of my army are not yours to take. You have no claim here.' Their mournful call ceased; the battlefield held its breath. Sea Mist snorted. Elodi leveled her sword at the chest of the opposing Reaper. 'Go back to your dark pits!' She unleashed a second bolt. The Reapers wavered and staggered back. Their eyes dimmed. Smoke billowed and swirled about their shrinking forms. Then their spirits fled back from where they had come, and their bodies fell as ashes, soon to be blown from the battlefield.

A sword clashed on a shield. Dorlan sat at the head of

Calerdorn's captured knights. He grinned. 'I admire your courage, Elodi. But that was just a taste of what will come. As a reward, I will allow you to return to your line. But this time, there is no place for you to run and hide.' He jabbed his sword at her. 'Your life is mine, Elodi. And I will take your head as a trophy for the walls of Calerdorn. But not before I have had—'

'I know of your past, Dorlan.' Elodi calmly replied. 'I pity you. I pity what you have become.' The great knight's mouth twitched. She continued. 'Today, we shall free you from the dark that enslaves your soul.' She swept her sword across the front line behind Dorlan. 'And all who dare to take one more step into our realm, will feel the pain of our steel.'

Dorlan scoffed. 'You shall eat your empty words before the day is out. I shall trample your army's bones into the plain, but as for you, *Lady Harlyn*. I shall take you back to Calerdorn and parade you before your people. Then I shall humiliate you, and then take—'

Elodi turned her back and kicked on Sea Mist, but only at a trot. She passed one of the hideouts behind the trench. The guard inside caught her eye. 'We held our position, ma'am, just as you commanded.'

She kept her eyes ahead and spoke as loud as she dared. 'Your bravery is surpassed by none. Await my signal. And may the Three be with you.'

Elodi reached her line. Those who had fled returned to their positions but could not look their leader in the eye. Elodi gazed upon them with pity. The fire still burned within. Her voice carried across the plain. 'Do not be ashamed of your fear. You were tested beyond your limits. But it is in such times we find our true strength. Stand now. Stand together. And stand firm.'

Bardon sat aghast. 'That was… if I ever… I don't think those creatures could have conceived you'd charge straight at them.'

She managed a smile. 'Neither did I. But by the Three, Bardon, those demons should have turned and taken their pick of the rotten lot behind—' A thunderclap ripped across the sky. Elodi looked up, convinced the dome had cracked. 'I think the pleasantries are done.' She steadied Sea Mist and cried out. 'For the Realms!' Another crack from the storm clouds drowned her words. The cold rain lashed on their heads. The enemy mass ranks advanced.

# 50. THE FIRE & THE FURY

Toryn rode with the six Amayans. Their horses galloped faster than he thought possible. They skimmed across the plain as if flying. But Toryn had little time to admire their agility. The towering black clouds to their right, swelled to such heights they would surely brush the faces of the gods.

Leagues ahead, lightning bolts flashed. Eryn cried out. 'It begins. Ah! The enemy summon the Reapers.' She shouted over to Toryn. 'They'll strike fear into your forces. We must arrive before all is lost.' Midnight surged, almost throwing him from her back. The air chilled as the clouds rolled over their heads bringing winter to Ormsk. He fixed his eyes ahead. Eryn assured him they followed the same path as the Amayan host riding to Draegelan's side centuries earlier. Toryn had to succeed. Eryn and her sisters would boost his strength yet further. With their help, he hoped to reach far back to summon the Verses of the Amayan charge. But the warlocks had to be engaged elsewhere if he had any chance to gain access to the Song. Toryn could only maintain the illusion for minutes at most. But if it worked, it would unsettle their opponents and help turn the battle.

A bright, blue light flashed across the clouds. Eryn roared. 'Amayan Fire! Lady Harlyn is truly an Amayan.' She yelled into the wind. 'Elodi challenges the Reapers! Our sister needs us. Ride on. Ride on.'

Elodi bawled against the howling wind. 'Sound the command!' The trumpeter raised the horn to his lips, but the instrument was wet and his mouth dry. He shook the water free and tried again. The call went up. It sounded weak in the din, but it reached the ears for whom it was intended. The call repeated along the lines. Elodi gripped her reins, willing the fuses to light in the downpour. Across the trench a few sparks flashed in the gloom. The first Ruuk reached the shallow ditch. Her jaw clamped tight. To her left, a cask erupted, quickly followed by three more, then two to her right. Great gouts of mud were flung high, along with many Ruuk, obliterated by the Shreeks' Rage. Elodi gaped at the destruction, knowing the brave souls lighting the fuses may well have shared the fate of their victims. She bellowed to her trumpeter. 'Archers!' His call echoed along the lines. Five hundred arrows streaked over their heads. In the face of the all-out attack, it seemed a paltry response, but every arrow that found a target would mean one less foe to fight. The arrows continued to fly, but as the mud and smoke settled from the blasts, Elodi groaned.

The cask in front had failed to ignite — a grinning Dorlan rode straight at her.

Elodi turned and yelled to Aldorman. 'We charge. We meet them at speed.' Her captain gave the command. The remaining Knights of Calerdorn leveled sixty lances and launched their attack. Elodi's blade burned hot in her hand as she urged Sea Mist towards Dorlan, looming large at the head of the dark horsemen.

The two ranks collided. Steel clashed upon steel, and knights on both sides fell. Dorlan wheeled Draego to drive at Elodi. She thrust out her sword and hurled a blazing bolt at the legend's chest. But his shield was equal to her attack. Sparks flew as he deflected her strike to take down a knight at Elodi's side. Sea Mist stumbled in the mud but held his ground. Dorlan swung his great blade. Elodi ducked under a blow that would have removed her head. She pulled back on the reins and sliced at his sword arm.

But Draego reared, taking Dorlan out of range. The huge horse kicked. Draego's iron shod hooves narrowly missed Elodi's face as Sea Mist swerved. She shot a glance behind. Her knights had the upper hand against Dorlan's imposters, but as he pulled Draego back to face Elodi, he felled two more with a sweeping blow. He turned and sprang at Elodi. She veered around the bloodied tip of his sword aimed at her throat, then swung back at his neck. But his armor easily resisted her blow. She cried out as her arm jolted as if she had struck a rock.

Nyomae shut out the dreadful cries of the battle. She was aware of arrows and rocks striking the shields of the First Horse encircling her, but she could not afford to be distracted. She calmed and entered the Song. Her way was clear, but Nyomae was certain the warlocks would come as soon as they sensed her intention. She found the Verse of the possessed Dorlan. His shadowy figure was encircled by a blazing light, defying any to enter; but enter she must. Elodi's Verse burned bright, but Nyomae feared the Amayan could not sustain her power for long. Behind Dorlan's form, a darkness laid its claim. It looked as if two giant hands guided him as an entertainer would a marionette. Nyomae saw what she had hoped to find: Dorlan's true soul was indeed trapped within his body. But his spirit appeared as a dim light, a flickering candle struggling against a breeze, powerless to act. He had the misfortune to witness what he had become, and the shameful acts he was forced to commit. Inside, Dorlan wept.

Nyomae began her journey. She surged back through the Song, passing from verse-to-verse through Dorlan's long life. The deeper she went, the brighter his entrapped spirit shone. It gave her hope. Nyomae found the Verse she sought and stopped. This was the moment Uluriel had captured him after centuries of serfdom had drained his strength. This was the moment Nyomae had a chance to undo the wrong.

Dorlan stood on a frozen plain in Nordruuk. His tattered clothes offered little protection against the bitter gales. A chain around his scarred neck tethered him to a large metal spike driven deep into the ground. He held a hammer. Before him was a mound of large rocks. Nyomae bit back the anger. The once mighty warrior was now a slave, forced to break stones and build walls for the Ruuk.

She readied herself for the fight to come. Her voice echoed as she spoke his name. *Dorlan.* But the one word uttered in the Verse, stirred Uluriel, and at once she knew Nyomae's mind. Uluriel's worldly form was far to the north. She did not partake in the battle, but what dark art she performed, Nyomae could not tell. But now her hand was forced. Uluriel would have to join the fight.

Her cry penetrated Nyomae's Verse to alert the warlocks at Roth's Doom. And they came.

The piercing screech threw many off their horses. Elodi clung to Sea Mist's neck as he reared. Dorlan roared as he charged. Elodi braced to meet the attack, but he wheeled Draego and drove at the First Horse protecting Nyomae. She circled her sword over her head. 'After him!' She kicked Sea Mist on. Ahead, the great warrior smashed into the line of knights. The three riders who turned to challenge Dorlan were flung from their saddles. But others readily took their fallen comrades place, reforming the shield around Nyomae. Elodi saw her. She stood amid the brawl with her head bowed as if in quiet study in Abernost.

Elodi rushed to the aid of the knights facing Dorlan. He bellowed his scorn, slashing, and jabbing his heavy blade at those in his way. More fell, but others rode at him, ready to sacrifice their lives to guard Nyomae. Elodi delved into her diminishing reserves to summon strength. Deep within she found the fire that burned bright in her race. It kindled once more. She drew it up her spine, into her arm, then launched a bolt through her blade at Dorlan. He swung his shield but was too late to block her strike. It slammed into his chest. He wavered, but as Elodi raised her sword, Dorlan recovered, turned, and aimed a blow at Sea Mist's neck. She hauled back on the reins. The blade missed, but Elodi was thrown from his back. She slipped in the mud as she clambered to her feet. The freezing rain drove into her face, stinging her eyes as she struggled to find Dorlan.

The hammer slipped from Dorlan's grasp as he beheld Nyomae. She revealed what would become of him if he did not aid her. He threw back his head and wailed as he saw his blade strike down knights fighting under the banner bearing his shield. He turned to Nyomae and appeared to recognize her kind. She spoke again. *I will free you from this torment. But I need your strength.* She gestured behind him. *A rider approaches. She will enslave you if we do not act.* A shadow sped across the plain. Uluriel of that time had come for Dorlan. But she was not alone. The air above her whirled as if a maelstrom drove her on. Nyomae knew it to be Uluriel's presence from the north. She had infiltrated Nyomae's Verse to assist her past self. Nyomae held her fear at bay as the cries of the warlocks from Roth's Doom drew near. It had to be now. Nyomae took Dorlan's cold hand. She reached back in his Verse to find him just before the battle at Talaghir. She only needed a remnant of his spirit to bring to this moment. But she needed Dorlan to be ready to accept the gift of his past spirit. *Open your mind, Dorlan. I bring you strength.*

But part of his broken spirit resisted, wary of the sudden power after the decades of servitude. Uluriel screamed. *Defy her, Dorlan! She brings only death. I offer you life.*

Nyomae pleaded with him. *You have seen what you will become. Trust me, Dorlan, and you will be free.*

Dorlan's gray eyes met hers. *Help me, Imaari. I wish to be free.* With his consent, his former spirit returned and reclaimed the warrior's broken body. He threw back his head and cried out. His bent back straightened, his shoulders widened, and his eyes blazed. Dorlan grasped his chains and tore the spike from the ground. He circled it over his head, then lunged and hurled the chain to ensnare Uluriel's horse. It stumbled, throwing its rider onto the frozen ground. Dorlan took up the hammer and charged at Uluriel. She regained her feet and swirled her arms in the air, desperate to mount a defense. But not in a thousand years of preparation could Uluriel stop the man hurtling towards her. As he ran, he regained his full stature and power, resembling the warrior who had challenged Ormoroth at Talaghir. Uluriel turned and fled.

But the battle was not yet done. Uluriel's dark form from the present took shape. She stepped out from the churning smoke. Nyomae staggered back. Uluriel's physical form had entered the Verse. For a moment, Nyomae thought she beheld a *Draedalak*, a demon of old. Uluriel had grown stronger, and more terrible, following her expulsion from the Archon. But the might of the Dark Verses consumed her mortal form, thus her flesh and bones suffered to wield its most dreadful power.

Uluriel's mouth gaped wide. Her eyes burned red. She threw out her arms and screamed. The air about her whirled, spinning faster and faster until the Verse itself screeched, pained by the chaos it had to bear. The vortex swelled. Above the dreadful din, Uluriel's fell voice shrieked, calling on the Evil One to strike down those who dared defy her.

A hand grasped Nyomae's. Dorlan stood at her side.

Together, they held their ground as Uluriel unleashed the tempest. The power of the Elorym ignited in them both. Nyomae shot out her hand. The bolt pierced the gale, tearing it asunder. It struck Uluriel. The air burst, throwing Nyomae and Dorlan from their feet. But Uluriel was gone, expelled from the Verse.

Yet still the danger had not passed. Nyomae spun around to face the two warlocks as they tore through the fabric of the Verse. But Ormoroth's captains had not foreseen who would stand against them. They hesitated. Before them, the mighty Dorlan of Talaghir, and at his side, a noble Imaari, burning with the blazing light of the Elorym. Not even ten warlocks could defeat them at this time. But Nyomae's strategy was revealed. As fast as they came, the warlocks withdrew, racing back to Roth's Doom to exact their revenge.

Elodi staggered over the fallen. Ahead, Dorlan had stopped. He sat upon Draego, gaping at the knights he had slaughtered. He held up his bloodied sword, then turned to see Elodi. Two knights charged at him. Elodi cried out, bringing them to a skidding halt. Nyomae had done it! Dorlan was free. And he lived. Sea Mist came to Elodi's aid. She leaped onto his back and drove on to meet Dorlan. His sword arm hung limp by his side. Tears streamed down his face to merge with the icy rain. He stared at the carnage. 'What have I done? With my own hands I have slain those riding under my banner.'

Elodi grasped his forearm as he moved to sling his sword away. 'You have been possessed by our enemy. But now you are free, Dorlan. You're free.' She pointed to the Ruuk stomping through the mire towards them. 'Ride with us! Fight, Dorlan. Right the wrongs the enemy have wrought upon you.'

Dorlan's eyes widened. He wheeled Draego and

leveled his great blade at the advancing enemy ranks. He bellowed. 'For Harlyn! For the realms!' The Ruuk front line faltered. Draego charged.

Elodi snatched Harlyn's banner from the ground. She held it high and cried out to her knights. 'Ride! Ride with Dorlan.' Sea Mist raced to join Draego. Her heart swelled as she rode side by side with Dorlan into battle. The line of knights stampeded at the Ruuk, but none could keep abreast with Dorlan and Elodi. Their swords blazed with a blinding fire as they sliced through the Ruuk. Dorlan roared his battle cry. His challenge echoed across the field, filling the enemy with dread, and his allies with hope. None could stand before him. Draego outpaced Sea Mist and Dorlan surged ahead, slicing through the Ruuk as if harvesting wheat.

At the rear, Uleva cowered, unable to evade Dorlan's eyes. A wall of Ruuk shields rushed to surround their commander. But they could not withstand Draego's charge. The wall shattered as his hooves clattered down on their shields. Dorlan slid from his horse and strode at Uleva. A green haze shimmered about her, but to no avail. Elodi caught up just as Dorlan brought down his blade to splinter the sphere… and split open Uleva's skull. The air erupted as she perished. All about were flung back, leaving Dorlan and Elodi to stand alone. But just as Elodi dared to hope they could win the battle, Dorlan's light began to fade.

But his deeds for the day were not yet done. He mounted Draego and drove on through the reforming lines of the Ruuk. Elodi did not follow. The sleet had turned into hail, hurling stinging ice into her face. She glanced down. The ground would soon freeze. The Norgog would come. Elodi surveyed the field through the blinding hail. The enemy's center was routed, but a fierce battle occupied both her flanks. To her left, the

Archonians held their ground against the Ruuk, but only just. Broon's mounted knights had outflanked the Ruuk, but their numbers were not enough to prevent their relentless push forward. And to her dismay, Elodi knew the hungry aralaks would soon be unleashed.

To her right, the Archonians and Galabrant's reserves had lost ground and veered inward to avoid being outflanked. But behind the Ruuk, the wraithlike creatures were ready to strike. Elodi searched for Dorlan but failed to find him amid the mayhem of battle. Sea Mist slipped. The ground was quickly turning to ice. It would not trouble the Norgog, but if her forces lost their footing it could prove pivotal. Elodi grasped Aldorman's arm and yelled. 'Reform! Reform the front line. The First Horse will join us.' She turned Sea Mist and gasped as the barrage of hailstones numbed her skin. The line withdrew.

The Archonians at the center had anticipated the Norgog advance and had formed a shield wall four deep. Elodi marshaled the last of her knights on the right flank; the First Horse took the left. Elodi knew the horses were vulnerable to a direct blow from a Norgog's hammer. Thus, it would be folly to attack the brutes head on. But perhaps she could trap them against the Archonian shields and strike at their flanks with their lances. Elodi turned. She had little in reserve at the rear. It would not be wise to split the three hundred Archonians standing ready, but where should they be deployed?

Bardon rode up. He gasped for air. 'Dorlan is lost?'

She yelled over the Ruuk cries urging on the Norgog advance. 'Alas, I believe his life has burned out. But he has done us a great service.' She glanced over her shoulder. 'What of Nyomae? Can she fight?'

Bardon shielded his eyes from the hail. 'She has collapsed. We have taken her to the healers. She lives, but I doubt she'll recover before the battle is done.'

'Then we fight on.' Yet Elodi was exhausted, and the Amayan Fire had all but burned out. She stood in her stirrups. 'I can see nothing in this storm. Our hope now lies with Toryn, the Amayans and the forces of Omstrad. But what of the west? Have our forces made it through the pass?' The ground trembled.

Aldorman cried out. 'Ma'am! The Norgog attack.'

'By the Three!' Midnight pulled up as they rounded the last hill. Toryn gaped. To their right, the fury of winter lashed the plain with hail, driving on the dark ranks of the enemy. Standing against the maelstrom, the forces of the realms braced to meet the onslaught. Their banners flailed in the wind, clinging defiantly to the poles staking their claim to the land.

Eryn pointed. 'Look! The realms push through the center. A great knight rides. And… an Amayan.'

Toryn's heart lurched. 'Elodi!' He knew she would lead from the front, but how would she fare amid the slaughter?

Eryn stood on Moonbeam's back. 'Ah, but the knight's strength fails. He's heading into a large force of Norgog.'

Toryn watched in horror as Elodi and her knights retreated. 'They must be almost spent. The right flank is almost overrun.'

Eryn clasped his arm. 'Then do it now, Toryn.'

Toryn shut his eyes and ears against the battle. 'My way is clear.' The woman he loved fought for her life. He had to be at her side. This was not just for the Five Realms. This was for Elodi. He bowed his head and tried to listen to his breath against the howling wind.

The hills turned green in the sunlight as he began his long journey. Time would slow down in the world where he stood, but he could not afford to linger in the Song. All could be lost if a warlock became aware of his plan. The seasons raced past as he sped through the Verses of the old hills as if flicking through the pages of a book. He slowed. Two great armies emerged on the plain below. He saw the mighty Draegelan; his presence burning bright in the Verse. Toryn flinched as he laid eyes upon Ormoroth. His dark form distorted the Song, stretching the sinews of his Verse as it strained to endure his presence.

Toryn twisted away to focus on the hills. He squinted into a blinding light. A force of more than a hundred Amayans charged across the lower slopes. He wove his hands around the shape of their formation. He could sustain the illusion for only a short time back in the present day, but that could be enough to turn the battle. His flesh burned as they seemed to ride through him. Eryn cried out. 'They come! Our sisters come!'

The Verse shattered and the sounds of battle assailed Toryn's ears. But now the realms had an ally they could never have imagined. Midnight whinnied. She tossed her head, then turned to join the Amayans of old as they raced across the plain.

The Norgog charged. Elodi clenched her teeth as their hammers smashed down onto the Archonian shield wall. The line buckled but shoved back. Despite the ice beneath their feet, the guards to the rear dug in and held the formation. But the hammers began to find their targets, splitting helms, cracking heads, and shattering shoulders. Elodi took a deep breath. 'Now!' Aldorman and her knights wheeled around the shield wall's left flank, while Bardon and the First Horse took the right. Sea Mist kicked out at the Norgog as Elodi jabbed down at the tough skins of their necks. The Archonians began to give ground as the great weight of the Norgog drove forward. Elodi hacked, while her knights drove their lances into the

Norgogs' thick hides. Her sword was now a mere mortal blade; the Amayan Fire was long spent. The skills learned from her master counted for nothing. Blades slashed, jabbed, and gouged. Lances pierced and twisted, but also snapped. Hammers swung and slammed down. Armor broke, flesh split, and bones shattered.

'Ma'am!' Aldorman yelled. She glanced up. It was if the sun rose for a second time that day. The Archon's words echoed in her head. *Rise and send these demons back to the darkness.* The sky cleared on her right flank. A ray of light blazed across the field as if a great beacon was lit. Elodi peered into the light. Her heart leaped as she beheld a great host of warriors racing down the slope. The Norgog faltered.

Elodi cried out. 'Fight on! The Amayans come.' The Archonians gained ground. Above, war raged as the blue sky fought to reclaim their territory from the winter clouds.

The battle raced towards Toryn as Midnight hurtled across the grasslands. The ground swelled, both remembering and welcoming the return of the Amayan host. At his side, Eryn and her companions burned with the Amayan Fire. Their swords blazed first blue, then with the brilliant white of a full moon. The air shimmered and crackled as the host raised their hundred voices. Toryn's spirit soared as their battle cry flooded his soul. But to the Ruuk, the Amayan challenge pained their ears and filled them with dread. Toryn could barely breathe. The Amayans surged as if a great wave, glistening from within, growing ever taller, ready to crash upon those who dared to stand in its way.

Ahead, the Ruuk on the flanks prepared to meet the attack. But none did so willingly. Even the hardiest Ruuk quailed in the path of the proud horses bearing fearsome warriors wielding flaming swords. The Ruuk in the front rank turned, desperate to fight their way through their own lines, choosing to take their chances against the Archonian shield wall. But many fled blindly in all directions, startled by the fierce light of the Amayan onslaught. But there was to be no escape. Deserters collided with the shreeks who smote them down with their fearful whips, forcing them back into the fight.

Toryn drew his blade. He yelled against the gale. 'For Elodi!'

Eryn roared. 'For Tanis! For Eleni!' She wheeled her sword above her head. 'And for Amyra!'

The host thundered into the Ruuk. Toryn braced as Midnight plowed four deep, trampling all before her. Caught in the glare of Amayan Fire, the Ruuk stood no chance. Wedged between Archonian shields and the great horses of old, they were crushed and slaughtered.

The left flank of the Ul-dalak army were routed, never to reform.

Eryn leveled her sword at the swirling darkness swallowing up the last of the fleeing Ruuk. 'To the shreeks!' Toryn's hold over the Amayans began to weaken. But the ghouls had to be defeated before they assailed the mortal Archonians. Eryn led the charge at the shreeks. This was a battle of the old powers, and not for the Archonians. The guards lined up and drove their shield wall into the flanks of the Norgog still battling at the center.

Toryn rode with the Amayans as they challenged the Ul-dalak's grim forces. Behind, a towering warlock commanded the dark ranks. Eryn cried out. 'Vordrak!' She urged Moonbeam forward. 'We shall avenge.'

Vordrak shot an arm skyward. A bolt erupted from the retreating clouds. It struck the ground and exploded, throwing up shards of ice and gouts of mud. But Eryn and her sisters would not be denied. They rode on through the debris, but a deep crater slowed their pace. Eryn cried out in frustration. The warlock and his beasts knew they were no match for the Amayans, choosing to flee to fight another day.

The light about Toryn dimmed, then vanished as the last of the Amayan army returned to their time. He tried to follow Eryn, but Midnight staggered. A spear had pierced her shoulder, and many arrows stuck in her flanks. Blood poured from her wounds. Midnight fell. Toryn slid from her back as the fearless mare took her last breath. But he had no time to thank her. To his left, the Norgog fought on, refusing to give ground without sacrifice. Hammers battered shields as Archonian steel thrust through the gaps.

Toryn desperately searched the carnage for Elodi. His heart lurched. Her red hair tussled in the breeze beneath a flurry of hammers seeking to crack her skull. Toryn slipped and stumbled over both the dead and the dying to reach her. But each time he lost his footing, he lost sight of Elodi. And when he did manage to locate her, she appeared farther away.

'Toryn!' He swiveled to see Gundrul and his force riding down the last of the Ruuk.

Toryn thrust out an arm. 'To Elodi.'

'Here. Take my hand.' Gundrul hauled him up onto his horse. The captain yelled over his shoulder. 'Looks like your surprise worked.'

'Maybe on this side.' He held onto Gundrul as his horse gained speed and lurched through the melee. 'But the battle rages to the west. We must reach Elodi.'

'Hammerskulls!' The captain bellowed. 'Ride on! Lady Harlyn's in peril.'

The Norgog heard the horses. They turned, squatted, and swung their cruel weapons to meet the charge.

Gundrul's front line collided with the Norgog. Toryn cried out as the iron hammer heads sank into the soft necks of their valiant mounts. Dozens were hurled from their screaming horses to be pummeled to death by the Norgog behind. Toryn leaped from Gundrul's horse and grabbed the hammer of a Norgog as it swung at an unhorsed rider. He drove his blade into its neck, then twisted to yank it free. But his opponent did not fall. It snarled, wrenched the sword from Toryn's hand and grabbed his throat. A horse stumbled on the boggy ground and crashed into them, freeing Toryn from the Norgog's grasp. Mercifully, the Norgog began to tire as the sun appeared in the clearing skies.

Toryn sensed the tide had turned. He and Gundrul slashed a path towards Elodi. He heard her call. 'They weaken! Drive them back.' But Toryn slipped and fell onto a stricken Norgog. Its large hands seized Toryn's neck. Dark eyes bored into him as its fingers dug into his throat. Lights flickered at the edge of his vision. His numb hand failed to get a grip on his sword. With his left, he fumbled for the Nordleng dagger in his belt. His sight blurred as his fingers closed around the handle. He pulled it free and thrust it deep into his assailant's side. Its eyes bulged; its hold released. But as Toryn fought to regain his feet, a large Norgog fell dead on top of him and pinned him into the mire. Mud clogged his mouth as he fought to breathe. Toryn writhed, knowing in seconds he could suffocate in the filth of the battle. He saw a patch of light and kicked out, dislodging another lifeless Norgog. A hand grasped his and yanked him free. He glanced up to see Amyndra. Blood streamed from beneath her dented helm, but her grip was strong. She ducked as a hammer swung at her head, then lunged, thrusting her sword at another behind Toryn. He spat out the mud, thanked her and rejoined the battle.

Ahead, Elodi fought on. Her eyes blazed through her mud and blood-caked face. The Amayan blade had dulled, but it rose and fell with renewed ferocity, cleaving any who broke through the few of her knights still on horseback.

The last of the storm clouds retreated. The strength of the Norgog waned in the sunlight and they struggled to fend off the blows from Gundrul's determined force. To Elodi's rear, Archonian shields pushed forward, forcing the stubborn beasts of Nordruuk back. Toryn ran to her side just as she slid from Sea Mist. He lunged and caught Elodi before the mud claimed her. He wrapped his arms around her shivering body and pulled her close. 'You've done it! You've all but defeated them.'

Elodi stuttered. 'Our left. What of the left?'

'The battle rages on, but the flank holds.' He turned as a wagon lurched across the mire. 'They bring water.'

Elodi gratefully accepted a flask, drank, and poured the rest over her head. She gasped. 'The horses. Don't forget the horses. Bring them water.' She recovered and stood without aid. 'Thank you, Toryn.' She managed a brief smile and clutched his hand. 'It's good to see you. But the day is not done.' She looked up and led Toryn and a limping Sea Mist to a nearby mound. 'What of the Amayans?'

Toryn pointed. 'They pursue the warlock who killed Amyra. But I could not sustain the others for long.'

Elodi sighed. 'Long enough. That was a decisive moment. We'd have lost the right flank had you not come.' She turned to the tents at the rear. 'Nyomae freed Dorlan. Together, we crushed their center. Alas, we could not keep up with him. But he slew Uleva. That is one less to fight another day.'

Toryn beamed. 'Good news indeed. Does he live?'

'I cannot be certain. Nyomae believed his life would be short following his release. We may have routed their center and left. But what of the west?' She sank to her knees. 'Can you see, Toryn? My sight and strength fail me. I'm spent.'

Toryn used the *farsight*. 'The Ruuk are retreating, but… ah! The Aralaks come.'

Elodi struggled to stay upright. 'Who commands them? Can you see Uldrak?'

'Yes, but he flees north. The spiders attack alone. I imagine their hunger drives them on.' He groaned. 'There must be five or six hundred. And there'll be more if they secure more food for their nests.'

Elodi grabbed his hand and pulled herself up. 'Then we must ride to aid the Archonians.'

Toryn held her. 'But you're weak. We cannot let you fall, not right at the end. You have achieved a remarkable victory at the center. I and Gundrul will deal with—' A dozen horns blared across the plain.

Elodi straightened. 'That is not a call of our enemy.'

Toryn searched. 'Spears, Elodi, spears! It must be Ruan. He's made it through the pass.' Their tips caught the last of the sun before it dipped behind the distant peaks of the Kolossos. And more followed. He grasped Elodi's arm. 'A force of at least a thousand are with them. They attack the spiders. Those creatures are no match for Ruan's spears. They scatter. And the riders pursue and hack them down. You've won, Elodi. You've won!'

'Then thank the Three.' Elodi turned to Sea Mist. 'We shall ride to greet them. Where's Aldorman? He and I should—' Her head dropped, and she slumped to the ground.

Toryn kneeled and took her hand. He whispered. 'I think Ruan will understand if you don't greet him just yet. Let him come to you, ma'am. You've deserved that honor.'

# 51. The Pain & The Glory

'There!' Dorlan lay surrounded by the dead slain by his own hand. Toryn stumbled across the bodies and crushed armor to the great warrior's side. His chest moved. He called back. 'He's alive.'

Elodi hurried over. She kneeled, removed his gauntlet, and took his trembling hand. 'Dorlan. Can you hear me?' She turned to one of the few knights of Calerdorn who could still walk. 'Please, get help. We must get him to the healers.'

Dorlan cried out. 'I am sorry, Elodi. I am sorry for everything—' His back arched in agony.

She stroked his hand. 'You have nothing to be sorry for, Dorlan. You were wronged. You have suffered long, and the enemy exploited your weakness. But today you have righted that wrong. You helped us achieve a great victory. Without you, the realms could have been lost forever.'

Dorlan's hand went to his face as the tears flowed. 'I slew many of your knights… I fought against my own. If only—' He coughed and groaned.

Toryn stared in awe at the giant warrior and legend of Harlyn. He kneeled and placed his hand on his broad shoulder. 'We saw your charge, Dorlan. You routed the enemy's center. Lady Harlyn is right. Without you' — he glanced to Elodi — 'the day would surely have been lost.'

Dorlan raised his arm and pointed. 'I… I killed her. I slew Uleva.' A shredded black cloak lay close by on a patch of scorched earth. There was no sign of Uleva. But Toryn knew she had gone for good, banished from the realm by Dorlan's sword.

Elodi retrieved Dorlan's blade and wrapped his fingers around the grip. 'She was a formidable foe. I thank you for purging this land of her evil.' Dorlan clenched his sword. Bright eyes stared out from his bloodied face. They moved but seemed not to notice Elodi or Toryn. His gaze went to the sky, perhaps seeing events from his long and painful life. He moved to speak, but his breath was weak. The light in his eyes dwindled. Lines appeared on his graying face as the years, long since held at bay, finally caught up with him. Elodi held back her tears. 'You will be forever remembered for your victories with Draegelan and today's momentous triumph. Go in peace, Dorlan. Take your rest, long denied you.' His eyes closed. His tortured spirit, unchained from its mortal vessel, departed for the realms beyond the sky. Elodi's shoulders slumped. She rested her head on Dorlan's chest and wept.

Toryn fought back the grief to comfort her. 'He is free now. His torment is over. And you rode with the noblest of knights as his equal. You won, Elodi. You have defeated the worst our enemy could throw at us.'

Elodi sat. She stared across the bloody aftermath of the battle. Many still cried out in pain. And many died alone without the words of a friend to ease them on their way. She looked to Toryn. 'Does each victory come with such agony and suffering? Why do we do it, Toryn? What drives us to slaughter and maim?' Her arm rose and fell. 'Are we not better than this? We must have lost close to half our strength today. Good souls trampled into the mud, never to see their loved ones again.'

Toryn clasped her cold hands. 'Alas, we have no other way to resist such evil. And if you had not made your stand here, many more would have died in the months to come.'

'Ma'am?' Four horseless knights arrived bearing a stretcher.

Elodi lowered her head. 'Alas, Dorlan has departed this realm. But please, bear his body to the tents. It is not fitting he lies bloodied and disheveled among our enemy. Ensure he is cleaned and made ready for burial.' The knights duly lifted Dorlan and placed him upon the stretcher. As they moved across the plain, many kneeled and bowed their heads.

A flash of lightning lit the last of the retreating dark clouds. Despite his exhaustion, Toryn turned and let the *farsight* take him north. He spoke to Elodi. 'The Amayans have found Vordrak. The fight to avenge Amyra begins.' He gasped. 'Another joins the struggle. Two warlocks confront the Amayans.'

Elodi closed her eyes. 'We cannot afford to lose them. How do they fare?'

'My vision is blurred. I can't see who prevails. But I sense it will be a challenge, even for six Amayans.'

'Ma'am?' Gundrul limped towards them.

Elodi groaned. 'Captain. You should not be on your feet. That is a nasty wound you carry on your neck.' She looked down and winced. 'But that doesn't begin to compare with that open gash on your leg. You're losing too much blood. How can you walk?'

Gundrul clasped Elodi's forearm and winked. 'I'm an Archonian, ma'am. Never a step back, eh. But less about me. I come to congratulate you on a great victory. When I stood with you the morning following the first attack on Calerdorn, we knew it was only a temporary reprieve. But this, ma'am. This was a rout. It will take many years for them to recover from the hurt you've inflicted today.'

Elodi sighed. 'Thank you, Gundrul. But the same could also be said of us. And I have yet to retake Calerdorn.'

'That may be so, ma'am, but we still have the reserves. We can reclaim the lands lost in Harlyn, and I believe we shall recover the quicker. And don't you fret. I will happily lead a force to take back your city. And after today, they will cower at the sight of Lady Harlyn leading an army their way.'

'Again, thank you for your kind words. But I will rest easier if you allow someone to attend to your wounds. You'll be leading nothing until you're fit.'

Gundrul grinned. 'You know me, ma'am. I'll be swinging my sword in no time.' He turned. 'Aha! Look who approaches.'

Elodi strode to meet him. 'Ruan!' She hugged him. Toryn laughed as the spearman flinched. Elodi stepped back and held his hands. 'Gundrul said you would make it. I don't know how we can thank you.'

He bowed his head. 'You're most welcome, ma'am. But it is I who should thank you. If you had not sent your fearless rider to Tunduska, we would have been trapped and slaughtered.'

Elodi glanced over Ruan's shoulder. 'Is Lena here with you?'

He nodded. 'That she is. She rode ahead to see our way was clear. I believe she's now tending to the injured horses at the rear. Lena's quite a rider, ma'am.'

'That she is. I will make sure she's rewarded for her bravery.'

Gundrul slapped Ruan's broad back. 'Better late than never, you old dog.'

The spearman managed to smile. 'It needed someone to squash those spiders.' He looked about him. 'But I must admit, Gunny, you and the good lady have done the greater damage. This day will be remembered for centuries.'

Gundrul grimaced. 'And I shall be bearing the scars with pride. And don't you worry about the finer details of the battle. You'll be hearing of my exploits at every opportunity from now until the day I die. And if you—' He stumbled.

Elodi steadied him. 'No more bravado from you, Captain. Time to get you to the healers. Ruan, would you be so kind to assist Gundrul? I fear Toryn and I lack the strength and would most likely drop him.'

'It would be a pleasure, ma'am.' Ruan hooked his arm around the captain. 'Come on, old boy. Time to stop pretending it doesn't hurt.' The spearman took Gundrul's weight. 'Go on then, Gunny. Tell me about your day. I know you can't wait…'

Elodi watched them leave. 'I doubt we would have come this far without those two. I would gift them land and wish them a long and peaceful retirement, but I doubt they would accept.' She turned to Toryn. 'Now. We must seek Nyomae and see how she fares. And I still need to find Aldorman. The last I saw of him he was pursuing the Norgog.' She turned to the north. 'And we will await the Amayans' return. Many have perished today. Every single one is a tragedy. But let us hope the Amayans can avenge Amyra without another falling.'

The two made their way through the mud in the fading light. The Archonian reserves lit torches to aid the retrieval of the wounded, but they also served to illuminate the pain frozen on the faces of the dead. Elodi stopped. Harlyn's banner lay discarded in the mud. She lifted it and wiped the filth from the torn cloth bearing Dorlan's shield.

She turned to Toryn. 'I will have this cleaned, but not mended. When I retake Calerdorn, this will hang in our Great Hall to honor all who have fallen today. All who made—' Her hand went to her mouth. She dropped to her knees. Beside the banner, the torchlight reflected on the armor of a knight lying face down in the grime. Toryn helped her to roll him over, but Elodi knew him before she saw his face. She had no tears left to shed, but her heart broke as the glassy eyes of Aldorman, the leader of the Knights of Calerdorn, stared vacantly at the sky. Elodi cleaned the mud from his face and cradled him in her arms. She rocked him gently, whispering words only for Aldorman. Her faithful captain had been at her side throughout the turbulent months, only to fall in the dying light as the battle was won.

Toryn quietly summoned the knights still able to stand. 'Please, take your captain to the tent where Dorlan lies. He has earned the honor to be at the side of Harlyn's legend.'

Elodi allowed the knights to take Aldorman. She looked up. 'Thank you, Toryn. He should be laid to rest alongside the man whose name he cried riding into the battle.' She declined Toryn's help and stood. She straightened, took a breath, and steadied herself. When she spoke, she sounded once more like Lady Harlyn, commander of the Five Realms' forces. 'Those whose tradition demand they be buried at their place of birth, shall be returned. Dorlan, Aldorman, and the Archonians shall be laid to rest where they fell. We will build a fitting monument to their memory in honor of their sacrifice. The enemy will be burned in a pyre, which I believe is their way.' She surveyed the field. 'Then we shall follow the way of the Nym.' Elodi waved her arm across the plain. 'Trees will be planted. From Roth's Doom to the hills in the east. Twice this land has endured a terrible battle. A forest will ensure it will not suffer again.'

## 52. BY DAWN'S FIRST LIGHT

Elodi and Toryn stood beside Nyomae's bed. She had collapsed upon freeing Dorlan and mercifully had stayed out of harm's way. Bardon and the First Horse had held fast against a determined strike by the Ruuk. But once the enemy became aware of Nyomae's intention, and Dorlan had joined the attack, their lines had come close to breaking. Had Nyomae failed to free Dorlan, none would have seen the day out.

Elodi turned to the healer. 'Thank you. We will sit with her through the remainder of the night. But please, tell me, how is Captain Gundrul?'

The healer gathered her bottles and herbs. 'I'm afraid it's not good news, ma'am. He worsens. The captain has a strong constitution, but I believe a poison troubles him, no doubt delivered by the foul blade that opened his leg.'

Elodi's hand went to her mouth. 'This is grave news. Please, see to it that he gets all the care he needs.'

She nodded. 'It is a poison I know well, ma'am. But my supply of tinctures runs low with so many requiring attention. I have done all I can. The rest is down to him.'

'Is Captain Ruan with him?'

'He is, ma'am. I instructed Ruan to talk to him. It may help the captain's spirit in his fight to overcome the poison.'

Elodi managed a smile. 'Then I trust the spearman has many a tale of their shared exploits. If any can help, I imagine it would be Ruan.'

The healer glanced to the other beds. 'There are others in need of my skills. Please excuse me, ma'am.'

'But of course. And please inform me if there is

anything I, or my captains can do to aid you.' Elodi sighed. 'To lose Aldorman is a great blow, but if Gundrul fails to see the dawn, that would be a loss difficult to endure. He has served without question, and an Archonian with a stout and loyal heart. So many have fallen this day. How many more will be lost this night?'

'He is strong. Gundrul will recover.' He smiled. 'If only to annoy Ruan.'

Nyomae groaned. Elodi looked down at her drawn face. 'Can you help her, Toryn?'

'I shall try. But I have little strength left.' Toryn placed his hands on Nyomae's stomach. He took a deep breath and let the warmth flow through his limbs. His hands tingled and grew hot, yet Nyomae remained cold to the touch. He redoubled his efforts but could not penetrate the icy shield about her. He dropped back. 'It's no use. I sense she's resisting my help, but I can't figure out why.'

Elodi kneeled. 'I cannot begin to imagine what she endured to wrest Dorlan from Uleva's grip. And the warlocks must have attacked.' She stroked Nyomae's brow. 'She is a remarkable woman. If we lose her…'

'Perhaps she shuts herself away from the world to heal herself.'

'I dearly hope that is the case.' Elodi looked up to see the thin canvas of the tent had turned pink. 'Dawn comes.'

Toryn and Elodi stepped out into a fresh breeze. But while the air was clear, the day's first light revealed the true horrors of the battle. The reserves had worked throughout the night to recover the wounded, but the countless dead still lay where they had fallen. Broken bodies, helms, breastplates, and weapons littered the plain for as far as they could see. Toryn looked to their faces. Some looked as if they slept, others still looked in pain. While he did not know many of their names, Toryn knew many by sight. It had been a gruesome fight for survival. How many did not even see the sword, axe or hammer that struck the fatal blow? And did others die defending his back? Toryn would never know if another had sacrificed their life to save his. Nyomae had chided him whenever he mentioned luck, but surely in the violence of battle, a weapon landing an inch one way or the other, made the difference between life and death. Luck had to play a part — unless the unseen gods deemed otherwise and deflected blows with unseen hands. Or did the Maidens' Song determine when your time had come?

Toryn's gaze fell upon the body of a young woman. No wound was visible, but she lay as if gazing at the sky on a summer's afternoon. Her hand still gripped her sword. Did she look into the eye of the warrior who took her life? Did she feel pain? Each casualty would have a story to tell, but it was unlikely it would ever be told.

Elodi's warm hand slipped into Toryn's. She whispered. 'Up there. I need to see the sun rise over unspoiled land.' She led him up the slope to the ridge where they could look across the hills. A mist clung to the valley below, masking the stream running through it. She leaned against Toryn. 'If only it was just the two of us. How I dearly wish we could watch the clouds float by and listen to the birds with an untroubled heart. Yet Nordryn sits in Keld with an army, warlocks escape to fight another day, and how many more Ruuk and Norgog yet live to avenge their defeat?' Her voice faltered. 'And I have yet to retake Calerdorn and free the people of Harlyn. And how did the Amayans fare? Will we ever be at peace, Toryn? And what of the spiders? If they rebuild their nests while we're still weak…'

Toryn pulled her close. 'You are strong, Elodi. But you must take time to recover. Let others take the burden from you for a while. You have saved the realms. Without your leadership, this region would have been lost, and the host heading south to take Archonholm. Take heart in your victory. As painful as it feels, it's still a victory. They had every right to believe they would destroy us, but you've proved otherwise. We can regroup and rebuild, and we have allies in Nyomae and the Amayans on their return. Together, I believe we can form a force the enemy will now fear.'

Elodi turned to face him. 'Thank you, Toryn. I note you fail to mention your vital role. We have much to do. I must free Harlyn and strengthen the borders. Nyomae and Gundrul must recover. And your father has to be found.' Reluctantly, she looked back to the battlefield. 'We may have inflicted heavy losses and reduced their numbers, numbers that may take many years to replace.' Her eyes wandered up to a cloud passing over the sun. The air chilled. Elodi sighed. 'I fear the ultimate victory will be won by those who can master and wield the old powers of this world.'

To be continued…

## Book 4: Crown of Sorrows

(Published January 2024)

You can sign up to my newsletter at

www.frontrunnerbooks.com/sign-up.html

Printed in Dunstable, United Kingdom

67382633R00251